HEIR OF THE CURSE

THE KYONA CHRONICLES BOOK ONE

DEBORAH GRACE WHITE

LUMINANT PUBLICATIONS

HEIR OF THE CURSE

By Deborah Grace White

For Ray, now and always.
Thanks for being my number one fan.
Without you, none of this would be here.

Kynton
Kerr
Pravat
KYON
Nerifa
MARSHLAND

Forest of Rune
Dragon Realm
VASILISA
Montego
GREAT RIVER
Argath
Alezae

CHAPTER ONE

Despite the familiar air of stress that so often gripped the village of Nerita at that time of day, Calinnae couldn't help but enjoy the walk down to the pier. As always, the faces of returning fishermen were heavy with anxiety as they inspected the day's catch, which never seemed sufficient.

There was no such weight on Calinnae's mind. He was just glad to be free from his father's workshop for the day, and the quiet coastal town was always at its most beautiful when lit by the golden glow of the late afternoon sun. Spring was thinking about summer, and the green of the hills surrounding his home gave a bright contrast to a sky clearer than he'd seen in months.

"Did you hear? Another new vessel tax."

Calinnae slowed his steps to better catch the conversation between the passing fishermen, a slight frown creasing his forehead.

"There's already a vessel tax. That's why I don't own me own boat."

"Nar, this is a new one. A tax on leasing them as well as owning them."

"What?? That's wicked, that is! How does His Royal High and Mightiness expect us to feed our families when he..."

The voices trailed off as the fishermen passed out of hearing range. Cal continued walking, his good mood dampened. He felt a familiar flare of anger at the mention of Kyona's young king. Another tax? On fishermen who didn't even own their own boats? How much could King Filip gain from targeting the kingdom's poorest subjects?

He took a deep breath, the bite of the fresh salt air familiar and calming. He knew there was no point fretting over things he couldn't change. But his steps were not as light as before. He felt suddenly less enthusiastic about joining his best friend at their favorite haunt, down by the pier. Calinnae's mind kept returning to the overheard conversation, and he knew that Jonan would have no interest in discussing anything as mundane as taxes.

Jonan would just have to put up with it. Who else was Calinnae supposed to discuss it with? He and Jonan did everything together.

As expected, he found Jonan standing at the end of the pier, his familiar figure and unruly dark hair impossible to miss. His friend's habitual restlessness was so evident from his posture that Calinnae barely held back a sigh. It was never a good sign when Jonan was in this humor. Calinnae couldn't count the number of times his friend's insatiable desire for adventure had gotten Jonan into a scrape. Calinnae usually had to rescue him, and he wasn't in the mood for it today.

"I know that look, Jo," he said lightly as he leaned on the railing next to his friend. "And if you're thinking of stealing another boat, you can count me out."

"How's that for loyalty?" protested Jonan, his mock outrage at odds with his easy grin. "You're supposed to be my best friend."

Calinnae snorted. "And since when has that made me willing to jump on board with your stupid ideas?"

"Go easy!" laughed Jonan. "I didn't actually suggest stealing a boat, you realize. What's gotten you into a mood, Cal?"

Calinnae acknowledged the accusation with a reluctant laugh. He ran a hand through his own tawny curls, trying to release the tension with a roll of his shoulders.

"Sorry. Father has been in one of his solemn moods all day, and it started to get to me. He's been going on endlessly about these latest rumors of another purge."

Jonan tilted his head inquiringly. "There's been another purge?"

Calinnae shrugged. "That's the rumor." He kicked a loose pebble into the water. "If it's true, King Filip is not only greedier than his father, but twice as stupid. King Hugo was bad enough, but I never heard of him being so paranoid. I mean, it's one thing to oppress peasants, but if King Filip keeps executing nobles who disagree with him, he's going to have his own court turning on him."

Jonan snorted. "Works for me."

Cal frowned into the water. "Do you think what that peddler said is true? About King Hugo's accident?"

"You mean that Filip was behind it?" asked Jonan, with a shrug. "Who knows, but it wouldn't exactly be a surprise, would it? Not with everything else we've heard about Filip. However stupid he is, I'm sure he was smart enough to hide his tracks, though. Maybe he just didn't want to wait another twenty years to become king. It would explain his paranoia about his court turning on him. They would only be following his example, after all."

Cal didn't respond. It wasn't that he disagreed—he had a horrible feeling that Jonan was right. But the casual indifference shown by Jonan—and the peddler—was almost as bad as the idea itself. Nothing showed better how low Kyona had sunk than the lack of surprise at the suggestion that their ruler had murdered his father.

Jo looked over and seemed to read Cal's continued concern on his face. "Lighten up, Cal! If you don't stop working so hard and worrying so much, you'll turn into your father before you're eighteen!"

Calinnae rolled his eyes. "Because you know all about the effects of hard work."

Jonan shrugged innocently. "Is it my fault that unlike your father, mine doesn't think I'm responsible enough to start training with him?"

"Yes," laughed Calinnae unhesitatingly. "It is."

Jonan grinned. "Well, since I don't want to be a wool merchant, I guess I won't complain."

"Very gracious," said Calinnae, grinning back. It was certainly hard to picture his impulsive friend taking over his father's small but respectable business.

"I don't know why my father thinks I would want to be like him," mused Jonan dryly. "He worries more than you and your father put together."

Calinnae frowned at his friend. "You say it like we're all being stupid to care, Jo. But Kyona is falling apart. Don't *you* care?"

"Of course I care," said Jonan impatiently. "But my father talks about nothing else. And what's the use of talking about it, anyway?"

Calinnae's frown deepened. "Well, what else is he supposed to do?"

"I don't know," said Jonan, clearly sick of the familiar topic. He gave a one-shouldered shrug, as if to dismiss the matter.

Calinnae felt a surge of irritation, but he didn't press the point. It was not exactly news to him that his friend didn't take the crisis in the kingdom very seriously. Well, Jo didn't really take anything seriously, as a rule.

"Your father came by the workshop as I was leaving, by the way," he said. "He wanted to talk over the rumors with my father."

Jonan made a face. "Meaning they're both going to sit there looking grave and shaking their heads for the next two hours. Then my father will start reminiscing about the old stories of how it used to be in the Golden Age, back before it all went wrong." He saw that Calinnae looked unimpressed and shot him a grin. "Come on, Cal, you know I'm right. You know my father as well as I do. Better, probably."

"Not quite," said Calinnae.

But Jonan wasn't too far wrong. The two boys' parents had been close since their own youth, and Calinnae and Jonan had been raised almost like brothers. It was true that Calinnae was nearly as close to Jonan's parents as to his own. Closer, he often thought, than Jonan was to any of them.

Calinnae gazed out at the ocean, watching the waning sunlight glint off the surface of the water. The last of the fishermen were coming in, their faces as strained as those of the men Calinnae had passed earlier.

"It's been ages since your father told us any of the stories," he said, almost wistfully. "I wouldn't mind hearing some of them again."

Jonan groaned. "Don't you start! It's a little early in the evening to be tucked in with a bedtime story!"

"A bedtime story?" said Calinnae incredulously. "Is that what you call your father's histories?"

"Histories?" Jonan snorted. "You're supposed to be the level headed one, Cal. How can you still believe Father's stories are true?"

"I suppose they can't all be true," Cal sighed. "But they

always felt so real. The details never changed. And I loved the way your father would come alive when he told them. I used to feel like I was really there." He shook his head, as if to clear it.

"But you're right, I'm old enough to realize that the stories must have been embellished. Too many generations have passed for that kind of detail to survive. Still, I don't see why the basic outline couldn't be true. I mean, in the two years since Filip succeeded his father, the rumors have only grown. It's not just your father now—lots of people are whispering that Hugo and Filip don't come from the true royal line. I know there are no written records of any line before theirs, but your father's account about the True Bloodline is as convincing as anything we learned in history class."

"If you say so," said Jonan, sounding amused. "Don't get me wrong, I'd love to think it was true that there's a hidden heir out there somewhere ready to storm the castle like a hero out of legend. I'd sign up to join his band of rebels in a heartbeat. It would be a real life adventure. But if it were true, where has he been hiding for the last couple of centuries? Or more to the point, *why* was he hiding? It's hard to get excited about the idea of such a chicken-hearted hero. I mean, according to my father, the last king's surviving heir was nicknamed Jonathon the Story-teller! What's the point of a royal heir who does nothing but tell stories? Jonathon the Conqueror, I could get behind. But Jonathan the Storyteller?" Jonan made a derisive noise in his throat.

For a moment Calinnae was silent. He felt defensive for the tales that had fascinated him all his life. They had given him a sense of importance, being inside a secret shared by few. And it irked him that Jonan, of all people, was laughing at him.

"I don't know why you're making fun of me for saying that the legends could be *based* on fact," Calinnae said, aggrieved. "At least I never believed in *dragons*, even when we were kids. But you were convinced they were real!"

"Yes, because Father's stories were full of dragons!" retorted Jonan. "Proving my point that it's all a load of nonsense."

"Dragons were barely mentioned!" contradicted Calinnae. "And in a general sort of way. I always thought the dragons were supposed to be symbolic."

Jonan snorted again. "Symbolic of what?"

Before Calinnae could answer, a shout drew their attention to a huddle of people standing near the start of the pier. The boys exchanged a frown, moving by unspoken agreement to join the group.

As they drew near, Calinnae could sense the townspeople's anxiety. Glancing around, he saw that a number of other small knots of people had formed in the immediate vicinity, and every face bore a look of alarm. The tone was unmistakable, and it was different from the everyday stress that was such a familiar part of village life. It was fear, and Calinnae felt an answering prickle of the emotion running up the back of his neck.

"What's going on?" Jonan demanded, as soon as they were close enough to be heard.

Everyone in the group shot the two friends panicked looks, and some of them gestured with their hands, clearly telling Jonan to keep his voice down.

"Soldiers," said an older man, in a curt response to Jonan's question. "There are soldiers here in the village. Just rode in from the direction of the capital."

"What do they want?" Calinnae asked sharply.

"No one knows. They rode down the main street, is what I heard."

Calinnae and Jonan exchanged an uneasy look. A visit from the king's soldiers was never a good thing—everyone knew that. Those who traveled regularly to the nearby trading city of Pravat sometimes brought back harrowing tales of the soldiers' brutality. But Nerita was a quiet, out of the way village. They had never before had soldiers actually in their town.

Jonan's eyes flicked toward the main part of town, although it wasn't actually visible from where they stood.

"Do you think my father is still with yours at the workshop?" His voice was low, and not quite as confident as usual.

Calinnae met his friend's eyes. With no need for words, they started quickly toward town.

Their way led them past their two houses, nestled together on the edge of the village, and Calinnae stopped.

"I'll go in first. See if they've come back already."

Jonan frowned impatiently, but before he could actually speak, the sound of raised voices reached them from Calinnae's house. Calinnae felt his unease growing. It was rare for there to be quarreling between the two families, but the voices of his mother Erryn and Jonan's mother Lynette were unmistakable.

"On second thought," he said quietly, "it doesn't sound like Father has come home yet."

Jonan was watching the house with narrowed eyes, a familiar look of determination on his face. It came as no surprise when Jonan moved toward the house, vaulting lightly over the low fence to avoid the squeak of the gate.

"Jo," Calinnae sighed, jumping the fence as well. "I thought you grew out of eavesdropping when you were about ten."

Jonan rolled his eyes. "Come on, Cal, they never argue. Something's going on. And you know they'll never tell us willingly. What if it's to do with the soldiers?"

"Why would our mothers know anything about the soldiers?" Calinnae asked, his forehead creasing. "What can they have to do with us?"

Jonan frowned thoughtfully, his voice low but firm. "I don't know, but Mother has been acting strange for weeks. She's as jumpy as a rabbit. Last time we heard rumors of a purge she burst into tears—right in the middle of the market! That night I heard her asking Father whether we were safe, and instead of reassuring her, he said nothing was certain! And now you tell me there's been another purge, and the same day royal soldiers come here. Come on, Cal! Soldiers in Nerita? Something is happening."

"Jo..." Calinnae hesitated. "What if you overhear something you don't like?"

But Jonan was clearly undeterred. He crept forward and crouched down on one side of a window, his back against the wall of the simple dwelling.

Curious himself, Calinnae hesitated for only a moment. Moving silently, he took up a position on the other side of the window, trying not to think how foolish they would look to any passersby.

He didn't need eyes to picture the scene. His mother had sat with Jonan's mother at their scrubbed wooden table more times than he could count. But their voices told him instantly that this time was different.

"Calm down, Lynette! What do you mean, they know? Who knows?"

"The soldiers!" cried Jonan's mother, her terror clear in her voice.

The eavesdroppers outside the window exchanged a startled look. *Did* their mothers know something about the soldiers?

"The soldiers don't know," said Erryn patiently. "They're probably here to enforce the new taxes. I'm sure it has nothing to do with Elam."

Calinnae frowned at the mention of Jonan's father. What did he have to do with it?

"They know, Erryn!" insisted Lynette, her voice becoming hysterical. "I'm trying to tell you—they've taken him!"

"What do you mean?" said Erryn sharply.

"The soldiers have just seized Elam, in town! The smithy's boy was passing and saw the whole thing, and he ran to tell me!"

There was a moment of stunned silence, and when his mother spoke again, her voice was more fearful than Calinnae had ever heard it.

"Save us all," she muttered shakily. "What do we do? Where's Nathan?"

She had seemed to be speaking to herself, but Lynette answered.

"They took him too!"

"What?" Erryn's voice was sharper than ever, and Calinnae felt his own fear mounting at this news of his father.

"Elam was with Nathan at the workshop, and they were both taken! We're on our own. What are we going to do?"

Again there was a beat of silence, but this time, Erryn's voice was stronger. She seemed to be making an effort to regain control of herself.

"We're not on our own, and you know what we have to do. You must tell him everything. We must tell both of the boys."

"No, we can't!" Lynette sounded like she was crying. "It's too dangerous! I can't do it! Elam was supposed to, Elam—"

"Elam may not be alive by morning," said Erryn brutally. Calinnae saw Jonan's involuntary start, but he remained frozen in place, unable to bring himself to meet his friend's eye as Erryn continued. "He's your son—you must do it."

"Wait, just wait!" Lynette cried, in the voice of a woman trying desperately to stop an unstoppable force. "You're not thinking about what's best for him. He's too young!"

"We don't have time to think it through!" Erryn countered. "We have to act now. For everyone's sake, he must be told the truth."

"I'm his mother, it should be my decision!" Lynette cried. "You and Nathan—"

"—have spent our lives protecting Elam's secret! We are the only ones he trusted with his identity. How could you question our commitment?"

"Not the only ones," said Lynette, evasively. "Elam said that he all but told the record keeper in Pravat. It was the only way to convince him to show him the records."

"You know what I mean," said Erryn impatiently. "Elam trusts our judgment, and so should you."

"But you said it yourself!" persisted Lynette. "We've spent our lives protecting Elam's identity and creating a hundred safeguards to make sure no one could find out. I don't understand why you want the secret out now of all times!"

Erryn spoke again, in a voice of forced calm. "The situation is changed now, you must see that."

Calinnae lost track of the conversation briefly, his mind racing as he tried to piece together the information he was hearing. Suddenly his mother's voice slashed through his thoughts, leaving a gaping hole.

"Lynette, we need to face the situation! Your husband might even now be dead, meaning your son is the only man remaining in the True Bloodline!"

CHAPTER TWO

For an endless moment, Calinnae's mind was blank, unable to make sense of the words.

The True Bloodline.

That's what she had said. Jonan's father was the heir of the true line of kings?

The ground seemed to be tilting under him, but he didn't tell himself it was impossible. He felt it to be true, as if he'd always known it. He had a fleeting image of Jonan's father, sitting in his old chair as Calinnae and Jonan sat on a rug by the fire as boys. Telling them the legends, the "bedtime stories". He had always taken on some extra quality when he spoke. Elam the Storyteller, like Jonathon the Storyteller. The stories had seemed true from his lips, like they were woven into who he was. Because they were. They were his own history, his own birthright.

And now Jonan's. Calinnae's eyes flicked to his friend. He could make no sense of Jonan's expression as he heard exactly what Calinnae had predicted—something they didn't want to know.

"How can you say it so calmly?" Lynette was saying, openly

crying now. "We don't know Elam's dead, it might not be too late!"

"Do you think I don't care as much as you do?" said Erryn, her own voice choked with tears. "They've got Nathan as well! But our first priority has to be the boys—we have to make sure they're safe! We can't go racing into town to—"

"Elam and Nathan aren't in town," Lynette interrupted. "The smithy's boy said the soldiers were taking them out of town, toward the copse on the hill."

A flash of movement caught Calinnae's eye, but it was a moment before he realized that Jonan was no longer next to him. He started to his feet, stumbling in his haste to reach his friend, who was already leaping over the fence.

"Jo!"

Jonan ignored him, and Cal pushed himself harder. He was taller than his friend, and his longer legs quickly compensated for Jonan's head start.

"Wait," he tried again, puffing as he caught up. "Where are you going?"

"Where do you think?" Jonan shot back. Following the trajectory of his gaze Calinnae realized that Jonan was making for the low hills that rose up to the north of the village, their crests lined with trees. The sky was starting to grow dark, and the tree line seemed menacing in the twilight.

"Jo, stop!" he tried desperately, grabbing hold of his friend's arm and pulling him to a halt. "You heard what they said!"

"Yes, I did!" Jonan said, his voice unsteady. "They said the soldiers took them both to the copse!"

"I know, but Jonan, I'll go! You have to stay safe!" Calinnae cried, his mind consumed with the thought of what it would mean if Jonan were to die.

Jonan gave no answer, his face stony as he shook free and once again took off running, Cal hard on his heels. Within minutes they had mounted the hill and reached the start of the small grove. Cal swallowed his protests, terrified that they would be too late if they wasted any more time arguing. Even more terrified that if the soldiers were indeed in the copse, any speech would alert them to his—and more importantly, Jonan's —presence.

They had barely stepped into the trees when they both checked involuntarily at the sound of an angry voice, some distance ahead.

"We know you have a son, traitor. Where is he?"

They couldn't see the speaker through the trees, but there was no mistaking the familiar voice that carried clearly through the twilight in response. Cal heard Jo's sharp intake of breath at the sound of his father's calm words.

"You won't kill my son."

"Won't we?" came the first voice, over the jeering laughter that met Elam's declaration.

"The usurper tried to wipe out our line generations ago," Elam said, his voice stronger than ever. "He failed then, and you will fail now. Our bloodline is protected."

"Your superstitions won't save your son any more than they'll save you," grunted the soldier.

Calinnae could barely hear the ring of steel over the drumming in his ears, but there was no mistaking the sound that followed. Calinnae stood frozen, his breath coming in short gasps as he heard the dull thud of a body hitting the grassy ground. It couldn't be real. Not just like that.

"Did you find the signet ring?" said the soldier's gruff voice, his casual tone making it seem impossible that he could have just killed an unarmed man in cold blood. "The king was convinced he would have it on him."

"We've searched him," replied a new voice. "He has no jewelry of any kind."

The first soldier grunted. "He must have already given it to his son."

Cal's body was still frozen in shock, but his eyes slid to Jonan's white and bloodless face. Their gazes locked, then all at once they both sprang forward. Cal was hardly aware of whether he was trying to reach the soldiers or stop Jonan from doing so. All he knew was that he couldn't stand still any longer.

"Let's go! Find the boy!"

The curt shout of the lead soldier was alarmingly close, and Jo put on a burst of speed. Cal reached out vainly in an attempt to stop his friend from running straight into the men who were hunting him, but Jonan was moving too quickly.

Fortunately, the soldiers were moving more quickly still. There was no sign of them between the trees, and Calinnae only realized that they had reached the right place when he stumbled over something in the gathering darkness and fell to the ground. Pushing himself up onto his knees he stared in horror into the motionless face of his own father.

The moment felt unreal, like a dream, and for the space of three long breaths he just stared, unable to take in the fact that his father was dead. Cal could only imagine that Nathan had died trying to intervene on Elam's behalf, but he supposed they would never know. A choking gasp brought him back to reality. He looked across, his mind still strangely emotionless, and saw Jonan, leaning against a nearby tree for support with his gaze riveted on Elam's body.

The two boys' eyes met, Cal still kneeling on the ground next to the body of his father, Jonan hovering over the body of his. Neither spoke. What was there to say?

Jonan sank to the ground as well. Watching, his mind strangely detached, Cal saw Jonan reach down and tug off one of his father's boots. He reached his hand into the toe and slid out a thin silver chain. Cal had never seen it before, but his thoughts were blank, incapable for the moment of either surprise or curiosity. Jonan didn't speak a word, just clutched the chain in his fist as he stared down at his father's face.

Cal had no sense of time, of how long they stayed that way. It was an interminable moment, in which Calinnae felt his childhood fall away from him like a discarded cloak. But a distant shout from behind them snapped them both out of their silent nightmare, turning their heads toward the village.

"They're looking for you," said Cal, his voice unfamiliar in his own ears as he pushed himself to his feet.

Jonan met his eyes, and Calinnae saw the moment when the realization hit.

"Home." Jonan pushed himself upright as Cal brushed past him. After hesitating for only a moment, Jo slipped the chain over his head. Then he stumbled forward, at Cal's side before he had gone three paces.

Calinnae had a vague sense that he should try to stop Jonan from coming, that there was an important reason for his friend to stay safe and hidden. But he couldn't seem to bring his thoughts into order enough to find the words. His whole mind was absorbed with the image of his mother, leaning against their kitchen table, talking to her closest friend with unaccustomed sternness.

As soon as they emerged from the trees, they could see it. Night had properly fallen now, and the orange blaze stamped their eyes violently. They checked for only a moment, their gasps intermingling. Calinnae outstripped his friend in seconds, his heart pounding in his ears to the exclusion of all thought, except for the one terrifying reality.

It was his house that was on fire.

Surely she had gotten out. Surely they both had.

Based on the shouts, a crowd had gathered outside the house. But the dwelling was on the edge of town, and Calinnae and Jonan were approaching from the grassy hills. No one stood between them and the building. As they neared it, Cal could see that the fire had only just begun to take hold, and the structure was still standing. He felt a swell of hope, painful after the numbness of the nightmare in the copse.

He burst through the back door, Jonan not far behind. Cal coughed as smoke rushed into his lungs, and raised his arms involuntarily to protect his face from the heat. Opening his mouth, he attempted to call for his mother, but he couldn't get the breath, instead coughing all the more violently.

His eyes, watering painfully from the smoke, were squeezed shut, and he jumped at a sudden pressure on his arm. Forcing his eyes open, he saw Jonan, his expression unreadable. Following his friend's gaze, Cal saw the sight he was dreading.

The two women were stretched out side by side on the floor. They had not been killed by fire or smoke. Filip's soldiers had dealt with them as efficiently as their husbands.

The heat of the flames licked at Cal's skin, threatening to consume him, and a creak from above told him that the roof was not going to hold for much longer. But he had lost all power of motion. He tried to step toward his mother's body, but his feet wouldn't move. He stared at her face, noting in a detached way that she looked peaceful in death, no sign of the strain of her recent argument showing in her features.

He turned away suddenly as his stomach heaved, its contents threatening to emerge. He realized all at once that Jonan was no longer standing beside him, and he cast his eyes around the burning room frantically, fearing the worst.

But a moment later he saw his friend through the smoke, in the act of seizing a rucksack that Calinnae recognized as his father's. He watched impassively, his mind too blank with shock to even be confused, as Jonan threw a few basic supplies into it.

An ominous groaning noise caused both boys to look

quickly upward. A second later, a whole section of the thatched roof collapsed with a crash.

"Jo!" he cried, but his friend didn't need to be told. Without another word, the two of them threw themselves back out the door through which they had entered, falling to the grass and coughing violently.

"Come on," said Jonan after a moment, his voice grim.

"What are you doing?" Cal asked, alarmed at Jo's look of determination.

"We can't stay here, Cal!"

"I know that!" Cal said. "But where can we go?"

Jonan had no chance to respond, because a shout from the street pulled them both to their feet.

"There!"

There could be no doubt that the soldier was looking at them. Abandoning his attempt to get answers from Jonan, Cal pushed all thought aside and simply ran.

Jonan seemed to have an idea of where he was going, but the thought did little to reassure Calinnae as he followed close behind his friend. They pushed through the crowd, darting between buildings in the darkness, trying to make use of the slim advantage that their familiarity with the town gave them.

They could still hear a commotion behind them, but no pursuer was in sight when Calinnae realized where they were headed. His breath tore at his lungs as they left the dirt road, directing their steps under the pier on which they had so recently stood.

"Jo, what are you doing?" he cried, as his friend began to untie a small fishing vessel.

"Quick, Cal, help me get it ready to sail!" Jo panted, by way of response.

"Jonan, there's nowhere to go!" said Cal desperately. "I know sailing across the sea to some land of adventure beyond is your life's dream, but we can't do it in this! It's not much more than a rowboat! If they don't catch us immediately, they'll easily be able to watch the coast for miles."

"I know," said Jonan curtly. "That's why we won't be in the boat."

"What do you—"

"Just help me!"

Cal abandoned his protests and began untying the heavy rope that connected the boat to the pier. It was absurd, but all he could think of was his flippant comment that afternoon that he wouldn't help Jonan to steal a boat.

Unlike his friend, he had never taken much interest in sailing. But with his help, the small vessel was soon ready to embark on the black water. In astonishment, Calinnae watched as his friend seized a tool from the boat's storage chest and bored several holes in the bottom of the vessel.

Just as Calinnae was about to demand an explanation, they heard the shouts of their pursuers.

"Come on!" Jonan cried, and the two of them launched the vessel, leaping in as they pushed off. Calinnae plied the oars to give them some small momentum as Jonan worked to bring the small sail upright. Glancing back, Cal could see a trio of soldiers setting to work on another boat, clearly intent on following them.

There was a light breeze, and as soon as their sail caught it, Jonan grabbed Cal's arm and nodded at the water. Cal nodded as well, and within seconds they had silently slipped from the boat into the cold sea. For a moment Cal stayed in place, treading water as he watched the little vessel sailing out into the expanse, unguided. It wouldn't stay on course for long, but hopefully it would be long enough.

Having grown up by the sea, both boys were strong swimmers. The journey back to the shore presented no difficulty, their only challenge being to remain unseen. Cal pushed out ahead with strong strokes. Glancing back, he saw that Jonan was swimming toward a sandy stretch of beach, and he tugged at his friend's arm in the water. When Jonan looked up, Cal shook his head and gestured further down the shoreline.

Jonan nodded his understanding and changed course, following Cal as he angled away from the pier. They tracked diagonally toward a stretch of uneven rock jutting out into the water, well out of town. Cal was exhausted by the time they reached firm ground, but it was worth every ounce of energy. They had avoided the soldiers, and they left no tracks as they clambered out of the water onto the rocks.

"That was clever," said Cal, watching their boat, barely visible in the darkness, as it continued away from shore. Was it his imagination that it looked lower in the water already? Their pursuers, no sailors, were still by the pier, wrestling with the vessel they had commandeered. "Even if it's still afloat when they reach it, they'll probably think we're in the water some-where. Maybe even that we drowned, if we're lucky."

"That's the idea," said Jonan curtly. Cal looked up quickly at his friend, alarmed by the unfamiliar hard note in his voice. Before he could say another word, Jo turned away, shouldering the dripping rucksack, and began to walk.

"Where are you going?"

Jonan looked at him, his eyes still hard, and said nothing.

"Jonan, talk to me!"

"Where do you think I'm going?" said Jonan, in a voice unlike his own. "Where do you think I should be going?"

Calinnae was silent for a moment, staring back at him. This was his friend, closer than a brother. But there was something unrecognizable in his appearance that terrified Calinnae for reasons he couldn't articulate. He reached out and gripped

Jonan's arm, dragging him behind a rocky outcrop, out of sight of the water.

"I don't know where you think you're going, but this isn't the time to do anything rash, Jo. We need to talk it through. We need a plan."

Jonan tried to pull his arm free, but Calinnae held on without difficulty. He had rarely had occasion to demonstrate it, but he knew that he was the stronger of the two.

"Talk? That's all you can suggest?" Jonan's face was still strangely hard, showing neither grief nor fear. "I don't want to talk, Cal. We need to act—we need to go. Well, I need to go. You don't have to come."

"Don't be stupid," said Cal absently. "You're not going anywhere without me." He took a deep breath. "But you're right —we do need to go. We have to get you out of here, and fast. Maybe if we head west...the coastal towns that way are supposed to be very isolated. We might even need to leave Kyona."

"Cal!"

He looked up in surprise, taken aback by the anger in Jonan's voice.

"Do you think I'm running away? That I'm going to hide?"

Cal felt panic rising within him at the look on his friend's face. "Jo, I know you're angry," he said desperately. "You think I don't want to kill Filip with my own hands right now? But you *have* to get yourself somewhere safe. You heard what—"

"Yes, I heard!" Jo shot back, his voice trembling with suppressed passion. "And you'd better believe I'm angry! How could he do this?"

Cal gave a hollow laugh. "It's not exactly news to us that Filip is the kind of tyrant to order the murder of defenseless women who were just—" His voice broke, and for a moment he was unable to go on, but it didn't matter. Jonan was already speaking over the top of him, his voice unsteady as his words tumbled frantically over each other.

"I'm not talking about Filip! I'm talking about my father. Don't you get it? He didn't just betray me by lying to me—he betrayed everyone! He *knew*! He knew his whole life that the real royal line had survived. He knew, and he did nothing, just like who knows how many generations before him! He let all those people live under a tyrant because he was too afraid to take action. *He* was the chicken-hearted hero in hiding! Well, I won't be!"

Jonan stopped for a moment, breathing hard. Calinnae stared in open-mouthed silence, stunned by the unexpected explosion of emotion. Jonan's words against his murdered father felt like a slap in the face.

"He turned it all into a bedtime story!" Jonan continued. "Just like Jonathon the Storyteller. Ever since Prince Jonathon chose to run instead of stand and fight, our whole line has been nothing but storytellers! Passing on the tale from generation to generation, lurking in the shadows, never taking action! I'm not going to make the same mistake. I didn't ask for this, and I don't want it, but if I'm the only one left, I'm going to do *something*."

For a moment Calinnae was still unable to speak. Whatever reaction he'd expected, that wasn't it. Fear, anger and confusion he could have understood, but this righteous indignation was foreign to him. Jonan's slur against the long-dead Prince Jonathon shocked him. Like Jo's father, Calinnae had always thought of the past kings with a respect bordering on reverence. But he couldn't deny that Jonan spoke not just with anger but with authority.

"But *what* are you going to do?" he asked weakly. "Storm the palace and take over the throne?"

"Maybe I will," said Jonan. His voice was calmer, but he was still breathing hard.

"Jo, you can't—" began Calinnae, but his friend cut him off.

"I'm going to Pravat."

"Pravat?" protested Cal. "That's on the road to the capital, Jo. I'm telling you, you need to hide, at least until the search dies down a little!"

"No, what I need is answers," said Jonan, his face set in uncompromising lines. "I can't ask the man who should have told me all of this, so I have to find them elsewhere. I'm not going to hide, Cal. You need to know that if you're coming with me."

"Don't be stupid, of course I'm coming with you. But we should be going as far from the capital as we can, not straight for it!"

"Didn't you hear what my mother said about the records?" Jo said impatiently. "She said the record keeper in Pravat knows who Father is—who Father was." He was silent for a moment, struggling with himself. "She said there were records. Maybe there's some kind of proof!"

Cal frowned. It was true that Kyona's Hall of Records was housed at Pravat, but it seemed like a stretch to think it held records proving Elam's royal ancestry. If there were such records, surely the truth would have come out before now.

"I don't like it, Jo. It's too dangerous."

Jonan shrugged. "Like I said, you don't have to come." His voice was low and serious. "And I mean that. I realize I'll probably end up dead. But they have no reason to hunt you if you're not with me. I'm not asking you to—"

"Stop wasting time, Jo," cut in Cal impatiently. "We both know I'm coming. You think I'm going to let you go by yourself? Would you in my place?"

Jonan gave a weak smile. "Of course not. And of course I know you're coming. It just seemed like I should...I don't know, make sure you know what you're getting into."

"Well, neither of us knows what we're getting into," responded Calinnae. "But we'll have a better chance together than you would alone."

"Then let's go," said Jonan. "I don't know how long our diversion will give us. It will take us all night to get to Pravat on foot."

Calinnae was still unconvinced, but Jonan was already moving, and they had lingered too long so close to the water as it was. Plus, the unexpected seriousness of his friend, usually so heedless, threw him off balance. He found himself falling in behind Jonan almost without knowing it. He wasn't thrilled at the idea of meekly following on one of Jonan's poorly thought-out plans, but he chose not to dwell on it. He'd always been there to pull Jonan out of trouble, and he wasn't going to abandon his friend now.

They gave the village a wide berth, moving at a jog as they traveled in an arc, heading for the northward road. For a moment Cal wondered if he would ever see his home again, then remembered with a jolt that his home had been destroyed. The memory of the dancing flames brought with it even more horrifying images, and he pushed them away, terrified of what would happen if he looked at them too closely.

He followed Jonan in silence, his wet clothes clinging to him and adding a chill to the mild night. There was too much happening inside his head to know where to begin. The grief and the fear were too near, too intimate, to discuss yet, so he sought refuge in the practical details instead.

"What exactly are you hoping to find at the Hall of Records, Jo?"

"I don't know," said Jonan quietly. "But if we're going to change anything, we need something more convincing than my father's histories."

"You mean the bedtime stories?"

For a moment Jo was silent. "I guess that was my mistake. I'm starting to wish I'd listened more carefully. I never dreamed it would really matter one day."

Calinnae tried to infuse a confidence he didn't feel into his voice. "Well, it's a good thing you've got me with you because I did listen carefully."

Even as he said the words, he felt his spirits lift. They had lost their homes and their families, they were being hunted, with nowhere safe to go. They had only the few supplies Jonan had thrown into the rucksack, and they had no plan to speak of. But they still had each other.

CHAPTER THREE

"What's on the chain, Jo?"

Cal hadn't spoken in hours, and his voice came out hoarse. He felt like he'd been walking for days, but it was still night, with no hint of dawn on the horizon.

Near the start of their journey they had agreed to push through the forest alongside the road rather than walk on the road itself. Other than that short whispered conversation, they had walked in silence.

"What?" Jonan seemed to come out of a daze at Cal's question. He looked as exhausted as Cal felt.

"The chain," Cal repeated. "The one you took from..." he swallowed, but Jonan clearly didn't need him to finish the sentence.

Jo drew the chain out from under his tunic, slowing as he stared at the shape dangling from it.

In the darkness, it was a moment before Cal could make out what it was. "Is that a signet ring?" he gasped, coming fully to a stop. "The one the soldiers thought your father would be wearing?"

Jonan nodded, stopping beside Cal without a word. Cal stared at the ring dangling from Jonan's hand.

"I've never seen your father wear a ring, so I thought they must be wrong." He spoke in a hushed tone. "But I guess he was wearing it after all." He frowned as he peered more closely at the ring. "Is that the royal crest? It doesn't look quite right, does it? Similar, but not the same."

"My guess would be that it's what the royal crest was before Filip's line stole the throne." Jonan's tone held none of the awe that Cal felt.

"You're probably right," Cal said after a moment's thought. "It's an intricate design. Without the original, they may not have been able to reproduce it exactly." He stared at the ring, a strange excitement rising up suddenly inside him, only to be quenched by a surge of guilt as the image of his parents' lifeless bodies flashed before his eyes. Surely it was wrong to feel anything but grief so soon. But still...he could hardly tear his eyes from the ring.

"Do you really think this belonged to Prince Jonathon?" he asked. "And to King Cael before that?"

"I do," said Jonan unemotionally. "Filip was convinced my father would have it, so it must be real. Or at least, he thinks it is."

Cal resisted the urge to ask if he could hold the ring. He felt confused and overwhelmed, and he wasn't sure what made him more uneasy—his own emotions, or Jonan's lack of them.

"How did you know it was in his boot?" he asked instead, as they started to walk again. "Did your father show it to you?"

Jonan shook his head. "No. He never told me anything about it." He gave a bitter laugh. "How could he, when he clearly didn't trust me enough to tell me his secret?"

"Jo..." Cal started. He was relieved when his friend cut him off with a shrug of one shoulder, because he wasn't sure what reassurance he could give. Not when it seemed clear to him as well that Elam hadn't thought Jonan responsible enough yet to know.

"How would he explain having an ancient and valuable signet ring with a crest suspiciously similar to the royal one?" Jonan pushed on. He glanced down at the object, still clutched in his fist, as he walked. "I knew he always wore a chain, though. He told me it was a keepsake from his parents, but I didn't realize anything was on the chain." Jonan shook his head, as if flicking off an insect. "You remember a few months ago, when that bull got loose and ran through town?"

Cal nodded silently. The ensuing chaos had provided a rare afternoon of excitement for the quiet town.

"Well, I happened to be with Father when we heard the sounds of the commotion. The moment he heard screams, he yanked this chain from around his neck and shoved it into his boot. When we realized what was going on, he was clearly relieved, but he didn't put the chain back on while I was there, and he never explained it to me. Just acted like nothing strange had happened." A note of bitterness had crept into Jonan's voice, and he paused for a moment before continuing. "When the soldiers mentioned a signet ring, I figured..."

His words and his steps trailed off, until he was once again standing still between the trees.

"What are you doing?" Cal's words came out involuntarily as Jonan pulled the ring from the chain.

"Keeping all this secret was my father's biggest mistake," said Jonan in a hard voice. "I told you, Cal, I'm not going to hide." He hesitated for a moment, as if the task was unpleasant, then slipped the ring onto his middle finger.

For some reason Cal found that he was holding his breath, but the moment was broken by another bitter laugh from Jonan.

It was an unfamiliar sound, so different from his normal carefree chuckle.

"Of course it doesn't fit," Jonan said. "It's too big. There's some kind of poetic omen in that, saying I'm not fit to fill my ancestors' shoes." Cal remained silent, and Jo glared at the ring, as if it was personally answerable for the sins of its owners. After a moment Jonan laughed again, with a recklessness that made Cal nervous. "Well, I defy you, omen! I'm more fit than my ancestors, because at least I'm going to try."

Cal breathed a silent sigh of relief as Jonan returned the ring to the chain and slid it back under his tunic. Jo might be reckless of the consequences, but Cal had no desire to advertise that Jonan was carrying a royal signet ring.

Their progress felt unbearably slow as they picked their way through the undergrowth beside the road. Calinnae's mind went to the one other occasion when he had traveled to Pravat. His father had rented two mares and taken Cal to the market. But thoughts of his father brought a lump to his throat, so he tried to push them away. He needed distraction, not endless hours of silent walking, if he was going to keep his mind off his grief and fear. He glanced around, but there was no comfort to be found in his surroundings. In the darkness before the dawn the forest on the left of the road hid sinister shadows, and the open fields on the right threatened exposure.

Thinking about their destination, he turned his thoughts to the legends that Jonan's father had told so often. They hadn't heard them much in recent years, but he remembered them well. Suddenly it was clear why Jonan's father was so engaged in the stories, and why his disappointment at his son's indifference was so great. He'd believed that Jonan would need to know some day.

Something about their silent journey beside the moonlit

road reminded Calinnae of one of the stories about King Cael. Cal had always felt an affinity with the last king before the Corruption. Perhaps it was because his mother had once told him he was named for this king, just as Jonan was named for King Cael's son Jonathon. King Cael, like all the kings, had lived in the capital of Kynton, nowhere close to the trading town of Pravat, but he had visited there more often than most kings. In fact, if there were records in Pravat that could help them as Jonan hoped, they were most likely left there by King Cael himself.

Cal remembered that the story about King Cael's own first journey to Pravat wasn't exactly a happy one. But for all his efforts to keep his mind on more positive thoughts, he was unable to stop himself from recalling the midnight ride of the long-dead king, under a moon just like this one.

KING CAEL RODE DESPERATELY, against the wind, his whole body thrown forward in the saddle as though to make the horse go faster. His fingers felt frozen to the reins in the winter air, but this was nothing to the numbness of his mind. He rode heedless of safety, an irresponsible young king taking off into the night without guide or guard. His own thoughts bitterly condemned his action, but he pushed on recklessly, urging his steed faster than would be wise even were his path lit by a friendly sun.

After several hours, as the darkness deepened in preparation for the far-off dawn, his rage and grief began to lull, and he remembered to take in his surroundings. By their very familiarity the landmarks around him were normally joyful reminders of his belonging to this land and it to him. But the darkness had taken them and turned them into shapeless, homeless shadows. The landscape looked hostile—it did not accept him as its ruler. But from the position of the stars in the sky, he must be about halfway to Pravat. As he focused on the world around him, he came out of his self-absorption and became aware of the heaving flanks of his horse. The poor creature was utterly spent.

Cael reined in and slowed to a trot, breathing deeply as if he himself had just run for hours. He felt as though he had. He tried with all his willpower not to allow his thoughts to return to Kynton, to the devastation that awaited him there, but involuntarily, he found his eyes straying back to the road he had just traversed.

Thalia, the first star in the sky of his youth. He closed his eyes and tried to will his thoughts forward to Pravat, to his task and away from his grief, but it was no use. With his eyes closed and the moonlit road no longer in his vision, all he could see was the fragile little body laid out on a funeral slab built for bigger royals, dwarfed by the bower of blossoms surrounding her. His daughter—the bloom that should have crowned his later years. The first child since his own youth to make the palace ring with happy laughter.

As his horse trotted gratefully on, the young king hung his head and finally allowed his grief to overtake him. He could almost hear its soft approach on the road behind, as though his slower pace had allowed it to come up alongside him at last, and wrap itself around his cold, tired body. He embraced it and wept silently.

Some time later, as the first rays of dawn were beginning to reach across the land like consoling hands, he heard hooves behind him. Mastering himself, he straightened in the saddle. He had expected pursuit. It was madness for the king to ride out alone into the night, and he knew it. He had anticipated a following of unbearable, well-meaning protectors.

It was with relief, therefore, that he turned his head and recognized, in the growing light, not a squadron of guards but a lone rider. Lord Damian Lindor, his closest friend since boyhood. Slowing to a walk, Cael allowed Damian to catch up.

Damian came alongside Cael on the dusty road, and slowed his horse to a walk as well. He reached across the gap between them and grasped the king's shoulder with his firm grip.

"Cay," he began, reverting to the nickname he had used when they were boys. "I'm sorry."

Cael reached his arm over and returned the grasp. Not for the first time he was thankful that his friend knew when to speak and when to be silent. Damian was not a man of many words, but his silent, solid presence was more of a comfort than Cael had expected.

Cael gave his friend a sidelong look and saw that Damian was looking at the road ahead, clearly ready to ride on to whatever destination Cael was making for. It was an incredible relief that Damian neither tried to turn Cael around, nor even asked him where they were going. The two men rode on, the first bird call of the morning and the steady thudding of the horses' hooves the only sounds accompanying their slow journey toward Pravat.

CALINNAE LOOKED SIDEWAYS at his friend as they walked. Did Jonan remember this story? Did he have a clear sense of purpose for what to do once they reached the Hall of Records, as King Cael had done?

They reached the city gate with the first glimmer of dawn and stopped before the end of the forest, looking up at the walls from the shelter of the trees.

"What do you think?" Jonan asked quietly.

"It's almost dawn," Cal replied. "The gates will open soon."

"Do you think that we can just go in? Should we try to pass unnoticed?"

Calinnae frowned as he considered. "I don't know. No soldiers passed us on the road, but if they went to Pravat before riding on to Nerita..." He trailed off, glancing back at the empty road. It was eerie in the pre-dawn, and beyond it, hidden from his sight, lay the little village home that he loved. He shook his head to clear it, wrenching his thoughts back to the formidable stone in front of him. "My instinct is to wait until we can be sure they're not already looking for us in Pravat."

Jonan shook his head. "Wait for how long? It might be too late by then. We can't afford to waste time. Once we're inside I won't know where to go, though. My father never brought me with him when he came for trading. Yours did, didn't he?"

Calinnae nodded. "Once."

"Do you know where the Hall of Records is?"

Calinnae nodded again. "It's right in the middle of town. We can't miss it."

"Good," said Jonan decisively. "Then let's rely on speed, not secrecy."

Calinnae felt uneasy, but he remained silent. Jo's instincts had always seemed backward to him, but he told himself that it was his part to obey now, however unnatural it felt. The idea of Jonan being his rightful ruler caused a curious reaction in Calinnae's mind, but he pushed it away.

The crowing of a cock relieved his mind from its inner wrestling. The little gates began to open slowly and laboriously, and soon two night guards came into view, looking tired and indifferent.

"How long do you think they'll be?" he heard one of them ask. "Should we wait or just go home?"

The other guard grunted. "We'll give them five minutes more," he said with a yawn. "But I'm not standing here a minute longer than that—the woman will have a fire going and something hot for my breakfast by now."

The two boys looked at each other in alarm. Calinnae was certain that Jonan was thinking the same thing he was—who is "them"? They waited in tense silence, but a moment later one of the guards grunted and nudged the other one, gesturing not out toward the hidden boys, but back into the city.

"About time," said the first guard, as two more men appeared at the gate.

"Angry boars can't drive you out of your bed at sunup when you have dawn watch, Maurice," one of the new arrivals answered lazily, but the night watchmen had already started down the street.

"The soldiers can't have been here already," whispered Jonan, "or surely the guards would be a bit more—"

"Awake?" interjected Calinnae dryly.

Jonan almost smiled. "I was going to say alert." He gave a determined nod. The need for action seemed to have had a galvanizing effect on his spirits. "Well, if the soldiers haven't been here then there's no reason why a couple of travelers can't enter the town after a long night's travel. I say we just walk in."

Calinnae nodded. He had already determined to follow Jonan's lead, and there was no point second guessing himself now. The two boys backtracked a bit then slipped onto the path as unobtrusively as possible.

As they passed through the gate, one of the new guards growled suspiciously, "You're about mighty early, young 'uns."

"Not as early as you, governor!" said Jonan cheerfully, and although Calinnae heard him mutter something about "cheek", the guard let them pass without any trouble.

As he led Jonan through the waking streets, Cal hardly knew whether to be elated or anxious that they had passed so easily into Pravat. The walls were thick and strong, and the main gate almost impregnable. Had they made it in only to be trapped inside?

The gate they had used was not the original city gate, and they had to wind through some back lanes to reach the main street of Pravat. But Cal was confident in his direction. As he had told Jonan, the Hall of Records was right at the center of the town. He remembered his father telling him that the city had been built hundreds of years ago specifically to house the Hall. It had been fortified because of the records.

But that had been a long time ago, and signs of disrepair were visible everywhere. The city clearly hadn't been intended to be large, and it was over-crowded. Cal could only suppose that people flocked there because of the illusion of safety created by the thick walls. But he couldn't help but reflect sadly, as he watched a filthy child playing on the street, that no fortifications could protect against the destructive influence of a corrupt ruler.

As he watched, the child's mother ran outside and carried the boy into a rundown home, scolding as she went. Before she slammed the door she threw a suspicious look at the two strangers. Calinnae glanced at Jonan.

"Cheerful place, isn't it?" muttered Jonan. Cal just nodded, aware of eyes watching them from windows of other dwellings. He had never felt so conspicuous.

Once they emerged onto the main street, it didn't take them long to reach the main square, where the Hall was located. When Calinnae had come years before, the imposing building had been obscured by the market tents and stalls filling the square, but now, early in the morning, he could see it as it was obviously intended to be seen, imposing and central.

It towered above the buildings on either side, with a square street front from which a tall structure rose. It had not been well cared for. The stone was grimy, and in places had begun to crumble. The large round window of stained glass reflected the morning light only dully, encrusted with the buildup of uncounted years. But even in its decay, the building was impressive. It had been intended as the focal point of the square—of the city—and it showed. The building looked proud, Cal thought, disdainful of its sordid surroundings rather than sullied by them.

"Is that it?" Jonan's voice pulled Calinnae from his dreamlike contemplation.

"Yes, that's it," he answered. "But it doesn't look like it's open."

"Was it open last time you were here?" asked Jonan.

"I'm not sure," Cal answered slowly. "I don't remember. What do you want to do?"

"I guess...I guess we go and knock," said Jonan, his voice not quite matching his confident expression.

Cal gave a nervous glance around him. Surely it wouldn't be long until the town started to stir in earnest. "Speed not secrecy?"

"Speed not secrecy," Jonan said, his voice firmer now.

The two boys made their way furtively across the square. They didn't speak, but they both tensed as they left the shelter of the street and started across the open square. They reached the door of the Hall of Records without anyone else appearing, however. Jonan didn't hesitate as he raised his hand to give two firm knocks on the old wooden door.

Calinnae could hear the knocks echoing in the empty space behind, but there was no answering flurry of activity. They exchanged uncertain looks then, after a minute, Jonan raised his hand and knocked again, more loudly. Even while his instinct was telling him to retreat and hide, Calinnae had to admire Jonan's confidence. And his persistence was rewarded. After a moment, they heard a slow shuffling sound, approaching from far inside.

Finally the shuffling stopped, and a wooden slat was pulled aside at head height. It was dark inside, and Calinnae could barely make out a face at the opening. He could only see the eyes, glinting in the early morning light spilling in from the square.

"Who is it? What do you want?" asked a quavering voice. "Are you soldiers?"

"No, we're not soldiers," said Jonan. "And we want to view the records."

"The records?" repeated that feeble voice nervously. "Well—well you can't. The Hall is closed."

"What time will it open?" asked Jonan impatiently.

"It won't," the voice replied. "The records are closed to the public by order of the king."

"What?" said Calinnae sharply. "Since when?"

The eyes, that had been focused on Jonan, darted quickly to him. "Since two weeks ago, when an express messenger brought an edict." The eyes seemed to look Calinnae up and down. "Who are you, and why do you want to see the records?"

For a moment both boys were silent. The eyes were still on Calinnae, and he felt that he was being measured somehow, that their entrance would depend on his answer. "Because..." he said slowly. "Because to embrace our future we must understand our past."

There was an intake of breath from behind the door. The eyes looked quickly between Calinnae and Jonan then suddenly disappeared as the slat slid shut with a click.

Disappointed, Cal turned to find Jonan watching him strangely.

"What was that?"

"What?"

"What did you say just now? It sounded like a charm or something."

"You don't remember it?" Cal asked in surprise.

Jonan shook his head, still looking bewildered, but he was prevented from replying by the creaking of the great door in front of them. Tortuously, it inched open no more than enough for them to slide through.

"Is there anyone else in the square?" asked the same voice out of the darkness inside the building.

Jonan swept a quick look around them. "No, no one."

"Come on," said the voice. "Quickly, now."

Without a backward glance, Jonan slipped through the door. After taking his own furtive look around, Calinnae followed.

CHAPTER FOUR

From the outside of the building Cal had expected the door to open into some kind of antechamber. However, he found himself instead coming into a narrow passageway lined with overflowing bookshelves. It was very dark inside, and they had to follow closely behind their guide through the winding corridors to see their way from his single guttering candle.

After a few tight twists and turns the low ceiling suddenly fell away to reveal the high ceiling the exterior of the building had suggested. Instead of opening into the wider space, however, the corridor continued narrowly across what should have been a spacious room. As they hurried along in their leader's wake, they passed openings that revealed rows of similar shelves in both directions.

Suddenly Calinnae realized that the dark corridors inside the door had not been lined by the shelves, but had been created by them. In fact the building seemed to have been originally made up of one enormous room that had been transformed into a labyrinth by the addition of a staggering number of shelves, each laden with books and scrolls.

They were guided along a well-worn track through the maze. In a few minutes they found themselves ushered into a small room, one that seemed to have actually been made with walls. Unexpectedly, the room was neat and orderly. A quick glance around revealed that the small space served as both office and home. Fleetingly Cal wondered if this man ever left the Hall at all. There was one chair, into which their host sank.

The two boys remained standing before him, a bit awkwardly. In the light spilling in through a window set high in the wall, Cal could see that the man was ancient, older than anyone he had ever seen. His face was lined and creased, and his hands, although steady, were knotted and warped with age. His surprisingly thick hair was as white as the snow that supposedly covered the mountains in the east of Kyona.

"So," said the man, his eyes on Calinnae. "So. You want to see the records."

"Yes, that's right—" began Jonan, but the man cut him off, still watching Calinnae.

"What did you boys say your names were?"

Cal and Jo exchanged a look, and Cal could see that his friend was containing his frustration with an effort.

"We didn't," said Jonan shortly. "But my name is Jonan, and this is Calinnae."

"Calinnae," said the man slowly. "And Jonan. Unusual names."

"Yes, well, that's not really what we came to talk about," said Jonan impatiently.

But their host seemed to be in no hurry, now that they were safely inside his lair.

"A name can communicate a great deal," he said.

"What's your name then, sir?" asked Calinnae. He felt less urgency than Jonan—they seemed safe inside the Hall, somehow—but he was becoming increasingly uncomfortable with the man's scrutiny.

"My name?" repeated the man, a bit vaguely. "My name is Aurelius. I am the record keeper."

"Well, Record Keeper," said Jonan curtly. "Are you going to show us the records?"

Aurelius transferred his gaze to Jonan and watched him for an inscrutable moment. Then he folded his hands in his lap and adopted a more businesslike manner.

"And which records do you wish to view?"

A quick look passed between Calinnae and Jonan. Calinnae tried with his eyes to communicate caution to his impulsive friend, but Jonan didn't seem to need the warning. He was uncharacteristically hesitant, apparently trying to decide how best to answer.

"What about your oldest records?" suggested Cal helpfully.

Aurelius's eyes flicked back to him. "My oldest records?" he said slowly. "My oldest records must be maybe a hundred years old. Very valuable manuscripts. From the time of the current king's great-grandfather. They are the oldest records in the country, not just in Pravat."

"Are they?" asked Jonan, his eyebrow raised. "Because my mother mentioned even older records. She mentioned you, actually. Unless there's another record keeper in Pravat."

"Your mother?" repeated Aurelius, surprise on his face.

"Her name was Lynette," said Jonan quietly, but there was no change in the old man's expression.

"I know I said that a name can communicate a great deal," said Aurelius blankly, "but I'm afraid that one means nothing to me." He looked between them again, a frown adding more creases to his already wrinkled forehead. "Where did you boys say you're from?"

"Nerita," said Jonan curtly. Cal saw a slight stiffening of the record keeper's frame. It seemed they had captured his interest, although his voice was quite calm when he spoke.

"Well, if you're looking for the history of Nerita, I can help you. It was settled only about seventy-five years ago, when trading with the South Lands was at its peak. It was intended to be a trading port, but it was too far west and captains preferred to dock at Alezae. Nerita became instead a fishing village. Very pleasant spot, I hear. I've never been there myself."

"We know all that," said Jonan impatiently. We've heard it all in school."

"You attended school?" asked Aurelius, his expression intent.

"Yes," interjected Calinnae. "Neither of our fathers was a fisherman. But even many of the fishermen's children go to school now, you know."

"This is all very fascinating, but we're not interested in the history of Nerita," cut in Jonan shortly. He took a deep breath, as though preparing to plunge into cold water. "We don't have much time, sir, so I'll get to the point. My mother said that you showed some records to my father, Elam. Does *that* name mean anything to you?"

Aurelius froze, his gnarled hands gripping the arms of his chair. He had been watching Calinnae with interest, but as soon as Jonan spoke, he transferred his unwavering gaze to him. "Elam of Nerita," he said, his voice barely a whisper. "Yes, I have met him. He comes here sometimes, to...buy goods."

"Spend a lot of time out in the markets, do you?" asked Calinnae dryly.

Aurelius's eyes flickered back to him for an instant but returned almost immediately to Jonan. "Elam is your father?"

A tiny quiver passed over Jonan, and he turned his head away slightly. "He was my father," he said, his voice suddenly husky. "He's—dead." Calinnae felt the knife twist again in his own stomach.

"Dead?" exclaimed Aurelius. He began to surge up out of his chair, then dropped back, a blind look in his eyes. "Dead?"

Jonan nodded curtly.

"When?" whispered Aurelius. "How?"

"Murdered," said Jonan, an ugly look entering his eyes. "By Filip's soldiers." Jonan looked back at the old man, his gaze seeming to assess the stricken look in Aurelius's eyes. Then, with his familiar recklessness, he pushed on boldly.

"I think you know who he was, sir. I didn't know until last night—there was no warning, you see, no chance for him to talk to me before...But I'm hoping the records you showed him might tell me some of the things that he had no time to tell me. I wondered if he might even have left a record of our ancestry with you."

Aurelius shook his head, the same look of distress still in his eyes. "He left no records with me, young man. He never even said, not openly, but I was almost certain, and he had the ring..." He trailed off, seeming to speak more to himself than to them.

"This ring?" asked Jonan, drawing the chain from under his tunic and holding the signet ring out so that they could all see the crest. Aurelius stared at it for an unblinking moment.

"Soldiers are looking for us," said Calinnae quietly, when the record keeper showed no sign of breaking the silence. "We don't know how long we have, but we need to know if you have anything in your records that will convince other people of what you—I think—already believe."

"I wish I did," whispered Aurelius, his eyes fixed on Jonan, although it had been Calinnae who had spoken. "I will show you the records I showed Elam, but I don't think you'll find what you're looking for. Come."

Without a glance at Calinnae, he hobbled forward into the main hall. Jonan followed. For a moment Calinnae remained standing where he was, thrown by the unexpected surge of annoyance, almost anger, he had felt when Aurelius had transferred his intent gaze to Jonan after discovering his identity. The emotion had been as brief as it had been intense, but it had taken Calinnae utterly by surprise. He could not remember ever feeling genuinely resentful toward Jonan in his life, and it seemed like a bad time to start.

Shaking his head, he tried to throw off his unease and hurried out of the small room. The elderly man led them through the labyrinth, right to the back wall. At what Calinnae judged to be about the center of the space, there was a raised dais. On it stood a statue of a man, seated on a simple chair. The model looked to be about in his mid-thirties. He had an attractive face with a peaceful expression, a scroll open on his knees. Calinnae had been at the rear, but when he saw that figure, he found himself pushing forward in his haste to get a closer look.

"Is that—" he stopped short as he read the inscription on the dais. It described the statute as "Lord Lindor, Restorer of the Hall of Records". The second part of the inscription was so worn it was hardly legible.

"Lord Lindor..." he muttered, half to himself, taking an involuntary step back. "It can't be." He turned to Jonan and saw that his friend looked lost.

"Surely you remember?" Cal said, a bit impatiently. "Lindor. There was Lord Damian Lindor, then his son, Lord Derek Lindor." He raised his eyebrows at Jonan, unable to believe that he had really forgotten such a crucial detail of the history. "Surely you know, Jo. He was the one who—" Cal broke off, glancing nervously at Aurelius. Did he really know the stories? What if it wasn't safe to speak in front of him?

"That is not Lord Lindor," Aurelius said, his voice vibrating with some suppressed emotion. "That inscription was changed."

"Who is it?" asked Jonan curiously. "Or is it a mystery?"

Aurelius didn't immediately respond, and Calinnae stepped

forward again, reaching out a hand to touch the marble form of the lithe young man. "For a moment I thought I recognized him," he said quietly, speaking to Jonan. "Stupid, isn't it? It's just that I've heard the stories so many times...I guess I created an image in my mind of what they all looked like, and this is just how I pictured..." His voice petered out.

"King Cael," Aurelius finished for him. Cal turned to look at Aurelius, fear and excitement mingling inside him, quickening his breath. It was the first time he had ever heard that name spoken by someone outside of his and Jonan's families.

"Yes," he said. "Exactly."

Jonan seemed to be finally catching hold of the magnitude of the conversation. He looked quickly between Calinnae and Aurelius. "And is it him? Is it King Cael?"

For a moment Aurelius didn't answer, and Calinnae jumped in eagerly. "It is, isn't it? He was the one who restored the Hall of Records. After his daughter died. Lindor had nothing to do with it. He just followed him here the first time."

Aurelius nodded slowly. "Yes. It is him. He spent years restoring the Hall and updating its contents." He looked around sadly. "But none of the records you see here are the result of his labors."

Cal couldn't take his eyes from the stone face of his childhood hero, but Jonan followed Aurelius's gaze around the room. "What are all these records, then?"

Aurelius shrugged dismissively. "Local history, trade agreements, agricultural information. Valuable information in its way. But not what King Cael intended."

Jonan looked back at the statue. Glancing at his friend, Calinnae found that Jonan was watching the effigy intently, as though searching for something.

"Strange," Jonan muttered, so quietly that only Calinnae

could hear. "Strange to think that he was my ancestor. Here I am, standing just where he stood, how many years later?"

Calinnae considered for a moment. "About two hundred and fifty, probably." He looked at Jonan and saw a heaviness on his friend's brow, an unlooked-for burden that had not been there this time yesterday. "Yes, it is strange."

"You seem so well-informed that I wonder whether it is actually true that your father had no time to tell you what he might have wished to." Aurelius's voice was so close between them that both boys jumped involuntarily.

Jonan paused. "I heard fantastic tales at my father's knee, just like any other child. But it's time to separate fact from fiction. I want to know what I can trust."

Aurelius smiled. "You should rather think about whom you can trust. Facts will not save you when you are in peril."

He pushed forward between the two of them and walked up onto the dais. Pausing for a moment to look up into the face of the stone King Cael, he shuffled behind the figure and bent low, as if grasping something at knee level.

Calinnae jumped back with a gasp as the statue began to move, the stone making a grinding noise as it slid slightly to one side. Underneath was revealed an opening barely big enough for a man to slip into, and a spiral staircase going down into a dark recess. He looked up in astonishment to see Aurelius watching their reactions with some satisfaction. Calinnae guessed that in all his long years Aurelius had rarely had the opportunity to show off this particular spectacle.

After a dumbstruck moment he realized that Aurelius was motioning for them to descend. He exchanged a startled glance with Jonan then moved forward, his excitement mounting once again at the thought of accessing records placed there by King Cael himself. Jonan was starting to look a bit excited as well. Knowing his friend as he did, Cal knew that a hidden staircase underneath an ancient statue could hardly fail to get some kind of reaction.

He slid himself into the opening, and found that a short ladder led down to the start of the staircase. His hand on the rail, he began to descend the stairs, aware of Jonan right behind him. It was pitch black below, and he felt a rush of cold air as he went lower. After a moment a flickering light from above told him that Aurelius had followed them down.

Calinnae could still barely see as he reached the bottom of the staircase. He reached his hand out, seeking a wall or structure of some kind to grasp, but his hand met only empty space. He stepped to one side to allow Jonan to join him on the flat ground, and the two of them waited while Aurelius made his way painstakingly down the stairs.

CHAPTER FIVE

W hen he reached the bottom the record keeper used the candle to ignite first one, then a second and third lantern placed on stands around the base of the stairs. He held one aloft, and in its stronger light Calinnae was able to take in the space into which they had descended. Suddenly the cold draft was explained. This was not a small hiding spot as he had assumed. It was a large room—Cal judged it to be about a quarter of the size of the one above it. It too was lined with shelves. The shelves were not as full as those in the great hall above, but there was still an impressive number of documents on display, most of the volumes and scrolls covered with a thick layer of dust.

Wordlessly, he turned to his companions. Jonan was looking about him with an expression that matched Calinnae's own amazement. Aurelius was looking at the room too, a sadness in his eyes.

"This is all that's left," he said quietly. "Of the records left by King Cael but also of the centuries of records that were here prior to his time. The rest have all been destroyed or lost."

The thought made Calinnae sad, too. How much irreplaceable history had been lost? But Jonan spoke in a bolstering tone, apparently immune to the somber mood that had taken his companions.

"This is amazing. Much more than I expected to find." He looked at Cal, his brow creased. "Maybe too much, actually, since we're trying for speed over secrecy."

Cal nodded. "You're right. The soldiers could come to Pravat in search of you at any moment. You could spend years going through all of this information."

"You could," said Aurelius with a smile. "And I have. I know everything that's in this room. And I think I know what will most interest you."

He turned to Jonan. "Let's speak more plainly. I knew your father, may he rest in peace. He was a good man. He approached me many years ago, when he first journeyed to Pravat after your family moved to Nerita. Like you he came seeking information from this hall. Over time, I came to trust him. I told him all I knew. There was no need. He knew it all already. He sought confirmation, and in him I found...companionship. For the first time since the death of my mentor, who trained me as record keeper, I found someone with whom I could discuss the terrible and wonderful knowledge this place holds.

"Had I ever found another person whom I felt I could trust to discuss these matters with, you would not find me as you do, with no apprentice to replace me." For a moment he paused, and a flicker of something passed across his eyes. Pain, or anxiety perhaps.

"But that is its own problem and no doubt will have its own solution," he continued briskly. "As for your father...he never spoke outright, but with all he knew about the True Bloodline, well, I formed my own suspicions. I have never heard the names King Cael, Queen Jacqueline, or Prince Jonathon outside the annals of this room. Except from your father."

The two boys were both silent for a moment, exchanging glances. It was strange to Calinnae also to hear a stranger talk in these terms.

"We, on the other hand," said Jonan, "have heard those names from our cradles. In both our households."

Aurelius looked at Calinnae with the first sign of interest he'd shown since discovering Jonan's parentage. "Your parents then are friends of the Line?"

Pushing aside the discomfort in his mind that he stubbornly refused to acknowledge as resentment, Calinnae nodded.

"Yes, that's right. My father never told the stories, but there's no question that he and my mother both believed them. I don't know how they met Jonan's parents, in their youth in Alezae I believe. But when Jonan's family moved to Nerita, so did we."

Aurelius was fascinated. "I never imagined such a network. Are there others in Nerita who believe in the True Bloodline?"

Calinnae shook his head vigorously. "No. As far as we are aware, no one else knows anything beyond the vaguest legends. Since childhood we've been forbidden to speak of it outside our families."

Aurelius nodded, seeming to talk more to himself than to his companions. "Cautious, that was Elam. Wise, probably, but still. Always so very cautious."

"Yes," said Jonan quietly, "he always was. About everything, not just about this." Calinnae watched, feeling helpless, as Jonan seemed to struggle with himself before continuing. "But especially about this. He never mentioned you to me, for example."

"Or you to me, young man," said Aurelius, giving Jonan a measuring look. "Quite an omission."

"The records, sir?" Calinnae interjected.

"Yes, the records," said Aurelius, returning to the present. He took a second lantern and led the boys to a small table with a chair next to it. He placed the lantern on the table and disappeared into the dust-covered shelves. He returned shortly afterward with a bound volume. It was clean, and had clearly been handled more recently than most of the manuscripts down there. Perhaps a favorite of Aurelius's, Calinnae reflected.

"Start with this," Aurelius said, dropping the tome onto the table so that it sent up a cloud of dust from the surface. Eagerly, Calinnae dropped into the chair and pulled it toward him. Jonan leaned forward, his arm on the table, watching as Calinnae opened the heavy front cover of the volume. Looking up, Calinnae happened to catch Aurelius's eye and saw that the old man was frowning reproachfully at him.

For a moment he wondered if he had breached etiquette in his handling of the manuscript. But as Aurelius looked between him and Jonan he suddenly realized that he was being chastised for taking the chair while Jonan stood. Chagrined, he jumped to his feet again. Jonan was apparently oblivious of the interchange and gave Calinnae a questioning look as the chair scraped backward. Calinnae just shook his head.

Aurelius shuffled off again, and the two boys turned their attention back to the document, leaning together over the table. The first page of the volume read:

Annals of Cael, King of Kyona

'To embrace our future, we must understand our past'

On this fourth day of the fifth month of the tenth year of my reign, I, Cael, King of Kyona, hereby commission that a project be undertaken to restore the Hall of Records.

Having visited the Hall in recent weeks I have discovered that the records therein contained have reached a state of disorder and disrepair, a situation undesirable for the people of Kyona, for whose benefit these records are maintained. It is of great public interest that the records be updated and organized so as to allow access by any individual desiring to know the history of our land and our ancestors.

I have appointed Senalda of Pravat as the Official Record Keeper, but I myself will personally oversee the restoration process.

"To embrace our future, we must understand our past," read Jonan aloud. "That's what you said! That's why he let us in. How did you know that phrase?"

"From the histories of course. From your father. It was King Cael's...philosophy I suppose. The story was that he had it carved above the doorway to this place."

"Yes he did," said Aurelius, reappearing from the nearest dimly lit corridor. "Or so I've been told. It's not visible anymore."

Calinnae nodded absently. "It's been a long time." He turned to Jonan. "You really don't remember?"

Jonan shook his head, looking a bit sheepish. "I only paid attention to the action bits, you know that. Restoring records halls didn't quite capture my interest."

Calinnae smiled slightly as he turned back to the document. "No big surprise there." There was nothing further on the first page, but before he could turn it over, Aurelius spoke.

"This, I think, is what you've really come for." He laid an enormous volume, bound in worn leather, on the table. It was not as orderly as the one Calinnae had in front of him. It had loose leaves sticking out at strange angles and seemed a bit more disheveled. Both boys looked questioningly at Aurelius.

"These are the private records of King Cael. He began to write them around the time he commenced restoration of the Hall of Records, but he wrote about things much further in the past as well as things that occurred from that point onward."

He paused for a moment and gave them a look strongly

reminiscent of their teacher in Nerita. "This is a precious record. Perhaps the most precious in all this place. I would not even admit its existence to anyone other than you, let alone allow them to view it. Handle it with great care."

Calinnae nodded, reaching out a hand reverently, but Aurelius gently slid the volume across the table himself, placing it in front of Jonan. Calinnae looked away as Jonan ran a hand over the cover of the tome. To distract himself he flicked quickly through a few pages of the previous volume. It seemed to be an official record, detailing the restoration work carried out at King Cael's instigation. He pushed it away and turned back to Jonan. He was surprised to find that his friend seemed to have been waiting for him.

"You open it, Cal."

"Why?"

"You were always the big fan of King Cael. You know I preferred Jonathon...at least until he lost his nerve."

Jonan was grinning, and Calinnae found himself smiling back, responding instinctively to the first genuine smile he had seen on his friend's face since the nightmare that was the previous evening.

Obediently he opened the book, supporting the front cover with his hand as it seemed only tenuously connected to the rest of the volume. A loose cover page had been inserted in the front of the tome as follows:

Annals of Cael, King of Kyona

'To embrace our future, we must understand our past'

On this eighteenth day of the tenth month of the tenth year of my reign, I, Cael, add this record to the records held in the Hall at Pravat. This record shall be updated by me upon future visits to the Hall of

Records. I entrust it to Senalda the Record Keeper. It is to be kept secure, separate from the public records.

Cal again felt his excitement mounting. It suddenly struck him that this was a page that King Cael had actually touched. His hand had actually written these words. He put the loose cover leaf to one side and began eagerly to read the first entry.

This volume I set aside for my private records. I am no record keeper, but I feel compelled to record recent events. The loss of Thalia, my eldest daughter, to a terrible accident has driven me to this place. There are no words to describe what I feel. She was in her twelfth year. In her death she protected her brother. But the loss of her future is a heavy price to pay for his future, and the future of our land.

I cannot change what happened. I have tried everything, I have asked personally. He said it must not be changed because the past is as precious as the future, and it must not be lost. With no offspring he can never understand. He who sold his future irrevocably. Since I discovered his secret I do not know whether I trust his wisdom as my father did, but it is not in my power to override him. And perhaps he is right. I am powerless to change the past, but if her future is lost, her past must be preserved. If the past is so precious, I must try to save it, as I cannot save her.

So I will break the tradition of my fathers, that the history of the kings, unlike the rest of our land's history, must be passed down by spoken word alone. When he is ready I will tell it all to my son as my father told me. But I will also record it here. I hope my fathers will forgive me. Life is too fragile. My son almost died this past week, and I know in my heart I will not have another. My father once told me that our line is protected, but still...I will not gamble all our long history on the survival of my line.

This record will never be made public. But perhaps some day, when I am in the ground, and Jonathon with me, these pages may be read by the right eyes to save our stories from oblivion.

For Thalia.

Even after he reached the end of the entry, Calinnae found himself staring at the bottom of the page. He felt a strange thrill, half horror, half excitement. Were their eyes the ones King Cael foresaw?

He looked across at his friend and saw his own confusion reflected in Jonan's eyes.

"Do you—" Jonan began, but Calinnae shook his head.

"No, I don't understand."

"Who is this 'he' who can apparently change the past?" Jonan looked unnerved, and Calinnae could understand why. Changing the past was something out of a fairy story, but since the life-altering discoveries of the last twenty-four hours, he no longer felt confident discounting anything as fiction.

"I don't know," he said aloud. "The whole thing is bizarre. I remember the story of Princess Thalia's death well enough, but the rest I can't make sense of. It reads as though he wrote it the night he rode here, even if he didn't add the record until later. I mean, he'd just buried his daughter, he was grieving…"

Calinnae trailed off before the disbelieving look on his companion's face. "No way, Cal," said Jonan. "You can't explain it away as an unbalanced frame of mind. Maybe he was rambling a bit, but he wasn't crazy."

"I didn't mean he was crazy," said Cal quickly. "I just thought maybe he was…I don't know, talking in riddles."

Jonan shook his head. "I don't think so. It's more like he knew something we don't, something big. And I for one want to know what it is."

"Me too," said Calinnae, mostly to himself. He was more

shaken than he cared to admit by the cryptic words of his hero. He ran his eyes back down the page. "How does someone sell his future irrevocably?"

Jonan shrugged but gave no other answer other than his own question. "Did you know that the royal history was supposed to only be passed down orally?"

Calinnae shook his head. "No. It seems like there's a lot I didn't know. But whatever King Cael intended, his descendants seem to have stuck to the old tradition."

"That's true, isn't it?" said Jonan thoughtfully. "Maybe I shouldn't have criticized my father for being a storyteller. He comes from a longer line than I knew."

Cal nodded absently, turning the page. For what was apparently the most precious manuscript in Aurelius's arsenal, the record was not well organized. The next page was a description of the history of King Cael's wife, Queen Jacqueline, and the page after an account of the battles between King Cael's father and the raiders who came from the South Lands. Calinnae gave his eyes a weary rub. The adrenaline of finding this place was wearing off, and he was starting to feel the effects of their sleepless night.

He flicked slowly through the pages, recognizing here and there the familiar stories that he knew by heart, embellished with details he didn't have time to stop and appreciate. Still, the familiarity of these accounts comforted him, reminding him that they weren't really starting from scratch.

"It's all here," he said quietly, after scanning an entry dated some fifteen years after the first, where King Cael recorded the appointment of Prince Jonathon to the responsibility over trade and border relations with the neighboring kingdom of Valoria. "Just like your father described it. It's all true, it must be."

Jonan met Calinnae's eyes, and for the first time since discovering his identity he looked as uncertain as Cal felt.

"It must be," he agreed. "But is there nothing about the time after King Cael's line lost the throne? Nothing that might help prove that I'm Prince Jonathon's descendant?"

Cal shook his head. "Not that I can see." He glanced at the chain around his friend's neck. "Nothing except for that."

"We already had this," said Jo heavily. "I was hoping to find something more."

"No," said Cal, "I mean—" he rifled through some pages, until he found one of the cover sheets. "Look."

Jonan leaned closer, frowning, and Cal pointed to the intricate symbol impressed into a circle of wax that appeared on the page, above King Cael's heading.

"Is that...?"

Cal nodded. "I think so. Compare it and see."

Jonan pulled the ring out from under his shirt and turned it so that they could see the crest. It seemed to match the indentation. After a moment's hesitation, he pressed the ring into the wax. It sank perfectly into the mold. The two boys stared at each other.

"Do—do you think that this mark was made by this very ring?" Jonan sounded shaken.

"I do," said Cal, his voice trembling with excitement. "So that's something, at least!"

"It certainly is," said Jonan. He was silent for a moment, considering. "It's not exactly conclusive, though, is it? I mean..." He hesitated, swallowing hard before continuing. "I took this ring from my father's dead body. Anyone could have done that. The soldiers would have if they'd known it was there."

"That's true," said Cal bracingly. "But it's a place to start. Just don't—don't lose it, or throw it away as an act of rebellion against your chicken-hearted ancestors, all right?"

Jo gave a hollow laugh. "I won't do that, don't worry."

Cal glanced back at the record in front of him, scanning it

idly until his eyes were arrested by an unfamiliar word. "What's that?" he said, speaking his thought aloud.

"What's what?" asked Jonan, peering over his shoulder. Calinnae pointed to a paragraph half way down the page.

"That. What's 'the Esvalere'?"

"No idea," said Jonan blankly. "Never heard of it before."

The two boys put their heads together, as Calinnae scanned the paragraph before, looking for clarity in the context.

I am proud of Jonathon. He is young for this duty, but already he is committed. He wears responsibility well. His mother will miss him as this role will require him to be frequently at the border. I tried to comfort her with the reminder that he will be in the region of her people, that she has long wanted all of our children to know the mountains and their roots there. She smiles and nods, but she doesn't hear me. She doesn't hear anyone anymore. She sinks daily deeper into a place I cannot reach. I know it makes her nervous to send Jonathon away, but he is a man now. Too much of his time is devoted to trying to ease her pain. I never wanted him to bear this burden, or to think of his life as bought by her sacrifice. I regret now telling him all that I did about his sister. It is time for him to look ahead. I can never believe that the past is more precious than the future. I tried to explain this to him, but all his response was to assure me that he understands the importance of securing the succession. It made me smile to hear him, still such a boy, talk of marriage and children.

But every day he is less the boy and more the man. I will watch him in the months to come. Maybe he will be ready soon. He is strong already, wiser than I was at his age, but still so young. The Esvalere is a heavy burden to bear. I am afraid of moving too fast. He may be strong, but he is gentle, and sensitive. He is more like his mother than like me. Daily I see her in him, as she used to be. Maybe that's why I love him so much. And why I fear for him in my heart. There is no

need to rush. I am still strong, with many years ahead of me. I will
watch, and I will wait.

Cal rubbed his eyes again. No explanation there, just more questions. He looked again at the date and felt a shiver go through him. If only King Cael had truly had many more years ahead of him.

"The Esvalere is a heavy burden to bear," Jonan read out quietly. "What does that mean?"

"I don't know," said Calinnae, his voice coming out more frustrated than he had intended. "I don't have any idea what he's talking about." He took a deep breath.

"I don't either," said Jonan, "but it seems important."

Calinnae considered the relevant paragraph again. "He speaks of it so casually, as though it needs no explanation. I don't think it can be the only time he mentions it in here."

He began flicking through the book again, more quickly now, past descriptions of the wedding of one of Jonathon's remaining sisters, battles, celebrations, genealogies. He had almost reached the back when Jonan spoke.

"There! That page, what's that?"

Calinnae pulled out the page in question. He had not needed Jonan's exclamation to note the page as different from the rest. It was loose, and looked older than the others. The writing was different, but at the top it said, in King Cael's writing, "The story of the Esvalere, as my father told it to me and his father told it to him". The entry read:

Once, long ago, when the race of men was high and noble, there
existed a friendship between the king of men and the dragon-ruler
Qadir. Such was the character of the king of men, that Qadir
entrusted him with a gift: the Esvalere. The glass sphere contained fire
to the eye of the ordinary beholder, but to the king of men it contained

sights that could nowhere else be seen. Qadir instructed the king in its use, and the king became the wisest of all rulers. A place was built in the castle of men to house the Esvalere, and none but the king could enter. The king swore an oath to Qadir that none but his heir, and those who followed after, would be allowed to look in the Esvalere, or be instructed in its use. It was said that a powerful enchantment was placed on the sphere by Qadir, so that none but the true king or his heir could wield it. If another tried to use it—

Calinnae came back to reality with a start as the book in front of him slammed shut with a loud snap. He looked up in surprise to see Aurelius, his gnarled hand resting protectively on the front cover, looking at the two boys with alarm in his eyes.

CHAPTER SIX

"You have to go!" the record keeper said in a strained voice.

"What?" Jonan beat him to it, his voice holding all the disbelief that Calinnae felt. "No, we were just finding answers."

Aurelius shook his head frantically. "You have to go now, the soldiers are here."

"Soldiers?" Calinnae repeated sharply. "Where?"

"In the square," said Aurelius impatiently. "I was standing watch, and I heard them."

The two boys exchanged looks. "What do you think?" Calinnae asked nervously. "Routine check?"

"No!" said Aurelius before Jonan could respond. "They're rounding everyone up for questioning. They know you're here somewhere. You were seen."

Calinnae felt a rushing in his ears as panic clouded his mind. He took in his surroundings with a glance. They couldn't get much more trapped than this dim underground cavern.

"Is there another way out?" Jonan asked sharply.

Aurelius shook his head. "There's only one door into the Hall, and it opens onto the main square, as you saw."

Jonan's eyes met Calinnae's, but he could read nothing but his own fear reflected back. Calinnae took a deep breath and tried to pull himself together.

"We have to think for a minute," he said. "Don't do anything rash Jo."

"I think rash might be our only option at this point." His friend's voice was sharp. "Unless you want to live here forever."

"Maybe staying here isn't such a bad idea." Cal was thinking aloud, but the more he thought about it, the more it seemed like the safest option.

"Surely you're not serious!"

"Not forever," Cal said quickly. "Just until nightfall. It will be easier to sneak out of the city then."

Jonan was shaking his head long before Cal finished speaking. "No way, that's madness. The soldiers can only just have arrived, there's no way they were here when those guards just let us wander in. They're going to put all of Pravat on lockdown as quickly as they can. Every second counts now, and it's not going to get any easier to get out."

Cal closed his eyes. His head was pounding, and he was still finding it hard to think straight. "Everything you just said makes sense, but I still think we should stay."

"What? Why?"

"Because...I don't know..." Cal wanted to say more, but somehow he was finding it impossible to articulate the intensity of the pull he felt to stay in their hideout, to stay safe. He opened his eyes and found his friend staring at him in disbelief. He tried again.

"Look, your survival matters now! In a way it never did before. You're only seventeen, you don't have a son—if you die, the Line dies with you. I know you've always thought Prince

Jonathon was wrong to hide, but this is why he did it—to ensure the continuation of something greater than himself."

Jonan made a frustrated noise. "We can argue about the choices of my ancestors another time. Right now we need to get out of here."

"But it matters right now, Jo, that's what I'm saying. Going out there is too risky!"

"Cal, every breath we take is a risk now," said Jonan. He looked at his friend in silence for a moment. "Look, I have no desire to tell you what to do," he said finally. "All I can tell you is what I'm going to do. And I'm not staying here."

Cal sighed. "Then neither am I." Despite the almost physical resistance he felt to taking the more dangerous course, Cal didn't hesitate. If he couldn't convince his friend, he could at least follow.

Aurelius had watched the exchange in silence, but he now stepped forward. "If you're leaving, I agree that you should do it now. I want to seal up the entrance to this room as soon as possible. It must be protected from discovery."

"Yes, of course," said Cal quickly. "Lead the way, Jo."

Jonan didn't need telling twice. He was up the staircase and grasping the bottom rung of the ladder before Calinnae had moved from his place. Hurrying to catch up, Cal soon emerged back into the main room of the Hall. Aurelius followed behind. Cal, his eyes on Jonan, wasn't watching the old man, but he heard the statue begin to grind back into place.

"Come," said Aurelius briskly. "I'll take you back to the entrance."

He led them through the labyrinth of shelves at a surprisingly brisk pace. When they reached the door through which they had entered, Aurelius slid back the wooden slat and peered out.

"The square is full of people," he whispered. "I can see

soldiers scattered throughout. It looks like they've rounded people up from their homes."

Cal joined the record keeper at the spy-hole. "I see what you mean. There are people everywhere." He turned to his friend. "That could work in our favor, Jo," he said. "Maybe we can blend with the crowd."

Jonan nodded. "I say we slip out one by one," he suggested. "Let's set a rendezvous point and meet up as soon as we can get away. The gate we came in through is probably the best option, since we don't know our way around any other part of town."

Cal raised his eyebrows. "You want to split up?"

"Just temporarily. If we were seen, they're probably looking for a pair of boys traveling together."

"That actually makes sense," Cal admitted after a moment's thought.

Jo rolled his eyes. "No need to sound so surprised," he muttered.

"Sorry," said Cal with a brief smile. "I'm not used to your plans being well thought through."

Jonan grinned back and put a hand on the door.

"Whoa, what do you think you're doing?" said Cal sharply.

"Isn't this the plan?"

"No way you're going first." Cal's voice was as firm as his conviction. He couldn't stop Jo from taking risks, but he would still do everything he could to protect his friend.

"It's my dumb idea to go out there Cal, it's only fair that I take the risk first."

"I don't care about fair," said Cal, pushing past his friend. "You're the one with a legacy to protect, remember? I'm going first." Without giving any more opportunity for argument, he opened the door as carefully as he could, and slipped out into the square.

For a moment he just stood there blinking, blinded by the

bright light. In the darkness of the secret record chamber, it was easy to forget that it was still only morning. He squinted around him, trying to be subtle without looking furtive. No one seemed to be looking at him. After getting his bearings, he sidled up behind a group of people part way across the square and tried to look like part of their number.

For a couple of minutes he kept his head down, focusing on each breath as he waited for his heart to stop thumping. When no one challenged him, he began to hope that he really had managed to escape notice. He looked up and took stock of his surroundings.

As he took in the scene around him, he could understand why no one had been paying him any attention. Everyone's focus was on the soldiers, and every face he saw held nothing but fear. Nerita was too small a town to attract the notice of the capital in the ordinary course of things, and Cal had never once seen a soldier there before the previous evening. The reaction of the people around him suggested more experience with the king's squadrons. The townspeople's fearful attempts to avoid notice filled Calinnae with apprehension.

Soldiers were moving through the crowd, shouting and shoving. At first Calinnae assumed that they were giving directions, but when he tuned in to the soldiers closest to him, he found that they were threatening rather than instructing. They apparently felt that moving people forcefully to where they wanted them would have better effect than words.

"Get over there! And watch yourself—I don't like that look."

Calinnae bristled in defense of the frightened looking group of peasant children who were being pushed into a corner of the square by a particularly large soldier. As far as he could see, none of them were giving the soldier any kind of look, their heads bowed, and their gaze on their feet.

Keeping a surreptitious eye on the Hall of Records, Cal saw

Jonan slip out a few minutes after he had. Jonan didn't look his way, but walked slowly and confidently in the opposite direction, stopping to lean against the wall of a building in a crowded part of the square. Cal had to admit to himself that he was impressed with how well Jonan pulled off the air of nonchalance.

Looking around, Cal suddenly realized that there was method to what had at first seemed like random bullying. The soldiers were herding people into age categories. The understanding came only a moment before the reality. Cal almost cried out in surprise when a rough hand grabbed his arm.

"You, this way! And don't give me any trouble."

In addition to the soldier who had grabbed Calinnae, two others had approached the group he had joined and were pulling other youths in the same direction. A very brief reflection convinced Cal that he gained nothing by resisting at this moment. He allowed himself to be pulled along toward the middle of the square.

Glancing up he caught a glimpse of Jonan and saw that his friend had half pushed himself from the wall where he was leaning, obviously debating whether to intervene. Their eyes met, and Cal gave the tiniest shake of his head. Jonan hesitated for a moment, then sank back against the wall, his muscles tensed for action.

The soldier who had hold of Cal released him after shoving him with unnecessary force into the group of young people already gathered in the middle of the square. A couple of them stumbled as he was propelled into them, but no one met his eye. Some of them looked frightened, but he also saw more defiance in the expressions around him than in anyone else in the square. He was heartened to think that some of the people of Pravat had some fight left in them.

"Get out of my way, you stupid old crone!"

Cal's attention was caught by a scene unfolding on the other side of the square. The same soldier he had seen pushing the children around had found an easy target.

"No need to round you up, no one's interested in you, are they?" The soldier gave a nasty laugh.

The man stepped slightly to the side, and Calinnae saw the object of his ridicule. An old woman was sitting on the edge of the square, her head bowed as if to avoid being seen. The tattered state of her clothing marked her as a beggar as surely as the blanket laid out in front of her, containing a few coins, obviously given by some of Pravat's more openhanded residents.

As Cal watched, the soldier leaned down and picked up a coin. "Pathetic!" he taunted. "This won't even buy me an ale. If you want to make amends for interfering with king's business, you'll have to do better than that."

Interfering? The woman hadn't even moved from her position against the wall. She still kept her eyes down, as if hoping that the brute in front of her would disappear if ignored. Cal felt his blood begin to boil. Was this the protection their king offered to the vulnerable in his land? Maybe Jo was right that it had been a crime for his father to let Filip continue as king unchallenged.

Thinking of Jo, Cal suddenly realized that if he felt angry, his friend would certainly be furious. And when Jo was angry, he usually did something impulsive and dangerous.

Cal's eyes flicked to Jo's position against the wall, not too far from where the woman sat. Sure enough, to his practiced eye every inch of Jo's taut frame showed that he was about to snap. Cal's hopes of remaining unobtrusive began to ebb.

He looked around and saw that soldiers blocked every exit to the square. Just as he was debating whether to push out of the middle and make his way to Jo, Cal heard a pained cry. His attention snapped back to the beggar woman. The soldier had kicked her, and was clearly about to do so again, continuing to harangue the woman verbally.

For a moment Cal forgot Jo's recklessness and the danger of their situation. He felt his own anger rise, and wanted to run to the woman's defense himself. But the impulse was instantly met by an even stronger and more intense urge. The desire to stay safe was so powerful it felt more like a need. Ashamed, Calinnae had no time to wrestle with himself, as another much stronger cry rang out across the square, jerking him back to his surroundings.

"Coward!"

For a shocked moment, Calinnae thought Jonan was talking to him, but he quickly pulled himself together. As predicted, Jonan had thrown himself into the soldier's way.

"Is that how the king's soldiers show their strength? By bullying defenseless beggars?"

Cal groaned internally, even while another part of him applauded Jo's words. They were in for it now. It was clear that Jonan had no thought for his own safety, but the sight of the slim young man facing off against the thickset soldier, armed with a sword, filled Cal with terror. With a rush of shame he was reminded that it should have been him interjecting. Jonan, much more than Calinnae, could not afford to draw attention to himself.

"What did you call me?" roared the soldier.

"I called you a coward," repeated Jonan, his voice calm but carrying. "Because that's what you are."

"We'll see how smart your mouth is once I cut out your tongue," growled the older man.

Jonan shrugged. "Perhaps we will, but attacking an unarmed youth won't make you less of a coward."

Calinnae felt a ripple pass through the group of young people standing around him. Someone even gave a low chuckle. He too admired Jo's courage, but for him there was no humor in his best friend facing his enemies alone. Cal started forward but was instantly restrained by a nearby soldier.

"Don't get any ideas, kid."

Cal tugged fruitlessly at the hold on him, but at that moment his attention was caught by a new voice. Another soldier had joined the first one.

"Hey, he is just a youth."

"So what?" raged the man whom Jo had insulted. "You think I care how old he is? If he's old enough to defy me, he's old enough to find out the consequences."

"No, I mean he should be in the middle with the others. You can settle your personal score later, but don't forget our orders."

"You're right," said the first soldier, turning back to Jonan with a very ugly look. "He fits the description, and he's got rebel written all over him. We should take him in for questioning." He cracked his knuckles meaningfully.

"We're looking for two, remember?" interjected the second soldier. "This one seems to be on his own. It shouldn't be too hard to figure out if he's a local."

He turned to the square at large and raised his voice. "Listen up! Two strangers came into town early this morning. They're troublemakers and criminals, and we're here to do you a favor by removing them before they cause you any problems. Anyone who can reliably identify them will be rewarded. Anyone who attempts to shelter them will be punished."

He strode forward and grabbed Jonan's arm. "Does anyone recognize this young man? Is he a local here, or a stranger?" There was silence. "Anyone? Anyone at all?"

Cal stood frozen in indecision. What should he do? He could hardly stand to see Jo standing there alone, with no one willing to speak for him. But saying that he knew him would only make things worse. The last thing he wanted to do was to confirm that Jo was one of two young men traveling through the town, not recognized by anyone else.

"He's a local!"

The voice, coming from right behind Cal, startled him enough to make him jump. He turned and stared in surprise at the speaker. It was the one who had chuckled at Jo's earlier retort, a young man about Cal's own age.

The soldier who addressed the crowd turned his attention to the unknown speaker.

"You there! You say he's a local?"

"Sure," said the youth casually. "He's lived on my street since we were children. His name is Fenton."

"That's right," chipped in another young man from the crowd. "We both run errands for the apothecary."

Cal's heart was thumping furiously. Was this going to work? Were they really about to be saved by the kind intervention of strangers?

"No he doesn't!" asserted a new voice disastrously. Cal singled the speaker out as a teenage boy standing not far from him. "No one else runs errands for the apothecary."

"Yeah," said a girl. "I've never seen him before in my life, and I know he doesn't live on your street, because I live on your street."

The first speaker glared at her, and she shrugged, saying more quietly, "What? He's a total stranger, and you heard the soldier. I'm not risking my life or my family's for someone whose name I don't even know, no matter how brave he is."

"Is that so?" said the soldier who had addressed the crowd. He eyed their would-be rescuer grimly. "We'll deal with you later," he promised.

"Not from around here, huh?" said the first soldier, stepping up to Jonan and grabbing the arm that was not already being held. "Where's your friend then? We know there are two of you. Our orders are to bring you both in. And it'll be all the better for you if you don't make any trouble about it."

Calinnae's mind raced, trying to think of a way out of this situation. What could he do to free Jo? If only their positions were reversed, Jo could probably have slipped away unnoticed. It didn't matter so much if Cal was caught. But even as the thought occurred to him, he dismissed it. Jo would never leave him behind, just as he would never leave Jo.

Cal was searching frantically for a solution when he heard Jonan's voice, as confident as ever.

"Orders? Whose orders?"

"By order of the king, brat," said the soldier. "So no amount of smart talking will get you out of it."

Jonan evidently thought otherwise. Cal saw him take an appraising glance around the square before he answered the soldier. He spoke loudly, his voice clear and carrying.

"King? Filip isn't the king."

A hush instantly fell over the scene. Every face turned toward Jonan. Cal found himself staring, as wide eyed as everyone else. For a moment even the soldiers had nothing to say, apparently stunned into silence.

"He's a usurper," Jonan continued boldly. "Like his fathers before him." He looked around at the crowd. "We've all heard the whispers. People say the true line of the royals is lost, but it's not. Just hidden from thugs like these." He nodded at the soldiers, who were still staring at him in shock.

Cal could hardly believe his ears. What was Jonan doing? He knew his friend was reckless, but this brazen declaration was beyond anything.

Jonan was still speaking, his voice rising to a shout. "Filip is not a good king—because he's not supposed to be king. And I for one say it's time to do something about it!"

As Jonan was speaking, Cal could feel a knot of tension building in the group of young people around him. For a heartbeat after Jonan delivered his challenge the scene remained frozen, then chaos erupted all around them.

CHAPTER SEVEN

The soldiers seemed to emerge from their stupor just as a collective shout rang out from most of the youths in the middle of the square, and a number of their elders around its edges. A multitude of people surged toward Jonan, and the two soldiers on either side of him turned their attention toward the suddenly hostile crowd. When they pulled out their swords, the unarmed townspeople slowed their advance. No one actually attacked the soldiers, but the momentum continued as raised voices filled the square. The words themselves were lost in the melee, but the anger was clearly communicated as a town's worth of pent up fear and frustration broke free.

In the confusion, Cal had no difficulty pulling out of the now slackened grip on his arm. He pushed his way through the crowd toward Jo, only to find that his friend had disappeared. For a moment Cal looked frantically around, afraid that he would see Jo being dragged away by soldiers. But as far as he could see, all the soldiers present were fully occupied with restraining the crowd. Try as he might, Cal could see no sign of Jo. It was hard to even get his bearings as he was jostled by the mass of people surging through the previously empty space.

Looking around, he saw a trader's cart, full of sacks of grain. Running to it, he leaped nimbly up onto the wooden structure, balancing on the edge. From his new vantage point he could see that a number of soldiers had abandoned their spots at the entrances to join the action in the middle of the square. Cal could still see no sign of Jo, but several other people were clearly taking the opportunity to make a clean exit from the scene.

Slipping away and meeting at their rendezvous point had been Jo's idea. Cal could only hope and trust that his impulsive friend had stuck to the plan.

Jumping down from the cart, Cal raced as quickly as he could toward the place where the main street entered into the square. He made it across the square unchallenged and had just started down the thoroughfare when a hand grasped his arm firmly.

"Where do you think you're going, young 'un? I saw you were mighty keen to join that troublemaker earlier."

Cal didn't need more than a second to recognize that talking was not going to get him out of this one. The man had Cal's right arm in a painfully tight grip, but unfortunately for him, he didn't know that Cal favored his left hand.

Not bothering to reply to the soldier's words, Cal pulled back his left arm and swung his fist forward with all his might, catching the soldier directly in his face.

Taken by surprise, the man staggered back for a moment, releasing his grip. That moment was all Cal needed, and he took off running at full speed. He heard the soldier's shout behind him, and he quickly dove off the main street into a random side alley, hoping desperately that he wasn't heading into a dead end.

Despite the danger, Cal couldn't resist a quick grin as he ran. It had been quite a while since he and Jo had sparred, and it was satisfying to know that he hadn't forgotten how to deliver a blow. Plus, after the constriction of the underground chamber, and the mounting tension in the square, there was a release in running as fast as he could.

The soldier pursuing him was much older and looked like he had indulged too much in his comforts. Cal soon pulled far enough ahead that he was confident that the soldier was always more than one corner behind. Still, it wasn't enough to outrun his pursuer to the entrance. Cal knew he needed to lose the man before he rejoined Jo if they were to have any hope of getting away from Pravat without a squadron behind them.

Cal was starting to pant himself when he saw what he'd been looking for—a concealed alcove not visible until you were alongside it. He pulled abruptly to a halt and threw himself backward into the space, crouching down as the soldier's pounding steps drew closer. He saw the older man race past, and remained crouching until all sounds of footsteps faded and his pounding heart had calmed to a steady throb.

He poked his head out cautiously. Seeing no one in the alley, he wasted no more time, racing back the way he had come. As he ran through the streets, he occasionally saw faces appear at windows of the houses, always pulled hastily back at the sight of him. Apparently news of the commotion in the square had spread, and everyone who had managed to avoid or escape the scene was keeping their heads down. After a few twists and turns he began to be afraid that he was lost in the labyrinth of back alleys, but suddenly he emerged again onto the main street.

He was quite a way from the central square, but he could nevertheless hear the continued shouting. He jogged away from it, toward the city wall, watching anxiously for a familiar landmark. He wasn't sure he would recognize the route back through the side streets to the gate through which they'd entered Pravat. Fortunately he didn't have to. Very soon, he saw a signpost labeled "To South Gate". He turned down the small street indicated and picked up speed, his heart thumping as he tried to think what he would do if Jonan wasn't there.

As he neared the gate, he suddenly remembered that there would be guards, and slowed his pace, sticking as close as possible to the walls of the buildings lining the street. Finally he saw it up ahead—the city wall. He stopped and peered around the final corner. There were two guards stationed at the entrance, looking anxiously back toward the main square.

The question of how to get past the guards tugged at Cal's mind, but he noted with relief that the gate itself was still open. Apparently the order for a full lockdown, that was surely coming, had not yet reached this quarter of the town.

Cal was so focused on what was around the corner that he had paid no attention to the empty street behind him. Consequently, it took all his willpower not to give away his position by crying out in shock when he suddenly felt a hand grab his shoulder.

He spun around, his fists already raised, then slumped with relief at the sight of his best friend.

"Easy there," whispered Jonan. "I expected you'd be mad about my stunt back there, but I didn't expect violence."

The fact that he was relieved to see Jo whole and unharmed did not prevent Cal from finding his cocky grin maddening.

"You're hilarious," he whispered back. "Mad is an understatement, but we can talk about that later. First we have to figure out how to get out of here."

Jo's expression instantly turned serious. "Yeah, I know. I was getting worried—I thought you'd never come!"

"Sorry," said Cal. "I got chased out of the square by a soldier, and I had to lose him before coming to find you." He permitted himself a brief grin. "Landed him a good blow first, though."

"Yes, Cal!" Jo kept his voice quiet with evident difficulty. "I was starting to think you'd lost your nerve, but I'm glad to know you've got some action left in you. I wish I'd seen it."

"Just because I don't look for trouble doesn't mean I can't hold my own. You know I always used to beat you in a fight," retorted Cal, feeling slightly stung by his friend's accusation.

"Not always," mumbled Jo. "Anyway, aren't we supposed to be figuring out a way to get out of here? I'd say we have very little time before the guards find out what's going on and that gate is locked."

"Yes, you're right," said Cal, deciding not to point out the obvious change of topic. "And you're the one who's put the whole place in an uproar, so what's your plan for getting out of here?"

"I haven't got one," admitted Jonan. "I kind of thought you'd be at your limit with my plans, anyway. I was hoping you might have a bright idea."

Cal peered back around the corner, chewing the inside of his cheek distractedly. "We could try to take them on, but I'm not at all confident that we could overpower them. Maybe if we were armed." He turned toward his friend but stared through him unseeingly, lost in thought. Something was tugging at his mind, but he couldn't place it. It felt like he was forgetting something important.

His mind strayed back to the Hall of Records. He knew it was hardly the time to be thinking about it, but he was so frustrated to have had to leave without getting to read those incredible accounts. He remembered flicking through King Cael's personal records, catching glimpses of all those familiar stories that he had heard a dozen times before.

"That's it!" he exclaimed suddenly, almost forgetting to keep his voice down. "The South Lands raiders!"

"What?" asked Jonan blankly. "What are you talking about?"

"The story," said Calinnae, "from the legends. Prince Cael

and Lord Damian, when they were young, before Cael was king. They went on a reconnaissance trip to find out the extent of the incursion by the raiders from the South Lands."

"Are you serious, Cal?" hissed Jonan. "This is not the time for storytelling! I know 'sit and wait' is your favorite tactic, but surely this time you see we need to move!"

Cal barely heard his friend, and didn't respond. He was still lost in his thoughts, recalling the details of the story, seeing it play out in front of him more vividly than his imagination had ever recreated it before.

Cael looked at his friend.

"Any bright ideas?" he asked quietly.

Damian said nothing, but gave him an expressive look from underneath his bloodied brow. Cael winced as he took in again his companion's bruised face. He knew he didn't look much better, but at least he didn't have to look at his own injuries.

"I know, I know, this whole thing was my idea, and I should be the one to get us out of it," he said sheepishly.

"I didn't say that, Your Highness," said Damian stiffly.

"Oh, don't 'Your Highness' me Damian," retorted Cael. "It's not like you were reluctant for a fight."

Damian sighed. "That may be true," he admitted, "but I still don't have any idea how to get out of this mess."

Cael shrugged. "It could be worse."

Damian threw an incredulous glance around the foul-smelling dungeon in which they were imprisoned. "Are you serious?"

"Of course I am."

"I'm sorry, but did you not notice our cellmate down here? You're telling me this is a good situation to be in?"

Cael winced again as he followed Damian's glance toward the rag-

covered skeleton who shared their accommodations. "I'm not saying it's a good situation, just that it could be worse. At least they don't know who we are. That's a significant advantage."

"That's true," said Damian bitterly. "They would never guess who we are because they wouldn't imagine for a moment that the heir to the throne would be foolhardy enough to attempt to personally take on a squadron of his own soldiers single-handed."

"Not single-handed," corrected Cael with a grin. "You were with me, Damian." His friend's only reply was a grumble, and Cael's own expression was more serious as he continued. "I shouldn't have attacked them of course," he acknowledged. "I lost my head a bit. I was just so enraged to discover that some of our own are in league with the slave traders. Selling out their own countrymen!"

"That was a blow," agreed Damian.

"But it does explain how the raiders have been having such success," mused Cael. "My father will be very interested in our report."

"For you to make a report we first have to get out of here alive," Damian pointed out.

"True," said Cael briskly. "There's a guard outside the door. How do we get past him? We could probably overcome him," Damian made a disbelieving noise, but Cael ignored it and pushed on, "but then we'd have the squadron down on us, and we wouldn't get far. We need to figure out how to get out of here without him realizing."

Cael fell silent for a moment, thinking hard.

"I have it!" he cried suddenly, then lowered his voice with a conscious look toward the door of their prison. "I have a plan. We can use my identity to get out of here."

"Cay—" started Damian warningly, but Cael shook his head, dismissing the other man's concerns.

"Don't worry, Damian, I've got this. It's going to work." His friend didn't look convinced by Cael's confident tone, but he nevertheless leaned in to hear the plan explained. With no other ideas, he had little option but to acquiesce.

A minute later, the guard outside heard a whisper through the bars set into the door of the cell behind him.

"Psst. Hey you!"

He grunted. "Keep it quiet in there."

"I need to speak to your leader. Take me to him!"

"Nice try, scum," laughed the guard. "You're staying right there."

"Ssh! Keep your voice down! Don't let him hear you! If he finds out, I don't know what he'll do."

The guard hesitated, his curiosity clearly roused, even though he was trying not to show it. "Who are you talking about, fool?"

"Him!" Cael jerked his head back toward Damian, sitting against the wall all the way to one side of the cell. "Don't you know who he is?" He flattered himself that he had hit just the right balance of incredulity and scorn in his tone.

The guard hesitated again as he peered into the cell, and Cael saw him take in the quality of his and Damian's clothes as he looked them up and down.

"What are you talking about?" he said gruffly.

"He's the prince," hissed Cael. "Sent to do reconnaissance by his father. The king." His emphasis on these last words was clearly not lost on the guard. "If you take me to your leader, I'll explain the whole thing. I'll tell you everything in exchange for my freedom. I wonder how happy your leader would be if you passed up this opportunity on his behalf."

The guard hesitated for a moment, then grunted again. "I'll take you to him, but the first sign of trouble, this goes through your throat." He patted his sword meaningfully.

Cael nodded eagerly. "No trouble! Take me to him."

The guard pulled a set of keys off his belt and unlocked the large padlock on the door. As soon as the door was open, Cael found a sword point at his neck. He put his hands up to show his cooperation. The guard kept his sword pointed at Cael with one hand while he used the other to click the padlock shut. This task complete, he gave Cael a shove toward the exit.

"Get moving."

Cael was young and strong, but he nevertheless fell hard to the ground upon being shoved.

"No need to be so rough!" he complained petulantly.

"Get up, you pathetic flower," scoffed the guard. Cael began to comply, grabbing at the guard to help pull himself up.

"Get off!" spat the other man, pushing Cael away. Cael fell back to the ground with a convincing cry of pain. "Get up and move NOW or you're going straight back in the cell!" the guard said, his face still etched with scorn. He clearly didn't notice the quick movement of Cael's hands as he pushed himself to his feet, or hear the soft chink of metal over the sound of Cael's loud complaints.

"You really are a pathetic dog," muttered the guard as he pushed Cael forward and the young captive preceded him down the corridor.

Cael didn't dare glance back, but he was sure he had managed to get the key close enough to the door that Damian would be able to reach it through the bars.

In a short time they had made their way up out of the dungeon level of the small complex the renegades were using as a headquarters. The guard led Cael into a large room, where a number of men were bent over a broad wooden table. Cael, born into a position of command and privilege, had no difficulty in instantly identifying the leader, even before he spoke.

The man looked up as they entered. Cael thought he seemed young to be in command of so many people. Perhaps forty. He must be affluent too. Cael's quick eyes noted the chain around the man's neck, disappearing under his tunic. It was an unusual sign of wealth for a man to wear jewelry. The leader took the newcomers in with a single glance and directed a look of calm disfavor on the guard.

"Well? I trust you have a reason for interrupting us."

"Yes, Liam, Sir," said the guard quickly. "This prisoner has information that he's willing to trade for his freedom, the cowardly dog."

The leader transferred his cool gaze to Cael. The disdain was evident on his face, and it took all of Cael's resolve to debase himself so as to maintain the deception.

"I have gold, Sir," he said quickly. "Lots of it. If you let me go, I can make you rich. And no harm done—I won't tell anyone what I've seen. I don't care what you do with my companion, kill him if you want to, just let me go!"

He felt the guard beside him start and relished his dismay as the leader turned to him with an angry look.

"Is this your idea of valuable information? All this tells me is that this man is a coward and a fool. That information is of no particular use to me."

"No, Sir!" said the guard quickly. "That's not what he said to me, that's not what I thought he would say. He said that—" The guard broke off as he looked back at Cael, who did his best to maintain the facade of desperation and cowardice. The guard faltered, and Cael could almost read the realization in his eyes of how foolish he would sound if he repeated the absurd deception by which Cael convinced him to let him out of his cell. "That is, he was—"

The leader, Liam, held up an imperious hand, silencing the guard's clumsy words. Cael noted with interest that there was an ugly scar on the man's palm, looking like an imperfectly healed burn. That was good—any identifying mark might be useful in tracking this Liam down later.

"Take him back to the cell," the leader was commanding. "I'll deal with him—and you—later."

As the guard led Cael out of the room, a more senior soldier broke off from the group around the table and followed them. Just outside the door, he accosted his subordinate.

"You idiot! I didn't think you were so green! You've made me as well as yourself look a fool in front of Liam. Once the prisoner is secure, report to me for processing and reassignment. Prison doors are no use when manned by a buffoon."

Cael managed only with difficulty to keep the grin off his face at this stroke of good fortune. This would speed things up considerably.

The guard kept up a stream of abuse all the way back to the cell, and Cael swallowed it with apparent meekness. All his senses were on the alert, and he didn't have any attention to waste on the man's words in any event. When they neared the cell, he saw the glint of silver that he had been looking for on the ground near the door.

When the guard reached for his belt, Cael threw himself onto the ground with sudden violence.

"What is this?" demanded his captor.

"Please Sir," said Cael with a sob in his voice. "Please don't throw me back in there to starve. I really do have gold, and it's yours if you let me go free." He grasped at the man in apparent supplication.

"Get your hands off me and get in there!" the guard said in disgust. "I hope they do let you starve. I wouldn't free you for all the gold in the kingdom."

Shaking the prisoner off, he retrieved the key from his belt and unlatched the padlock. He shoved Cael back into the room and locked it again. He didn't peer through the bars this time, his mind clearly on his impending punishment.

When the guard disappeared, Cael settled down in a corner of the empty cell, but he didn't have to wait as long as he expected. A familiar face appeared at the bars almost immediately.

"That was quite a spectacle," said Damian, his tone disapproving.

"It was, wasn't it?" agreed Cael cheerfully. "I don't think I've ever actually knelt before anyone before. It was quite an interesting experience."

Damian rolled his eyes as he began to fiddle with the lock. "You're incorrigible."

"What, don't tell me you've found the other key already?" said Cael. "That was quick! When I saw the guard's keys on the ground *where I left them I was worried that you never reached them in the first place."*

Damian shrugged, trying first one, then another key in the lock. "I thought it would be easiest for you if I left them close to the door. And you were quite right—there was a guardroom with extra keys close by. Let's just hope one of these works."

As he said it, there was a loud click as the key he was trying turned in the lock.

Cael strolled out casually, slapping his friend on the shoulder as he passed. "Thank you, My Lord," he said with a grin.

Damian returned it, apparently unable to resist. "You're welcome, Your Highness. I have to admit, as crazy as it sounded, that was a good plan. To look at you, no one would suspect how good a pickpocket you are."

"Thank you," repeated Cael with unconvincing modesty. "It was simple. Divide and conquer, and include just enough truth to sell it."

"And boldness to the point of being brazen," added Damian in playful reproach.

"Precisely. Now enough talk. The quicker we get back to Kynton, the better. I'm looking forward to another encounter with this Liam when we return with the royal guard."

"One step at a time, Cay," returned Damian. "We still need to get out of here."

Cael laughed. "Easy. When you and I put our heads together, when have we ever failed to get out of a tight corner? And since our charming hosts seem to like the idea of letting us starve, with any luck we'll be halfway home before anyone comes to check on us."

Damian shook his head, but grinned back at his friend. "I'd say you rely on luck too much, but I'll refrain because somehow yours never seems to run out."

~

"CAL! Wake up—where are you right now?"

Cal pulled his attention back to his surroundings with difficulty. Jo was watching him with evident frustration.

"Divide and conquer, and include just enough truth to sell it…" he muttered. "And boldness to the point of being brazen. Well that's your part, obviously."

"What? What does that mean, what are you talking about?" Jonan was looking at him like he'd lost his mind. "Cal, this is no time for riddles. I say we rush them and take them by surprise. We might get lucky and overpower them."

Cal shook his head. "No, we need to get out without them realizing, or we won't get far."

"How do you propose to do that?"

"I have an idea," said Cal.

"All right," said Jo, still sounding incredulous. "Let's hear it."

"It requires both of us," said Cal quickly. "Let me explain."

As he rapidly outlined his plan, Jo's expression changed from concern to approval. "I didn't think you had it in you, Cal," he said, eyebrows raised.

"Don't compliment me until we pull it off," said Cal dryly.

And without further conversation, he threw himself around the corner and ran toward the guards. They both jumped, startled, as he appeared, and one put out an authoritative hand.

"Stop!" he shouted. "Who are you and what's your business?"

Cal bent double, leaning on his knees and breathing hard in an attempt to look as though he had been running for some time.

"There's a commotion—" he panted, "—in the main square. They've sent me to ask for all available guards to assist."

For a moment they stared at him blankly.

"What are you waiting for?" he urged.

"We can't leave our post unmanned," said the guard who had accosted him.

"Of course not," Cal said impatiently. "No one is asking you to. But surely you don't need two of you to man this tiny gate."

The two guards looked at each other. "I can manage," said the one who hadn't yet spoken. "You go and find out what's happening. The suspense is getting too much anyway."

The first guard nodded curtly and turned to Calinnae.

"I'll come with you."

Cal shook his head. "I'm not going back to the square now, I have to run to the other gates with the same message. I got delayed coming here, and that big soldier will have my hide if I don't finish delivering my message. Surely you know how to get to the main square."

The guard grunted and took off back the way Cal had come. He hoped fervently that Jo hadn't wasted any time in getting into position for his role.

Without a backward glance at the remaining guard, Cal took off south along the wall, ostensibly headed for the next gate. In reality, he doubled back as soon as he was out of sight and found a vantage point from which to watch Jo's performance.

Mere seconds after Cal had left, Jo appeared from the other direction.

"Hey! Where's the second guard for this gate?"

"What's it to you, kid?" growled the remaining guard.

"I've been sent around to all the gates to give the word that we're supposed to go on full lockdown. No one in or out. They're going to send reinforcements to double the guard at each gate. They won't be happy to find there's only one of you here!"

"Are you sure?" The guard looked uneasy. "An errand boy was here just a moment ago, telling us to send a guard to help in the main square."

Jo closed his eyes in feigned frustration. "What a disaster!"

he said. "That order has been overridden, I thought someone went after that errand boy to call him back. How long ago did the other guard leave?"

"Only a moment ago."

"Run after him, and call him back!"

"You do it!"

Jo shook his head. "I would if I could, but I have to get to the rest of the gates. And I need to catch up to that other idiot errand boy before he puts all the gates at half guard! Which way did he go?"

"South," said the guard, looking thoroughly alarmed now. "But—"

"Thanks," said Jo, cutting him off. He turned toward Cal's hiding spot.

"Wait!" said the guard. "That's all very well, but who'll call back my other guard? I can't leave my post."

Jo shrugged. "Then don't. If he's only just left, I would, but it's up to you. You're the one who'll have to explain yourself to the soldiers when reinforcements arrive."

Without a further glance, Jo took off at a swift run and was soon out of sight. From his hiding spot, Cal saw the guard hover for a moment indecisively, before running after his companion, shouting for him to come back.

Cal could hardly believe his eyes. It had actually worked! Now they had not a moment to lose. He looked around for Jo, and almost instantly his friend joined him, having doubled back just as Cal had done. They exchanged a purposeful look, and without further discussion they checked that the coast was clear and sprinted for the gate. Within moments they were outside the city.

CHAPTER EIGHT

Once clear of the gate, the boys looked at each other again.

"What now?" they said simultaneously, and Cal smiled briefly before remembering that it was anything but amusing that neither of them had a clue what to do.

"We should get as far away as we can as quickly as possible," said Jonan.

"But not toward Nerita," Cal said quickly. "That's probably where they'll look first."

Jo nodded his agreement. "Let's go the opposite direction."

Cal looked around them. "Do you think it's safe to go along the outside of the wall?"

"Nothing is safe, but it's no crazier than any other course. And less crazy than most of what we've done in the last hour."

"You're not wrong," muttered Cal, trying not to think about everything that could have gone awry with his unexpectedly successful scheme.

"Let's stick as close to the wall as we can," Jo was saying. "Didn't I see a forest on the northeastern side of Pravat as we were coming in? We can lose ourselves in the trees."

Cal nodded. "It's more of a grove than a forest, but better than nothing. And the land beyond looked hilly. That might help us stay out of sight."

"Let's give it a try," Jo said, and began to jog along the wall.

They reached the grove without passing any more gates. Cal had expected one on the eastern side of the city, but maybe the trees made the location undesirable for a road. The road coming from Alezae to the east must bend around and enter Pravat through a different gate.

Once they reached the trees, they struck out as close to northeast as they could judge, trying to head in the opposite direction from Nerita. Each step away from their home pulled at Calinnae. His exhaustion was beginning to catch up with him, and he was hit anew with the realization that they could not go home, perhaps ever. Could it really be less than twenty-four hours ago he had been walking down to the dock to meet Jonan, enjoying the mild weather with barely a thought for the future? Now it seemed doubtful they even had a future. How drastically everything had changed.

CAL WOKE as dusk began to creep over the hills. He stood up cautiously, stretching his stiff limbs. Casting his eyes around, he took in the details of the landscape. He had been so anxious during their flight from Pravat that he hadn't really taken it in. But a few hours of sleep had buoyed his spirits considerably, and even though the anxiety was still there, he was able to appreciate the beauty around him now.

And it was beautiful. It was different from the seaside charm of Nerita, but the rolling hills, stretching out apparently endlessly, created their own sense of peace and calm. Long green grass rippled under an errant breeze, and summer wildflowers dotted the slopes with spots of blue, purple and white. He supposed that Jonan would find the vista boring, but to Cal it was comforting in its constancy, a reminder that there were some things even an evil ruler couldn't corrupt. Cal's own life might be uncertain, but Kyona had been here long before Filip, and would continue long after him.

With a sigh, he brought his mind back to their present predicament. Jonan sat nearby, looking as though he had been awake for some time.

The boys had continued at a jog until they passed out of the trees and into the hilly country beyond. After an hour or so of skirting around hills to keep out of sight of the walls of Pravat, they judged that it was safe to stop. Well, as Jonan had said when they left Pravat, nothing was really safe. But by then the sun had been at its zenith, and their exhaustion gave them little choice.

Neither companion was used to the type of travel they had been forced to undertake, or to going without sleep for a night. Once the excitement of their escape from Pravat began to wear off, they could barely continue to put one foot in front of the other. So they had found as sheltered a hollow as they could, and had settled down to sleep, with the intention of continuing once it was dark.

"Did you sleep at all?" Cal asked, joining his friend where he sat on a gentle slope.

Jo nodded. "A few hours, I think. But I stirred about an hour ago, and once I'd seen that, it was pretty hard to just drop back off."

Jonan hadn't made eye contact while he spoke, and it was only as he inclined his head pointedly that Cal realized Jo was staring back the way they'd come. Following his friend's gaze, Cal put his hand over his mouth in an involuntary gesture.

They'd traveled some distance, but even in the dim light of

the gathering dusk, they could clearly make out a thick column of smoke, rising from the vicinity of Pravat.

"They set the city on fire?" Cal whispered in horror. "Because of us?"

Jo shrugged. His expression was stony, but Cal knew him well enough to recognize the emotion hidden inside. "From the size of the smoke cloud, I don't think it can be the whole city burning. It's fading a little now, but when I woke up it was quite a distinct line billowing up. I can't be sure of course, but my best guess is that they didn't burn everything, just—"

"The Hall of Records," Calinnae finished quietly. "Of course they did." He was silent for a long moment. "Do you think Aurelius—"

"I don't have any information you don't have, Cal." Jo shrugged again. The gesture was casual, but his tone was terse.

"I hope he's all right," said Cal, mostly to himself. "And all those records...perhaps the underground chamber survived." After a moment's thought he continued, still thinking aloud. "I wonder if the soldiers were under orders to destroy the Hall anyway. It seems like Filip's biggest fear is information getting out. Maybe he wasn't willing to trust that his ancestors successfully purged all relevant records."

"Why don't you just say it?" said Jo, and Cal turned to him in surprise, raising an eyebrow as he took in Jo's belligerent stance.

"Say what?"

"That if they weren't planning it before, my exhibition in the square made sure of it."

Cal gave his friend a measuring look, but said nothing, so Jo continued.

"I know you think this is my fault, that I was crazy to make a scene, but I couldn't think of any other way out of it. I could see in the people's eyes that they were on the edge. I just took a gamble that they would respond if given a little push."

Cal sighed. "Well, you were right about that." He looked at Jo seriously. "But you're wrong if you think I blame you. None of what's happening is your fault. And I shouldn't really be surprised. Slipping away was a nice idea, but being inconspicuous has never been your strength, has it? Besides, although at the time I was...alarmed, I couldn't think of any other way out of it either."

Jo smiled briefly at Cal's understatement, but when he answered, his tone was serious too. "It was more than just wanting a way out of a tight corner. You said Filip's biggest fear is information. What you mean is Filip is afraid of the truth. Everything I said was the truth. That's surely what he fears most, and I thought it was about time he and his bullies were the ones to feel afraid."

"You're right there," said Cal, his voice hard as he looked at the smoke pillar now barely visible in the gloom. He glanced back at his friend. "And anyway, you don't have to justify yourself or answer to me."

In the gathering darkness, Cal could just make out Jo's raised eyebrows. "Since when? You've chewed me out over my hot head more times than I can count."

Cal shrugged one shoulder. "Since yesterday."

"Don't do that, Cal," said Jo sharply. "You've never been a follower. This sudden...deference is frightening me more than all the rest of it. We've been best friends as long as I can remember, and I can't recall a single time you were willing to just follow along with my crazy schemes. Admit it—you always thought I should follow you, that you had better ideas of how to get into mischief, and better ideas of how to get out of it. And you were only sometimes wrong."

Jo grinned briefly, but Cal had no answering smile. He only wished he could truthfully deny Jo's words.

Cal's silence seemed to irritate his friend. "I'm serious, Cal," Jo continued. "Stop acting like..."

"Like what?" Cal prompted.

"Like I'm your king!" Jo burst out.

Cal was still for a moment, then he looked his friend in the eye with an effort. "But you are."

Jo looked away quickly, and Cal could only be glad. The long silence that followed was awkward, and he was relieved when Jo broke it.

"Speaking of good ideas, that was amazing back there. The way you used the legends to get us out of our predicament. I never would have thought of it. It was like they were a...a tool you could use at will."

Cal gave a tight smile. "It turns out it pays to listen carefully to bedtime stories."

"Well, I'm just lucky you're here with me. Even if I had listened better, I don't think I'd ever know the stories like you do. It's like they're always there, isn't it? Always just below the surface of your mind, waiting for you."

"I'd never thought of it that way," said Cal. "But yeah, I guess you're right."

Jonan shook his head, clearly impressed, as he picked up his rucksack. In unspoken agreement the two boys started walking, continuing in the same direction as before.

"Like I said," repeated Jonan, "I'm glad you're with me."

Cal smiled. "So am I."

And he was. But he was also troubled. As he walked in silence beside his friend, Cal couldn't deny that Jo had been right in what he'd said. They had both always had strong ideas. In some ways their friendship was an unlikely one, as each might have been expected to prefer a friend who would be happy to follow. But perhaps that was the beauty of their combination—neither of them eclipsed the other's strength of will or character.

Besides, their friendship had been predetermined not only by the friendship of their parents, but by the shared secret that had created a unique and permanent bond between their households. Jonan had been present for every escapade of Calinnae's childhood and youth, and he couldn't even imagine life without his friend.

But if he was honest with himself, it wasn't much easier to imagine a life of serving Jonan. He wished Jonan hadn't articulated the thought. But he had, and now Cal had to fight harder than ever not to dwell on it.

Because he did think he was a better leader. More sensible, more clear-thinking, not so hotheaded. He could only hope that Jo didn't realize just how great Cal's struggle was. The last thing Jo needed was to think his only friend and ally was doubting him and his leadership. Besides, Cal was ashamed of his own resentment and didn't want Jo to know about it.

As he felt the sting of shame, he was suddenly reminded of his inaction in the square, and his skin prickled as a fresh surge of chagrin passed over him. It took more than clearheadedness to make a good leader. He had always thought he was as brave as Jonan, just less reckless, but he was proving himself wrong. Somehow the crisis that precipitated this mad adventure had triggered a new fear in him, creating a desperate need to stay safe and hidden. It wasn't just fear for himself, it was fear for Jonan and the bloodline he represented.

Thoughts of his friend and of the lineage they were protecting steadied him. Bloodline or no bloodline, Jo was his best friend. And as much as this shameful new fear might cripple him from taking risks for himself, Cal would never hesitate to come to Jonan's aid. And on top of that, whether Jonan wanted to admit it or not, he was the heir to the throne. Calinnae might struggle with his new background role, but his reverence for the true royal bloodline that Jo had always mocked ensured that he would follow Jonan's decisions.

To whatever end might come.

CHAPTER NINE

They had been walking for at least an hour before Jo broke the silence. Cal started at the unexpected sound. They had traveled through much of the night and slept a few more hours after dawn. Cal was no longer blinking in the now bright sunlight, but he still felt groggy.

"What are you thinking about, Cal?"

Cal took a moment to answer, thinking how glad he was Jo hadn't asked him that question while they walked the night before. He had no desire to share his previous musings. Not that his present ones were much more palatable.

"Actually, I was thinking about...your father. He would have made a good king."

"I've been thinking about him too," said Jo quietly. "When we stopped to sleep." He paused. "I know I seemed harsh before, when we found out what happened. But I...I didn't mean...I would never..."

"I know, Jo," said Cal quietly. "You don't have to explain. I know you loved him, and your mother. And they knew it too."

"I hope so," said Jo, almost too softly for Cal to hear.

For a while, they walked on in silence. Cal felt his throat

tighten as his thoughts continued to circle around his memories of a man who had been both gentle and strong and had always treated him with great kindness. It was painful, thinking about Jonan's father, but much less painful than it would be to let his thoughts drift where they kept trying to go. By focusing on the calamity of the death of Prince Jonathon's heir, he could almost distract himself from the much more intimate devastation that threatened to overwhelm him every time he remembered the sight of his own father's still form, or his mother's peaceful face.

He couldn't help but think that it was fitting, in a twisted way, that the two couples had died together. As though the closeness of their friendship in life had carried on into death. Just as he and Jonan, having shared every aspect of their childhood, had shared the brutal end to their innocence. He would never have wished for the death of Jonan's parents, of course. But even though it was clear that Jonan didn't want to speak about it any more than Cal did, there was still a kind of mutual comfort from sharing the same sorrow.

But Cal knew they couldn't risk being swallowed up by their grief. They had a task to do. He felt almost afraid to let the grief in. He thought back to the stories. King Cael had known plenty of heartache. He seemed to have coped as well as could be expected with the death of a daughter in her childhood, but the same couldn't be said of his wife, Queen Jacqueline. She had never recovered, and had declined from that point on. And her early death in turn had been more than King Cael could shoulder.

Cal felt a shiver go down his spine as he remembered how King Cael's grief over his wife's death had weakened him, blinding him to what was happening in his kingdom enough to pave the way for the betrayal that led to so much loss and destruction.

Grief was a distraction they couldn't afford.

Cal looked over at his friend. Jonan looked as tired as he felt, and Cal regretted bringing up Jo's father.

"Why do you ask?" He tried to inject a lighter note into his voice. "What were you thinking about?"

Jonan sighed. "I was thinking about what to do next. We didn't exactly find what we were looking for at the Hall of Records, did we?"

"No," Cal said heavily. "We didn't. It was always unlikely, but I was hoping we would find more answers in Pravat than we did."

"So was I," said Jonan, turning toward him. Calinnae was astonished to see a grin spreading over Jonan's face, and he immediately felt a familiar apprehension begin to build. "Which is why I grabbed this on the way out."

As he spoke, Jo reached into his rucksack and pulled out a rolled up piece of parchment. When he recognized the ancient account they had been reading when Aurelius interrupted them, Cal came to a sudden halt.

"Jo!" he said explosively. "Even for you, that's outrageous! You just stole what is probably the oldest and most valuable manuscript in Kyona!"

Jo waved a dismissive hand. "Accounts are written to be read, Cal. It's of more use to us out here than hidden away in a stuffy vault."

Cal made a grab at the document, but Jo held it out of reach.

"It's not intended to be read by just anyone, Jo!"

Jonan made an impatient sound. "I'm not going to distribute copies throughout the countryside. But why shouldn't we read it?" Cal opened his mouth to protest further, but Jo cut him off. "Stop making a fuss, Cal. Where's that deference I didn't want earlier?"

Cal's only response to his friend's smug grin was to shake his head disbelievingly. Jo was incorrigible.

"Well? Is your righteous indignation going to extend far enough to prevent you reading it with me? I can keep the contents to myself if you like, on principle."

Cal narrowed his eyes, but refused to be baited. "Just stop waving it around like that, you're going to rip it."

Jo snorted, but complied. The two boys sat side by side on a nearby boulder, Cal pulling the last of their food out of Jonan's rucksack for them to share while Jonan smoothed the document out across the stone. In a moment, both heads were extended over the parchment, picking up right where they'd left off.

It was said that a powerful enchantment was placed on the sphere by Qadir, so that none but the true king or his heir could wield it. If another tried to use it, its power would be unleashed in destruction, marking the usurper for what he was. Qadir warned that in such an event, he would return and reclaim the Esvalere, for its power was not to be entrusted to the wrong hands. Qadir further warned that should the king allow such an event to occur, he and his line would suffer the dragonwrath, for the gift of the sphere was not given lightly or without cost. Nevertheless, such was the friendship between the two rulers, that Qadir promised that even if it became necessary for him to take hold of the Esvalere, he would not destroy it, but would keep it safe for the king or his heir to once again wield, if he could convince Qadir that the dragonwrath had been lifted.

At the bottom of the page was another note in King Cael's handwriting, reading, "This is the entirety of the first account of the Esvalere. So the sphere has passed, father to son, in unbroken line, until it was received by me from my father's hand when his passing was near. Like all my ancestors, I was vouchsafed this gift only upon swearing to keep it safe from all but my true heir. One day it will pass to my son, and he will swear the same. May the dragonwrath never touch our line."

When Cal had read the rest of the entry, then read it over again from the top, he looked up to see Jonan frowning down at the page. Jonan looked up, and their eyes met.

"What is the dragonwrath?" Jo's voice was uncharacteristically subdued.

Cal just shook his head, with no answer to offer. He could see fear on his friend's face and wondered if his skin had also prickled when reading the ominous-looking word.

Jonan rubbed his eyes in frustration. "No help at all. Just more questions, always more questions! When do we get some answers?"

"I wish I knew," said Cal with a touch of bitterness. Jo was always talking about how well Cal knew the stories, and he himself had felt he was well versed in the secret history of Kyona's royals. But all they had read in Aurelius's records was making him feel like he knew nothing at all.

"Come on," Jonan sighed, looking at the sun. "We'd better keep moving. Who knows how long until soldiers are roaming these hills?" He rolled the parchment up again and replaced it in his rucksack.

Cal followed Jo mechanically, thinking over what they'd read.

"I can't figure it out," he said slowly. "This Esvalere—King Cael talks about it like it's central to his rule, like it's at the heart of what it means to be king. How can we never have heard of it in all the stories?"

Jonan just shrugged, clearly still disgruntled.

"What did that other record say?" Cal persisted. "The one where we first saw the Esvalere mentioned?"

Jonan thought for a minute. "It said, 'The Esvalere is a heavy burden to bear.'"

Cal nodded. "And King Cael said that he would tell Jonathon

when it was time, that there was no rush, but it was only a few years later that everything fell apart."

Jo looked at Cal, understanding dawning in his eyes. "Wait, you think that didn't happen? You think—"

"He never told Jonathon, yes!" Cal was growing more certain the more he thought about it. "It makes sense, doesn't it? If Jonathon never knew of it, he never told his son, who never told his son, and so on. Your father didn't mention the Esvalere because he'd never heard of it either. That's why it isn't in any of the stories."

"I think you're right," said Jonan, once again sounding impressed.

"Well," said Cal, trying not to sound too satisfied with himself. "If nothing else, that information alone makes it worth having gone to Pravat. Just think! There might be no one else alive other than us and Aurelius who knows about this object!"

"Well," said Jonan with a grin, "us and this dragon ruler."

Cal rolled his eyes. "Of course it's all about the dragons with you. But be serious. You said yourself you don't believe in dragons anymore."

"I do now, obviously!" said Jonan, his surprise evident in his tone.

Cal stared at him. "What? Because of this record? It's an ancient legend, Jo!"

"Kept by King Cael!" Jo countered. "Your hero! Are you saying you think he was crazy? Or just a gullible fool?"

"Neither, of course!" protested Cal.

Jo made an exasperated noise in his throat. "But he wrote himself that he had received the Esvalere from his father. And he spoke about the dragonwrath! Do you really think he was making that stuff up?"

Cal was silent for a moment, frowning. "No, of course I don't. I think the sphere must be real. And he was clearly afraid of some kind of magical consequence if he misused it, something that was traditionally called the dragonwrath. But he didn't write himself about any interactions with dragons, did he? He's just recording the legend of how this powerful object came to be in his family line. Maybe the dragon ruler with his sinister warning is just a metaphor for...I don't know, caution against becoming power-hungry or negligent."

"That doesn't even make sense, Cal." Jonan no longer sounded impressed.

Cal shrugged, untroubled by his friend's criticism. "Well, it's no harder to believe than that this Esvalere thing was given to King Cael's ancestor by an actual dragon."

"Yes, an actual dragon," affirmed Jo, studying the manuscript, which he had pulled back out of his bag while they spoke. "Qadir, to be exact. I wonder," he mused. "Could he still be alive? How long do dragons live?"

"Jo," said Cal, fast losing patience, "this is getting ridiculous."

"It's *all* ridiculous," said Jonan, looking at Cal with unusual seriousness. "But that doesn't mean it isn't true. If you can believe that there's a magical object with power to make a king the greatest ruler of all time, why is it any harder to believe it came from dragons? Even my father's stories included dragons!"

Cal frowned. "All the stories said was that the true line of kings were known as friends of the dragons. I thought it meant that they had unusual power and wisdom, that kind of thing. They never said anything concrete like what this account says."

"Because Jonathon didn't know this stuff!" said Jo excitedly. "Like you said. His father meant to tell him when the moment came, but he ran out of time. So it's not in the stories. But it's real!" He turned to Cal with a shining face. "It's real, Cal, I'm sure of it."

"All right," said Cal slowly, finding Jo's sudden eagerness disconcerting. "Even if I agreed, how does that help us?"

But Jo wasn't listening. He was staring straight ahead as he walked, obviously deep in thought. "Do you think...do you think this Qadir, this dragon ruler, could be the one King Cael was talking about in the other record? The one who could apparently change the past?"

Cal's first instinct was to make a sarcastic reply, but the memory of that entry in King Cael's journal sobered him. He had been as unable to make sense of it as Jo had been, and he couldn't deny that it was hard to explain its meaning without magic.

"I don't know," he said instead, feeling suddenly even more weary, as though the rise in Jonan's energy was draining his own.

"Well, that doesn't matter right now, anyway," said Jonan. "Cal." There was such earnestness in Jonan's voice that Cal couldn't help but meet his eye. "This is it. This is the answer."

"What do you mean?" asked Cal, his voice wary. Jonan's face was still aglow with excitement.

"We need to find them."

"Who?"

"The dragons!"

For a moment Cal was silent, too astounded to respond. "Jo... that doesn't make any sense," he said eventually. "I thought you wanted to storm the castle and take back the throne this minute. Now you want to go on the wildest wild goose chase imaginable? To sidetrack for a dragon quest?"

To Cal's annoyance, Jonan just laughed. "A dragon quest. Yes, I like that!"

"Jo—" Cal tried again, but his companion cut him off.

"Don't you see, Cal? It's not a sidetrack. This is how we storm the castle and take back the throne."

"What, you think you're not only going to find dragons— mythical creatures no one has believed in for generations—but you're also going to be able to convince them to attack Filip for you?"

Jonan shook his head. "No—I think I'm going to convince them to give me the Esvalere."

"What do you mean?"

"I mean I think I know what happened. If King Cael never told Jonathon about the Esvalere, then Jonathon never had it. Think about it. If he'd taken it with him, it would not only be in the stories, it would be in our hands right now! Such an item would have been carefully protected and faithfully handed down from father to son, like the stories were."

"Yes," Cal agreed slowly, "that's true. I don't think Jonathon can have taken this Esvalere when he fled."

"Which means it was left behind. Which *means*," it was Jo's turn to sound pleased with himself, "that other guy, the usurper, probably found it when he took over the king's position, and probably tried to use it."

"Which would mean..." continued Cal, "...the dragon ruler would have reclaimed it."

"And he, or whichever dragon ruler succeeded him, would be holding it for the king's true heir to claim," Jonan finished excitedly.

"Jo..." Calinnae wasn't sure how to phrase what he wanted to say, but it terrified him to see Jonan clinging so enthusiastically to such an impossible source of victory. He took the page from his friend and scanned it. "Even if all that were true, even if you're right, what about this dragonwrath? Why aren't you suffering from it now, whatever it is? Why didn't your father?"

"Didn't he?" said Jonan, and Cal saw with mixed emotions that he had succeeded in sobering his friend. "Jonathon was exiled, and all his descendants along with him. My parents couldn't settle in the place where they grew up, they had to move, as did my father's parents, and my father's grandparents...

always on the run, never able to really have peace or security. Cal," Jonan looked at him seriously, "my father was just murdered. And I'm a seventeen year old running for my life, with no idea what to do next. Believe me, this inheritance is not what I wanted for my life. Maybe this is the dragonwrath— misfortune dogging each generation."

Calinnae wasn't sure what to say. He wasn't convinced, but neither could he come up with a better explanation for what they'd read, or a more sensible plan. As they crested the slope they'd been walking up, he looked away from Jonan and gave a small cry. "Look!"

Jo quickly followed his gaze, and they both stopped for a moment, staring ahead. They had been wandering through grassy slopes since they left the trees outside Pravat, but they finally seemed to have reached the end of the hills. Ahead of them the land stretched out on a flat level, and a road could be seen curving in from the west and running east toward a sizable town.

"What do you think?" said Jo, and Cal was glad to see that his friend was stashing the scroll safely back into his rucksack. "Should we make for the town?"

Cal looked around him, then up at the sun. "If we pick up the pace we could get there by nightfall, and it will be easier to hide in a town than on this open pastureland."

Jonan nodded. "Let's do it," he said decisively.

They began to walk more quickly, and before long, they had joined the road. There wasn't a lot of traffic, but they passed the odd traveler or tradesman's cart heading toward town as well. Few were heading out into the open so late in the day.

"What town do you reckon this is?" Cal asked quietly, as they passed a trio of rough-looking men who were laughing a little too loudly at some private joke.

Before Jonan could respond a signpost appeared ahead, as if in answer to Calinnae's question.

KERR

3 LEAGUES

The two boys looked at each other in wordless dismay. Cal had forgotten that Kerr was one of the towns out this way. He may not have known much about the area, but everyone had heard of Kerr. It was notorious for its violence and crime.

"Do we leave the road and head back to the pastureland?" Jo asked.

Cal looked around. "We can't go back toward Pravat," he said, trying to lower his voice even more as he saw one of the three rowdy men watching them with interest. "And this road presumably leads back to the capital, which is the last place we want to head for right now. I don't know where else we'd go."

Jo followed Cal's gaze and nodded. "It's probably more conspicuous now to leave than it is to continue into town. I guess we push on."

Cal nodded, although he felt very uneasy. He wished they could shake free of the band of men who had noticed them, but as they walked on, he and Jo couldn't seem to get out of reach of them, no matter their pace. And it was impossible not to notice the unsavory nature of a number of their other fellow travelers.

By the time they reached the town, darkness had almost fallen. Calinnae was exhausted, yet, when confronted with the actual sight of Kerr, the idea of camping in the open didn't seem so bad. Perhaps it would be better to brave Kerr in the morning. After all, night was surely the most dangerous time. But the gates were open, and Jonan showed every sign of continuing on into the town.

CHAPTER TEN

They kept their heads down as they passed through the gate. Trying to look like they knew were they were going, they followed the main street for a while. Most of the shops were already closed, but the taverns were just picking up for the evening. Jonan nodded toward a large one up ahead, its lights spilling out onto the darkening street.

"Should we go in there?"

"Why?" asked Cal dryly. "In the mood for a drink?"

"More like for a room to stay. That tavern looks large enough to have rooms attached. And if it doesn't, surely they can direct us to where rooms can be found. I just hope we have enough coins."

"We'd better," agreed Cal as they pushed through the door into the tavern. While he didn't love the idea of asking for help from anyone in this crowd, which was growing more disorderly by the minute, he liked the idea of spending the night on the streets of Kerr even less.

They approached the bar, and waited for the tapster to direct his attention toward them. Calinnae tried to seem natural, but he could tell that they stood out. A quick glance around the room showed way too many eyes fixed on them. He had hoped that this tavern was big enough for outsiders to go unnoticed, but it seemed he had been wrong.

After what felt like an eternity, the tapster finally came over to them. Jonan began to inquire about a room, but after an appraising look, the tapster cut him off.

"You're a bit young for our tastes here, mate. The youths are more welcome at the taverns on the other side of town."

His tone was derisive, and the rebuff was met with guffaws on all sides.

"Haven't seen you around here before, have I?" drawled a new voice. "Saw you on the way in, looking mighty unsure of whether you wanted to be here." Cal turned to see one of the men from the road. The man had an ale in his hand, and from the look of him, he hadn't wasted a minute of the short time since they'd all entered town.

"Where are you from, anyway?" asked one of his companions. This one was not yet inebriated. His expression was keener, and Calinnae didn't like the calculating way he was looking them up and down.

"None of your business," said Jonan gruffly.

The man raised his eyebrows. "Like that, is it?" His eyes darted between them shrewdly. "I saw you on the way in too. Coming from the west, hey? Heard a rumor there were a couple youths who got smart with the king's soldiers back in Pravat. Shooting off their mouths about being from some long-lost royal bloodline. Big reward being offered, I hear."

Calinnae threw Jonan a reproachful glance. Of course, Jo hadn't actually claimed to be from the royal bloodline back in Pravat. But Cal wasn't exactly surprised to learn the tale had grown in the telling. What a stroke of bad luck that these travelers had brought the tale to Kerr.

At that moment there was a commotion in a corner of the

tavern. A quick look between Jo and Cal was all that was needed. In the brief moment when everyone's attention was diverted by the beginnings of a routine brawl, the two of them slipped back out the door as unobtrusively as possible.

"That got ugly fast," said Cal tensely as they hurried further up the main street, trying to put some distance between themselves and the tavern. "Do we try another tavern, do you think?"

Before Jo could answer, they heard a shout behind them. Glancing back, they saw that half a dozen men from the tavern had followed them out, their interrogator in the lead.

"Come on," shouted Jonan, and Cal followed him as he sprinted down a side street.

Cal and Jo were young and fit, but they were also exhausted, and the men from the tavern were neither as old nor as slow as the soldier whom Cal had so easily outstripped back in Pravat. It was evident from the shouts of their pursuers that they were quickly gaining on them.

"We need a plan, Jo!" panted Cal as they ran. "We can't outrun them, and we have nowhere to run to even if we could."

"Maybe we stand and fight," returned Jo.

"Are you mad? Two of us, and six of them, with plenty more where they came from!"

"Better than being run down like rabbits!" said Jo mulishly.

The street they were running down ended abruptly as it opened into a back street that ran perpendicular to theirs. They hesitated only a moment, then darted to the left. In moments, however, they realized that they had made the wrong decision. The street was a dead end. As they heard the voices of their pursuers, almost at the corner, they threw themselves behind a broken cart, piled with refuse.

They couldn't see the street from their hiding place, but they could hear the men slow down when they reached the corner.

"Which way'd they go?" shouted an unfamiliar voice.

"Doesn't matter," said another one with a guffaw. "Dead end either way."

Cal groaned quietly, wishing he could calm the pounding of his heart. Surely then he would be able to think more clearly, to find a way out.

"Come on out, *Your Majesty*," continued the second voice. "You're needed on, uh, royal business." His words were met by drunken laughter.

"Yeah, what's the matter?" taunted another man. "I heard you gave a lovely speech in Pravat. Don't you got nothing to say to your subjects here in Kerr?"

The men were moving up the street in each direction, kicking things over and generally making a ruckus. They didn't seem to be in a hurry, confident that they had cornered their prey. But still, they were drawing steadily closer.

"Any ideas?" muttered Jonan to Cal.

"Not this time. You?"

Before Jonan could answer, a hiss sounded nearby, much closer than their pursuers.

"Psst! Over here!"

They turned to see who was hailing them. It took Cal a moment to realize that the speaker was above them, looking down at them from a second story window.

"Psst! Quickly! The door directly below me!"

Calinnae looked with uncertainty at the ragged girl who was beckoning to them. She was leaning half out of the window, frustrated at their slow response.

"Come on, Cal!" Jonan urged.

"Can we trust—?"

"This is no time for your infernal skepticism!" When Calinnae still didn't move, Jonan added, "We don't have much choice!"

Reluctantly Cal responded to his friend's shove, and the two boys slid out from their hiding spot as stealthily as they could. Immediately the girl disappeared from the window. They raced to the doorway, covered by the darkness from the sight of the men further down the street. By the time they reached the door, the girl was there, pulling it open and ushering them inside.

She led them rapidly up a flight of stairs and into a small dark room, containing a table, two chairs and several cushions on the floor. After she'd shut the door behind them and lit a couple of candles she indicated that they should sit. They did so awkwardly, and Cal shot a sidelong glance at Jonan, conveying the fact that he remained unconvinced.

The girl was leaning on the table, staring at them curiously. She was scrawny, and her clothes clearly marked her poverty.

"So they're after you."

The boys remained silent.

"You're the troublemakers from Pravat, are you? I've heard about you two."

"It seems our fame has spread," muttered Jonan ruefully.

"Your fame," Calinnae corrected, still eyeing their hostess with mistrust. He instantly regretted his words when he saw the shrewd way the girl's eyes darted to Jonan. She was clearly measuring him up now that Calinnae had identified him as the one who had made the rumored claims. Entering Kerr had been a huge mistake.

Jonan frowned at him, then turned his attention back to the girl, who was cheerfully continuing to discuss their fugitive status. Cal thought she seemed surprisingly unafraid, either of them or of the gang that had been chasing them.

"Apparently you're wanted for murder and treason."

Jonan's eyebrows rose. "Is that what they're saying?"

"Yes. That's what *they* are saying." Suddenly she grinned at them. "But I've heard different rumors."

Jonan grunted non-committally. "Have you?"

"Yes," the girl continued. "Rumors about the king. That his is not the true royal bloodline."

Cal tried to keep his voice light. "Those rumors have been around for a while. We've heard them too. I think everyone has."

"I'm talking about more recent rumors." Apparently their rescuer was not to be deterred. "I heard about the disturbance in Pravat. I heard that...someone...is claiming that there's a living heir to the real royal house." There was a gleam in the girl's eyes as she looked between them. "That this heir might even be walking among us. That he might be getting ready to challenge King Filip for the throne."

Cal barely suppressed a groan. News certainly traveled fast. He had thought they'd been unlucky to run into the one other traveler who knew that soldiers were on the lookout for fugitives in the area, but this girl made it seem like the story of Jonan's declaration in the main square of Pravat had already spread throughout all of Kerr.

"That's quite a tale," was all he said, his tone discouraging.

She seemed disappointed at their reticence, but clearly wasn't going to give up easily.

"Well, will you at least tell me your names?"

Cal was about to insist that she do so first, but Jonan spoke before he could.

"I'm Jonan, and this is Calinnae. We come from Nerita."

Cal glared at his friend. Why not just tell her their whole life story? Jonan's mouth twitched, as though he could read Cal's mind, but he continued speaking without looking at Cal.

"You said we're wanted for murder and treason. Who are we supposed to have murdered?"

Cal cut in before the question could be answered. "First of all, seeing as you seem to know so much about us, how about you tell us who you are?" He thought he sensed, rather than saw,

Jonan roll his eyes, although his friend mercifully refrained from commenting.

She pondered Calinnae for a moment before answering. "My name is Elnora," she said. "I come from Alezae. And if there's any truth to the rumors about you two, you can count me a friend."

"Alezae?" Jonan was unable to hide his surprise at the mention of the affluent seaside town. "How in the kingdom did you end up here?"

Elnora's smile didn't slip, but her eyes took on a look that surprised and almost frightened Cal. There was no longer the fire of life in her expression—she looked almost dead. Yet at the same time, he could discern a fiercely defiant gleam lurking there.

"What?" she said quietly, "don't you like Kerr? Isn't this the kind of place you'd like to grow old in?"

As he studied her changed countenance, Cal felt less suspicion and more sympathy with their strange rescuer. He realized, after a quick assessment, that she was older than he had first thought, perhaps sixteen or seventeen. Not much younger than himself. Like Jonan, Cal found himself wondering how she'd gotten there.

Elnora pulled Cal out of his musing with a question. "Where are you two going next?" Her tone was businesslike—evidently the conversation had been getting too personal for her liking. "I guess you'll be heading for the capital."

"Why would we be going there?" asked Jonan, in a passable attempt at indifference. Whatever he had noticed, he spoke as if he was not aware of the tension that had entered the room.

She eyed him in some amusement. "All right, so we won't talk about it. You can stay here tonight, anyway. It's very unlikely that you'll be found."

Jonan seemed relieved to find a haven. He looked at Cal

inquiringly, but Cal was satisfied now to trust Elnora, even when she slipped out as they lay down for the night.

"So she passed the test?" Jonan asked through a yawn.

"She seems to be genuine," answered Calinnae, equally exhausted. "What made you trust her so quickly?"

"I don't know, I could just tell."

Cal rolled his eyes in the darkness, but didn't bother to reply. He was well used to his friend's inexplicable instincts. Personally, he preferred to place his trust in more reliable sources, like sight and sound.

And yet, as he drifted into sleep, he pictured Elnora's face and the sudden vulnerability he'd seen there when she met his eye. In that moment he'd felt that they could trust her, and he couldn't entirely explain it in any concrete way.

Whatever instinct Jo had, maybe it was rubbing off.

CHAPTER ELEVEN

Before sunrise, Cal was awakened by Elnora's persistent poking.

"We have to move, the soldiers are all over the city." She shook Jonan awake. "Come on! Gather your things." In seconds they were outside, creeping through the dark. There was no moon, but Calinnae knew that his breath was making a cloud around him in the cold morning air, even if he couldn't see it.

Elnora seemed tense and alert as she led them down the cobbled streets, which was probably a good thing, the two boys being still half asleep, with no idea what direction they were heading in.

Cal was certain the boys would never have made it out of the city without Elnora. She led them confidently to the other side of Kerr, where the city backed directly onto a rocky peak, and there was consequently no wall. At a glance, the rocky crags looked just as effective. But Elnora took them up the cliff by a route that, while it followed no obvious path, presented no difficulty for three young and agile travelers.

Once they were clear of the city, Elnora made straight for a spot on the other side of the peak where they were partially protected by a rocky overhang. Cal suspected that she had been here before, probably many times. She set about lighting a fire.

"Should we stay here?" asked Jonan in concern. "Won't the soldiers come after us?"

Elnora shook her head. "They don't know you were in Kerr."

"I thought you said there were soldiers everywhere!"

"There were. They arrived during the night, and by dawn they'll have taken up positions all throughout the city. I asked around while you were sleeping—apparently there are soldiers stationed now in every town within fifty leagues of the capital."

Calinnae and Jonan exchanged looks of alarm, but Jo recovered quickly. He strode confidently to Elnora and began to help her with the fire. "Well then, it's a good thing we're not going to the capital, right Cal?"

Elnora looked up in surprise. "You're not?" Her gaze shifted between the two of them. "Then where are you going? Are the rumors not true after all?"

"Rumors rarely are, wouldn't you say?" Cal knew his evasiveness would probably annoy Jonan as well as Elnora, but he was still reluctant to trust Elnora so quickly. After glancing between them one more time, she sighed in resignation.

"I can't blame you for not wanting to confide in me. You have no reason to trust me. But I meant what I said last night. I've heard the rumors that King Filip isn't a true royal, just like everyone. And honestly, it's comforting to think that there might be a reason why he's such a terrible ruler. And I've seen my fair share of soldiers' bullying—I mean, I live in Kerr. But this is something different. The manhunt the king has underway for you two...Well, no offense, but you don't look that dangerous to me. But if the rumors about your heritage are true, then I can see that you'd be very dangerous as far as King Filip is concerned."

She snorted. "If the king was a bit smarter, he'd realize that showing the country how desperate he is to find you will only convince everyone that he, at least, thinks your claim is legitimate!" She paused, but neither of the boys spoke. "Anyway," she said, her tone milder, "I know better than most how little the king, or his father, has ever done for the people he should be protecting. If there's even a chance that someone else," her eyes lingered on Jonan, "someone better could be the rightful king, that person could count me as a friend."

The two boys exchanged a look. "Thank you," said Jonan, a bit awkwardly. Cal suspected that, like him, Jonan didn't really know how to respond to Elnora's unexpected burst of eloquence.

The three of them sat around the fire in silence and watched the sun inch over the rim of their world, each lost in their own thoughts, perhaps seeing in the new day a future very different from that of the others.

Cal again found his thoughts slipping unbidden into the stories he had grown up with. One story in particular had been pulling at his mind since the moment he read the name of the town on the signpost the afternoon before. Kerr was notorious enough in their present time, but it had been little better even before the Corruption.

Cal remembered how Jonathon had fled alone to Kerr after the takeover. Not for the first time, they seemed to have found themselves in a situation remarkably similar to one he had heard about in legend. Cal's thoughts strayed back over the details of that incident, wondering if it could once again provide some wisdom for a situation that seemed hopeless.

Jonathon strode quickly down the darkened streets. Everywhere around him he could hear the sound of drunken celebration, as the revelers of Kerr welcomed in the new year. It wasn't so much raining

as misting, and Jonathon's feet slipped a little in the mud as he picked up his pace, eyes darting down every dark alley, whether in search of a friend or an enemy he wasn't sure. The rightful king checked again to make sure that the hood of his cloak was up. It took all of his mental strength to remain focused on where he was, and not to succumb to the horrific images pushing at his weary mind.

A dog snarled at him as he turned a corner into an even smaller and dingier side street, trying to look as if he knew where he was going. Suddenly, as the noise from the main road taverns grew further away, he heard it. The unmistakable sound of following footsteps that he'd listened for in fear for the last two days. He didn't dare to look back, but sped up, going as fast as he could without running. The footsteps matched his pace. He quickly decided that, as it was a single pursuer, his greatest hope lay in an early confrontation.

Turning a corner, he stopped abruptly, and as soon as the spy hurried around, Jonathon grabbed him and pinned him against the wall with surprising ease. As he peered into his captive's face in the semi-darkness, the reason for the lack of resistance was obvious. The man had to be at least seventy. Still, Jonathon knew better than to let this surprise disarm him completely.

"Who are you, and why are you following me?" he hissed fiercely.

"My name is Leon, Your Majesty."

Jonathon took an involuntary step back. "What did you call me?"

"I was following to make sure nothing happens to you, Sire."

Despite his alarm, Jonathon couldn't help but feel slightly amused at the offer of protection from someone who looked at first glance as though a sudden gust of wind would blow him over.

"I think you have me confused with someone else," he said brusquely, releasing the old man and turning to leave.

"I don't think so, Sire. I would know a king of Kyona anywhere." Leon looked at him with sad eyes. "Even in Kerr." The two men regarded each other for a moment.

"I can offer you somewhere to stay tonight."

Jonathon hesitated. The idea of finding a friend in this forsaken place did not seem likely, however much he wanted it to be true. But he didn't know what other options he had. Jonathon decided to go with his instinct.

"Take me there."

As the two figures hurried furtively through the dirty streets, Jonathon noticed the speed and steadiness of his guide's pace. Leon's glory days were long over, but there was life left in his unusually supple legs, and his arms had the memory of strength.

Leon's home was so humble that Jonathon felt ashamed of his own opulent background, but the old man didn't seem to regard the contrast. Jonathon's presence in his house was undoubtedly the greatest honor his sunset years had seen.

"Please sit, Sire. I will bring you some food."

"No, don't trouble yourself," Jonathon began, but his host had already disappeared. When he returned with some bread, Jonathon took it meekly and continued. "And please, call me Jon. I don't believe titles will be necessary for me anymore."

Leon again looked at his guest sadly, with eyes that seemed weary of seeing. "As you wish, of course."

Jonathon had a vague impression that a reproach was concealed in Leon's words, and was quick to change the subject.

"How were you so sure of my identity? I was doing my best to conceal it."

Leon smiled. "I served many years in the Royal Guard under your grandfather. You look remarkably like him, and when you walk, you're hardly distinguishable. Those were the best years of my life," he added reminiscently. "I remember the day your father was born."

A heavy silence fell at these words, both men momentarily lost in painful memories. Suddenly the elderly man spoke again, his voice choked with emotion, yet fierce. "I want you to know, Sire, that my loyalty will always be with your family, and I'm not the only one. Never forget that, wherever you find yourself."

Jonathon nodded his gratitude, but could find no words to respond to this declaration. Soon after, he lay down for what he expected would be a wakeful, watchful night. However, several hours later he was awakened by a shout in the street, probably the last drunken rioter being thrown from the last closing bar. He saw Leon standing at the one small window and was certain that only one of them had slept.

"I need to leave," said Jonathon suddenly. The sun was coming up —he should have been gone by now. This city would not welcome him by daylight.

Leon nodded. "I can show you the way."

"There's no need, Leon, I can find it."

He remembered from the hurried journey of the night before that Leon's home was only a few streets from the city gate. He looked at the old man. What kind of a life would Leon live here for however long he had left? Jonathon hated to leave the man with nothing, and searched his mind for an appropriate means of thanks. He didn't see what power he now had to improve Leon's life.

Fleetingly, the possibility of inviting the old man to come with him flashed through his mind, but he refused to acknowledge it. He couldn't afford to be accompanied by the reproach he had seen in his host's eyes when he denounced his title.

Jonathon held out a few coins in a feeble attempt, but Leon backed away, a pained expression on his face.

"I will never take gold from my king."

Jonathon felt an unreasonable frustration as the older man's words confirmed his thoughts. "I am no king, Leon!"

"You are, Sire, you know that you are. Father is followed by son, to become father, to be followed by son."

Jonathon frowned at the old adage, the blessing spoken over each future king at birth. Blessing? he wondered, thinking of the fate that had befallen his father. Or curse?

"No Leon," he said, "my father was king, but I will never be." He

turned and almost ran out of the door before his rescuer could respond,
with a miserable sense that he had failed his grandfather's servant in
more ways than one.

CALINNAE FOUND himself shivering at the memory. That story had made Jonan indignant, he recalled. Jo had said that Jonathon had mistreated the old man. He considered it very unkingly to leave the man in that way, and then to go into hiding when all his people were looking to him for deliverance. Cal remembered that Jonan's father had gotten a strange look in his eyes when Jonan went on a tirade about the story, and now it made perfect sense to Cal. Without realizing it, Jonan had been speaking against his own father.

Cal had to admit that he had always sympathized with Jonathon, personally. He didn't see what Jonathon could have done for Leon. And Cal still thought that, in Jonathon's situation, going into hiding was the wisest and the safest course. Still, the legend always left him with a dissatisfied feeling. It made him uncomfortable, especially now that he and Jo found themselves in a similar situation.

Cal looked up to see that Elnora was putting more wood on the fire. Jonan stood several feet away, looking north toward the distant capital, presumably trying to figure out their next step. Cal caught his eye with a questioning look, and Jonan nodded, clearly as keen to get moving as Cal was. Cal turned his attention back to Elnora. Although she was looking down, he had the distinct impression that she had observed the silent interchange between the boys.

He noticed that a hollow look had come into her eyes, and her movements were mechanical. Glancing back toward the awakening city, he could easily understand why. However tough and independent she seemed, this was no place for her to live her life.

"What are you doing here?" he asked softly. She looked up, seeming surprised at his gentle tone. He remembered a bit ashamedly how suspiciously he had spoken to her the night before.

"Trying to live, I suppose," her voice was so quiet he hardly caught her words.

"But how did you end up in Kerr?" Cal persisted. "Surely Alezae is a better place to live."

She shrugged. "It's better in some ways, but it's not what it used to be. And there was nothing left for me there."

Cal hesitated, curious about her story, but not wanting to pry. "What do you mean, it's not what it used to be?"

"It's not as out of control as Kerr," she answered. "Not yet, at least. But it's full of fear, and the crime is growing. The traders have everyone on edge, and they're taking over. I left two years ago."

"Traders?" Cal started, confused, then he registered the rest of what she'd said. "Two years ago? You must have been little more than a child. You came here on your own?"

She shrugged again. "I may have been young, but I don't think I was really a child. Not since my parents died. I guess I grew up in a hurry."

"I'm sorry," said Cal quietly. He wanted to say more, but nothing came. Her words touched too closely on his own loss, and for a moment he struggled with the now familiar feeling of trying to outrun his emotions. It was a welcome relief when Jo approached.

"Cal, can I speak to you for a minute?"

Cal jumped up a little too eagerly, and he and Jo stopped just out of hearing range of their young guide.

"We need to get out of here, Cal, and quickly."

"I agree," said Cal. "If there are soldiers all throughout town, it won't be long before someone speaks to those men and decides to come looking. The trouble is, where do we go?"

"I think I have the answer to that," said Jo unexpectedly. "But you're not going to like it."

Cal raised his eyebrows, but Jo hurried on before he could speak.

"There's another question, though, before we get to that."

"What question is that?"

Jo nodded toward Elnora, trying to be discreet and failing. It was clear to Cal as he glanced back that although she couldn't hear them, Elnora was following their exchange as closely as she could.

"What about her?" Jo continued.

"I've been wondering the same thing," said Cal quietly. "She probably saved our lives, it seems like we should do something for her. But what?"

"We could invite her to come with us," said Jo.

"Jo, that would...that would change—"

"Everything," finished Jo. "I know."

"Plus," said Cal, "we can't promise to keep her safe. We don't know if we'll be alive by this time tomorrow."

"I know," said Jo again. "But we can tell her that. I'm just saying we should offer her the option. I mean," he glanced back at Kerr. "It just feels like—"

"Like we can't leave her here," said Cal. He spoke with sudden decision. "You're right. If we leave her here, we don't deserve her help."

He felt a deep sense of satisfaction, almost elation. As he'd promised himself, he would have followed Jo's decision anyway, but it sure felt good to wholeheartedly agree with him.

Jo inclined his head toward Elnora again. "Do you want to...?"

Cal shook his head. "You're in charge here, remember?"

Jo grimaced but didn't argue. He led the way back to where Elnora was standing by the flickering fire, her arms wrapped tightly around her thin frame, as if trying to hold herself together.

"Elnora," he began, and she looked up at him. Her eyes were blank again, and it made Cal shiver. "We have to leave right now. It's not safe for us to stay here."

She just nodded, returning her gaze to the fire. "I assumed as much. You're right that Kerr is not safe for you. Honestly, you were foolish to come here. You won't find many friends in this town. Here," she added, pushing a bundle toward them that Cal hadn't even realized she had been carrying. "There's some food in there, for your journey." She took a deep breath and spoke quickly, without looking up. "There's no need for any big speech. It's best if you just go. I don't do goodbyes well, even with people I've just met."

"Do you want to come with us?" The words burst out without Calinnae's permission. He had fully intended to let Jo do the talking, but the hopelessness radiating from this strange girl tugged at his heart.

Her head snapped up, and she looked between them, clearly astonished. "Come...come with you?"

"It won't be any safer than being here," Cal hurried on. "Less safe, probably. We're being hunted, as you already know. And we don't really have much of a plan. We're making it up as we go. We have no idea what will happen to us, or to you if you come with us. You should know that."

He wasn't really sure Elnora was listening. The expression of astonishment had slowly given way to an enormous grin. He noticed that it changed her features considerably.

"Yes. Yes, I want to come with you. I don't know if I can help much, but I want to do what I can."

"Are you sure?" Cal asked uncertainly. Her sudden enthusiasm threw him slightly off guard. "You don't know us, or anything about us."

She laughed. "You don't know anything about me, but you're still inviting me."

Cal and Jo shared a glance, but both refrained from pointing out the obvious fact that the two of them together had much less to fear from this scrawny young girl than she had to fear from them if they were to turn on her.

"Well, if you're sure," said Jo, "then we really should get going."

"Do you think you can get in and out of the city safely, to gather your things?" asked Cal, but Jonan shook his head.

"I don't think we have time for that, Cal," he said.

"It's not necessary anyway," Elnora cut in cheerfully. She pulled a little pouch out of the folds of her skirt and strung it over her shoulder. "I have everything."

The boys looked at each other. Apparently she had come prepared, just in case.

"So," Elnora continued, still seeming elated. "If we're not headed toward the capital, where are we going?"

Jo took a deep breath and looked between the two. "We're going back to Pravat."

CHAPTER TWELVE

Cal suppressed a sigh as he stretched his limbs, stiff and sore from another night sleeping on the ground. The sight of rolling hills behind and in front of him—that had so recently filled him with admiration—now did nothing to improve his mood. It was maddening to be covering the same ground he and Jo had traversed just a couple of days ago.

He refrained from complaining though, for a couple of reasons. One was that he had said it all when Jo had announced that he wanted to return to Pravat, and nothing had convinced his friend to change his mind. Cal had to admit he might have been more convincing if he had come up with an alternative plan. And having acknowledged that Jonan had the right to lead, he couldn't refuse to follow.

The second reason was Elnora. The endless walking at an exhausting pace, the scant food, the discomfort of sleeping in the open—she had borne it all not only without complaint, but with cheerfulness. Cal didn't like to think that a teenage girl was tougher than he was. *And*, said a small voice in his mind, *you don't want her to think badly of you.*

He ignored the thought. Nevertheless, the more time he

spent with Elnora, the more he had to acknowledge that his reaction to her was unexpected. His initial suspicion had disappeared quickly, replaced by a desire to help her. But that had been because he felt sorry for her. And somehow her cheerfulness and obvious capability made it difficult to sustain sympathy, despite the hardships of her situation. She had impressed him.

"Good morning."

The cheerful voice of the girl herself broke into his thoughts about her, and Cal hoped that he didn't look as self-conscious as he felt as he acknowledged her greeting. Although Jonan was just stirring next to Cal, Elnora had clearly been awake for a while. She looked more fresh than anyone on the run had any right to look, and she had prepared food from the dwindling supply in Jo's rucksack. She had a way of making it stretch that suggested she was used to living on little food.

"Ready to continue on our dragon quest?" she asked brightly, and Cal made no attempt to hold back a groan as Jo grinned in response to the question.

Elnora had listened with impressive passivity to the argument between Cal and Jo when the latter had announced that they needed to go back to the Hall of Records in the hope that the hidden chamber had survived, and they could search the ancient manuscripts for clues about where to find dragons. But of course she wanted an explanation once they were on the road.

Much to Cal's annoyance, she had latched onto his sarcastic comments about a "dragon quest" and seemed maddeningly delighted to be taking part in one.

"I know you're baiting me," he said now, with a long-suffering sigh. "But I still have to ask the question—do you genuinely think Jo's right that there are dragons, and that we might actually be able to find them if we just look hard enough?"

She took a moment to think before answering him. "I'll admit I was skeptical when you first told me about the legend of dragons, and how Jo thought they might be able to help him. But once I saw the manuscript..."

Cal looked down at the hard chunk of cheese he was eating to hide the involuntary frown that came to his face. He had no wish to offend Elnora, and it wasn't her fault that Cal vehemently disagreed with Jo's decision to show Elnora the ancient record. Jo had insisted that it was impractical to keep details from her when they were now traveling together, and Cal hadn't known how to talk him out of it with Elnora present.

But the Esvalere was so secret an object that by rights, even Cal shouldn't know of its existence. He had been relieved when Elnora had only glanced briefly at the account, and hadn't asked about the unfamiliar word. Jonan hadn't actually mentioned that his aim in finding the dragons was to reclaim the sphere, and Cal dared to hope that Elnora hadn't grasped what it was. Still, Cal felt very uncomfortable about the whole thing.

"Well," Elnora was still speaking, apparently oblivious to Cal's reaction. "I have to admit I'd never imagined such an ancient record could exist. Not to mention Jo's signet ring, and how it perfectly matches the mark at the top of the manuscript!" She gave a light-hearted laugh. "To be honest, up until then I was only *mostly* sure that you were who you're rumored to be. But having seen the ring and how it fits into the wax..."

Cal smiled in spite of himself. "I did think you believed Jo was legitimate a little too easily. I mean," he shot his friend a smirk, "he looks more like a vagabond than a royal."

Jonan grinned, as unbothered by the observation as Cal had known he would be, but Elnora ducked her head slightly, her smile strained.

"I was more surprised that *you* were willing to trust *me* so quickly. If we're going to talk about vagabonds...I'm not exactly fit company for royalty."

"Nonsense," contradicted Jonan, frowning. "Whatever's in my blood, I didn't grow up in some stuffy court full of self-important nobles. If I thought I was too good to be your friend, I'd make a terrible king."

"I agree," said Cal quickly. "That may be what Filip is like, but from everything we heard in the stories Jo's father told us, the true royals were never so obsessed with their own status."

Elnora smiled more genuinely at him. "Speaking of the stories, that's the other reason I don't feel confident to discount Jo's dragons altogether. Your stories are so convincing, but I'd never heard any of that stuff before. There's so much I didn't know about. It would be arrogant to assume something couldn't be true because it's outside my experience."

Jonan let out a laugh that he hastily turned into a cough. Looking at him in surprise, Elnora followed his gaze to see Cal's rueful expression. Somehow managing to look apologetic even while laughing, she hurried to correct herself.

"Not that I'm saying you're arrogant Cal! You have more reason to trust your knowledge of these things than I do."

He sighed. "No, I don't. And when you put it like that, it sounds so simple. But I'm still not sure whether I can believe it."

She smiled. "Well, that's why we're investigating, isn't it? To see if there's any truth to it. I guess I agree with Jo that just because we've never seen a dragon doesn't mean they're not real."

Cal frowned at her mention of agreeing with Jo. He looked at his friend accusingly. "Just don't let it go to your head that we've somehow managed to find the one person in the country who doesn't think your schemes are crazy. Why do I have a bad feeling that this alliance you two are forming against me is going to get us into more of a scrape than we're already in?"

"No scrape," said Jo with a grin. "Just a dragon quest."

"If that's not a scrape, what is?" muttered Cal as he shouldered the rucksack before Elnora could insist on carrying it, as she frequently attempted to do. He didn't really expect an answer, but Elnora sidled up to him as they started walking.

"I never actually said I don't think his ideas are crazy, you know," she said quietly, a sparkle in her eyes.

Her smile was hard to resist as he looked down at her. When she smiled, her face lost the pinched, defensive look that had characterized her in Kerr. Mollified, he couldn't help but return it.

"Tell me more of the stories," she continued eagerly. "King Cael was about to get married, not long after ascending to the throne."

Cal couldn't help smiling again. Elnora's enthusiasm for the stories was perhaps what had warmed him most to her. She had at first asked Jonan to tell her about how things were before the Corruption, and Cal had struggled to bite his tongue at Jo's constant inaccuracies. Fortunately, Elnora's endless requests for details had soon defeated Jo, and he had laughingly washed his hands of the process, directing her to Cal and his incredible memory.

"Well, they were married in Kynton with great fanfare, and everyone celebrated. The king's advisors had been unsure about the marriage, because the mountain region had such a mixed reputation. There was a lot of superstition back then. People thought the mountains held magic, and were wary of the mountain folk, whose ways were different. But the future queen wasn't just anyone. She was the daughter of the chief of the mountain people. With the mountain region so close to the border, and relations with Valoria not always free of tension, it seemed like a desirable alliance, to make sure the mountain people didn't turn on their country."

"Enough with the politics, Cal," interjected Jo. "Get on with the action."

Cal gave his friend a sudden shove, and grinned when Jo almost lost his balance.

"Anyway," Cal continued as if there had been no interruption. "It turned out to be a popular choice. Queen Jacqueline captured the hearts of the people, and the princesses were apparently enchanting. King Cael had been an only child, and it was a long time since the castle had been home to adorable little girls. First there was Thalia, born just a year after the king and queen were married. Then Sarai, then Parmida, and finally Avalyn."

"Just princesses?" asked Elnora. "Were there no sons?"

Cal smiled. "Yes, there was a son. Jonathon. He was...well, he was everything. The apple of his father's eye, so the story goes. The hope and future of Kyona." His smile faded, and for a moment they all walked in silence. Elnora glanced between the two boys, taking in their somber expressions.

"Things didn't go quite as planned," said Jo quietly.

"Not quite, no." Cal felt suddenly weary. Glancing down at the uncertain look on Elnora's face, he made an effort to pull himself together. "But that's getting ahead in the story. We were talking about when Jonathon was born. And that day," he smiled, "was a good day."

*J*ACQUELINE HELD *out arms weary but eager to take her newborn son. A son at last. She held him with a firm grasp, as if to assure herself that he really was there, and would not disappear back into the desperate hope from which he had come. Yes, this boy was certainly a*

child of hope. That's exactly what Jacqueline saw when she looked at his tiny red face—the hope of the country, and most of all, that of her husband, fulfilled.

King Cael leaned against the battlements not thirty feet from where his wife lay. His face was free of the anxiety one might expect in a man waiting to hear if he had an heir. He surveyed the landscape before him peacefully. The day would have been very fine if not for the strong wind blowing in from the distant coast. Cael didn't mind the cold at all, and he leaned into the wind and let it make an unkingly mess of his hair. When he heard the infant's scream he smiled but otherwise remained motionless, eyes now closed against the gale.

It was a son, he was sure of it—in fact he'd known for quite some time. Everything they'd hoped for would now unfold in its season. After four daughters, the monarchs had finally secured one of the oldest existing royal bloodlines.

His thoughts turned to the mother of this incredible new being. A gentle but resilient beauty from the mountains, she had been unreservedly loved from the moment she became the young king's bride. She was only seventeen when he met her, but Cael had loved her for the fortitude and strength that had already made her a woman.

However, after their first daughter was born, Cael had quickly realized that to his people she would remain not a queen, but a sweet girl bride until she produced an heir. Now that this was done, he suspected much would change for her. He thought of his four beautiful little daughters and wondered how their lives would change also.

He opened his eyes suddenly and appraised what he could see of his country again. The wind was still forceful, but the sun shone even more brightly than he'd realized. The crying had stopped. He'd go to his wife when she wanted him, which would be when they could be alone. As for the newborn, there was no need to seek him out. His son would soon be brought to him for his blessing, a blessing he would joyfully give.

"Jonathon..." said Elnora pensively. Her gaze traveled over to Jonan, who gave her a quick smile.

"Yes, I'm named for him. All very secretly of course."

"Wow," said Elnora. She sounded impressed, and Cal had to suppress a sudden urge to tell her that he was named for King Cael.

She had soaked up every detail of the early years of King Cael's rule, how his marriage had heralded a time of great peace and prosperity, with relations with Valoria stronger than ever, harvests more plentiful than they had been in years, and no more sign of incursions by raiders from the South Lands.

Jonan couldn't help but comment, as Cal had heard him do before, that it was anticlimactic to hear about the impulsive young prince becoming a responsible and sensible father of five, receiving diplomatic envoys instead of undertaking daring escapades with his closest friend, Lord Damian Lindor.

But Elnora didn't seem to think so. She just laughed at him.

"I liked the stories about the young Prince Cael too," she assured him. "But I think that when he became king, it was time for him to become a man and stop indulging in mad adventures." Perhaps she noted the suddenly haunted look that came into Jo's eyes, because her next words were spoken in a lighter tone. "Besides, little Jonathon has some promise, and how can he get a turn unless his father steps aside? I'm looking forward to hearing about his reign."

It was embarrassing, Cal thought, the tightness he felt in his throat at her words. Jonan had always made fun of him for being too invested in the stories. He looked away as he answered, to hide his emotion.

"He didn't get one, I'm afraid. King Cael was the last king before the Corruption."

"What? That's so sad!" Elnora had obviously not realized they were getting so close to that stage of the story. "What happened?"

"Oh no," said Jo, the humor in his voice pulling Cal out of his heaviness. "That's still a while off, and Cal the stickler won't like telling the story out of order."

Cal rolled his eyes. "It's not altogether out of order," he corrected. "We were up to Jonathon's birth, and the seeds of the problem were already being sowed by then. No one else could see it, but Queen Jacqueline could." His voice dropped to a mutter as his thoughts branched off in a different direction. "Maybe the mountain people really did have some kind of magic." His eyes glazed over as he pondered Queen Jacqueline's strange premonitions...

"She is far too consumed by love."

Cael looked at his wife in surprise. The weakness that had succeeded the childbirth was now but a memory, weeks old. Her rosy cheeks and dark-haired loveliness were as full and engaging as ever. He had been removing the tunic that he wore when not engaged in formal duties, the traditional Kyonan blue laced with gold, while she watched him from the bed. But her comment about his best friend's wife made him turn.

"For Damian? Do you think so?" He finished his task and made his way to her side. "Organza loves him, certainly, but it has always seemed to me as if she could not give him her full support." He refrained from expressing more of the reservations he had felt when Damian had made his choice, five years previously.

Jacqueline seemed to understand him, however, and she smiled as she answered, "Yes, you've put it very well. I did not mean love for

Damian but for Derek." Cael was surprised at the mention of Damian's four year old son.

"I think Derek is a fine lad. I hope he and our little Jonathon can be friends. You should have seen Damian's face when I told him we had been granted a son." Cael smiled at the memory. "He was almost as delighted as I was."

And indeed Cael's own delight at finally fathering a boy had been magnified by the knowledge that his closest friend shared it. And he knew that Damian shared the hope he already had that in each other their sons might find a friendship like they had known.

He nodded to himself as he continued his train of thought. "Yes, Derek is an engaging child. He takes after his father. Thankfully."

The last word was muttered, but Jacqueline's knowing smile showed that she hadn't missed it.

"I don't think Organza was quite so pleased when she heard," she said quietly. "I think she believed we would never produce an heir."

Cael was going to ask his wife to elaborate, but after a glance at her face, he decided against it. She had a faraway look in her eyes that Cael had come to know well. Sometimes she went into these moods, and it seemed like she was in another world. She often came out of that other world with surprising predictions and reflections. Cael admired her insight, but he somehow felt further from her in these moments, as if she was on a level beyond him, where he could not reach her.

She didn't seem to notice his scrutiny, and when she spoke, her gaze remained unfocused.

"A woman enslaved by love for her husband is not capable of anything near the damage that can be done by that all-consuming love for her son."

Cael smiled at his wife's pensive expression. "Don't look so serious, love. What could be more right than that a mother should love her son?"

Jacqueline shifted her eyes off whatever fascinated her so deeply, onto him, and she smiled warmly. "You're right, of course. It's the most natural thing in all creation."

"You should know, after all," her husband added, kissing her. "You made me the father of a son."

"CAL. CAL!" Jo's voice broke through Cal's reverie only when accompanied by a hard poke.

"What?" Cal hadn't intended to speak so sharply, but he had been deep in thought and came back to reality only with difficulty.

Jo didn't speak in response, just nodded ahead. Following his gaze, Cal saw what they had been looking for. Trees were starting to appear as the slopes began to decline.

They had made it to Pravat.

CHAPTER THIRTEEN

The three travelers crouched in their hiding spot, pausing their whispered conversation by unspoken agreement as a sentry became visible in the moonlight, walking behind the top of the wall. Only when the soldier was out of sight did Jo continue the protests he had been making all afternoon.

"I still don't like this plan. I think I should go in, and Elnora should stay."

Cal sighed. "We've been over this, Jo. It's too risky for us to both go back in, everyone's on the lookout for two teenage boys traveling together."

"Besides," chimed in Elnora. "I'm far too afraid to stay out here all alone in the dark. You're much braver, so you have to do it." She gave Jonan a cheeky grin in response to his glare.

Cal shook his head, but couldn't help smiling at Elnora's attempt to lighten the situation. They all knew perfectly well that Jo was galled by the idea of taking the safer role while letting them take risks on his behalf. Somehow Elnora's ribbing seemed to take some of the sting out of it. She had a remarkable way about her, Cal reflected. And she seemed to understand instinctively the way Jo thought.

Cal sighed again, and when his friend continued his attempts, Cal found his patience dwindling.

"Fine, I still say Elnora and I can go, and you can be lookout here, Cal."

"I think you're forgetting," Cal said with a bit of a snap, "just how conspicuous you made yourself last time we were in town. You're staying here."

"I thought I was supposed to be in charge," grumbled Jo half-heartedly.

"Tell me I'm wrong on this, and I'll follow your lead." Cal raised a challenging eyebrow. After meeting his glare for a few pregnant seconds, Jo subsided, although he clearly wasn't happy about it.

"Of course you're not wrong," said Elnora briskly. "A young couple will be less likely to attract attention if we're seen." Calinnae was glad of the darkness as he felt a slight flush rise at her words. "Cal and I will climb up the wall, Cal can direct us to the Hall of Records—"

"If there's anything left of it," Cal muttered. Elnora's pointed glare silenced any further interruptions, and she continued.

"—then we'll find this manuscript about the dragons, return the manuscript Jo stole—" she held up a hand to forestall Jo's protest as he opened his mouth, "—get back to the wall, give the signal, Jo can throw up the rope, we'll climb back over, and we'll all be out of here with no one any the wiser."

Her speech was met with ringing silence. The two boys exchanged a look, and Cal could see that Jo was thinking the same thing he was. They had spent the afternoon devising this plan while waiting for darkness to fall. But when it was laid out all at once like that...well, so much could go wrong.

Cal was more glad than ever that he had insisted Jo stay

back. Jo clearly knew it was because Cal considered Jo's life more valuable than his own. But it was difficult for Jo to refute that idea when Cal wouldn't articulate it, and instead came up with endless other valid reasons for Jo to stay.

So here they were.

"It's not going to get any darker than this," Cal prompted. "There's no reason to delay any longer."

Elnora nodded. Cal thought she looked nervous, and for a moment wondered if they were asking too much of her. But she moved with such confidence as she started toward the wall that he shook the thought from his mind and followed her, pausing only to give Jonan one last reminder.

"Remember, if we get separated for any reason, or if we're late, *don't come into the city*. We'll find a way out, and we'll meet you—"

"Over at that clump of trees, I know, I know." Jonan gestured with his head as he spoke in a long-suffering voice.

Cal turned away, but Jo's quiet voice drew him up short.

"Be careful."

Cal directed an incredulous look back at his friend. "Am I hallucinating, or did *you* just say the words 'be careful'?"

Jo rolled his eyes, but Cal didn't miss the slight smile on his friend's face, and couldn't help smiling himself as he moved toward the wall again.

They had found a section of the perimeter where the trees grew right up to the wall, and creepers could be seen growing all the way to the top. Such a situation would hardly arise in a genuinely well-guarded city. But no amount of doubling or even tripling the guard now could undo the effects of Pravat having been considered unimportant for decades.

Still, as they hid behind a large tree, waiting for the sentry to pass again, Cal couldn't help but compare their approach with the way he and Jonan had casually strolled into the same city a week ago. For better or worse their adventure was changing things drastically, and not just for them.

Careful observation throughout the afternoon had taught them how long they had between sentries, and when one next passed, both Cal and Elnora sprang into action. Elnora reached the wall first and began to test the creepers, looking for a strong trunk. Cal pushed her hand aside gently.

"I'll go first," he whispered. "In fact," he wondered why this hadn't occurred to him earlier, "I could take the rope and throw it down to you once I'm up."

"Nonsense," Elnora hissed. "Then we'd have to untie it and throw it back to Jo. Think how much extra time that would take! Stop messing about, Cal, there's no time for chivalry."

Without another word, she grabbed a section of vine at shoulder height and heaved herself up. Cal quickly followed, hoping that if she were to fall, he might at least have a chance of catching her on the way down. As he climbed close behind her, he had to admire how well she seemed able to pull herself from branch to branch. She was far from heavy, certainly, but the feat still showed impressive strength.

The walls were solid, but not high like they might be in a military city. They reached the top without incident, but Cal paused just below the rim, putting out a hand to stop Elnora. She looked at him questioningly, and he mouthed the word "wait".

She nodded her understanding, and they both remained frozen, suspended in position, holding on like squirrels clinging to a tree trunk. They had both had the strength they needed to climb, but it had taken much longer than expected. Over and over again they had to search for handholds among the foliage, with the increasing height making it imperative that they test each branch before transferring their weight. He knew Elnora's arms must be as sore as his were, and holding on while staying still was somehow much harder than holding on while climbing upward. But by his estimation, they only had a few minutes before the next sentry came. That wasn't enough time to get over the wall and find a staircase down to the ground.

Sure enough, after about three minutes, just as Calinnae's arms were starting to shake from the pain of holding his body up, they heard footsteps just above them. They both shrank against the wall. A glance at Elnora's face showed Cal that she was in as much pain as he was, and he just hoped that she could hold on until the sentry was out of sight. He was alongside her now, and would be no help at all if she were to fall.

But within moments, the footsteps faded, and he saw Elnora looking to him expectantly. He nodded, and they both began to move stiff limbs, pulling themselves up and over the top of the wall. Even in the intensity of the moment, Cal had to admit to himself that, in Jo's absence, he was enjoying being the one expected to take the lead. He immediately felt guilty for the thought, and hoped that Jo was staying safely out of sight.

The moon had momentarily passed behind a cloud, and once they were on top of the wall, it was several moments before Cal could make anything out in the gloom. He felt Elnora draw close to him, and a soft touch on his arm made him look up.

She was nodding in the direction the sentry had gone, and as he followed her gaze, his heart lifted at the sight of a stone staircase descending to the ground below. They were fortunate to have unknowingly picked a spot close to one of the staircases that appeared only sporadically along the perimeter.

They were at the head of the stairs in a flash. Elnora began to hurry down them, but looking ahead, Cal reached out a hand and pulled her to a stop. She wobbled for a moment, her balance thrown by the sudden movement, and Cal grabbed her shoulder with his other hand to steady her. Several steps ahead of her had crumbled away, and she had been about to place her foot on unevenly sloping rock. It would almost certainly have led to a tumble over the edge.

Taking in the situation, she nodded her thanks, and Cal quickly let her go. They proceeded more cautiously down the stairs, and soon found themselves on level ground again. Beckoning for her to follow, Cal set off away from the wall, trying to be as quiet as possible. At first he thought Elnora hadn't followed, but glancing back he saw her right behind him. She surely had more experience of trying to stay unnoticed than he did. Her footsteps were all but silent in the still night.

He knew they'd come in on the eastern edge of the city. If they could continue straight out from the wall, they should be able to wend their way through the back streets toward the center of town, and the square that housed the Hall.

As they crept through the streets, Cal noted the absence of any other people. Possibly there was an enforced curfew, which wouldn't help if they were noticed.

The closer they came to the central square, the more nervous Cal became about what they might find there. When they finally saw a large open space ahead of them, Cal's heartbeat sped up frantically, even as his footsteps slowed. He took a deep breath, then peered around the last building into the square.

Relief warred with shock as he turned his gaze to the right and took in the Hall. Much of the structure was still standing, so the hidden chamber might be intact. But the sight of the blackened shell of the once-imposing structure nevertheless filled him with dismay. So many decades, even centuries, that building had stood. And now it was destroyed because of the fear and greed of their usurper king. Cal felt anger building inside of him.

Looking around, he saw that no other buildings seemed to have burned. The soldiers specifically burned the Hall then.

They must have controlled the blaze before it spread. Still, such a gamble had been taken with the homes and lives of the inhabitants of Pravat. The fire could have destroyed the entire city. But Filip wouldn't care, far away in his stolen castle, surrounded by his ill-gotten wealth.

Calinnae's anger grew into a flame of its own, and it made him bold. He took Elnora's hand and strode confidently across the square, trying to look like a couple of local youths out for a stroll, too young and foolish to take a curfew seriously.

She didn't speak, but followed willingly enough as they walked the length of the square until they were standing right in front of the ruined building. Cal glanced up briefly, noting that the stained glass window had been shattered, leaving only a round hole high above the door. Then he strode boldly in through the yawning opening where the door had been, Elnora at his side.

Everywhere he looked, charred remains of shelves, books, and scrolls could be seen. The walkways constructed of bookshelves were gone, replaced by mounds of rubble and debris, with the occasional white corner of a page visible.

It took some time for them to pick their way through, but without the maze of shelves, it wasn't hard to find their way straight across to the back of the structure.

Cal felt another ripple of relief when he saw the statue, and not just because they needed it to get to the room below. He felt a fierce satisfaction in knowing that the effigy of his idol had survived the inferno. The stone King Cael had a few blackened spots, but was clearly still sound. And Cal was even more gratified to see that the fire had destroyed the inscription falsely naming the model as Lord Lindor.

"How do we get underneath?" Elnora's whisper was quiet, but it still seemed to echo in the large space.

Calinnae shook his head. "We didn't see exactly how he did

it." He walked behind the statue. "He came back here and manipulated something, then the whole statue moved."

She looked at him with wide eyes, and he couldn't help but smile.

"I mean it slid to the side. It didn't come to life or anything."

She nodded, embarrassed, but Cal could understand her reaction. This place had awed him when he saw it during the day, fully intact. Its hollow shell, with moonlight slanting through the broken roof, held an eerie kind of magic.

Elnora joined him behind the statue, and the two of them poked around for several minutes, pushing and pulling at any bit that jutted out. Cal was beginning to despair of finding the secret entrance when Elnora gave a low cry.

"I think I found it!" she whispered excitedly. "There's a lever of some kind here." She pulled it, and the statue began to move. The grinding noise made them both wince, but Elnora at least was quickly distracted by the sight of the opening below. She turned to Cal with awe on her face.

Cal didn't know of any way to close the entrance behind them, or indeed to open it again from below, so he knew they had to be quick. Just the thought of accidentally revealing this chamber to unfriendly eyes made him sweat a little, even in the chill night air.

They were into the underground room in no time. Cal saw with relief one of the lanterns still burning. He looked around the empty room, puzzled—he had hoped to find Aurelius hiding here, but he could see no one.

But there was no time to worry about that. Seizing the lamp, he lit a second from its flame and handed it to Elnora.

"Let's spread out," he said, glad to be able to talk at normal volume again. "I know there are a lot of records, but we can start with the ones on that table." He pointed to the table they had used previously, which still had a number of tomes scattered across it. "Just look for any mention of dragons."

Elnora looked surprised. "You do the searching, Cal," she said quickly. "I'll keep watch at the entrance."

Cal looked at her suddenly uncomfortable expression in confusion. "No, I think it's better if we both look through the manuscripts. Otherwise we could be here all night. Standing guard won't give us enough warning to be worth it."

She swallowed. "No, I really think I'd slow you down. I wouldn't know what to look for."

"I told you, look for the word dragon."

"Cal..." He waited, but she hesitated, apparently unsure how to continue.

"Come on Elnora," he said impatiently. "We don't have time to argue. This is what we came for, so let's get it done."

"I can't." She spoke so quietly he could hardly hear her.

"Can't what?"

"I can't help you." She cleared her throat, not quite meeting his eye.

"Why not?" Cal was utterly mystified. Elnora had been so eager to help them from the moment they'd met that he'd found it a little hard to believe. Why would she choose this moment to be obstructive?

"Because I can't read."

In the silence that followed, Elnora stared at the ground, and Cal stared at her. When he saw her embarrassment, he mentally kicked himself for being so slow to understand. He realized that it was up to him to speak first.

"I'm sorry, I didn't realize...I mean, you never mentioned. When we showed you that manuscript, you were so impressed by it..."

She shrugged. "I was too ashamed to admit that I couldn't read it when you both obviously could."

"Elnora," he spoke quietly now too. "You have nothing to be ashamed of."

She laughed bitterly. "How would you know that?"

"What I mean is, you have nothing to prove to me or to Jonan. You have no need to be embarrassed around us. Lots of people can't read."

She turned away from him. "That's easy for you to say. You say you're from a small fishing village, but you both can do a lot more than read. You don't realize how...humble my background is. Like I said earlier, I'm not exactly a logical companion for anyone exalted. And now I'm suddenly traveling with the two of you. I mean...Jonan is royalty! Or he should be. And you—" She glanced at him then looked away quickly. "You're more impressive than you realize."

Cal looked away himself, unsure how to respond. It was true that he and Jonan had received additional education at Elam's hand, considerably beyond that of their peers in Nerita. The reason for Elam's determination to take Jo far beyond basic teaching was now clear. And Cal had simply benefited by extension. Of course he had been part of these additional lessons. He and Jo had always done everything together.

"I'm sorry," Elnora continued after a moment. "If I'd realized how many records you'd need to look through, I wouldn't have insisted on coming in Jonan's place. I just thought it was most important for him to stay safe."

"So did I." Cal sighed. "I hope he's lying low, like he's supposed to." He looked at Elnora. Her face was still flushed with embarrassment. "And there's no need for you to apologize. We'll find what we need to. You can hold the lantern for me, and help me decide which books to look through. We want ones that look old."

Elnora glanced around. "They all look old."

Cal laughed anxiously. "Older."

Elnora nodded with determination, and started hunting through the shelves nearest to the table. She pulled a few tomes out, piling them on the table as she went. When she had added about a dozen to the books already there when they arrived, she came over and took Cal's lantern out of his hand, holding it aloft for him to read by.

Cal had already scanned and discarded three titles. He saw King Cael's name mentioned a number of times, as well as Jonathon, and more occasionally one of the princesses, but the records also stretched back further than the stories Cal knew. No mention of dragons, though.

When he had flicked through all the books on the table without success, Cal had to fight a feeling of rising panic. Elnora showed no sign of discouragement, but flitted back to the shelves and pulled more volumes out.

"These look old," she said, clearly making an effort to sound positive.

Cal smiled briefly at her, then took the records she held out and began to search them. He was on the fourth one when his heart suddenly leaped at the sight of the word he'd been looking for.

"Here!" He had to remind himself to keep his voice down. "Dragons!"

Elnora had been back at the shelves, but she raced over, staring at the page so eagerly that Cal almost forgot that she couldn't read it.

"Here," he continued. "It's in King Cael's handwriting." He started to scan the page, then remembered that he should read it aloud for his companion's benefit, although he left out the mention of the Esvalere.

Even before my father told me of the Esvalere, I had heard rumors of dragons. The legends are rarely told here in Kynton, but in the mountains they are still common tales, spun around the fire on a cold night. I heard them when I made my extended stay in Montego some years ago. My advisors had encouraged it, saying that we would do well to strengthen ties with the mountain folk. With them so close to the border many fear that if there is trouble with Valoria, the mountain folk will forget that they are Kyonan, and may be lured to side with our neighbors. My advisors told me to look past the strange ways and unearthly speech of the mountain people. Since I brought Jacqueline home, they would not dare to make such comments to me anymore. I don't think anyone intended for me to meet my bride during my sojourn in the mountains...but she has won their love in her own right now. And not just because she is the mother of my heir. My beautiful mountain girl—how could she fail to captivate the hearts of my people with her sweetness and goodness?

Cal glanced involuntarily at Elnora and saw that she was watching him with rapt attention, clearly engrossed by the narrative. He felt an unexpected embarrassment at reading aloud King Cael's reflections on the loveliness of his wife. He glanced back at the page and was relieved to see that the author was getting to the point.

But the dragons. The mountain people talk about them still, claiming that they used to be widely believed in by their ancestors. Some even claim to have seen them in recent times. At that I only smile. There can be no doubt, however, that the stories of dragons spring from the mountain region. When I was in Montego, I could understand why. The place seems magical, in a way that no other part of this beloved country of mine can quite match. It is a wild and beautiful landscape, and the people are different from my other subjects. There is an indefinable quality about them. I had expected the mountain people to be offended by the superstitious talk of them having an unnatural magic about them, but they own it readily. Many of them claim that their magical quality stems from living on the doorstep of the dragons" realm, being gradually soaked in the magic of the beasts over many centuries. I'm sure that those in Kynton would rather say that the legends of the dragons arise as a way to explain the unusual quality of the mountain people. It is this quality that some like to call magic, but I would not quite give it that name.

It is hard in such cases to know where these stories originate, or where myth ends and history begins. Although they meant it well, many times have I been frustrated in my attempts by the tradition of my ancestors that royal history should be passed down only orally. I have chosen to break that tradition, but often all I can record is rumors or legends, only guessing myself at what truth lies within them.

Of course, there are other things that I know more of, but even I am not willing to commit to paper. Not every royal secret is mine to share.

So I will content myself with recording only the legends of the dragons, as are still recounted by the legend-tellers, the mountain folk.

"Is that all there is?" asked Elnora, when Cal stopped speaking.

He nodded. "Yes, that's all."

He wished King Cael had been clearer, but he had stopped short of saying that dragons did not exist. The contents of this document would not convince Jo that his quest for dragons was a waste of time.

"Well, that's enough, isn't it? Now we know our next step." Elnora sounded excited. It took Cal a moment to remember that their mission had been to figure out where to go to find these supposed dragons, not to find information to disprove their existence to Jonan.

When he didn't respond, Elnora spoke again. "Surely we head for the mountain region now."

He nodded slowly. "Montego, specifically. That would be the

place to start." He had heard of the mountain city, the center of the area occupied by the mountain people, but he had never imagined going there.

"We did it!" Elnora's elation suggested to Cal that she had not been as confident in the plan as she previously conveyed. "We found information on where to go to follow up the stories of dragons."

"We did," Cal nodded again. "And now we need to get out of here." He pulled out of the rucksack the original manuscript that Jo had taken and placed it on the table. It would be safest here.

He was the one who had said they had to leave, but he lingered for a moment, wishing once again that there was time to stay and read all these incredible records. As he cast one last longing glance around the room, he saw it. An arm lying across the floor, protruding from behind a bookshelf not far away.

Aurelius was in the hidden chamber after all.

CHAPTER FOURTEEN

The two trespassers quickly confirmed that Aurelius was alive, much to Cal's relief. But the elderly man was clearly in bad shape. A quick scan of the area revealed that he had retreated down here with food, water, and oil for the lanterns. He had obviously anticipated that he might be trapped down here for some time, but for reasons that were not immediately obvious, he had lost consciousness.

After a few minutes of attempting to rouse Aurelius, Cal began to be very anxious. They had not factored into the plan time to care for an injured record keeper. They could probably survive down here throughout the day until it was dark again if they needed to. But he didn't know what rash action Jo might take if they failed to appear for the planned rendezvous.

Before he had time to think about contingency plans, Aurelius stirred, lifting his hand to his head with a groan and blinking in the light of the lantern. As awareness returned, he looked back and forth between the two of them, first with confusion, then with sudden recognition at the sight of Calinnae.

"You! You've come back!" Aurelius tried to sit but only

groaned again, resting his head back down on the ground for a moment.

"Are you all right?" asked Elnora in concern. "Did you hit your head?"

Aurelius stared at her uncomprehendingly. "Who are you?" He looked around, realizing who was missing. "Where's the—" He glanced again at Elnora, then transferred his gaze to Cal. "Where's your friend?"

"Jonan is outside the city," Cal assured him quickly. "Staying safe." *We hope.* He refrained from saying it aloud. Aurelius looked worried enough as it was.

"Thank goodness for that," the old man said, closing his eyes for a moment. He quickly opened them again, however. "Why are you here? The soldiers are looking for you. They searched everywhere. They burned the Hall!"

"We know," Cal said gently. "I'm so sorry."

Aurelius managed to push himself to a sitting position, assisted gently by Elnora. "It's all right, young man. It wasn't your fault. I saw the whole incident in the square." He pursed his lips for a moment. "Your friend is rash. Brave, but rash."

"Yes he is," agreed Cal. "But that's not important right now. How did you end up trapped down here?"

Aurelius winced as he gingerly touched a hand to one shin. "It was never my intention to be trapped. But when I realized they were going to destroy the Hall, I decided that my best course was to hide down here, to protect the records. Unfortunately, I'm not as young or as nimble as I used to be. In my haste I fell as I descended the ladder. I think my leg is broken, and I hit my head. It was all I could do to close the entrance, and hobble over here. There's no way I could climb back up the ladder on my own. I had brought food and water for several days, but my water has run out, and I was starting to despair of making it back to the surface."

"We can help you," said Elnora.

"Who is this young lady?" Aurelius asked. Cal wondered if it was his imagination that Aurelius's voice held a hint of reproach.

"This is Elnora," he said quickly. "She's been traveling with us since we left Kerr. She won't tell anyone about this place," he added, when Aurelius didn't respond.

"Of course I won't," said Elnora reassuringly, but Aurelius did not look reassured.

"You live in Kerr?" he asked, clearly suspicious.

"Not anymore," said Elnora with her usual cheerfulness.

"We need to get out of here before dawn," Cal cut in. He suddenly remembered that Aurelius had lived in the Hall. "Do you have somewhere to go?"

The record keeper nodded. "I have a niece who lives in the city, not far from here. She'll take me in."

"I think we should go without delay," said Cal, and was relieved when Aurelius readily agreed.

"Yes indeed. I would be most grateful. I've seen quite enough of this room."

It was slow going, but with assistance from both Elnora and Calinnae, Aurelius was able to ascend the staircase and then the ladder. When he emerged into the ruined Hall above, Cal heard a sharp intake of breath from the elderly man, but Aurelius did not comment on the extent of the destruction.

Once they were all above ground, the record keeper directed Cal on how to close the secret entrance, and the three of them began to slowly pick their way across the rubble-strewn floor. Cal hoped that Aurelius had been telling the truth when he said that his niece's house wasn't far away, because even with assistance, it was clear that every step was painful for the old man.

When they reached the entrance, Cal saw with relief that the square was still deserted in the darkness. Aurelius directed them down a side street. Cal and Elnora exchanged glances, but neither commented on the fact that they were going the opposite direction from the city exit.

Their progress was maddeningly slow, and long before they reached their destination the first hints of dawn began to creep up the sky. It was hard to keep track of time in the dim underground room, and they had been away from Jonan longer than he had realized. By the time they reached the house, it was clear that they were not going to be able to keep their rendezvous. Cal gritted his teeth in frustration, but there was nothing to do but to push on.

Aurelius's niece took so long to answer the door that Cal wondered if anyone was home. When she answered, she looked between him and Elnora with such fearful suspicion that he thought they would be turned away. But when her eyes fell on Aurelius, she gave a hastily stifled cry and ushered them inside. They crossed the threshold just as a cock crowed somewhere nearby, and Cal had to hold back a groan.

Things had not gone according to plan.

It was a long morning. Although clearly suspicious, their hostess allowed Cal and Elnora to hide in her home at Aurelius's request. They huddled in a room with the curtains drawn, conferring in whispers about what to do next. Elnora maintained her calm quite well, but Cal was fretting himself into a state of distraction within an hour of their arrival.

Elnora told him that Jo would be fine, and they just needed to trust that he wouldn't do anything foolish. Cal felt no such confidence. He knew Jonan much better than Elnora did. Elnora's first suggestion was that they lie low at the house until dark, and make their way back to the meeting point. After some discussion, however, she seemed to realize that whether or not

Cal's concern was well founded, he was not going to cope with waiting out the entire day in suspense. Not with Jonan's whereabouts a mystery.

Aurelius's niece told them that the city was not on full lockdown. The gates were open during the day, but anyone entering or exiting was thoroughly searched, and sometimes questioned.

They decided that their best course was to leave openly, trusting in the fact that no one was on the lookout for a boy and a girl together. Cal hoped fervently that they wouldn't run into the one soldier who had taken note of him last time, or the guards they'd tricked into leaving their post unattended.

Upon asking, they discovered that there was always a long line just after sunup, as people wanting to leave the city for the day waited their turn to be searched. So they decided to wait for a few hours before making their attempt. The less time anyone had to scrutinize them, the better.

Their hostess brought them some food, which they ate gratefully, but she was clearly reluctant to engage more than absolutely necessary. She had settled Aurelius into a bed and made it clear that he was not to be disturbed.

So they had nothing to do but wait.

As much as Cal knew he needed to take his mind off his stress, he was too distracted to initiate conversation, so they sat in silence for a long time before Elnora's soft voice broke into his thoughts.

"Why did King Cael restore the Hall of Records?"

It took Cal a moment to register her question, deep in thought as he was. "Well...it was because the records of the country's history had become outdated and fallen into disuse."

"Yes, I understand that, but why was it so important to him? When you spoke of it before, you made it sound like it was his life's work."

Cal considered her words for a moment. "I suppose it was his life's work, in a sense. It was after his first daughter died that he began the restoration."

"Thalia," said Elnora. "I remember. But you never told me how she died. Or why that would make him want to go to the Hall of Records."

Cal was silent for a moment. As much as he loved recounting the stories, he took no pleasure from the thought of telling this particular tale.

"It wasn't so much because Thalia died that he wanted to record the royal history. It was because Jonathon almost died. He was afraid that if he was somehow prevented from passing on the history to his heir, it would be lost forever. I didn't know before we first went to the Hall that the royal family only passed down its history orally. But now I understand better than ever why King Cael cared so much about the Hall of Records. His only son and heir almost died as a small child."

"What happened?" Elnora prompted gently, when Cal fell silent.

"There was an accident. Or at least," his voice dropped to a mutter, "that's what they thought at the time."

Elnora's forehead creased in confusion. She opened her mouth, clearly intending to ask for clarification, but Cal hurried on before she had the chance. He didn't really want to get into all that now, not while he was so stressed about their predicament.

"Jonathon was a child, like I said. Maybe six or seven. Thalia was the oldest, old enough to care for him. He was playing in the castle grounds, below the ramparts, when a whole section of the parapet above crumbled. Thalia saw what was happening, and she pushed him out of the way. She was crushed, and died immediately.

"She protected the lineage. She bought his life with her own." The words felt heavy as they came out. Fleetingly, Cal realized that in insisting that Jo stay behind and he and Elnora go in his place, risking capture by Filip's soldiers, he had been ready to do the same. And not only with his own life, but with Elnora's. It was a grim business, this royal blood. A heavy burden for more than just the heir.

"That's so sad," Elnora said quietly. "How awful. It would be horrible to be Jonathon, living with that knowledge all your life, that someone had died to save you."

"Maybe it made him live his life more fully," said Cal in response. "Perhaps he didn't want to waste her gift."

Elnora shook her head, and Cal was surprised by the certainty in her voice. "No, more likely it would have poisoned his life. He would always feel the guilt of it. He would always feel like his life wasn't worth the high price that was paid for it."

Cal thought about her words for a moment before responding. "I don't think that's true," he said slowly. "That his life wasn't worth it. It obviously was."

Elnora met his eyes, her own expression troubled. "You mean because he was the heir?"

Cal shook his head. "No, that's not what I mean. I mean that his life obviously was worth such a high price because Thalia was willing to pay it." Elnora still looked confused, so he pushed on. "I came to the market here once with my father. My mother wanted to make a new dress, and the merchant we bought cloth from was selling silks from Valoria. I couldn't believe how expensive they were, and I asked my father if any material could really be worth so much. He said that goods are worth whatever someone is willing to pay for them. The price set by the merchant is meaningless until someone actually hands over the coins."

Cal shrugged again. "I just thought that whether Jonathon thought so or not, the fact that Thalia was willing to buy his life with hers meant that his life was worth that cost, at least to her."

Elnora was silent for a long minute, her expression unfocused as she processed Cal's words. "I would never have thought about it like that," she said at last. "I wonder if Prince Jonathon did. I wonder if he still felt the guilt for the rest of his life."

"I'm just guessing of course. I don't know how it affected Jonathon, really," said Cal thoughtfully. "Some good came out of it in that King Cael began to record the history, which is helping us now. But honestly, I think the heaviest price was paid by Queen Jacqueline.

"She was never the same after her firstborn daughter died. Even before they knew the full story of what happened, she seemed to know a bigger shadow was beginning to envelop them. And she couldn't forget the cost that had been paid for her son to live, and the Bloodline to continue."

Cal's eyes misted over as he once again lost himself in thoughts so familiar they felt like memories.

When King Cael returned from Pravat, his heart still troubled but his mind again at peace, he found his wife shivering on her bed and went straight to her. She did not look at him, but leaned wearily against him.

"I do not love him less, Cael. Or resent him in any way." Her soft voice surprised him. When he had left, after the funeral, her grief had been beyond words.

"I know, love, of course I know."

"But I don't just mean because of this. I have never loved him less, or cared less for him than the girls." She turned her grief-stricken face toward his. "I'm his mother."

Cael looked down at her in surprise. He had never mentioned to her the difference he noted between her relationship with their daughters and with their son. The difference was definitely there, but it was so subtle that he had wondered if it was just a mother's bond with her daughters. He had no sisters, and no experience to confirm or contradict his thoughts. But now he could tell that there was an answer forthcoming. He waited in silence.

"When Jonathon was born, I knew at once that it was not the same as the girls' births. I knew that he could never be to me what they were. He was the fulfillment of Kyona's hope and yours, but not mine."

Seeing Cael's confusion, Jacqueline hastened to add, "You must not misunderstand me. I did not then, nor have I ever, loved Jonathon less than the others. But to be his mother is not the same task as to be the mother of our daughters. At each of their births I rejoiced while the nation worried, knowing my day of sacrifice was put off a little longer. From the moment they began life, they were all mine, but it was not so with Jon...already he knows it. He treats me with love, kindness, respect. Yet although he does not understand it, he senses that I am not of the same fabric as him. I am not his equal."

Her last comment elicited an exclamation from her husband. "Jacqueline, surely you cannot believe anybody thinks this of you!"

"I do not care what others think of me, Cael. I care what is true. I do not mean that I am less of a person, but Jonathon has a greater purpose, his future is of greater value. He is the steward of your bloodline, he belongs to that power and responsibility, and so he can never fully belong to me." She turned her eyes again to her husband and added softly, "Just like you."

"Jacqueline!"

"It is true, although I know you don't like to hear it." She smiled softly at his unhappy look and put a gentle hand on his cheek. "Don't look so. I am yours, and that is enough for me. I have given all I am to your life's purpose, and now I know that I am part of whatever you achieve. And you have loved me Cael, as I have never been loved."

Cael held her tighter. "This is not right, this grief, this sacrifice. There must be a better way."

Jacqueline shook her head. "Not everything can always be right. There is a shadow over this place. We have been touched by a dangerous combination of love and death, and now it has entered our lives."

Cael could give no response to words he did not fully understand, but he held his wife as she slept, dry eyed. Whether this was because she was too strong for tears or simply too weary, he could not tell.

FOR LONG MINUTES after Cal's tale, neither companion spoke. But a shout from outside jerked Cal out of his reverie. It sounded as though it was simply an altercation between a pedestrian and a merchant whose cart was blocking the street, but it served to remind both Cal and Elnora of the world beyond their hiding place.

"We should go," said Elnora quickly.

Cal nodded. "I was thinking the same thing. I'll be much easier in my mind once we find Jonan."

Although she sniffed disapprovingly at the intrusion on the old man's rest, their hostess allowed them to say farewell to Aurelius. They waited until they couldn't see anyone passing through the front window of the small home, then slipped out onto the street and began to walk quickly back toward the central square.

A couple of streets away from the house they passed a merchant's cart trundling by, also on its way to the square. It was piled high with fresh bread. In a movement so swift Cal almost missed it, Elnora toppled a few loaves into Cal's open rucksack, and retightened the drawstring. He was surprised, but didn't comment.

When she did the same with some dried meats from a cart further along the street, however, he gave her a pointed look.

She shrugged. "What? We're almost out of food, and we won't make it to Montego with nothing to eat." When he still didn't speak, she added, "I don't usually steal."

He raised his eyebrows, and a quick grin broke through her guard.

"Well, not anymore, anyway." After a moment she grew serious. "I did when I first got to Kerr. But it's been a long time now since I've needed to resort to it."

Calinnae didn't comment. He'd been brought up with strict morals about such things. But he'd also been brought up with a roof over his head, and food provided by someone else every day of his life.

Calinnae would have preferred to avoid the square—he didn't like the idea of all that open ground. But they weren't confident they could find their way back to the gate without it. They skirted around the edge of the space as unobtrusively as they could, but Cal still saw a number of people looking at them curiously. He tried to look less nervous than he felt.

A number of times they encountered pairs of soldiers patrolling the streets, but they managed to avoid catching the interest of any of them. The soldiers didn't seem especially alert. It appeared that they thought, correctly, that the fugitives had made it cleanly out of Pravat long ago. And, Cal reflected ruefully, why would the soldiers think them foolish enough to return?

They had decided to make their way out of the small southern gate that Cal and Jo had originally used on their approach from Nerita. From there they could follow the wall until they found the trees, where Cal hoped rather than expected to find Jonan waiting patiently at the appointed meeting place.

When they neared the southern wall of the city, Elnora cast

an appraising look up and down Cal. He felt suddenly self-conscious.

"No offense," she said, "but you're not very good at looking inconspicuous."

She reached out a hand. Before Cal could figure out what she was doing, she'd taken hold of his arm and drawn it around her shoulders. If he hadn't been self-conscious before, he was now.

He fought a flush as they rounded a corner and joined the back of a small queue waiting to get out of the south gate. Cal was relieved to see that he didn't recognize either of the guards on duty. Nevertheless, he wondered just how many times he would have to sneak through this particular gate.

"Try not to look so worried," Elnora muttered to him. He glanced down at her quickly.

"Sorry," he said. "How are you so good at this?"

She gave him a dry smile. "A lifetime of blending in. Just keep talking to me."

Somehow Cal found that with his arm across the shoulders of a pretty girl who wanted him to talk to her, it was difficult to think of anything to say. His own thoughts pulled him up short. When had he started thinking of Elnora as pretty? She had seemed the most ragged urchin imaginable the night he met her. Perhaps it was the way her smile softened her face, or the sparkle in her eyes.

"Cal?" Elnora raised her eyebrows at him, and he pulled himself together.

"So, Montego," he said quickly. "I guess we're headed for the mountains."

"Looks like it," Elnora agreed, her brow slightly furrowed.

"What is it?" Cal asked, trying not to smile at her thoughtful expression. "Nervous about meeting the infamous mountain people?"

She laughed self-consciously. "Maybe a little." Her tone turned dry. "I suppose they can't be worse than the friendly residents of Kerr." She shook her head. "But growing up on the coast, I guess I was always taught to be wary of people who live in the mountains. Just like people who live in the forest."

"People who live in the forest?" Cal repeated, distracted. "You mean the Forest of Rune? I didn't even know anyone lived there. What's wrong with them?"

Elnora shrugged. "Nothing, probably. Most likely it's just a tall tale. But people say to avoid the forest, because the foresters are dangerous. Some claim that they live by their own laws, and even the king leaves them alone."

Cal snorted, thinking of what he knew of Filip. "That seems unlikely."

"Probably," Elnora agreed lightly.

Cal gave her a sideways look, his mind returning to the original topic of conversation. "Elnora, I was thinking. How well do you know the map of Kyona?"

"Well enough, I think," she answered. "Why?"

"It's just that if we head for Montego, we probably shouldn't go back through Kerr."

"No," Elnora agreed emphatically.

"So I guess we'll be going through—"

"Alezae," said Elnora, suddenly catching on. "Oh."

Cal was trying to decipher the expression on her face when they were hailed by the guard.

"You two! Where are you off to?"

"Nerita." Cal immediately berated himself for the answer. He had been so distracted by the conversation with Elnora that he hadn't realized they'd reached the front of the line, and the guard's question had taken him by surprise. His home town was the first place that came to his mind.

"Nerita?" The guard was immediately suspicious. "Haven't

you heard? Nerita is occupied by the soldiers now. No one comes or goes. Apparently that's where the trouble makers come from."

Cal tried to hide his dismay at this information, but there was a ringing in his ears that made it hard to focus. Elnora came to his rescue, her voice smooth, with just the right amount of insolence.

"Of course we've heard. Hasn't everyone? We're not going to Nerita, just taking the road toward Nerita. My uncle's farm is only an hour or so out of Pravat, down that road."

The guard looked between them with narrowed eyes. Cal schooled his face into what he hoped was a look of nonchalance. His arm tightened involuntarily around Elnora's shoulder as the guard called to his fellow on duty.

"What do you think about these two?"

The second guard grunted as he strolled over. "What's their story?"

"They claim they're going to a farm an hour down the road toward Nerita."

The newcomer shrugged. "There's farmland out that way. What's your concern?"

"I don't know, something just doesn't seem right about them to me."

"We're right here, you know," said Elnora. "We can hear you."

"Shut your mouth, girl," said the first guard. His hand twitched, as though he was considering striking her, but it remained at his side. "Don't give us any attitude, unless you want trouble."

Cal bristled at the man's rudeness, and once again spoke without thinking. "We're not afraid of a little trouble."

The man eyed him up and down, his look measuring. "What do you reckon?" he said, again speaking to the second guard as though they weren't there. "Should we take them in? Ask a few more questions?"

His companion grunted again. "And spend the rest of the morning waiting for the soldiers to get to us? My shift's almost over. We're supposed to be looking for two teenage boys. No one said anything about a girl. Let them go."

The first guard was clearly still reluctant, but he waved them through. "I'll be on the lookout for you," he threatened, his eyes lingering on Calinnae who was still staring aggressively back at him.

They started down the road, walking quickly but not running. For a few moments they were silent. Cal's ears were still ringing, the strength of his anger toward the antagonistic guard surprising even himself.

"Are you all right?" Elnora asked quietly. It was only as he looked at her that Cal realized he was glowering. He tried to calm his features.

"He almost hit you, do you realize that? He was thinking about it."

She shrugged. "It wouldn't be the first time. It's common, isn't it? Guards and soldiers, anyone with a small amount of power. They have to keep convincing themselves that they have power by punishing anyone vulnerable enough to be in their reach."

Cal looked at her in silence for a moment, not wanting to admit that prior to the devastating events the night he had left Nerita, he had never had experience of either guards or soldiers in his sheltered seaside town.

"Well, it would be the first time such a thing happened when you're with me," he finally said. "And once would be one time too many."

She looked at him in surprise. "Thanks for the concern, Cal, but I can take care of myself. I've been doing it for a long time."

"I know you can," he returned. "But you're not by yourself now. We can all look out for each other."

She smiled but didn't respond. Cal thought she looked a bit reserved, like she wasn't willing to count on it. It troubled him, but he didn't know what else to say.

Elnora glanced back at the gate. "They're not watching us," she said. "Should we head for the trees now?"

Cal nodded, and they veered left off the road, picking up the pace as they headed for the grove of trees where they had arranged to meet Jonan if they were delayed.

A shout behind them made them turn. Cal saw in dismay that the distant figure of the guard was pointing in their direction, a mounted soldier behind him. As they watched, frozen, the soldier urged his horse out of the gate, followed by a second soldier, also in the saddle.

Without a word, Cal grabbed Elnora's hand and began to sprint toward the trees. She kept pace with him. Glancing back, Cal saw that the soldiers were riding after them. He looked at Elnora running beside him, then ahead. They would be lucky to make it to the trees, but then what? They couldn't outrun horses on foot.

He didn't want to lead the soldiers right to where Jonan was, but with no other idea of what to do, Cal continued to run toward the grove, his breath coming in pants, conscious with every step that the soldiers were gaining on them rapidly.

They reached the shelter of the trees with the sound of hoofbeats mere feet behind them.

"Hey, you! Stop in the name of the king!"

They started to wend their way between trunks. Cal and Elnora were separated briefly as they dashed around trees, coming back together occasionally. The horses were hampered by the undergrowth and the trees, but it wasn't enough to slow them down significantly. Cal was still trying to think of a way out when he heard a sharp cry behind him.

He turned to see the closest soldier, who had almost reached him, toppling to the ground. He watched in astonishment as the man, who seemed to have too many limbs, struggled and writhed where he had fallen.

"Cal! Grab the horse!" The familiar voice jerked him out of his confusion. Jo disengaged himself from the stunned soldier, and Cal realized with a glance upward that Jo had dropped from a nearby tree straight on top of the man. He hastened to do as Jo had said, and grabbed the bridle of the horse, which was prancing nervously nearby.

"Where's Elnora?" he asked sharply.

"I don't know," Jo began. "She was right behind—" The rest of his sentence was lost as his legs were grabbed from behind by the soldier he had attacked. For a moment they struggled, but looking around Cal saw a sizable branch on the ground. Without giving himself time to think, he grabbed it and hit the soldier on the head as hard as he could. The man went down hard and didn't stir.

Jo picked himself up, panting. "Thanks."

"He's not dead, is he?" asked Cal nervously.

Jo made a quick check and shook his head. "No, just unconscious. We'd better hurry."

Straining their ears, they quickly heard the sounds of a nearby altercation. They ran toward it, Cal still leading the horse. The other soldier had caught up to Elnora. He had dismounted and seized her by the arm. She was struggling, but he was clearly much stronger than her.

Once again, Cal didn't think. He let go of the horse and ran at the soldier with a shout. The man turned a bit too slowly to avoid the blow Cal aimed at his face. Momentarily stunned, the soldier stepped back and shook his head to clear it. His expression hardened into anger as he took in his young attacker, and his fist shot out in a move that Cal barely ducked in time to avoid.

The older man reached for his sword, but before it was clear of the scabbard, he was tripped from behind by Elnora. He managed to stay on his feet, but he staggered for a moment, trying to keep his balance. That moment was all the boys needed. Cal and Jo rushed him together. He raised his arms defensively, but they once again aimed for the head, and with the combined impact of both their blows, he was soon lying prostrate like his companion.

Breathing hard, Cal looked up at Elnora. "Are you all right?"

She nodded, her gaze on the soldier. "I'm fine. You came just in time, I think. Where's the other soldier?"

"Cal knocked him out," said Jo, sounding a little stunned himself. "Who knew you could be so ferocious?"

"You can make fun of me later," said Cal shortly. "First let's get out of here." He strode over to his friend. They clasped arms briefly. "I'm just glad we found you, and in one piece."

"Likewise," returned Jonan. "I was frantic when you didn't come back before dawn. I've been hiding up in the trees all morning, trying to watch the road, in the hope that I'd see you if you came out through the gate sometime today. Much longer and I would've come looking for you myself. I was trying to think of how to sneak past the guards when I saw the commotion."

"I'm impressed you lasted that long," said Cal dryly. "As soon as we were held up, I realized we didn't have much of a backup plan."

"We can talk about this later," cut in Elnora. "More soldiers will come when these ones don't return with us in tow."

"You're right," said Jo quickly. "But which way do we go?"

"Toward Alezae," said Cal, with a quick glance at Elnora. "We'll explain later."

"I say we take the horses," said Jonan. He turned to Elnora. "Can you ride?"

She shook her head. "Can you?"

Jo shrugged. "We've ridden a few times. Cal's more confident than I am, but with horses as well-trained as these, we should be fine."

Cal nodded. "You can ride with me, Elnora," he said. "We won't be able to outstrip pursuing soldiers, not with one of our horses carrying two, but it will give us a little head start."

Elnora took a deep breath. "I have an idea for how we could lose them," she said. "But it's a bit dangerous."

"I'm in," said Jo quickly, and Cal rolled his eyes.

Elnora grinned at him, but her expression was serious as she turned to Cal for his response. "Do you trust me?" she asked quietly.

He looked at her for the briefest of moments before responding.

"Yes, I trust you. Let's do it."

CHAPTER FIFTEEN

Cal watched with regret as the horses cantered away. He was not experienced enough to make riding comfortable, but it had been gratifying to cover ground so quickly after so many days of endless walking. Still, he thought Elnora's plan to send the horses on down the road toward Nerita was a good one. When the soldiers found the horses wandering aimlessly, it would hopefully make it harder to track where the fugitives had gone. They had even dismounted on a rocky outcrop, hoping not to leave tracks.

And they had benefited from the saddlebags, their food supplies being significantly increased now, with the valuable addition of water skins, and a couple of extra blankets.

Jo was watching the horses too, his expression glum. "I still think we should have taken the soldiers' swords," he said.

Cal shook his head. "They're heavy and cumbersome. Not worth the extra burden when we don't know how to use them."

"I do," said Elnora unexpectedly. The boys both turned to stare at her.

She was standing some distance away. Cal had intentionally put a bit of space between them when they all dismounted, after sharing a horse all the way from Pravat. It wasn't that he had disliked riding double with her. On the contrary, if he was honest he'd enjoyed having her perched in front of him, as he reached around her to hold the reins.

At least until he'd seen Jonan with eyebrows raised and the hint of a grin on his face. Cal had just scowled in response, but he'd felt self-conscious after that and been glad when the ride was over.

"What do you mean?" he asked now.

"I know how to use a sword, a little," said Elnora brightly. "It's been a while, but I remember the basics."

"How?" asked Cal as Jo said, "Why didn't you say anything back there?"

She shrugged. "You didn't ask," she said, in response to Jonan's question. "And I didn't particularly want to carry one of those soldiers' huge swords all the way to Montego. A small fighting knife might have been worth it."

She looked at Cal. "As for how...well, I was part of a...a scavenging group for a few years before I left Alezae. I learned a lot of things from them, including how to use weapons. Like I said, it's been a while."

"A scavenging group?" repeated Cal skeptically. "You mean a gang?"

She smiled briefly. "I guess you could call it that. We weren't as intimidating as that makes us sound. Still, it wasn't a good situation. That's why I left and made my way to Kerr."

"Did you say Montego?" asked Jonan, distracted. "I thought Cal said we had to head toward Alezae. Montego is in the mountains, isn't it?"

"We can tell you everything on the way," said Cal. He turned to Elnora. "You said it's not far to the start of this marshland. Let's get moving."

She nodded. "Follow me."

. . .

CAL LOOKED around at the bog, wondering when he had stopped noticing the stench. After two days, his nose seemed to have adjusted. True to her word, Elnora had led them swiftly across a rocky plain to the start of the swamp. At first Cal had felt his spirits lift when a fresh breeze and the familiar smell of salt reminded him that they were drawing close to the coast.

But thoughts of home quickly turned his mind to memories he didn't want to think about. Unbidden, his father's face rose before his eyes, colorless in the moonlight, succeeded by an image that was anything but colorless, orange flames dancing fiercely against a black sky...

As was his custom, Cal had tried to chase away the horror by focusing on practical details. Instead of talking about the murder of their parents, he had recounted to Jonan the guard's words. Jonan hadn't commented on the military occupation of Nerita. Their situation had changed the lives of everyone they had ever known, and not for the better. But Cal could see in Jo's eyes the same suppressed panic he felt, an overwhelming sense of careening down a path not of their choosing, at a speed that was quickly growing out of control.

Mercifully, the reminder of all they had left behind was short-lived. Once into the marshland the breeze quickly disappeared, all similarities to their former home further along the coast disappearing with it. The air was thick and hazy, the ground underfoot mushy and uncertain, and the smell...well it was for the best that they'd become accustomed.

As they passed from the rocky plain into the beginnings of the swamp, Cal had briefly told Jo all that had happened in Pravat. Jo was relieved to learn that Aurelius had survived. As Cal had predicted, Jo interpreted the manuscript differently. Cal recounted it as best he could remember, and Jo didn't see any reason to think that King Cael was implying that dragons were a myth. Excited at the hints of magic in the mountains, he readily agreed that they should head for Montego.

For much of the journey there had been no conversation—it required all of Elnora's concentration to find their way. Even following her lead, the boys had to focus carefully on where they were placing their feet, leaving little attention for chatter. They all knew how dangerous such swamps could be. If Elnora failed to accurately find whatever invisible trail she seemed to be following, they could easily become lost or cornered in the bog. Such an event could only have one outcome. Elnora had not been lying when she said her plan was dangerous.

But now they were trudging through a welcome patch of slightly firmer ground. Their boots had long since become soaked through, but they squelched less with each step, and it was a pleasant change. The three of them were even able to walk abreast for a while, and Cal drew alongside Jonan to listen to his friend's conversation with Elnora.

"So you obviously know a way through this mess," Jo was saying. "Is that something you learned from this street gang too?"

Elnora nodded. "We used to smuggle things in and out of Alezae, sometimes to the coast, sometimes to the road, where others would take them to Pravat."

"Seems like a well organized operation for a bunch of kids," said Jo.

"I never said it was a bunch of kids. A number of us were very young, but the leaders of the group were adults. They recruited kids with nowhere else to go. Kids who wouldn't be missed, so they could get us to take all the biggest risks."

"Sounds horrible," Cal chipped in quietly.

She shrugged. "It was bad, but at least there was some level of protection. Better than being completely alone, knowing you'd probably fall afoul of the traders."

"What do you mean by traders?" asked Jo, just as Cal remembered Elnora's cryptic reference to traders in their conversation outside Kerr.

"Slave traders," said Elnora matter-of-factly. "From the South Lands."

"Slave traders?" Cal spoke more sharply than he intended. "I thought that hadn't been happening in generations."

Elnora stopped walking and turned to look at the two boys, who were watching her in consternation.

"You're serious? I thought Nerita was on the coast. You genuinely don't have a problem with raids there?"

They both shook their heads speechlessly.

"Wow." Elnora's eyes glazed over for a moment, apparently lost in the dream of life in a quiet coastal town without fear of seafaring abductors. "If I'd known other coastal towns didn't have the constant raids, I definitely would've headed along the shore to somewhere like Nerita instead of inland to Kerr."

"I wish you had," said Jonan brightly. "Maybe we could've joined forces earlier."

Elnora came out of her reverie to give him a skeptical look. "Somehow I doubt you would have befriended me."

Cal tuned out the good-natured argument that started.

Jonan seemed to take it lightly, but Calinnae was deeply troubled to discover that the South Lands traders were again becoming bold. The state of the kingdom was worse than he'd imagined. He hadn't realized how sheltered they were in Nerita —Jonan's parents had chosen well.

The country needed a strong king. One who would care about the needs of his people. One who would be wise as well as bold. Cal looked at Jonan, laughing with Elnora, and the sight did nothing to dispel the sense of frustration building within him.

Why didn't Jonan take the news of the raiders more seriously? If they survived this, would he really be able to take on the mantle of kingship? Jonan had never loved Kyona the way Cal did. Cal hadn't exactly been discontented in Nerita, but he had always thought that when he was older he would like to travel further inland and see more of the country. But not Jonan. A trip to the capital was what everyone did. It was too tame for Jonan. For as long as Cal could remember his friend had always wanted to board a ship, sail across the seas, and find new lands far from Kyona.

With an effort Cal turned his thoughts from this resentful track. It would lead nowhere good. Jonan cared about Kyona, and its people. He just had a different way of showing it. Cal would have to help him cultivate more of a love for the land, that was all.

Still, Cal couldn't quite bring himself to join in the banter. Before long they were forced to go single file again, and conversation ceased.

When they stopped for the night and Elnora told them that they would reach Alezae the next day, he responded only with a nod. There was no wood in this marshland to build a fire, but as they settled for the night Cal sat at a little distance from the others. He didn't intend to draw their attention, he just didn't feel close to sleep. He was surprised when Elnora came and sat next to him. Jonan seemed to hesitate for a moment, then came and joined them.

"Can I ask you something?" Elnora's soft voice broke the silence.

"Of course." Darkness was falling, but he could still see that her expression had grown serious.

"Did you say before that Princess Thalia's death wasn't really an accident? That they only thought it was?"

Cal looked at her in the semi-darkness but said nothing.

"So..." Elnora spoke hesitantly, seeming to pick up on his reluctance. "So what actually happened?"

Cal sighed, looking away. "I was hoping you wouldn't ask about that," he said.

"Why?"

"Because," Jonan chimed in, "it's not a very nice story. Even I remember this one."

Cal turned to find them both looking expectantly at him. He sighed again.

"All right," he said. "I guess I can't leave it there." He paused, his eyes unfocused as he stared at the swamp before him.

"A year passed after the accident before anything came to light. King Cael was troubled at the change in his wife, but things had otherwise more or less gone back to normal. Well, as much as they ever can after something like that. He had no way to know that their real problems were just beginning..."

King Cael stared at the remains of the parapet that had crushed his daughter almost twelve months before. He knew that he should have attended to its repair well before now, but somehow he hadn't been able to bring himself to address it.

"What am I looking at Randolph?" He tried to keep his annoyance out of his voice as he addressed his steward, but he was eager to be away from this cursed spot.

"It was one of the builders, Sire," said Randolph, his expression carefully neutral. "They commenced work yesterday, at your instruction. The man came to me this morning. He said that he had found something."

Randolph hesitated, and Cael felt a prickle of frustration. It wasn't like his steward to be less than forthright.

"What did he find, Randolph?"

"Well, Sire...he said that he is strongly of the opinion that the damage could not have happened accidentally."

"What?" For a moment Cael just stared stupidly, unable to process the significance of Randolph's words. "What do you mean?"

"He said, Sire," Randolph's voice was unusually gentle, and it was adding unreasonably to Cael's irritation, "that he believes someone sabotaged the stonework. That someone intentionally made it collapse."

There was a ringing in Cael's ears that made it hard to hear his steward's voice. "You're saying...you're saying that someone did this? Intentionally? You're saying that my daughter wasn't killed by accident, that someone meant to do it?"

But even as he said the words, he realized that it was not Thalia but Jonathon who had been under the parapet when it had fallen. Suddenly the anger building inside him was checked as a cold shot of fear lanced through it.

"I am not qualified to say, Your Majesty," Randolph answered cautiously. "I have no experience in such matters. But the builder who came to me is someone whose knowledge of such things I respect. And I trust him. In such a...delicate case, he would not approach me with his conjectures unless he was very sure."

"We must find the truth of this, and quickly," said Cael. "How could I have been so foolish as to leave this unattended to for a year? It will be so much harder now to pursue this information."

"Indeed, Sire," said Randolph, his voice regaining a slight measure of the dry tone that Cael was used to hearing. "If it is of assistance, the builder said that he believes that the person would have had to be present at the time of the collapse to have any confidence that it would fall at the intended time."

"When my children were underneath it, you mean," snapped Cael. His steward remained silent as Cael's thoughts raced.

"I will undertake this investigation myself, Randolph," he said quickly. "Arrange for me to meet with this builder, but do not mention the matter to anyone else. And arrange for me to meet with the nursemaid who was the first on the scene." Cael looked at his steward as the man gave a curt nod. "I am trusting in your discretion in this matter, Randolph."

"Of course, Sire," the older man said quickly.

As the steward hurried off, Cael found himself pacing back and forth across the ground where this horrific crime had apparently been committed. He could hardly marshal his thoughts, but two strains were dominant. One was a blazing determination to keep his son safe. The other was a numb dread as he wondered how he would tell Jacqueline of this news. He would find answers first.

By the end of the day he had met with both the builder and the nursemaid. The former confirmed everything Randolph had told him. Cael's instinct was that he was a trustworthy source.

The nursemaid had at first seemed less helpful. She was clearly very flustered at being called before the king himself, and she became very distressed when asked to recall the horrifying events that occurred a year earlier. As the nursemaid twisted her skirts in her hands, Cael remembered with disapproval the way the woman had been in hysterics when she ran with the news straight to Queen Jacqueline. And he remembered all too clearly the deathly white of his wife's face as she ran, without a word, to the castle grounds.

For a moment Cael was tempted to dismiss the woman from his presence. In her nervousness she was hardly more coherent than she had been on that terrible day, and it seemed unlikely she could have any useful information to offer. But he remembered the steward's words, echoed by the builder, that the perpetrator would have had to be close at hand at the time of the collapse. Taking a deep breath, he tried to summon some patience.

"When you approached the scene, did you see anyone else nearby?"

She gulped. "No, Sire, there was no one else nearby on the grounds. That's why I ran straight over."

"What about up on the ramparts?" the king persisted.

"On the ramparts, Sire?" she repeated. "I don't know...I don't think I looked up to see."

Cael sighed. If only he was conducting these inquiries a day after the incident, rather than a year.

"Although..." Cael looked keenly at the nursemaid as she spoke again. "I did see Peter coming down the stairs from the wall a little further on as I ran to get the queen. I'd forgotten, but now I think of it, I thought it was odd that he was going away from the children, not toward them. A few people had gathered by then, but I still would have expected him to go over to see if he could help."

"Peter?" Cael tried to keep the sharpness out of his voice. This woman seemed like a rabbit, at risk of being startled out of her suddenly sensible conversation.

"Yes, Sire. He doesn't live in Kynton anymore, but he worked for Lord and Lady Lindor for many years."

Ah yes. Cael had been wondering why the name sounded familiar. He wouldn't have been able to recall the man's name, but he could picture his face.

"Did he speak to you?"

"No, Your Majesty. At least, I don't think so. I might have said something to him, but I...I wouldn't recall..."

Cael grimaced internally as she trailed off. Yes, he could imagine the hysterical nature of any conversation she might have conducted in that moment.

"How did he seem? Can you recall anything about his demeanor?"

She thought for a moment. "Well, Sire...he seemed...shaken. I mean, I didn't know him well personally, but we'd both worked in the castle for many years, so I'd seen him around plenty. He was always very collected. I remember feeling shocked by the look on his face that day. He was horrified. But so were we all."

"Indeed," said Cael, but his mind was elsewhere. The information was hardly conclusive, but it was worth further investigation.

He did remember this Peter. He even remembered that he had left Kynton. Damian had mentioned it. Cael remembered because his friend had been very surprised, even a little upset, about Peter's sudden decision to return to his rural home. Apparently he was a trusted servant who had been with Damian's household for a long time.

Cael had not remembered the timing of Peter leaving, but now he thought about it...had it been soon after Thalia's death? The weeks following the tragic accident were a blur in his memory.

Accident? Maybe not. He gritted his teeth. It was sure to be an uncomfortable conversation, but he would get to the bottom of this, whatever it took.

When his friend walked into Cael's private receiving chamber an hour later, Cael wasn't so sure. Damian's relaxed posture and friendly greeting made it hard to know where to begin.

"Sire," Damian said pleasantly. "Randolph said you wished to speak with me." He took in the look on Cael's face, and his expression became concerned. "Is all well?"

"Actually..." Cael grimaced. It was unlike him to be at a loss for words, but "uncomfortable" had been optimistic. No part of his experience as prince or king had prepared him for an interview like this.

He took a deep breath and pulled himself together. "Thank you for coming, Damian. I need to talk to you about the day Thalia died."

Damian's expression softened. "Of course. The date is coming up, isn't it?"

Cael swallowed. "It is, but that's not why I called you here."

When Cael failed to elaborate, the nobleman prompted him gently, his face still showing concern and compassion. "What is it, Sire? How can I help?"

Cael steeled himself. "You can help by telling me about Peter."

"Peter?" Damian said blankly. "You mean my former servant?"

Cael nodded. "Yes. He was seen in the area at the time of the...incident."

Damian's expression was still blank. "I don't understand."

"You should know that I received a report this morning." Cael turned away from his friend to look out the window. "As I'm sure you'll understand, it has disturbed me greatly. The builders have begun work on repairing the parapet, and they are of the opinion that the damage was intentionally done."

"Intentionally...you mean..." There was a sharp intake of breath as understanding dawned. "Someone meant for it to be fatal? Surely not!" he protested when Cael nodded tersely. "Why would anyone plan such an attack on the princess?"

"You recall the details of the incident," said Cael, his voice tight. "There is reason to think that the target was not Thalia, but Jonathon. I can imagine there might be a number of people who might wish harm to come to my heir."

"Yes, I suppose you're right," said Damian slowly. His attention turned suddenly to the king's face, and when he spoke again, his voice conveyed his shock. "But this is terrible, Cay. I'm so sorry. And to discover this, after all this time."

"Indeed," Cael couldn't quite look his friend in the eye.

"But, Sire," Damian said, seeming to suddenly remember the previous question. "How is Peter mixed up in all this? You said he was seen in the area? Ca—Your Majesty, you don't think he was involved?"

Cael at last looked at his friend. Damian's face showed nothing but blank astonishment.

"I don't know what to think, Damian," said Cael, again looking out the window. "But I remember that you told me he left Kynton suddenly. When was that?"

Damian thought for a moment. "It was soon after the princess's death, you're right," he mused. "If he was nearby that day, and saw what happened...perhaps it was too much for him." For a moment he was lost in thought. "And yet I wouldn't have thought him likely to be easily overwhelmed."

"I remember you were surprised by his sudden departure," prompted Cael.

"Yes," Damian acknowledged, "I was. I had no idea that he was thinking of leaving us. He had a great deal of responsibility in our household, and his sudden departure was inconvenient as well as unexpected. It was most unusual that he left without taking his leave."

Cael looked up sharply. "He didn't even speak to you? He ran away, effectively?"

"No, no," corrected Damian hastily. "He didn't run away, Sire. It's true that I didn't speak to him personally, but he spoke with Organza. He told her that his father's health was failing, and he felt he should be back in his hometown. She relayed it to me at the first opportunity, of course, but she didn't feel right to prevent his leaving when he was so set on it."

There was a moment of awkward silence as Cael pondered Damian's words. There was certainly more to be explored here.

"Your Majesty," said Damien, when Cael didn't speak. To Cael's ear his voice held concern, but not fear. "I realize as I say it that the circumstances of his departure are unusual. I didn't know he was in the area when the accident happened, but if he was I understand that you may wish to inquire further of him about his sudden decision to leave Kynton.

"But I trust Peter. I would have said that Organza and I would trust him with our lives. And he had always doted on Derek. Never would I have hesitated to leave the boy in his care. I cannot believe that he could have been involved in anything like this."

He hesitated at Cael's impassive expression.

"I realize you will not wish to simply take my word for it—"

Cael sighed, the look of uncertainty on his best friend's face breaking through his reserve. "I trust your word, Damian, of course I do. It is hardly pleasant for me to pry into these matters further. But I must find the truth of this." His face hardened as he thought of his little girl. "And I will, Damian, whatever is necessary for me to do so. I'm sure you understand that."

"Of course I do, Sire," agreed Damian readily. "I would not wish you to do less. And I am ready to assist in whatever way I can. My household is at your disposal. Should you wish to interview any of my servants, I will ensure that they cooperate. And I will discover the precise details of Peter's hometown in case you wish to ask him further questions."

Cael gave his friend a pointed look. "Organza won't like her household being disrupted."

Damian shook his head, his expression serious. "She will understand. I will speak to her, and make it clear that this is necessary."

Cael just nodded. It was appealing to think of having his best friend and advisor at his side in this investigation, as would normally be the case. But the situation was delicate, and he needed to proceed with caution.

"That is all I wished to ask you today. We will speak more of this."

"Yes, Sire," said Damian. He hesitated for a moment, then reached out to clasp Cael's arm in a wordless gesture of support and condolence. Cael nodded an acknowledgment, but could not bring himself to speak, instead turning away as his friend left the room.

Jacqueline was expecting him. And he had a feeling that this next conversation would be no more comfortable than the last.

When Cael again found himself in his private receiving chamber early the next morning, he felt immeasurably weary. He had slept little. Jacqueline had received the new information without outward display of emotion, but the look in her eyes had haunted him throughout the small hours.

He had intended to go for a ride this morning, to clear his head, before embarking on any further investigation. But this time it was

Damian who had requested the meeting. Cael knew that for his friend to ask to see him at such an early hour, it must be important. So he waited, unsure whether to be hopeful or anxious.

He was not kept long in suspense. When Damian was shown into the room, Cael saw at once that something was drastically wrong. The contrast could not have been greater between the nobleman's relaxed demeanor the day before and his deathly pale countenance now.

"Damian, what is it?" He could not keep the anxiety out of his voice.

Damian swallowed twice before managing to speak. "Sire, I have come to...to confess."

"Confess what?" Had Damian bungled his inquiries in some way?

"I did it." Damian's voice was barely more than a whisper.

"What did you do?"

Damian swallowed again, and his voice became stronger. "I did it, Sire. I planned the attack and ordered Peter to carry it out."

For a long moment there was silence, Damian's words seeming to echo throughout the still room.

"I don't...understand," said Cael slowly. Damian's declaration seemed like gibberish. He could make no sense of the words, but the look of anguish on his friend's face terrified Cael.

"I am ready to face the consequences," said Damian, his voice clear but his expression still tormented.

"You...you did this? Impossible. Why would you say such a thing? You cannot have done this!"

Damian only bowed his head, remaining silent.

Cael felt like he was supposed to be angry, but there was only confusion and astonishment in his mind. He couldn't make sense of any of it.

"This is madness, Damian. Of course you're not behind it. Why would you wish to harm my family?"

"It was for Derek, Your Majesty." Damian's head was still

bowed. "I know you understand that a parent would do almost anything for love of a son. So—so many years you had no heir. So many daughters born, while my son grew older and stronger. I—I thought that if you never had a son, Derek might one day have a chance."

Cael stared at his friend in disbelief. "You expect me to believe that you covet my crown? I've known you all your life, Damian. I can't believe it—I don't."

"Not for myself, Your Majesty," said Damian quickly, looking up. "Never have I coveted it for myself. Only for—for my son."

Cael shook his head, still unable to throw off his stupor. "Yesterday you stood here and told me you had no knowledge of this. That you and your household would fully cooperate with the investigation. And this morning you come in here and tell me that you were personally behind it?"

"My conscience convicted me, Your Majesty. I thought I could carry on the lie, but I realized last night, after we spoke, that I could not."

"Your conscience?" Cael's voice was deadly calm, even as the missing anger began to rise. "You speak to me of conscience, as you stand there telling me that you're responsible for my daughter's death? You have been my closest friend since childhood! You tell me you know I understand a father's love for his child, even as you confess that you tried to murder my son to benefit your own?"

"Cay..." there was desperation in Damian's voice. "Cay, I'm sorry. I'm sorry."

"Silence!" Cael's voice was a roar. "I will countenance neither your insolence nor your apologies." He strode to the door and wrenched it open. "Guards!" The men on either side of the doorway sprang to attention. "Take this man to the dungeons. I cannot bear to look at him." True to his word, he turned his face from the sight of his friend being led away, deathly pale but unprotesting.

For a moment after they had left, Cael paced the room frantically, trying to outrun the myriad emotions threatening to overwhelm him. Shock, confusion, disbelief, anger, grief, betrayal.

He could not outpace them for long. King though he was, he covered his face in his hands and wept.

He had again wondered how he would tell his wife, but castle gossip made it unnecessary. She confronted him a few hours later, as he prepared himself in his chambers for the midday meal.

"What's happening, Cael?" her frantic voice almost overset the cold calm that had succeeded his breakdown. He didn't think he could handle her distress in addition to his own.

"They're saying that you've locked Damian in the dungeons. They're saying he's to be executed!"

When Cael didn't answer, she clutched the front of his tunic, forcing him to look at her.

"Is it true?"

"Yes." His voice was unrecognizable, even to his own ears.

"Cael! Tell me what's happening, right now!"

As briefly as possible, Cael relayed what Damian had said to him that morning. Jacqueline stepped back, releasing her grip as if his clothes had burned her.

"So you see, I had no choice," said Cael, his voice strained.

"Damian didn't do this," said Jacqueline quietly.

Cael turned away from her. "He says he did."

"Cael!" Jacqueline's voice was rising. "You know as well as I do that Damian is incapable of such a thing! You cannot have him executed!"

"He confessed Jacqueline! Speak to him yourself if you wish."

"Cael, you know he didn't do this!"

"He—"

"Don't keep telling me he confessed! If I can see why he confessed, so can you!"

"What can I—?"

"It was Organza!" Jacqueline's voice was passionate, a frenzied *look in her eyes. "You know it was! She did this! If someone ordered that servant to kill our child, it wasn't Damian! Organza would do anything if she thought it would elevate Derek."*

For a moment her words were met by silence. When Cael spoke again, his voice was once again quiet.

"I don't know what you would have me do, Jacqueline."

"Not this!"

"Damian confessed. He holds to his confession. How then can any other sentence be passed? Would you have me leave Thalia's killer unpunished?"

"No! But I would not have you hold the wrong person to account."

"Even if what you say is true—"

"You know it is!" Jacqueline interrupted.

"Even if I do, Damian has made his choice! If he chooses to take responsibility for his servant's actions, to confess and bear the consequences to protect the real culprit, then it is out of my hands."

Jacqueline only stared at him, clearly not knowing how to answer.

"He looked me in the eye, Jacqueline," Cael whispered. "My best friend. He looked me in the eye and told me our child was killed for the sake of his."

For a moment she just met his look, then she placed her hand gently on his cheek. "What can we do Cael? How can we bear this?"

"I don't know." He had nothing else to offer. "I don't know."

She leaned toward him, and he pulled her close. As they held one another wordlessly, Cael wished desperately that he had an answer to her question. Crown or not, he had never felt so powerless.

~

CAL GLANCED at Elnora in the silence that followed his tale. He looked away quickly at the expression on her face.

"So what happened?" she asked, her voice barely above a whisper. "Was Lord Lindor executed?"

"Yes," Cal confirmed heavily. "There was a brief investigation, but no trace could be found of Peter, the servant. And without him, there was no evidence whatsoever to contradict Lord Lindor's account, or to implicate Lady Lindor, however much people might whisper. Lord Lindor stuck to his confession, and the news quickly spread. The court was consulted of course, and they agreed that once the confession became public, there was really only one possible outcome.

"He was executed almost immediately. Lady Lindor took their son, who was about ten years old by then, and left straight away. She returned to the town where her father had his estate. Apparently she made quite a scene first. Perhaps she hadn't really believed the king would bring himself to have his best friend executed. In any event she forgot herself when it happened, making all kinds of threats and accusations."

"How could she dare?" breathed Elnora, indignation in her tone. "When she was the one who..."

Cal shrugged. "Some people think they have the right to do whatever they can get away with."

"Jonan was right," said Elnora, a small shudder running through her slight frame. "That's not a very nice story."

"No, it's not," agreed Cal. "Why do you remember that one so well, Jo?"

He looked over at his friend, but saw that Jo was spread out on the ground next to Elnora in the darkness. He had obviously fallen asleep while Cal talked. It didn't matter. Cal was pretty sure he knew the answer to his own question. That part of the story had always hit home for both of the boys. Something about the betrayal of such a friendship was hard to forget.

Cal returned his gaze to Elnora. Her face looked uncharacteristically strained, and he again wondered if they were asking too much of her.

"Are you feeling anxious?" he asked. "About going back to Alezae, I mean?"

She sighed. "A little. I never planned to go back there. There are bad memories waiting for me. And more than that. I left because I wasn't safe there."

"Well, you're not going back alone, at least," said Cal. She smiled, but it didn't reach her eyes. "Still, I wish we weren't dragging you somewhere you don't want to go."

"No one's dragging me," she responded quickly. "I want to be part of this quest. It's worth braving Alezae again."

"I'm glad you feel that way," said Cal quietly. For a moment he watched her in the dim moonlight. When he spoke again, his voice was soft. "Can I ask you something?" he said, echoing her earlier question.

"What is it?"

"How did your parents die?"

She looked down at her hands. "That's not a very nice story, either."

"I would imagine not," Cal tried to speak gently. "And you don't have to tell me anything of course. I just thought it might help you to talk through it before you find yourself back there." He paused. "But it's up to you. I don't mean to pry."

She was silent for so long that he thought she'd decided not to answer, and he regretted asking the question. But suddenly she drew a deep breath and began talking.

"I was a child at the time, ten years old. We never had a lot of money, but we had a small home, and my parents were good people. They were intelligent, too, especially my mother. She may not have been able to read, but she taught me many things. My father was a laborer at the docks when there was work, but it was never reliable. We were often hungry, but never desperate, like many others.

"It was a particularly rough time with raids. A number of

other children my age disappeared. My parents were terrified that my sister and I would fall afoul of the traders." She paused at Cal's involuntary utterance of surprise. "Yes," she acknowledged quietly. "I had a sister. Constance. She was three years older than me.

"We used to go down to the docks sometimes to see our father at work, but we weren't allowed to go near the water anymore. We lived not far from the docks, though, and raiders had been known to come further in than our home. They were getting bolder. At first they would sneak in during the night, rely on stealth. But they became more and more violent. They would sometimes come in large groups, often armed.

"One day Constance and I were out at the home of one of the other children from our neighborhood. It was my idea."

Elnora paused, her voice small.

"We weren't supposed to be out so late in the afternoon. But the girl said that her brother had taught her how to fight like the boys did. I wanted to learn. It was stupid. We didn't intend to stay long, but time ran away.

"By the time we headed home, it was almost sunset. We realized before we reached our street that some men were following us. There were three of them. We ran, but they caught up with us before we got to our house. Our mother had come home, and she was standing in the doorway, looking for us.

"She saw them grab us, and she shouted for help. None of our neighbors came, of course. People weren't willing to risk their own families for each other, not in that part of town. But my father was close, on his way home from the docks. He appeared around the corner, as if from nowhere. He looked so determined that for a moment I thought we were saved."

Her voice trailed off as she stared straight ahead, lost in her memory. After a moment she gave her head a little shake.

"But he never had a chance. We hadn't even realized that the men had knives—they didn't need to use them to overpower a couple of children. But my father was unarmed. He ran at them and landed a couple of good blows, but that just made them angrier. My mother ran over when he went down, but all it achieved was her death as well. Still, in the struggle the men let go of us, and we knew what to do then. We ran so far and so fast I thought my lungs would burst. We didn't stop until our bodies could go on no longer. We managed to get away.

"We waited hours before going back. The raiders were long gone, and our parents were there, side by side." Elnora stared down at her hands. For a moment Cal wondered why she looked so surprised. It wasn't until he followed her gaze that he even realized that he was clasping one of her hands in a strong grip. It had been an unconscious reaction to her story. She didn't say anything about it, and he didn't let go as she continued her tale.

"We managed to stay in our home for six months, eking out a living as best we could. My sister looked after me." Elnora smiled sadly. "She seemed so grown up and responsible to me at the time. Now I'm grown, I can hardly believe she was only thirteen.

"But as bad as things had seemed, they got worse. Some of the locals started working for the traders, giving them inside information on vulnerable targets."

Cal made an angry noise, but Elnora just shook her head. "I know it's awful, but most of them did it in an attempt to protect their own families. Things were bad. Alezae is known as a wealthy town, but that's only in the merchants' sector. There are many wealthy families there, and you can be sure they weren't ever targeted by the traders. But the authorities weren't interested in reports of children and teenagers being abducted in the dockside district. There's no doubt that the crown was turning a blind eye to the trade, at the very least. But the traders became so bold...there are rumors that the crown might even be behind the trade...that the king profits from it."

"What?!" hissed Cal, unable to help himself. He was already feeling a strange mixture of anger and helplessness as he listened to Elnora's story, and this suggestion produced a surge of rage stronger than he had ever felt. He sat back, letting go of Elnora's hand. "Do you think that's true?"

Elnora shrugged. "I don't know, but I wouldn't be surprised. Not with some of the things I've witnessed from the king's soldiers. I've seen with my own eyes times when soldiers could have prevented the traders taking someone, and didn't. Either way, we all knew better than to go to them for help. Everyone had to look out for themselves.

"And two young girls, living alone, near the docks? We quickly realized we weren't safe there. But once we started trying to live on the streets...well, that was no better. It was inevitable that the traders came across us. We were lucky to last as long as we did. The only reason I'm still in Kyona is that there was only one man the second time. He was built like an ox, and he grabbed us with one hand each. Constance bit his hand and told me to run for it. So I did.

"He couldn't chase me and restrain her. So he let me go." Elnora's voice was so quiet Cal found himself leaning forward to hear her. "I didn't even look back. I knew he would take her to the ships, but I just did what I had been taught to do and ran as far and as fast as I could. I never saw her again. I knew I couldn't survive on my own, so I joined a gang at my first opportunity. It wasn't exactly like having a home, but they did protect me from the traders."

She fell silent, her tale apparently finished, and for a long moment Cal didn't know what to say. The trauma of his own parents' violent deaths was still so near that he couldn't bear to look it in the face, but it suddenly seemed much less agonizing than what had happened to Elnora. He remembered that she had said, the night they met, that she hadn't really been a child since her parents died. And he remembered how he had felt, after finding his father's body, that his childhood was suddenly and irrevocably over. How much more horrifying for Elnora to have experienced that at the age of ten.

"I'm so sorry for everything you've been through," he said eventually, his voice quiet. "And more sorry than ever that we're headed back to Alezae."

Elnora sighed. "The truth is, I'm not sorry. Honestly I think I should be going back there. I think it was cowardly of me to leave."

"Of course it wasn't! What happened to your sister wasn't your fault. You did what you were supposed to do."

She looked at him incredulously. "Didn't you hear me, Cal? I didn't even try to help her. I ran away and left her."

"What else could you have done?"

"I could have tried," said Elnora simply. "At least if we'd both been taken we might have stayed together. I appreciate what you're trying to do, but what if it had been you in my position? What if Jonan was in trouble, and he told you to run? Would you do it?"

"That's different," said Cal quickly.

"Yeah? Why?"

"I'm not a child, for one thing! No one would blame you for running away. You did well to manage even that."

Elnora shook her head. "I've been running away all my life. I don't want to run anymore." A small shiver ran across her features, despite her determined tone. "I just hope we don't run into any traders while we're in Alezae."

"You're just like Jonan," mused Calinnae, almost to himself.

"How so?" Elnora sounded surprised.

Cal spoke with a hint of ruefulness. "He doesn't believe in running or hiding either. And he's brave, like you."

Elnora laughed, a touch of her normal lighthearted attitude returning. "Thanks for the compliment, but I'm also very unlike him."

"What do you mean?"

"Well, for one thing, I know my lineage, and I can promise you there's no royalty in it."

Cal returned her smile. "Well, yes, Jo is special in that way."

Elnora settled herself for sleep, a yawn interrupting her next words. "Honestly, I'm still amazed he's even willing to befriend an urchin like me. Imagine knowing you have the same blood as people like King Cael and Prince Jonathon."

"Yes," said Cal quietly, "imagine that."

Elnora had closed her eyes, but he continued watching her for a minute as she lay on the ground next to Jonan. How could anyone not want to be her friend? She was hard on herself, but she was incredible. After all she had been through, she had not only managed to survive, but had retained an attitude of cheerfulness, and a willingness to risk her own safety to help others.

As he settled for sleep himself, he felt sobered. He had so much still to learn.

CHAPTER SIXTEEN

The travelers looked down at Alezae from the rocky hill that had succeeded the swamp.

"It looks beautiful," said Jo, sounding surprised.

Cal understood what Jonan meant. After their time in both Kerr and Pravat, it was strange to see a city not surrounded by a wall. Alezae was larger than Cal had expected. The central district stood out even from this distance, its pale stone walls rising above the rest of the city. But the buildings that sprawled out around it in every direction continued further than he would have guessed. The outlying buildings at the western edge of the town began not far from where they stood.

Their elevated vantage point gave them a good look at the layout of Alezae as well as the size. The central area, which Elnora had called the merchants' sector, looked clean and prosperous even from afar. The further from the center the eye traveled, the grimier things became. The city looked like it had a big X drawn through it by two major thoroughfares running diagonally across the space. The roads created four triangular districts to the north, east, south, and west of the central merchants' sector. Cal knew from Elnora's descriptions that most of the dwellings were in these various districts. Even at this distance Cal thought that the southern one, where the trading dock was located, looked by far the most run down.

He glanced at Elnora and saw that her gaze was also directed toward the south, her expression hard to read.

"We don't have to do this, you know," he said softly. She looked at him in surprise.

"Of course we do," she said briskly. "We're almost out of supplies. Besides," she added, raising her eyes to his, "I want to. I told you, I'm sick of running."

He nodded.

Jonan had watched their interchange with a slightly puzzled look on his face, but he didn't ask any questions. "We'll follow your lead, Elnora," he said instead, gesturing toward the town.

"Wait, let me look at you first," she said.

They turned toward her, and she stepped back, subjecting them both to close scrutiny. Cal was suddenly acutely aware of how long it had been since he had bathed, and how filthy his traveling clothes had become.

Elnora seemed to be thinking the same thing as her eyes traveled over his person. "It's not ideal," she sighed. Cal felt his face grow hot, but a low chuckle from Jo told him that his friend was not feeling self-conscious. Jonan had endured Elnora's assessment with a grin, and his voice held its usual impudence when he spoke.

"I'm always telling him to smarten up and get in shape, but will he listen?"

Cal's hand shot out with the speed of old familiarity, but Jonan sidestepped the intended shove easily.

Elnora scowled at him. "You're no better, Jo," she said reprovingly. She looked back toward Alezae. "The thing is, we'd be smartest to avoid the dockside district altogether, but to cut straight through town, we'd have to go through the merchants' sector, and we won't exactly blend in. The two of you look like beggars."

Jonan looked at her pointedly. He opened his mouth, but at a nudge from Cal he seemed to think better of it, and closed it again.

Elnora just gave another sigh. "No need to be polite. I know I look just as bedraggled. Days of trudging through a swamp will do that."

"Aren't there a couple of spare tunics in the rucksack?" suggested Cal.

Jo shrugged. "Sure, but none of them are clean by now."

"They're surely cleaner than these." Now he really looked at Jo's and his own clothes, he realized that Elnora was right. The bog had not been kind to their wardrobes.

"Good idea," said Elnora briskly. "You should change."

Cal expected her to turn around or something, but she didn't. And when Jo pulled a tunic out of the bag and stripped off his current one without hesitation, Cal felt it would be churlish to request it.

Elnora's gaze was measuring as she assessed Jonan's new look and gave him a curt nod. But when she turned to see Cal fishing a tunic out of the bag, still bare-chested, he thought he saw a slight flush rise up her cheeks. It was the first time he had ever seen her blush, and he wasn't quite sure what to make of it.

Jo, of course, had no trouble knowing what to say.

"Being on the run agrees with you, Cal," he said cheekily. "You're fighting fit."

"Oh shut up," grunted Cal without malice. He had expected Elnora to laugh at Jo's banter, as she usually would. But she remained silent until Cal was finished putting his grubby tunic away, then spoke in a businesslike tone.

"Let me look at you both."

Jo jumped to attention with another grin, and Cal couldn't

help but chuckle a little himself at her stern expression. She ignored them both, narrowing her eyes.

"Definitely better." She stepped forward and smoothed Jonan's hair into some semblance of order. The sight created a strange reaction in Cal, one he refused to articulate. Elnora turned to Cal. She hesitated for a moment, then turned away, saying brusquely, "You should do the same, Cal."

Cal hastened to comply. He couldn't help but notice that Jo, who had seemed unaffected by Elnora's gesture, looked quickly between his two companions. His expression was suddenly more serious.

"Now my turn," said Elnora, glancing down at herself with a grimace. "I suppose I should try to look more like a girl."

Jo was chuckling again. "No offense, Elnora, but you always look like a girl."

She narrowed her eyes at him. "Why would I be offended by that?"

He shrugged, still grinning. "I don't know, but you didn't sound excited about it."

She sighed. "It's just the skirts I'm not excited about. Long-standing habit. So much harder to run quickly in the stupid things. But girls in the merchants' sector don't worry about that kind of thing, so if I want to blend in…"

She trailed off as she wrestled with her clothes. She wore a dress, but it was usually hitched up above her hips, so she could benefit from the increased mobility of the thick leggings she wore underneath.

After letting down her skirts, Elnora did the same to her hair. It had hitherto been tightly confined at the nape of her neck, and when she loosed it, Cal was surprised to see that the waves ran down well below her shoulders. It was lighter in color than he had realized, too, the sunshine glinting off the golden strands.

Elnora bent to briefly scrub her hands and face in a tiny stream that trickled past nearby, bubbling down the rock to feed into the marshland. Her task finished, she turned back to the others.

"Well? How do I look?"

Different, Cal thought, but he wasn't sure if it would be polite to say so. There was a moment of silence, then Cal realized that Jo was looking expectantly at him.

"Uh…" Cal fumbled for a moment. "Like a girl."

In his peripheral vision, he saw Jo roll his eyes. "Smooth, Cal," his friend muttered.

But Elnora seemed pleased with the response. "Good." She gave a small smile but didn't look Cal in the eye. "Now as soon as you two make use of the stream, we can be on our way."

The two boys quickly washed faces and hands, and the three of them refilled their water skins. Then they made their way carefully down the rocks—Elnora grumbling about her skirts all the way—and set off toward the center of town.

It was delightfully easy, Cal reflected, entering a town without a wall surrounding it. The fact that they were now in a part of the country where, as far as they knew, no one knew they were fugitives, didn't hurt either.

Alezae was much bigger than Pravat, and the three strangers did not attract any particular notice as they wandered through the west district of the city. The district was mainly made up of houses, but there were official buildings too. As they got closer to the central sector, the dwellings were more frequently interspersed with shops. Cal tried not to gawk. He had never seen a true store before, only merchants' stalls.

The plan was to make the most of Elnora's familiarity with Alezae to buy some food and other provisions. They still had the scanty collection of coins Jonan had grabbed from Calinnae's house as it burned. They hadn't needed to use them yet. As Cal pointed out, Elnora had provided them with free accommodation in Kerr. Not to mention the "free" food she'd gotten in Pravat.

At the look Cal gave Elnora when he made this comment, Jonan insisted on hearing the story. He was very impressed by Elnora's sleight of hand. He all but dared her to give a demonstration as they entered the bustling merchants' sector, with goods for sale wherever they turned. But she shook her head firmly.

"No way, Jo. It takes more than quick hands to pull that off here. I should know. And aren't we supposed to be trying not to attract attention? I have no intention of stealing anything, especially now I know you actually have coins." She glared fleetingly at Cal. "Something Cal failed to mention in Pravat."

Cal made a spluttering protest. "It's not like you asked my opinion before you started swiping stuff!"

"Oh, get off your high horse, Cal," grinned Jo. "It's not like you were hesitant to raid the soldiers' saddlebags."

Cal could think of no response and simply scowled at his friend.

Elnora took the lead in the purchase of food and supplies, being much more familiar with their surroundings. Her shrewd bartering showed her companions a new side of her—Cal was certain that he and Jonan would have paid much more for the same goods without her help.

Cal couldn't help but be distracted by the varied sights and sounds of the market district. It was unlike anything he'd ever seen—so much more impressive than the square in Pravat. He wondered how its current state compared with the days when Alezae had been at its height. Back when Prince Jonathon had been appointed as Border and Trade Protector, Alezae had been a frequent base of his. Back then the slave trade had been quelled, brought down by King Cael before Jonathon's time. The city was so wealthy and so beautiful that travelers coming from other lands often never made it to the capital, content to make Alezae their new home.

Cal felt a strange pang go through him at the thought of the city's former glory, back when it was a gateway between Kyona and everywhere else. It filled him with pride to think of Kyona as it had once been, prosperous and peaceful, attracting immigrants and visitors and wealthy traders. But the pride was inevitably accompanied by sadness as he thought of how far things had fallen. No one from other lands seemed inclined to seek a new home in Kyona in recent times.

But Alezae evidently still attracted enough trade to make it a bustling city, and there were still signs of wealth, especially in this part. Mindful of Elnora's words, Cal was aware that he was seeing only Alezae's best side, and that the prosperous facade was not the reality of life for many of the city's residents. Still, he couldn't help but be impressed.

Apparently Jonathon had loved it, too. Seeing the appreciation in Jo's gaze as he took in the constant bustle and activity of the place, Cal wondered if something of this proclivity had been passed down through the generations. Was that why Elam and Lynette had chosen Nerita for a place to live? Was there some vestige of love left in Elam's blood for life by the ocean?

As he saw other young people wandering past, laughing and enjoying food freshly bought from the vendors, Cal imagined what it might be like if they weren't on this mission. He had always wanted to see more of Kyona, and here he was, exploring one of the kingdom's largest and most interesting cities. He would have loved to wander through the markets with Jo and Elnora just for fun, without jumping at every shout, or wondering how they would find somewhere safe to sleep that night.

But they had a job to do, and they didn't have time to get distracted.

Once Elnora declared them restocked, Jo suggested they look for lodgings. Elnora smiled a little bit indulgently as she shook her head, and Cal and Jo exchanged knowing looks. Someone was enjoying being the one with the answers.

"Believe me," Elnora assured them, "we can't afford any accommodation in this area." Her expression grew more serious as she glanced around. "I know we're all sick of sleeping rough, but in all honesty, I don't think it's wise for us to stay the night in Alezae. Or at least," she looked down at her feet. "It's not wise for me to stay the night."

"Too many bad memories?" asked Cal sympathetically.

To his surprise, Elnora gave a rueful chuckle. "The memories I can deal with. My concerns are more flesh and blood." Cal frowned, but she pushed on, clearly not intending to elaborate. "I think we'd do best to continue on through the east district and look for a place to camp outside town."

"As you like," said Jonan. "Lead on, and we'll follow."

They had spent a couple of hours in the merchants' sector, but there was still plenty of daylight left when they entered the east district. They were blending in so well that Cal had begun to relax, and conversation was flowing freely as they walked down the smooth streets. He was therefore taken completely by surprise when someone hailed them from the other side of the way.

"Ellie?" The voice sounded incredulous. Elnora's head snapped up, her posture tensing immediately as her eyes quickly found the source of the call.

"Sketch?" She squinted uncertainly at the young man approaching them. He gave her a broad grin, but she didn't return it, still looking ill at ease. "Wow," she said instead. "You got big."

His grin widened. "Yep. My growth spurt came a little late. You look the same as always though." He regarded her for a moment, his gaze taking her in from top to bottom. "Maybe a bit older, actually."

Cal shifted slightly, and the man's eyes flicked to him briefly before returning to Elnora.

"What are you doing here? I never thought you'd come back."

"I didn't plan to," said Elnora concisely. Cal couldn't help but notice how uncomfortable she seemed, one of her arms wrapped around her slender body.

"Yeah, that's what I thought. You were quick that day, the way you slipped away from me." The improbably named "Sketch" shook his head, his smile sliding away. "The boss wasn't happy when you left. He wasn't happy at all."

"I know, and I'm sorry. I know he would have blamed you."

"He did." Sketch's countenance was grim now, and Cal was amazed at how menacing the previously jovial youth suddenly seemed. Cal took a step closer to Elnora, and Sketch's eyes again flicked to him.

"Well, like I said, I'm sorry," said Elnora, a spark of defiance in her voice. "I didn't mean to get you in trouble, and I couldn't help what he might do afterward."

Sketch regarded her steadily for a moment, then in a sudden motion he waved a hand dismissively, his cheerfulness apparently restored. "Don't worry about it, it was, what? Two years ago? Bygones, Ellie, bygones. How have you been?"

Elnora smiled faintly. "Never mind that. How are you?"

"Never better," he said with a broad smile, gesturing to his tall frame. "I'm the picture of health, as you see."

Elnora gave a small chuckle. "You never did take anything seriously."

"You haven't told me what you're doing here, little one. Can I help in some way?"

Cal didn't at all like the young man's familiar tone, especially as it was clear that Elnora wasn't sure how to respond to it. He could feel Jonan's tension beside him as well, but for the moment both of them held their peace, waiting to see how events would unfold.

"We're just passing through," Elnora was saying, "not looking to stick around Alezae."

Sketch nodded. "I figured. But you look like you're wandering. What do you need?"

Elnora hesitated, clearly unsure whether to tell any part of their plans to the young man. Cal's instinct was strongly in the negative, but he had to trust Elnora's judgment over his own in this unfamiliar situation. Plus, there was no way to communicate privately with this Sketch determined to stick so close.

"Let me help you out, Ellie," said Sketch winningly. "For old times' sake."

"There's nothing much to help with, honestly," said Elnora. "We were just wanting some lodgings for the night." Cal kept his face carefully blank at the falsehood. "Somewhere cheap."

His face brightened. "Of course! I can help. I work the east district a lot these days. I know all the spots. Let me show you."

"Well..." Elnora glanced meaningfully at her companions. "Thanks, I guess."

"No problem," Sketch said cheerfully. "Happy to help. Come with me."

They started walking after him, but Cal held Elnora back slightly with a touch on her shoulder. She looked at him questioningly.

"You don't trust him, do you?" he asked as quietly as he could.

She looked troubled. "Honestly? I'm not sure. He can be

unpredictable, but..." her eyes glazed over, "there are also good memories there. He helped me out of a tight spot more than once." She shrugged. "I didn't know what else to do. If I'd refused his help outright, maybe things would have gotten ugly right then and there. It's probably best to let him show us this place. If something feels off, we can slip away as soon as we get the chance."

Cal just nodded. He felt very uneasy, but he could think of nothing to say. He looked at Jonan, and his friend's expression told him that he also had no faith whatsoever in this Sketch person.

They walked on for about ten minutes, heading east. Cal and Jo were silent, but Sketch kept up a steady stream of cheerful conversation, which Elnora responded to more reservedly.

"How much further, Sketch?" she asked eventually.

He smiled. "Actually, we're here," he said. As he spoke, they rounded a corner and found themselves in the middle of a group of five young men and women.

"Hey Sketch!" One of them hailed their guide immediately. "Finally! How did you go with the target?"

"Ah, I lost him," said Sketch dismissively. "But look who I found instead!"

The man stared uncomprehendingly at the three newcomers. They had instinctively drawn into a huddle, realizing immediately that their suspicions had been well founded.

"Who's that?"

"Oh yeah, you weren't here then, you wouldn't remember," said Sketch. "This is Elnora."

"Elnora?" said the only girl in the group. She stared at Elnora. "I remember you. Left in a hurry, didn't you?"

Elnora turned to Sketch. "Look, we don't want any trouble. I know I put you in a tight spot when I left, but I truly didn't mean you any harm."

The other girl scoffed. "A tight spot? You know how the boss is when someone tries to leave. We were on half rations for a month."

Sketch waved an airy hand. "I'm not holding a grudge, Ellie. I told you, bygones. Forgive and forget."

Elnora's voice was quiet. "We both know the boss doesn't forgive or forget."

"Well, then, you know he won't have forgotten you, little one. I'm not sure what he'll say about you coming back! It will take everyone by surprise I think."

"Come on Sketch," said Elnora, a pleading note in her voice. "Can't we just be on our way? We're only passing through."

"Now, Ellie, you know I can't do that." Sketch's words were apologetic, but his tone remained cheerful. "This has to be reported."

"Look," said Jonan suddenly. "I don't know what your problem is, but we have better things to do than chat with you lot all day. I don't know what right you think you have to stop us going about our business."

Instead of responding, Sketch measured Jonan with his gaze for a silent moment, then addressed himself to Elnora again.

"Who are your friends, kid?"

Elnora jumped in quickly. "They're just some friends who've been traveling with me." She gestured at Cal. "This is Isaac. The other one is Tom."

Cal kept his face carefully impassive.

Sketch nodded slowly as he took in every detail of their appearance. "They'd better come too, I suppose." He jerked his head in the direction they'd come from. "Let's not waste any more time."

"Finally," grumbled one of the men who hadn't spoken yet. "I'm starving." The group started moving off in the direction indicated, only Sketch staying behind to shepherd the three of them. Elnora started to follow him, but Cal grabbed her arm.

"What are you doing?" he hissed.

She shrugged. "You heard him, he's not going to just let this go."

"Elnora, you're not on your own this time. You don't need to go with him."

"Yeah," Jo chimed in. He glanced at Sketch, who was standing some distance away, apparently confident enough of the outcome that he was happy to patiently wait out their discussion. "The three of us could take him on, easy."

Elnora shook her head frantically. "That would be a mistake, trust me. These guys know the city better than anyone. I'm sorry you're being dragged into this. It's the last thing I wanted. But now that they know I'm here, we wouldn't make it far if we tried to just leave. I'm sorry," she said again. "If we'd made a break for it back there, maybe we could have gotten away with it. I shouldn't have given him a chance, I suppose." She frowned, her eyes glazing slightly as she stared unseeingly over Cal's shoulder. "But it might still turn out all right. The gang can be precarious, but they have their own code of honor. They can be reasoned with."

"I don't like this," said Cal, still gripping her arm. "Who is this boss he's talking about?"

He felt a slight tremor go through Elnora's frame. "He's the one running the gang," she said. "His name is Bryant."

"So why is he unhappy with you?"

Elnora looked at the ground. "Remember how I told you I don't do goodbyes well?"

"Yes," Cal said.

"Well, I didn't do goodbye well when I left Alezae. I didn't do goodbye at all." Cal must have still looked confused, because she pushed on impatiently. "I ran away, Cal. I planned it carefully and ran away. The thing is that once you join the gang, you're not supposed to leave. Ever."

Cal and Jo exchanged a look. "I thought you joined the gang to *avoid* being sold into slavery," said Cal dryly.

Elnora acknowledged the point with a grimace.

"So what do we do now?" Jonan asked.

She shrugged. "I guess we find out what Bryant wants, then figure it out from there."

"You seem very calm about it," Cal observed.

She met his look evenly. "I don't know what other choice we have. I managed to get by all right for the years I was in the gang, didn't I? I'm older and smarter now. I'll figure something out. I'm just sorry you're getting mixed up in this. Especially you, Jo. Truly."

"Especially me?" Jonan sounded like he was getting irritated, so Cal cut in.

"Don't be ridiculous, you've followed us into our scrapes, the least we can do is stick together now."

"Ready to go?"

Cal felt his hands ball into fists involuntarily at Sketch's deceptively pleasant tone. But Elnora just nodded and followed Sketch down a side street. Exchanging a look, the boys followed close behind.

It quickly became clear to Cal that Sketch was now leading them toward the infamous southern district, near the docks. And it was equally clear that for all her brave words, the further south they went, the more unsettled Elnora became.

Their guide led them through the entrance into some kind of compound. Glancing around, Cal realized that either Elnora had downplayed the nature of the gang, or things had escalated since her departure. She had said that the group was not that intimidating, but this was clearly a full scale operation. Young men and women milled around the open area, including the ones who had been waiting for Sketch earlier. And the ones standing guard at the entrance and outside various of the buildings were armed.

He gave Elnora a sideways glance, and saw that surprise was mingling with the growing uneasiness in her expression. So things had changed.

Sketch disappeared into one of the buildings without breaking stride. With one last apologetic glance at Cal and Jo, Elnora followed him. Hurrying to keep up, Cal emerged into a larger room than he had anticipated. There were a number of people inside, but he had no difficulty identifying Bryant. The man radiated authority and control. He was leaning against the far wall, in conversation with another man, when they entered.

"Boss!" called Sketch. "Look who I found wandering around the east district."

The man turned, the movement unhurried. As he faced them, Cal could see in the shaft of late afternoon sun slanting through a nearby window that he was probably in his forties. Certainly older than everyone else Cal had seen inside the compound.

He took in the three newcomers. His gaze hardened as it fell on Elnora, but when he spoke, his voice sounded light and pleasant.

"Elnora. This is a surprise. I thought we'd lost your good company forever."

"Bryant," Elnora acknowledged tersely.

"You were most unkind to leave without saying goodbye, you know," said Bryant. "I don't know what I had done to deserve such treatment. After I took you in, gave you food, protection, a place to live, good honest work—"

Jo let out a snort, apparently unable to help himself. Bryant turned his eyes toward Elnora's companions calmly, taking careful stock of both Cal and Jo before speaking again.

"Can it be that you wish to make amends? Have you brought me a peace offering, replacements in effect?"

Jo started forward, but Cal put out a restraining hand. He was angry, too, but this was not a good time for Jo's hot head to get the better of him. Bryant took in the identical blazing looks in Cal's and Jo's eyes and sighed.

"Apparently not. That's a shame. You both look young and strong. But I have no interest in initiating members whose loyalty I cannot trust." He turned away, apparently losing interest in them. "Which brings us back to Elnora."

He walked slowly up to her, and Cal had to admire the way she stood still and calm.

"You've grown since you left, Elnora," he said. "In more ways than one. I'm pleased to see how your confidence has increased." He reached out a hand and touched her hair. "And your hair has grown longer."

Cal saw red as Bryant contemplated the strand between his fingers. Most of him ached to take a swing at this man, but Jo's presence held him back as strongly as an anchor of iron. If this situation deteriorated into a bloodbath, what would become of his friend, and the Bloodline he represented?

"You've changed too," said Elnora quietly. "When did your little gang become a military operation?" When Bryant merely smiled, she tried again. "What do you want from me, Bryant? If you have no interest in members who don't want to be here, what use am I to you?"

Bryant stepped back, a look of surprise on his face. "Oh, I don't want you to join us again, Elnora. I think that ship has sailed," his eyes lingered on her face, "so to speak."

"Then let us be on our way," said Elnora reasonably. "You can have no reason to keep us here."

"Ah, but you owe me, my dear, don't you? There's the little

problem of the debt you ran away from. Food, lodging...protection."

"I don't have any gold to speak of, Bryant," said Elnora tersely. "None of us do."

He took them in at a glance. "I would imagine not. We must find another way to settle our accounts, mustn't we?"

"Well, my friends have nothing to do with this. Why don't they go back to their business, and you and I can figure something out?"

"An excellent notion," agreed Bryant. He turned to Cal and Jo. "She's quite right. I have no reason to take up any more of your valuable time. Elnora can stay here, and you can feel free to go."

"No," said Cal flatly, dimly aware that Jo had spoken simultaneously. "I don't think so."

"Isaac," said Elnora warningly. For a moment Cal just stared at her blankly, then he remembered that she had given them false names.

"We're not going anywhere, Elnora, so don't even try." Cal's voice was uncompromising.

"By all means, you're welcome to join her," said Bryant, a touch of humor in his voice. "Three is certainly more effective than one, but one will do the job, you know."

"I told you, Bryant," said Elnora. "We're just passing through. We're not interested in a job."

"Not that kind of job, my dear. It just so happens that your arrival is most conveniently timed. You have a debt to me, and I happen to have a debt of my own you can help me pay."

"What do you mean?" Elnora sounded uneasy.

Bryant nodded toward the man he had been speaking to when they entered. "This gentleman over here has come as an envoy. He represents my business partners. They have a ship sailing tonight, you see, and like I said, I owe them a debt. You will do very nicely."

"A ship?" Elnora's face was as white as a sheet. "You mean… traders?" When Bryant just smiled blandly at her, she shook her head. "No, I don't believe you. You're trying to punish me. You don't deal with the traders. You never have. You make a point of it, with your so-called code of honor—that's the only reason I joined your group in the first place!"

"Things change, Elnora," said Bryant. "Times are harder than they were. We do what we must to survive."

"I'll die first," said Elnora, her voice choked with passion.

"Let's hope for better, my dear," said Bryant mildly. "I hear that two thirds survive the journey. You never know, maybe your sister even did. Perhaps you can be reunited with her," his eyes glinted with a very nasty light, "one way or the other."

Cal heard a low growl go through the room at Bryant's words, and it took him a moment to realize it had come from his own throat. Jo glanced over at him, but Elnora's eyes were fastened on Bryant, as if hypnotized. If possible, her face was even paler than it had been, and if Cal didn't know how tough she was, he would have thought she was about to faint.

Bryant's gaze lingered on Calinnae for a moment. Then he nodded to the man he had indicated. "What do you think? Will it answer?"

The man nodded. "Aye, it'll answer."

"Then go ahead," said Bryant, and the man started toward Elnora, three others peeling away from the wall behind him to assist.

Cal and Jo both raced forward, placing themselves in front of Elnora. But even as he raised his fists, Cal could see it was hopeless. They were impossibly outnumbered, and surrounded on every side.

"Enough," said Bryant, apparently losing patience. "Remove

them." Cal drew his arm back, ready to swing at the first person to come within his reach, but he was suddenly grabbed from behind. He struggled furiously, but strong arms held him fast. He could see that Jonan was in the same situation, multiple men holding him back.

The trader and his men again approached Elnora.

"Stay away from her!" Cal shouted. He kicked and fought with all his might, all thoughts of his own, or even Jonan's, safety forgotten. He managed to break free for a moment, but he was quickly overwhelmed again.

Elnora also fought, but there were far too many aggressors for it to have any effect. Once the trader's men had her under control, Bryant waved them all out with a lazy hand, clearly done with the distraction.

They were dragged outside of the building with infuriating ease. At first Cal didn't understand what the men intended—he thought he and Jo were also being taken to wherever Elnora was destined for. But once they were clear of the compound, the reality became evident. The two boys were merely restrained by Bryant's men, while the traders forced a still-struggling Elnora into a cart.

Jo and Cal shouted and fought, but they were powerless against the two dozen gang members who had come to watch the spectacle.

"Elnora!" Cal shouted pointlessly. "Elnora!"

She met his eyes, and he saw the moment she decided to stop fighting. *Go,* she mouthed at him. He struggled harder, but she shook her head. Her eyes traveled across to Jonan, then back to Cal meaningfully. *Go.* He knew she wasn't making a sound, but it was almost as if he could hear her quiet voice in his head.

She was accepting the outcome in an attempt to protect them, and the secret they guarded. She was giving up.

CHAPTER SEVENTEEN

Cal was pretty sure the men had intended just to leave him and Jo outside the compound. But when it became clear that they were ready to run after the cart, the gang members changed their minds, instead dragging the boys a few blocks away. They roughed them up a little, as if it was more a matter of routine than personal malice, stripped them of their one pack, and shoved them into the muddy footpath.

"You're lucky the boss was in a good mood," one of them spat as he turned to leave. Cal started up from the ground, desperate to take his fury out on someone, but Jo grabbed his arm.

"Forget them, Cal, they're not important!"

For a moment Cal could hardly see his friend's face through the red haze obscuring his vision. But Jo maintained his grip on Cal's arm, staring his friend down until Cal's thoughts came back into focus.

"Come on Cal, breathe. We need to be smart."

"What, now you want to be cautious?" Cal knew there was no good to be gained from shouting at Jo, but he couldn't keep it in. "Now you want to wait and hide? Next you'll tell me you think we should run away and leave Elnora to the traders!"

Jonan shook Cal's shoulders, his own voice rising. "How dare you even say that!? As if I would ever consider such a thing!"

"You don't understand, Jo!" shouted Cal. "Don't you remember what she said last night? This is her worst fear! Her worst nightmare!"

Confusion flashed across Jo's face, and Cal suddenly remembered that his friend had slept through the entire conversation the night before. Cal took a deep breath and tried to pull himself together.

"Did you see her face? She decided to give up fighting so we wouldn't get drawn into it." Cal gritted his teeth. "She might have given up, but I never will! We have to get to her before that ship sails."

"Of course we do," said Jo matter-of-factly. "That's what I was trying to say. We have to be smart and figure out how to find the ship. We can't afford to waste time picking a pointless fight with Bryant's men."

Jo was right. As his heart rate slowed, Cal's blind fury began to subside as well. He took in the blood on Jo's face, and the bruises already beginning to form. Suddenly he remembered the real reason for Elnora's sudden capitulation, and his own forbearance back at the compound.

"Not you," he said quickly.

"What do you mean?"

"You shouldn't be risking your life with the traders. We'll make a plan, and I'll go in there, but you need to stay out of sight, like at Pravat."

"Don't start this again, Cal." Jo sounded angry.

"I mean it, Jo," Cal said warningly. "Your life is more important than just you. What good will it do Kyona to have a true king who's dead, or sold into slavery in the South Lands?"

"That's enough!" said Jo. He was definitely angry, his voice ringing with unexpected authority. "I've had enough of this! You and Elnora both. Bloodline or not, my choices are still my own. I don't want to be king, but if I have to be, I should at least try to be one worth following!" He paused, breathing hard, and the two friends stared each other down for a silent moment.

"I know you mean well, Cal," Jo said eventually, his voice calmer. "But you have to stop trying to protect me and let me be who I am. Besides, I care about Elnora too."

Cal turned away. Jo's last words sent a shard of ice through his heart, but he couldn't think about that right now. It was clear that he wasn't going to convince Jo to sit this one out. There was nothing to be gained by wasting more time.

"At least tell me they didn't take the signet ring when they took the pack," he grunted.

Jo touched his hand quickly to his chest, feeling the place where the ring sat on its chain, hidden under his tunic.

"No, I still have it."

"Then let's go," Cal said tersely.

"Did you see where they went?" Jo asked.

Cal shook his head. "No, but I'm guessing it won't be too hard to find the docks." He glanced at the sky, taking in the lowering light. "If the ship is sailing tonight, we can't waste a minute. We can figure out the next step once we get there."

Without another word, the two boys took off at a quick jog. They gave the compound a wide berth, heading south. The further they went, the rougher their environs became. Cal felt the hairs on the back of his neck prickle. The dwellings were small and dirty, and packed together more closely than he had ever seen. The smell was nothing to admire, either. Not as bad as the marsh, thankfully.

He felt extremely uneasy, and the sight of Jo jogging beside him, apparently unconcerned, did nothing to reassure him.

Jonan's gauge for danger had always been faulty. Everywhere Cal looked, he saw eyes watching their passage, observing curiously from the street, or peering surreptitiously from dwellings. In none of them could he detect a hint of friendliness. It distressed him to think of Elnora growing up here.

But not as much as it distressed him to think of her being packed onto a slave ship bound for the South Lands. He gritted his teeth and picked up the pace, pushing himself harder.

They reached the water so abruptly that both boys had to pull themselves up short to avoid running straight into it. The gloom was deepening, and when they suddenly shot out from between grubby dwellings, they almost missed the ankle high stone ridge that ran along the edge of the walkway. Peering down, they saw the water lapping against the rock, black in the gathering darkness.

Cal looked quickly to the left and right. They needed to find the quay before night truly fell. Somehow he didn't think asking for directions from anyone in this neighborhood would end well.

"There," said Jonan quickly, pointing to their left. Following his gesture, Cal could just make out a large dark mass further down the walkway. They took off toward it, moving more cautiously now.

By the time they reached the wharf, the daylight was gone. Cal wasn't sure if this would make their task easier or harder. The dockyard was huge, making the port at Nerita seem like a child's miniature in comparison. Cal felt overwhelmed as he peered at the numerous ships lying at anchor in the harbor. It was clearly not a busy time of day, but there were a number of dock workers still going about their business.

"What do you think?" he whispered to Jonan. "How will we know which is the right ship?"

Jo narrowed his eyes, also scanning the area. "I don't know.

Do you think they'll be trying to remain hidden, or is the trade so accepted here now that they don't have to?"

"Elnora would know, but I have no idea."

They were both silent for a second, then Jo continued.

"I'm guessing most ships don't set sail at night," he mused. "We should look for one where the activity is ramping up, not settling down."

"What does that look like though?" said Cal impatiently. "You spent much more time at the quay at home than I did."

"This is hardly Nerita," said Jo dryly. "We never had ships this big."

"A good thing too," said Cal in a hard voice. "Or we might have grown up in fear of the traders like Elnora did."

Jo gave Cal a puzzled look. "What was all that talk about her sister?"

"She had an older sister who was taken by the traders," said Cal concisely. "That's why she joined the gang, so she wouldn't be alone. Their parents had already been killed trying to stop them being taken."

There was a moment of heavy silence, and when Jo spoke there was anger in his voice. "We can't let them take her."

Cal didn't answer. While they spoke, they had been cautiously making their way through the dockyard, trying not to attract notice. They found a vantage point, tucked away behind some large crates, and tried to take in as much information as possible about the ships around them. They watched in silence for some time, but there was no obvious preparation for immediate departure. Cal began to feel panicked. Was it possible that they were too late, and the ship had sailed before they arrived? If not, it would surely be leaving soon.

And even if they could identify the right ship, how would they rescue Elnora? How would they avoid ending up as slaves themselves?

Without warning, the same fear he had felt in Pravat rushed up within Cal. He was suddenly reminded with blazing force of the reality of the danger they were in, and he knew a strong impulse to slink away, to look for safety. Shame gripped him, but it didn't erase the fear.

And even while he felt afraid for himself, he felt frustrated with Jo. Cal might see his own hesitation for the cowardice it was, but had Jo decided to remain safe, it would have been a different matter. Jonan had a responsibility to more than himself, and he shouldn't be taking unnecessary risks.

It was ironic, he thought bitterly. The very bravery that made Jo better suited to be king would likely be just what would prevent him surviving long enough to ever take the throne.

With the shame, Cal felt a rush of anger. Anger at himself, anger at everyone else. How had they ended up in this situation?

He ground his teeth in frustration. If only Elnora had known better than to give Sketch even the smallest amount of trust. It had been obvious to both Cal and Jo that he wasn't sincere. Cal had thought they should trust Elnora's judgment, but her history here had colored her thinking, making her easier to take advantage of, not harder. They couldn't be too careful who they trusted, Jo especially. It wouldn't be the first time misplaced trust had led to devastating results for a member of the royal family.

For a moment Cal forgot that they were supposed to be carefully observing the scene in front of them. He closed his eyes against the onslaught of memories from the legends. For the first time, he wished he didn't remember them so well. The depressing story of Lord Lindor's confession and execution, followed by the harrowing account of Elnora's childhood, had left him weary.

Perhaps it was because of being in Alezae, or because of his bitter reflections on Elnora's misplaced trust. Either way, he couldn't seem to stop his thoughts sliding back through time to a past that seemed to have become hopelessly intertwined with the tangled mess his present was becoming.

King Cael strode forward eagerly as the arriving party began to dismount in the castle grounds. His eyes skimmed over the servants and knights, looking for the one figure that held any interest for him. When he saw who he was seeking, he broke into a broad grin.

"Jon! Welcome home, my boy."

Jonathon looked up at his father's greeting, and it did Cael's heart good to see the genuine gladness in his son's eyes as Jonathon responded with a smile of his own.

"Father! It's good to see you."

The two men met, clasping arms in a brief greeting, before Cael stepped back, gripping his son's shoulder.

"Let me look at you." He regarded his son with satisfaction. Jon was the picture of youth and strength. His new role became him; he had shouldered the responsibility well. But the absences were longer than his parents would have liked. He had been gone three months this time.

But Cael well remembered what it was like to be young and full of energy, and how little he would have appreciated his own parents trying to curtail his adventures because they missed him.

"You look well," he said instead.

"I am well," Jon laughed. Cael grinned responsively. He had missed that laughter.

"How's Mother?" asked Jonathon.

Cael's expression flickered for only a moment before he answered. "She is well—and she will be overjoyed to see you."

Jon's curt nod told Cael that his son understood. "There's something I would like to tell you before I go to her," said Jon. "I brought someone back with me. A friend who I met in Alezae. Or not met...rediscovered."

"Who?" asked Cael. "Any friend of yours is welcome here, Jon, you know that."

Jon hesitated for a moment. "I'm glad to hear you say that, Father," he said, glancing back at the bustle behind him. "Because he is very unsure of his welcome."

"Why?" asked Cael, following the direction of his son's eyes. When he got a good look at the figure standing off to one side, just out of earshot, his eyes widened. "Damian," he whispered involuntarily.

His gaze slid back to his son's face, which now showed concern and uncertainty. Cael blinked, trying to clear his head and return to reality. He knew it wasn't Damian. He had himself been the one to confirm the success of the execution. The image of his former best friend's lifeless body was as fresh in his mind as if it had been yesterday, instead of years ago.

"Can that be...is that Derek?" he asked Jonathon, his voice a whisper.

Jon nodded slowly. "It is."

"How he has grown," said Cael, mostly to himself. "Of course he would be a man now. And he looks so like his father."

"Perhaps I should not have invited him," said Jon quickly. "I do not wish to cause you pain, Father. But he has been a friend to me these months. And I could not but feel for his situation. He is Lord Lindor now, but he has not been able to fully claim his birthright for fear of returning to Kynton. After all, he was exiled through no actions of his own."

Cael shook his head, trying to clear the fog of years that seemed to have descended on his mind. "If he has been a friend to you, of course you were right to invite him to accompany you home. He was not exiled. His mother chose to leave and not return."

"If you are certain," said Jonathon hesitantly. "He and I were only children when he left, of course, but I didn't think he'd been told not to

return. We used to be such friends when we were small...remember how I used to follow him around? It drove him crazy at the time."

Cael did his best to respond encouragingly to his son's smile. He did indeed remember how as a child Jonathon had hero-worshiped Derek, four years his senior. The memory filled him with a strange mixture of fondness and terrible pain as he recalled his own friendship with Damian.

"Of course I am certain," he responded with an effort.

"Thank you Father," said Jon, a shadow lifting from his eyes. "I knew you would be generous."

Cael's smile was more genuine as he again clasped his son's shoulder. "Come," he said. "Your mother will want to see you straight away."

However great Jacqueline's delight in being reunited with her son, it was clear to Cael before the evening's meal was over that she was less enthusiastic about their guest. Of course she showed him no incivility—she had gracefully and capably filled the office of queen for many years now, after all—but Cael knew her too well to miss the underlying distress.

When they were alone in his chambers he expected her to have a great deal to say about it. But she said little, receiving his account of Jonathon's invitation almost without comment.

"What do you really think about this?" she asked when he had finished speaking.

He shrugged. "I'm not sure what to think. But I couldn't refuse Jon, not when the impulse was so honorable."

"And where does Organza fit into this picture?" asked Jacqueline, her voice uncharacteristically hard.

"There has been no mention of Organza returning," Cael assured her quickly. "That I could not countenance so readily. But Jon is right—Derek should not be punished for someone else's actions."

Jacqueline regarded her husband for a long moment. "Perhaps the son would not be so readily forgiven his mother's crimes if he did not so strikingly bear his father's face," she said quietly.

Cael shrugged, uncomfortable. "What do you want me to say, Jacqueline?"

"Do you regret it?" she asked softly.

He shrugged again, turning slightly away from her. "I hardly know." His voice was barely a whisper. "I regret everything about that situation. But I'm still not sure I see how I could have changed the outcome."

His wife said nothing, merely coming up behind him to place her hand on his arm and lay her head on his back. He turned and encircled her in his strong arms. It felt good to know that she saw him as strong and safe, that she still looked to him for comfort and protection.

"I'm worried about Jon," she said at last.

"Jon will be all right," said Cael bracingly. "He's strong, and he's smart."

And as the weeks passed, Jonathon's energy and cheerfulness seemed to confirm Cael's faith. He was so glad to have his son back at the castle, full of humor and activity, that he almost became accustomed to Derek's presence, almost ceased to see Damian every time he looked at him. Almost.

It helped that Derek was not much like his father in personality. He was polite and respectful, but reserved. Cael often saw the two young men laughing together, seeming relaxed, but in the presence of the king or the queen, Derek had little to say.

However, while Cael became less concerned, his wife became more so.

"I don't like this friendship between Jon and Derek," she said to him one afternoon, two months after Jonathon's return.

Cael looked up, surprised at how troubled her tone had become. "Why? I admit it still feels strange at times to see Derek, but it is not as though he has caused any trouble."

She shook her head slowly. "It's difficult to explain, but I don't *think it will end well. There's something in Derek's manner, something I cannot trust. He is so reserved around us."*

"Can you blame him, given the circumstances?"

"It's more than that," said Jacqueline. "Jon still sees his childhood hero, but Derek has changed. He is not the warm and engaging child who left Kynton. There is something cold about him, something calculating."

"I have not seen it. Are you sure your perception of him isn't simply prejudice because of his mother, love?" Cael spoke gently, but the look Jacqueline gave him was both sharp and shrewd.

"Are you sure your perception of him isn't simply blindness because of his father?" she returned. When he didn't answer, she continued. "I think you should speak to Jon, encourage him to keep a bit more distance."

"How can I do that in good conscience?" asked Cael quickly. "Would you have me punish him for the crimes of his parents?"

"It is good to extend your generosity to him in recognizing his claim," said Jacqueline. "But inviting him into the inner circle of our trust as Jon has done...I do not think it is wise."

Cael shook his head. "Speak to him if you will, but I will not willingly replace my son's generosity of heart with suspicion." He turned to leave, but his wife's quiet voice checked him at the door.

"Do not let any regret you might feel about taking drastic action in the past prevent you from acting as decisively as you should in the present circumstances."

He did not respond, walking from the room with a falsely purposeful step. As always, his wife's insight was too sharp for his comfort. Nevertheless—although he was unsure whether it was for the sake of his son or his dead friend—he could not bring himself to do as she asked.

~

"THERE!"

Cal opened his eyes, startled by the sharp voice of his friend. He was alarmed to see that the dockyard had become noticeably emptier, most of the workers presumably having gone to whatever dubious welcome awaited them in their humble homes. How long had he been distracted? Any delay could be disastrous.

He followed the direction of Jo's gaze and saw a small knot of men moving toward the end of the dockyard.

"What about them?" he asked in a whisper.

"Their bags, look."

Cal looked more closely and realized that Jo was right. The men were carrying full sized packs over their shoulders. They didn't look like they were going home for the night. More like they were about to set out on a voyage.

The two boys exchanged significant looks, then slipped out of their sheltered hiding place and followed the men at a discreet distance. They walked the entire length of the wharf, then continued on past the breakwater that extended out on its far edge. Looking ahead, Cal realized that there was a ship docked right on the other side of the breakwater. It was outside the true port, but the waters were not too rough, still partially sheltered by the wharf.

In contrast with the other docked ships, the deck of this one was a bustle of activity. This was it, it had to be.

"We found it," said Jonan. "Now what do we do?"

In the distraction, Cal had almost forgotten his former frustration, but the danger of the situation came rushing back to him. He looked at Jo's determined face and gave his head a small shake. He could not change Elnora's previous decision to trust the wrong person. But he could choose to take action now, even when his fear was telling him to run in the other direction.

He remembered Elnora's face in the moonlight as she

described her fear of the traders—the monster in the night that haunted her childhood. That image drove away the last of his lingering hesitation.

The men ahead of them would soon be within hailing distance of the ship. Cal glanced around him and saw a length of abandoned iron. Ignoring Jo's startled half-cry, he seized it and started toward the men, propelled by anger and determination.

"We put up a fight," he said grimly.

CHAPTER EIGHTEEN

"What is it, Jo?" Cal asked for the third time. "I know the jacket doesn't fit properly, but we just have to make do."

"No, the jacket is fine," said Jo mildly.

Cal glanced at his friend. He thought that if no one was looking too closely, the heavy pack, jacket, and cap that Jo had donned made him look passably like one of the traders, ready to set sail. He hoped his own borrowed raiment was as convincing.

"So why are you looking at me like that?" Cal spoke in a whisper as he tied a makeshift gag around the mouth of the last unconscious trader, worried that their voices would carry to the ship docked a short distance away. Considering what they did for a living, he was tempted to roll the men's inert bodies into the dark water and be done with it. But he'd never killed before, and he couldn't bring himself to do it.

"It's just...that was impressive. And a little bit frightening."

Cal raised an incredulous eyebrow at his friend. "You're scared of me now?"

Jo rolled his eyes. "No, *I'm* not scared of you. But do you realize that you just set into three grown men with a metal bar and single-handedly beat them senseless before any could even raise an alarm?"

Cal shrugged, a bit uncomfortably. "What should I have done?"

"I don't know…that, I guess. It's just…when did you become so fierce?"

"Well, if we're going to save Elnora from slavery, we need to be fierce, don't you think?"

"Oh, I approve wholeheartedly," Jonan hurried to clarify. "I just didn't expect it from you."

Cal shrugged again, saying nothing as he and Jo dragged the final unconscious man behind a large packing crate, where he joined his fellows. Aloud he might make light of Jo's surprise, but in truth he himself was unsettled by the powerful rush of anger that had surged through him the moment he decided to act instead of to run.

But there was no time to think about that now. Both boys turned toward the ship. Surely it would not be long before it set sail, and then they would have missed their window.

"Do we just brazen it out?" Cal asked, trying not to sound nervous. He wished he could recapture the rush of passion he had felt. But attempting to infiltrate a trading gang by casually strolling in wearing stolen clothes was not something that could be done in a fit of rage.

"Nothing else I can think of," said Jo. "How can we plan further when we have no idea what we'll find inside?" Jo didn't sound at all nervous, and Cal had to suppress a sigh. Catapulting himself into dangerous situations without a plan was Jo's specialty, after all.

"Let's go then," he acquiesced.

Hoisting the heavy packs over their shoulders, they walked with false confidence toward the ship. There was still plenty of activity on the deck, which Cal hoped would make their entrance less conspicuous. They both ducked their heads instinctively as they walked up the gangplank, caps pulled down as low as possible over their eyes.

"Finally!" said a rough voice as they stepped onto the deck. Cal had never heard someone from the South Lands before, and the accent sounded heavy and unfamiliar. He turned partially toward the speaker without raising his head. "Only the two of you?" the man continued. "Isn't there a third?"

Cal hesitated, but Jo grunted beside him. "Coming," he said concisely, his voice unnaturally deep.

The man who had addressed them made an irritated noise. "He'd better hurry. The captain is eager to be off. If your friend thinks he's indispensable, he'll realize his mistake when we leave without him. I have no idea why the captain took on so many of you Kyonan deckhands this time. We can manage just fine without you, so remember that. If you don't pull your weight, you'll go below too."

Cal breathed a silent sigh of relief. It was an incredible stroke of luck that the men they were impersonating were apparently not from the South Lands, and not necessarily familiar to the other sailors.

"Well, get your stuff below, and get to work!" prompted the man when neither Jo nor Cal spoke or moved in response to his lecture.

They hastened to comply, trying to look as though they knew where they were going as they moved across the deck. It was a bit easier to see on the ship, with flames illuminating the space from many lamps attached to the vessel in various places. Cal glanced around him, trying to take in as much information about the ship as he could.

There were over a dozen sailors on the main deck, and no doubt many more below. How they would extricate themselves after finding and freeing Elnora he had no idea. He looked up at the part of the deck that sat on a higher level, with stairs leading up from the deck on which they stood. He could see a large wooden wheel with a man standing behind it, looking confident and important.

"Is that the captain?" he muttered to Jonan.

His friend had spent a lot of time throughout their childhood sneaking onto the smaller vessels that frequented Nerita, attempting to stow away to adventurous lands beyond. Calinnae used to wonder why Jo's parents weren't more concerned every time Jo was caught at it, until his mother explained with a smile that any ships coming to little Nerita were small vessels bound for other Kyonan ports, nowhere near big or hardy enough to brave an ocean crossing. Jo had been crushed when Cal relayed this information to him.

Following Cal's gaze, Jonan shook his head. "No, that would be the helmsman. The captain will probably be in his quarters until the ship is actually ready to leave."

"How do we get below?" Cal asked, his voice still a murmur.

Jo nodded in front of them. "There's the staircase up ahead. The sailors will have their berths below. And that's where the cargo will be too."

"Cargo?" retorted Cal. "You mean people."

Jo shrugged. "In this case, yes. But there may be other cargo, too."

They reached the rough wooden stairs and descended them without being accosted. The space below was just as much a hive of activity as the deck had been. They found themselves buffeted by sailors going to and fro, obviously preparing themselves for a long voyage. Following the stream, it was easy to find the several berths full of bunks and swinging hammocks where the hands must sleep.

A quick glance into those chambers was enough to show that they didn't lead to any cargo hold, however. Cal and Jo hurried on further into the bowels of the ship, hoping that their failure to settle their belongings in the deckhands' quarters didn't attract attention.

Immediately after the berths, they passed a few small cargo holds, but they were clearly filled with supplies rather than people, so the boys pushed on.

As they traveled further down the narrow walkway on the ship's lower level, the number of other hands bustling about decreased. As the hubbub of preparation faded, a new sound began to be heard, one that sent an involuntary shudder down Cal's back.

Low moans and metallic clanking, punctuated with louder sobs or wails, told them they were heading in the right direction. Cal imagined one of those cries coming from Elnora, and his feet unconsciously sped up.

He was therefore in front of Jo when he came out into the open space at the end of the walkway. They were clearly at the back of the ship now—he could see the curved wooden wall that formed the inside of the stern. For a moment his feet faltered, as a wave of horror overtook him at the sight in front of him.

The space was filled with two large cells, metal bars forming unyielding squares. Large though the cells seemed, each one had far more people than the space could comfortably hold. All of them were young, no one much above his own age, and many considerably younger. Their feet were shackled, long chains linking them together as they huddled against the walls, or in small clumps. Some were openly weeping, but others were clearly made of sterner stuff, glaring defiantly out through the bars, their spirits not broken. Yet.

Cal's eyes darted over the cells, searching frantically for Elnora. He expected to recognize her in one of the tougher captives who stood erect despite their chains, their posture challenging the two newcomers. But with rising anxiety he failed to spot her anywhere.

"Hey, you two! What are you doing here?" The accented voice caused Cal to jerk his head around. In his horror at his first sight of a slave vessel, he had failed to even notice the trader standing guard between the cells.

"We're two of the new deckhands," said Jo, covering Cal's lapse. "Just arrived."

"Kyonan?" grunted the man, squinting at them in the dim light.

Jo nodded, and Cal turned in surprise as several of the captives spat angrily on the ground.

"Come to see it for yourselves, huh?" said the trader with grim mockery. "Well, you wouldn't be the first. Take a good look, and don't forget it. If you get on the wrong side of the captain or that first mate of his, you'll be in there with them faster than you can say 'goodbye Kyona'. And as you see, they don't take too kindly to fellow Kyonans who've turned on their own to work with us."

The prisoners bore out his words, many of them giving the two boys looks that spelled death. Cal couldn't blame them. His own ire began to rise at the very thought of any Kyonan taking part in this heinous trade.

"But how will they throw us in there if they've run out of leg shackles?" said Jo, his voice trembling with what Cal knew to be suppressed fury, but the trader appeared to take as fear. The man grinned.

"Oh places will free up fast enough. No way all of them make it through the crossing. You can pick which ones aren't strong enough." He nodded to the back of one of the cells, where a number of younger captives were huddled against the wall, hugging their knees, many of them crying.

Cal longed to wipe the filthy smirk off the man's face, but

he forced himself to breathe deeply, keeping his anger in check. He needed to take better stock of the situation before doing anything rash. He heard the soft chink of metal, and glanced down to see the ring of keys hanging from the trader's belt.

"How long until we sail?" he asked, trying to sound natural.

"Any minute now, I would think," the man answered. "We're behind schedule already from what I know." He nodded back the way they'd come. "You two had better stow your belongings and get back on deck, or the first mate will have your hides before we're even on open water."

Cal nodded and turned as if to leave. He exchanged a look with Jo as he did so, and not for the first time on their adventure, was glad of the lifelong friendship they shared. There was no need for words to confirm that they were of the same mind.

The moment the trader turned away from them, they sprang into action. Cal's hand was over the man's mouth before he could move, stifling his startled cry. Simultaneously, Jo jumped at the man from behind, wrapping his arms around the deckhand's neck. The man flailed frantically, but fueled by their rage, the two boys both held on grimly, Jo squeezing the man's neck with all his might while Cal covered both mouth and nose. The man's scrabbling hands went from his neck to his face and back again many times before he stilled.

Some of the captives cried out in shock when the boys rushed the foreigner, but they were quickly shushed by their more savvy companions.

When Cal and Jo finally lowered the trader's still form to the ground, they were both panting hard. Calinnae saw at a glance that the man was still breathing, although his face was deathly pale. Cal glanced up to see every eye on him and Jonan. All sounds of crying had stopped, and a new light was springing into many faces.

He quickly knelt down and fumbled with the man's belt, trying to get the ring of keys free.

"Did you see Elnora?" he asked Jonan quickly, and his friend shook his head, still breathing hard.

"I couldn't spot her."

"Me neither," said Cal, his voice troubled. "How are we going to get past the rest of the deckhands? There are only two of us."

"Sorry to interrupt," said a rough voice, "but there are a lot more than two. Unless you intend to free whichever friend you've come for and leave the rest of us in here."

Cal looked up and met the speaker's eye. He was a boy close to their own age, and his eyes were aflame with rage and defiance.

Cal hastened to fit first one key and then another into the enormous padlock on the door of the boy's cell. "Of course we're not going to do that," he said quickly. "It's just that there must be three dozen men on this ship, and some of them are armed."

"There are sixty of us," said the boy. "And believe me when I tell you, swords won't stop us." Looking at the young man's blazing expression, Cal didn't doubt it.

"Aye!" agreed another captive. "Better to die fighting our way free here than as slaves in the South Lands." His words were greeted by many murmurs of assent, but Cal couldn't help but notice that there were also plenty of terrified expressions among the group. He didn't think everyone was quite as confident as the ones who had spoken up.

But none of that mattered. They had little time, and there was nothing to be done but free them all and let events unfold from there. He had no illusions that these youths were going to follow any directions he or Jo might give them. Cal hardly cared what they did, as long as he could find Elnora. The fact that she hadn't stepped forward and identified herself alarmed him greatly. Surely she was here—surely there wasn't more than one slave ship sailing from Alezae tonight.

The lock finally opened with a satisfying click. The first speaker strained toward the open door, but was pulled back by the shackle on his leg. Cal turned to Jo.

"They're individually shackled," he said quietly. "It will take forever to free everyone."

"We don't have forever," said Jo grimly. "Give me the keys, I'll open the other cell."

"Undo our shackles first!" came a sharp voice from the already opened cell.

Cal looked with uncertainty at the group before him. The situation was clearly volatile. Most of these kids had surely grown up on the streets, and the group could easily become an angry mob if he and Jo didn't manage this rescue to their satisfaction. Cal again searched fruitlessly through the crowd with his eyes. Where was Elnora? And if only there was more than one ring of keys, he lamented to himself.

As if reading his mind, the boy who had first spoken up said authoritatively, "Undo my feet, and I'll help."

Cal hesitated for a moment, but the unflinching gaze of the speaker held an earnestness he instinctively trusted. He fumbled with the keys again. Once he found the right one to unlock the rod containing the heavy chain that ran through all the shackles, it was easier to find the right one for the next step. The locks for the shackles were small, the key correspondingly tiny. There were two tiny keys, suggesting that one would do all the shackles in the other cell.

As soon as he was free, the young man grabbed the keys from Cal's hand. He hung the ring over a protruding metal rod that formed part of the latch on the cell door. The edge of the rod looked sharp to Cal's eyes. Without a word, the former captive raised his heavy shackle, now open, high above his head and brought it crashing down on the ring once, twice, three times. With a crack, the thin metal ring splintered, and the keys fell loose.

Jo didn't waste any time. He grabbed a handful of keys and raced to the other cell, undoing the padlock much more quickly than Cal had done. Cal didn't pause to watch after that, instead moving quickly with one of the small keys to undo the shackles on the rest of the prisoners in his own cell.

The first couple to be freed began to race for the door, but the capable one who had broken the keys free ordered them to wait in a voice of fury.

"We all go, or none of us go!" he roared. "We need our numbers to rush the traders, or none of us will make it out of here."

He clearly had the respect of his fellows, because to Cal's relief no one questioned him. Cal had freed two thirds of the prisoners in his cell when he was brought up by Jo's sharp voice.

"Cal! Get over here!"

He hesitated for a moment, looking at the ten or so youths who were still shackled. Then one of those he had already freed stepped forward and held out a hand wordlessly. Cal handed over the key and pushed his way through the mass of people to get out of the cell and into the one across from it.

"Back here," Jo called. Cal hurried toward his voice, noting as he did so that someone else had also taken over from Jonan. When he reached his friend, he felt a surge of relief followed instantly by the acrid taste of fear in his mouth.

"Elnora!" he cried, dropping to his knees next to Jo.

Elnora didn't respond. It was her sure enough, but something was very wrong. She had already been freed from her shackle, although Cal could see the red marks on her ankle where it had been. She didn't respond to Cal's voice. He had thought her gaze was locked on Jonan, but once he was down at her level, he saw that she was staring blankly ahead, her eyes fixed on the middle distance, no recognition or emotion in her expression.

"Elnora!" he tried again. "Come on, we have to get out of here!" He was dimly aware that the process of freeing everyone was almost complete, and he knew that if they didn't join the first rush of exodus, their chances of getting out would decrease dramatically.

"Elnora," Jonan was saying. "It's all right, you're free now. We have to go!"

Still she didn't respond, just continued to huddle against the wall, her arms wrapped around her knees and her face expressionless. Jo looked at Cal helplessly.

"Go," said Cal quietly. "Check where the rest are up to."

Jo hesitated for a moment, then obeyed, leaving Cal and Elnora alone, or as alone as it was possible to be in the depths of a crowded cell.

"Elnora," he said softly, taking her hands and trying in vain to catch her eye. "It's Calinnae. We've come to get you."

She still didn't respond, but something flickered in the back of her eyes in response to his quiet voice. Seeing it, he continued more confidently.

"You need to come with me now. If we don't go soon we'll lose our opportunity."

She started to draw her hands back, but he held fast.

"Elnora, I swear to you that while my heart is beating, I will not let the traders take you across the sea. But I can't get you out of here without your help. Right now I need you to wake up." He raised his voice slightly. "Wake up, Elnora!"

He saw the moment something shifted, as she shook her head slightly and blinked, as if trying to shake off sleep. Her eyes found his, and there was wonder in their depths.

"Cal?"

"Yes, it's me," he said, squeezing her hands encouragingly.

"You came for me."

He nodded. "Of course we came for you. Now we need to get out of here."

She swallowed and nodded, allowing him to pull her to her feet. She looked around her with wide eyes. Still gripping her hand, Cal pulled her to the front of the cell and out into the walkway. Jo was standing next to the ringleader from the other cell.

"Are we ready?" Cal asked them. "Everyone free?"

They nodded, and the local boy turned to the group.

"Ready to show them what we're made of?"

There was an answering roar, but he continued in a loud voice. "I don't care whether you want to make them pay, or just want to run for your home, we rush the deck together."

Everyone nodded, and the boy shouted, "Go!"

Cal had expected him to be at the front of the rush, but as everyone else started running down the walkway with a shout, the boy turned back to the unconscious trader, the rage still simmering in his eyes. He reached down and put his hands on either side of the man's head. With a movement that was alarmingly quick and practiced, he wrenched the head to one side. The resulting crack as the man's neck broke gave Cal a sick feeling in his stomach that he had never felt before.

As he watched in shock, the boy looked up and met his gaze. His eyes held nothing but confident defiance. Cal swallowed hard but said nothing. He was more shaken than he cared to admit, but what right did he have to cast judgment on this almost-slave?

Instead he joined the group running for the exit. He still held Elnora's hand, but he had lost Jonan in the melee, and that realization sent a shot of fear through him. The escapees shouted as they ran, a wild and dangerous sound. They raced for the stairs, the startled exclamations of the few deckhands still below being swallowed up as the stampede overwhelmed them. There was a brief bottleneck at the stairs, then Cal and Elnora burst out on the deck above.

The scene was one of utter chaos as sixty youth, many bearing unlocked shackles as weapons, clashed with the sailors. Some broke free and ran immediately for the gangplank, taking off into the night, but many seemed ready to stay and do battle with their would-be captors. Cal searched the crowd frantically for Jonan. He knew Jo wouldn't have taken off down the gangplank without them. Sure enough, he soon spotted his friend banging furiously on a door set below the upper deck. Cal's heart plummeted as he realized what Jonan was doing.

Stifling an oath, he did the only thing he could, and rushed to his friend's aid.

"Come out, you coward!"

A momentary lull fell over the scene as the captain appeared in the doorway of his cabin. The man was tall and commanding, and Cal saw the dangerous gleam in his eyes as they took in the action on the deck, then came to rest on Jonan.

"What is this mutiny?" he demanded, his clear voice somehow carrying across the uproar.

"No mutiny," spat Jonan, balling his fists. "We are no crew of yours. Just justice. Time for you to answer for your crimes."

The man looked amused as he glanced down into Jonan's furious face, his eyes gliding over the youth's lean frame.

"And who are you to pass judgment on me and my crimes?"

For an infinitesimal moment, time seemed to pause as Cal watched the scene before him. Jo stood bravely before this cold-blooded monster, a light glowing in his eyes. In a flash Cal saw past all Jo's boyish impetuosity and restlessness, and glimpsed the king he could be.

But he also saw the danger Jo was in. They were all in

danger. With the appearance of the captain more of the freed captives had fled, and he couldn't be sure that the traders wouldn't be able to subdue and recapture those that remained. And that wasn't even counting the danger Jo posed to himself.

Cal stepped forward, intervening before Jo's hot head could betray him into another unwise declaration.

"We're Kyonans, that's who we are," he growled at the captain. "And we're not going to stand by while you enslave our countrymen."

"You're a few foolish children with rash courage and a double dose of luck," snarled the captain. He waved a hand at the various figures disappearing into the night. "You've cost me my cargo for now, I'll grant. But don't think you've won a victory. All you've done is let them loose tonight so we can catch them tomorrow."

With a stab of anger, Cal realized the man was right. They may have made a difference in the lives of the prisoners who were even now back on home soil. But suddenly it wasn't enough. Not when they could do nothing about the plague this trade had become.

"Is that so?" Jonan's voice was as determined as ever. He turned to his friend. "Cal, hold him."

Before Cal could ask what Jo meant, his impulsive companion had disappeared back down the stairs. At the same moment, Elnora pulled away from Cal. Distracted, he tried to both see where she had gone and keep an eye on the captain.

In a movement so quick he didn't see it coming, the older man darted forward and grabbed Cal by the throat. Grasping at the firm grip with his hands, Cal tried to kick out with enough force to deter his attacker. He couldn't feel his foot connect with anything at all, but suddenly the hold on his neck was released.

Cal stumbled back, gasping, trying to regain his balance ready for another attack. Looking up, he saw that the captain had instead raised his hands and stood motionless, a sword tip pressed against his own throat, pricking the skin so that a single drop of blood glistened at its end. Gripping the hilt with firm and confident hands was Elnora. Cal realized that she must have read the man's intentions much more quickly than he had, and managed to retrieve a weapon from one of the downed sailors. Judging by the sheath lying at her feet, the trader in question hadn't even had a chance to use it before he was knocked to the ground.

Before Cal could even thank his rescuer, Jonan appeared back at his side. He saw with confusion that his friend grasped two large clay pots in his hands. Jo glared the captain down.

"Maybe more traders will come, but you won't be rounding anyone up tomorrow," he said grimly. Then he turned and threw the pots with deliberate force, smashing one right below his feet and hurling one further down the deck. A thick liquid poured out and flowed freely across the gently pitching surface.

Suddenly Cal understood. "Come on!" he shouted to Elnora, "we need to get off this ship!" He turned to the various scuffles still taking place elsewhere on the deck. "Get off the ship!" he shouted to their allies. "Now!"

The ringleader from the cells, laying into a deckhand nearby, looked around quickly and took in the situation at a glance. "Off the ship!" he roared. The other locals took his order much more seriously than they had taken Cal's, and they began to run for the gangplank even as Jonan seized one of the lamps mounted on a nearby beam and threw it at his feet.

"No!" the captain shouted, as the flames leaped onto the deck, licking up the oil with devastating eagerness. Cal saw that Elnora was still standing in place, holding the captain at bay.

"Come on!" he shouted to her again.

She still didn't budge, as the captain turned to them with

hatred in his eyes. "You think this changes anything?" he spat. "Your friend is right—more will come. You can't stop it."

For a moment Cal forgot their perilous situation. He could no longer feel the heat from the glowing blaze, eclipsed as it was by the red hot rage that once again filled him.

"Change is coming," he said to the captain, his voice ringing out strong and clear. "Sooner than you think. And when the true king sits on the throne, your day will be over."

He had expected the captain to scoff, but the man seemed to hesitate before the look in Cal's eye. Cal didn't wait for further conversation. He grabbed Elnora's arm and pulled her toward the gangplank. Jonan was running ahead of them, grabbing and dropping more lamps as he went. By the time they reached the gangplank, the ship was well and truly ablaze, traders and captives alike scrambling to disembark. Some of the sailors even jumped off the other side of the ship into the water to escape the flames.

The three companions made no effort to stick together with any of the other escaped prisoners as they took off into the night. After a short distance, a lingering smell of burning made Cal turn around. He gave a cry and careened to a stop.

"Elnora! Your dress!"

She glanced down and quickly began to stamp at the hem of her garment, extinguishing the glowing edges that were threatening to turn into a flame.

"I told you skirts were impractical," she muttered, and Cal felt like laughing with relief at hearing her normal humorous self surface for a moment. But then he looked up, and the laughter died on his lips.

The other two followed his gaze, and the three of them stared in silence at the sight before them. Men were continuing to scatter, crowding the gangplank or jumping off the edge of the burning deck. Although they had intended to cause the fire, somehow the sight of the ship fully aflame, the leaping orange light reflected on the black water, was still terrible to behold.

Cal felt an involuntary shudder pass over him as he watched. For a moment, the scene was eclipsed by his mental image of another fire, and he was back in Nerita, watching the merciless flames devour the only home he had ever known. He knew the memory that would come next, and he wrenched his thoughts back to the present.

The screams of the sailors were suddenly drowned out by an explosion as the flames apparently reached more of the oil stores Jo had raided below deck.

"Time to go," said Jo grimly. They glanced across the nearby quay. Some of the youths could still be seen sprinting across the dockyard. Presumably they all had somewhere to go, however humble it might be.

"I think we should go the other way," said Cal quickly. He tried not to think about the fact that they not only had nowhere to go, but now had no provisions at all. He and Jo had shed their heavy stolen packs down in the cells.

Jonan just nodded, and the three of them took off at a run, heading away from the dockyard. They had only gone a few streets, however, when Elnora spoke up, her voice coming out in gasps.

"I'm sorry, I'm not sure I can keep going much longer at this pace."

The two boys slowed, turning to look at her. Cal suddenly noticed for the first time that she was limping significantly.

"What's wrong?" he said sharply. "What happened?"

"It's my ankle," she said through gritted teeth. "Where the shackle was."

Cal found that his teeth were clenched too as they all pulled themselves to a stop. The fire inside him was not yet fully extinguished, but he pushed his anger aside, unable to afford the distraction. His eyes met Jo's over Elnora's head as she bent down to gingerly feel her ankle. Neither of them was strong enough to carry her for any distance, and they wouldn't make it far at this rate.

The dockyard wasn't far away, and the sounds of the commotion could still be heard clearly in the still night. In the midst of the chaos, they didn't hear the sound of an approaching cart as they hesitated in the middle of the road, uncertain what to do next. Before they knew what was happening, the cart had swung around a corner ahead, traveling way too fast. They barely had time to leap out of the way as the horse reared, its plunging hooves flailing where they had been gathered a moment before.

"Whoa!" the man driving the cart shouted as he attempted to regain control of his horse. When he successfully brought the cart to a stop, Cal saw that a woman was sitting next to him. They both looked thoroughly alarmed.

"What's going on, what are you doing in the middle of the road?" the man asked them anxiously. When they didn't answer, he barreled on, seeming to forget in his nervousness that he was addressing strangers. "What's happening at the dock? We were just leaving on our way out of town, but we saw the flames break out. Is there a ship burning in the quay? Do they need help?"

"Robert, look!" his wife whispered beside him, raising the lantern she held and casting its light in their direction. "Look at their clothes!"

The man glanced sharply at the three of them, taking in the singed edge of Elnora's dress and the ash sprinkled across their clothing. He seemed to note the wary looks in their eyes as well, and his next words were accusatory.

"See here, where did you come from just now? What do you know about this fire?"

Elnora stepped forward, but whatever she had been about to say was lost. As she put her weight on her injured ankle, it finally gave out, and she collapsed with a little cry of pain. Reacting instinctively, Cal reached out and caught her before she fell, supporting her in a firm grip.

The man's eyes traveled down Elnora's disheveled person and settled on her ankle, visible below the torn and muddied hem of her dress. Even in the dim circle of lamplight, the bruises could clearly be seen, and the skin was rubbed raw in a distinct band.

"What kind of ship is alight back there?" he said, his voice suddenly much sharper. "What kind of cargo?!" he demanded when they didn't answer. Still none of them spoke. "Traders?" His tone was grim.

Cal nodded, his eyes not leaving the man's face as he continued to hold Elnora up. If only he knew who to trust.

"Get in," the man said tersely. "The back is full of goods. Hide under the cover."

Cal looked at his companions. Elnora's eyes were squeezed shut against the pain in her ankle. Jo met Cal's look and gave a small shrug before starting toward the cart. Glad to let someone else take the lead for the moment, Cal lifted Elnora in his arms and carried her in Jonan's wake. Her eyes flew open in surprise as her feet left the ground, her startled gaze landing on Cal's face. He said nothing, merely handing her as carefully as he could to Jo, who had already clambered into the cart.

Cal followed, and the three of them crawled beneath the cover as directed. The cart was full of fresh produce, clearly headed for an early morning market far enough outside of town to necessitate a late night departure.

The driver was already swinging the horse around, ready to head away from the docks.

"Which way do you need to go?" he called back to them.

"North," said Jo concisely.

"Then north we will go."

CHAPTER NINETEEN

Cal looked up at the mountains looming ahead. He felt a small thrill go through him. He had never seen mountains before, and even from here, their sheer size was impressive. Another treasure of this beautiful kingdom that he had only heard about and was now seeing with his own eyes.

Looking down again, Cal felt another surge of gratitude at the sight of the small rucksack full of food. As if the appearance of sympathetic strangers at that crucial moment in Alezae hadn't been miraculous enough, the kindness of their rescuers in taking them so far north and then providing them with supplies almost brought tears to his eyes. Cal was emboldened to hope that for every citizen like Bryant in Alezae, there were two others like the two who had come to their aid.

Still, after days of riding in the back of the cart, he was happy to be on his own feet again. And even happier to finally be within striking distance of the foot of the mountains that had seemed so impossibly far away when they first glimpsed them in the distance the morning after leaving Alezae. Montego was less than a day's trek away. Their new friends had assured them that with the lengthening summer days, if they kept to the path and were fit enough for the steady ascent, they should reach the mountain town before sunset.

Cal could sense a similar lift in mood in Jo, standing on his right. He felt rather than saw Elnora approach him on his left, stopping far enough away from him that they could both have stretched an arm toward the other without their fingers touching.

"Good morning," he said politely, not meeting her eye. "Ready to go?"

She nodded, looking determinedly straight ahead instead of toward him. Jonan remained silent as they started walking, but with a glance in his direction Cal saw his friend roll his eyes at the carefully formal exchange between his companions.

Cal sighed. It was easy for Jo to make light of it all, but Cal couldn't see how to restore his easy friendship with Elnora the way Jo seemed to have done. And it wasn't just coming from him. It gave Cal a pang to think of the familiar good-natured banter he had witnessed between Jonan and Elnora in the last few days, when she had barely exchanged a word with him. She didn't even look him in the eye if she could avoid it.

But then Jonan hadn't been the one to call Elnora out of her trance in their moment of crisis. He hadn't been the one to grasp her by the hand as they ran from the foul cage in the bowels of the ship, and as they fled the inferno through the streets beyond. He hadn't been the one to carry her in his arms, however briefly, as they accepted the offer of sanctuary. And most importantly, he hadn't been the one she had turned to as the cart rumbled out of Alezae.

Even now Cal had to resist the urge to glance sideways at Elnora as he remembered the look in her eyes as she had turned toward him wordlessly. It had almost seemed like she wanted to thank him, and he had not been able to countenance such a thing. When he had reached for her, he had intended nothing more than to check if she was all right after her imprisonment and injury. But just like his voice inside the ship, his touch had seemed to unlock something within her, and she had thrown herself into his arms, her inarticulate cry of pain piercing his heart more effectively than any words could have done.

The strangest thing was that he hadn't felt in the least awkward at the time. He had certainly felt grief and anger in response to her pain. But somehow it had felt both natural and easy, holding her in a strong clasp while she sobbed desperately inside the circle of his arms, years' worth of pain and fear and loneliness pouring out.

Her exhaustion had eventually overcome her, but even after she had cried herself into sleep, her head remained against his chest, one hand clutching his tunic. Not for the first time in the last few days, Cal felt his heart rate increase as he recalled how it had felt to support her small form in his arms as she slept through that long night.

The awkwardness had come later. Huddled in the cart in the darkness, with the trauma of recent events hard on their heels, Elnora had not seemed self-conscious. But in the gray light of an uncertain dawn, it was a different matter. The ash might still cling to their clothes, but the fragility that Elnora had allowed herself to reveal disappeared with the stars.

And now, even after the passage of days, she would barely look at him.

Jonan had been there throughout that night, certainly. He had met Cal's eyes across Elnora's still form, his expression inscrutable. But it wasn't the same. If anything could clearly demonstrate that fact, it was the casual tone he and Elnora had quickly recaptured.

"How's your ankle?" Jo was asking Elnora now, his light words seeming designed to confirm Calinnae's reflections.

"It's fine," she said, apparently just as relaxed. "Much better."

"It's lucky it wasn't broken or sprained," Cal interjected, trying to match the tone.

"Yes," said Elnora concisely after a beat of silence.

Cal sighed and dropped behind his companions, giving up on the attempt to join the conversation. Jo had begun showing Elnora the basics of reading during their time rumbling along in the cart, and while Cal thought he could do a better job of teaching her, he had the good sense to stay out of it while Elnora was in this mood. He quickly tuned out the discussion happening ahead of him regarding Jo's latest lesson.

Looking around, he tried to refocus on his previous exhilaration at being finally at the start of the mountains. He had been astonished to see that their peaks were white even now, heading into summer. He had never enjoyed cold weather and could only be glad that they hadn't discovered Jo's life-changing secret at the start of winter. He suspected that a trek through the mountains would be a different story then.

For a short while their path continued level, giving ample opportunity to marvel at the peaks ahead. Even when the ground began to slope upward, their way still led through grassy turf, the last of the spring flowers blowing in the gentle gusts of breeze. It was a very different type of beauty from either the coast or the plains, but it was no less glorious to Cal. He had always loved this time of year. Somehow the knowledge that had gradually grown on him throughout their adventure—that Kyona's descent into fear and decay was much further advanced than he had imagined—only made the intense beauty of this beloved kingdom more poignant to him.

There was so much of value in Kyona, and he could not bear to see any more of it lost. Since leaving Alezae he had frequently been dogged by the memory of the trader captain's sneering face as he told them that they could not stop the many more ships that would come. They had to find a way through this. Somehow, impossibly, they had to get Jonan on the throne at Kynton where he would have the power to put an end to the suffering.

If only he had some idea of how to achieve this impossible feat. Since Cal didn't believe for a moment that they would find dragons in the mountains, he couldn't see how going to Montego would get them any answers. But he had not raised any further objections when Jo directed their rescuers to bring them north. He would like to think that he was becoming better at following, but in truth it was more that he had no other suggestions to make.

And quite apart from all of that, he couldn't be sorry to find himself on this road. The closer he got to the mountains, the more he found himself wanting to experience the strange quality about the place and the people that King Cael had described in his records.

Whether he wished it or not, the ground continued to rise steadily under their feet as they walked. Before long they couldn't see the peaks of the mountains anymore. The gentle grassland fell away, and the path wended its way through rocky ground. The occasional clump of color still appeared as flowers burst their way out of the patches of turf dotted throughout the rocks. These bright flashes became less frequent as they climbed, however, and by the time they stopped to eat around midday, they were well and truly surrounded by outcrops of stone.

They settled themselves a little way off the path. They hadn't passed anyone else since setting out, but they knew there was a reason the road had been smooth and well-tended thus far. It was the main route in and out of Montego, and they had no desire to get trampled by passing traffic.

Cal set out food from the pack gifted to them by the man and his wife. The three of them gathered around the supplies, no one speaking for a moment. They had maintained a fast pace all morning, and he could see he was not the only one feeling weary.

He cast a surreptitious glance at Elnora, and caught her in a wince as she shifted her legs under her. He was not surprised to see this evidence that her ankle was giving her more discomfort than she admitted. Glancing up, she caught him looking and diverted her gaze quickly, an unreadable expression on her face.

Jonan stood up abruptly. Startled, the other two looked at him. He hadn't eaten much, but he still had some food in his hands.

"I'm going to scout up the path ahead a little way," he said. "See what we have to expect as the slope gets steeper."

For a moment Cal was bewildered, but when Jo lingered to give him a significant look before leaving, he understood. He had to suppress a sigh as he watched Jonan disappear around a corner up ahead. He knew Jo was trying to help, but if Elnora wasn't willing to talk to him, he couldn't see what there was to be gained by manufacturing an opportunity for them to be alone.

He looked cautiously over at her. She was determinedly avoiding looking up, her body angled away from him as she ate. She sat in an unnatural posture, the sword she had taken from the downed trader on the ship still strapped around her waist. Cal had not even realized until they were out of Alezae that she had showed the presence of mind to grab the sword and its sheath as he pulled her off the ship. He remembered her saying after they left Pravat that swords were cumbersome, and she didn't want to carry one on the journey to Montego. Apparently their run in with the traders had changed her mind.

It didn't seem to give her any security now, though. She sat slightly hunched over, as if by turning in on herself she could keep the outside world out. The stance had become familiar, and he hated to see it. He felt a fleeting desire to lean forward and wrap his arms around her slim frame as he had in the cart. To hold her firmly and assure her that she was safe and he would protect her from everything and everyone. But the thought passed quickly. He couldn't promise any such thing.

Nevertheless, looking at her uncomfortable posture, he realized that Jonan was right. If they were all going to continue to travel together, he and Elnora needed to break this awkward silence, for everyone's sake.

But where to start? He looked around him as he tried to find the right words, and was momentarily distracted by a small bunch of flowers growing nearby.

"Dianmons!" he said involuntarily, and Elnora looked up in surprise.

"What?"

"These must be dianmons," said Cal, moving closer to the blooms to get a better look. "Sometimes called the flower of Kyona. I'm sure you've heard of it."

Elnora nodded, but didn't speak again.

"They're beautiful," said Cal, speaking mainly to himself. "They really do look like snowflakes." The small white blossom was indeed striking against the gray mountain rocks. Its petals curved out from the center, layering over one another, their ends crenelated. Deep purple veins ran through each petal, erupting from the heart of the flower. It was delicate, intricate, new details becoming evident as he looked more closely. But to thrive up here, it must be hardy as well.

Just like Elnora. He looked back up at his companion.

"Apparently it used to be so popular with the royals that it was a sort of emblem for the kingdom once," he said, keeping his tone light. "But it only grows in the mountains, so I've never seen it before. I've always wanted to."

After a moment's hesitation, he picked one of the flowers and handed it to Elnora where she still sat.

"Here, see for yourself."

"It's nice," said Elnora colorlessly, after only a cursory look.

But Cal kept his hand outstretched. "Take it," he insisted. "Who knows if you'll get another opportunity to see one up close?"

She just stared at his hand for a moment, but when he didn't budge, she reached out and reluctantly took the flower.

Cal sat down again, the interaction over the dianmon having given him an excuse to resettle himself much closer to Elnora. He considered her in silence for a long moment. She gave no intentional sign of being aware of his scrutiny, but the rising color in her face betrayed her.

"I'm sorry," Calinnae finally said, his voice coming out more quietly than expected.

She looked up, startled. "For what?" He had succeeded in getting her attention, at least.

"For all the trouble we've brought on you," he said.

For a moment she stared at him, nonplussed. "All the trouble *you've* brought on *me*?"

He nodded. "You wouldn't have been in that situation in Alezae if it wasn't for us. You wouldn't have been foolish enough to put yourself in that danger on your own account. And it wasn't the first time you were in danger because of us either. I've been selfish, dragging you into trouble in my attempt to protect Jo."

She had been staring at him in surprise, but at his last comment she managed a small smile. "Trying to protect your friend is not exactly selfish," she pointed out.

He shook his head, not wanting to be distracted now that he had managed to start expressing some of what had been circling around his head for the last few days.

"I mean it," he said. "I'm more sorry than I can say. I know you left Kerr because your life there was miserable, but at least you weren't being hunted and attacked at every turn. We should never have asked so much of you."

Now it was her turn to shake her head. "I feel like you're stealing my words," she said. "I'm the one who should be apologizing, and I've been trying to figure out how to do it for days. You would have passed through Alezae unnoticed if it wasn't for me. I'm the one who brought trouble on you, and I can hardly bear the thought of how much danger you put yourselves in just to rescue me from my own stupidity."

"'Just' to rescue you?" said Cal incredulously. "As if that wasn't more than worth the risk!"

She shook her head harder. "No, it wasn't. I could have been the reason that Jonan died or was enslaved, and then this whole quest would be for nothing. Everything would be lost." She hesitated for a moment. "And you...well I couldn't bear to be the cause of you being hurt or killed either, Cal."

She hadn't said his name in days, and his heart did a strange kind of jump at the sound of it.

When he didn't respond immediately, she continued in a subdued tone. "You should never have come for me. Of course selfishly I'm glad you did. But you shouldn't have."

Cal took her hands gently. "We would never have left you, Elnora. You're not on your own, you're with us now. You should've known we would come for you. There was never any question."

She was staring down at their hands. She looked like she was fighting tears, and when she spoke her voice was small. "I was so afraid Cal. And now I'm so ashamed."

His hands had tightened on hers at her first words, but he almost let go now in surprise.

"Ashamed? What do you mean? What can you possibly be ashamed about?"

She still didn't look at him. "About the way I fell apart. I don't know what happened. I hardly remember anything between when they threw me in the cart and when you...woke me up, or whatever you did. It's all a blur, like I'd fallen into one of my nightmares, but it just went on and on."

She squeezed her eyes shut, and Cal could see moisture clinging to the end of her lashes. "All the horrors I'd imagined about being caught and put on one of those slave vessels were more real than my imagination could paint them, and I knew that if my nightmares were going to turn into reality, then much worse was still coming." She drew a shuddering breath.

"I just...I'm embarrassed that you witnessed whatever that was."

"Elnora." Cal had to fight to keep his voice level, because he felt an unreasoning anger. "You don't ever have to be embarrassed in front of me. Not for any reason."

She swallowed hard. "But I am. And I'm embarrassed in front of myself, too. I never thought I'd be someone to fall apart in a crisis. Hardly the person you want with you on a journey like this one."

"*You* are the person we want with us on a journey like this one," said Cal firmly. "And you are not someone who falls apart in a crisis. Don't forget that wasn't exactly the first crisis I've seen you in. What happened in Alezae...that was different. Not many people have to face their very worst fear in the flesh."

She still wasn't looking him in the eye, and he could see that she didn't quite believe him. He felt more helpless than ever.

"Elnora," he said quietly. "You don't think you're worth it, but you are. We won't let anything happen to you if we can help it." Cal was suddenly unsatisfied with hiding behind "we". "*I* won't." He willed her to look up at him. "Elnora, when I saw you in those chains...one ship is nothing. I would have burned the whole South Lands to the ground if that's what it took."

She finally met his eyes, surprise mingling with something

else in her expression. He again knew an impulse to lean forward and put his arms around her, but he remained where he was. For several endless heartbeats their gazes were locked, then she blinked rapidly, as if trying to clear away the intensity.

"What, if you'd been too late to stop the ship, you'd have sailed across on the next one, would you?" Her tone was joking, but Cal wasn't quite ready to let go of the moment.

"Yes. I would have," he said, his voice still serious.

As she stared back at him he noted for the first time just how very blue her eyes were. But he also noted that they were unnaturally round at this moment, and he could see that he'd unnerved her. He suddenly remembered that the point of this conversation was to try to clear the awkwardness between them, and he let go of her hands, trying to lighten his tone as well.

"I mean, I would have tried my very hardest to stop Jonan racing off to a likely death, but I would have come on the next ship myself."

She laughed unconvincingly. "That would have been ironic. You're the one who wants to stay here, and all Jo ever wanted was to sail across the sea, right?"

Cal turned away with a tight smile. "Yes, well, we don't always get what we want, do we?"

"Rarely, in my experience," said Elnora, regarding him steadily. Now that he had looked away, she seemed much less reluctant to look at him, and her gaze was all too perceptive.

For a moment there was silence as Cal returned to his abandoned food. But she surprised him by being the first to speak this time.

"You were wrong before, you know."

"What do you mean?"

"I didn't leave Kerr because my life there was miserable. I mean, it was pretty miserable," she hastened to add as Calinnae raised his eyebrows. "But that's not the main reason I wanted to come with you. I guess that just made it easier to leave."

"So why did you want to come with us?" he asked.

"What you two are doing is important, and it's good. I could see straight away that this was it. This was my chance."

"Your chance?" Cal prompted when she failed to elaborate. "Your chance for what?"

She shrugged. "Just...my chance. Everyone longs for their chance, don't they?"

"I'm not sure I know what you mean."

She looked away for a moment, apparently trying to figure out how to articulate whatever was in her mind. When she spoke, her eyes remained focused on the mountains ahead.

"Everyone's lives matter to them, of course, but some people's...really matter. Surely everyone wants that, wants to be part of something greater. And it's not just that. It's not about wanting to be important. It's about wanting to discover who you are."

She looked over at Cal finally, and smiled at the wry look on his face.

"I don't mean finding out you're secretly someone important, like Jo did. More like finding out if you're of high enough quality. I think deep down, we all wonder if we're strong enough to be purified by fire instead of destroyed. And as much as fear of the answer holds us back from asking the question, I think some part of everyone longs for their chance to be tested and to prove their character."

She shrugged. "As soon as I met you, I knew that if there was any truth to the rumors about what you were doing, I wanted to help. I knew it was my chance."

Cal was silent. Again she watched him steadily.

"Haven't you ever felt that way?" she asked after a prolonged silence, her voice a little bit wistful.

He looked back at her. "Yes," he said finally, "I suppose I have. I'd never thought of it in quite those terms, but I do know what you mean. I think I just assumed my 'chance' would come in some form or another. It never occurred to me to go chasing it. That's more Jonan's philosophy."

Thinking about his friend sent his thoughts in another direction, and he couldn't quite hold back a bitter laugh at his own expense. Elnora looked at him questioningly, and he sighed.

"I suppose I never thought I'd be the backup in my own story. I'm ashamed to admit it, but I would have expected that my chance to prove my mettle would involve me being the hero at the center of it all, not the reinforcement hanging back on the edges." He suddenly thought of the shameful fear that had almost crippled him throughout their journey, although he could find no trace of it within himself at that moment. "And I would have hoped I would do a better job of it all."

Elnora gave him a thoughtful look. "If you ask me, I think you're doing incredibly. You may not have royal blood, Cal, but you were born to lead as much as Jonan was. And you're braver and more confident than you think you are. Yet you never complain about having to follow Jo."

"I thought I just did," said Cal dryly, trying not to look too pleased at her compliments. She just shook her head with a smile and continued.

"It's not an easy thing to just swallow that longing for greatness and choose instead to support someone else."

"I don't think I've ever longed for greatness, exactly," interjected Cal quickly. "But Jo..." He made a noise of frustration before he could stop himself. "The irony is that Jo doesn't even want any of it! He doesn't even seem to feel the enormity of his heritage. I think I feel it more for him than he does for himself. It's like you said—all he's ever wanted was to go on some great adventure beyond our borders." He sighed. "But I love this place." He gestured at the beauty around them. "It's home."

Elnora gave a sad smile. "Well, I've never longed for greatness either, but I do know what it means to long for home."

"Well, maybe it's no surprise that this is Jonan's chance to prove himself, not mine. Maybe adventures belong to those who long for them, not those who just value home and security."

"I don't think so, Cal." Her serious tone compelled him to meet her eyes. "I think this is your chance to prove yourself as much as it's his. How can our quality be tested if we're not asked to make sacrifices? Kerr wasn't great, but it was a home of sorts. And I had to give it up to come with you. And Jo is giving up what he really wants too.

"Maybe this is your test. Not to see if you have what it takes to be great, but to see if you have what it takes not to be. To be strong enough to give yourself to making Jonan strong, instead of yourself."

"Maybe," he said quietly, captivated by the intensity of her expression. "And if so, it really is a test, because sometimes I don't know if I do have what it takes."

She reached over and gave his hand an encouraging squeeze. His skin seemed to burn from the contact, and she quickly let go. "It takes a different kind of courage," she said. "But it's no less than the courage Jo has to show. Both of you are sacrificing what you really want."

She sighed. "From my observation, life is all sacrifice. I think some pernicious fate rules over everything, with the aim of denying us all what we want. And our character is demonstrated by how well we can handle it."

Cal frowned at her. She had once again surprised him with the depth of her insight, but he didn't agree with her last words. Despite everything that had happened, and all they had seen, he couldn't bring himself to believe that some malicious fortune was running their lives, and that he could expect nothing but hardship from his future.

Before he could respond, however, Jo came into view. His entrance was so well-timed that Cal wondered uneasily if Jo had been listening to their conversation. He hoped not—he didn't want Jo to hear the things Cal had said about him. But he shook the thought away. It wasn't his to worry about. He seemed to recall having told Jo once before that if he eavesdropped he might not like what he heard—and look how that had turned out.

If he had heard anything, Jo didn't comment on it. He had nothing of particular interest to report about the path ahead, and the three of them were soon organized and back on the track. Cal could see Jo's relief as he observed the much more natural way in which Cal and Elnora were interacting. He realized guiltily that he had been too absorbed in his own situation to consider how uncomfortable the sudden coolness must have been for Jonan as well.

With open communication restored, the afternoon seemed to pass much more quickly and pleasantly than the morning, despite the increasing difficulty of the walk. The path climbed steadily now, and the air began to feel crisp well before the sun started to sink. Conversation gradually declined as they needed all their breath for the effort of climbing the steeply sloping path.

The sun was very low in the sky when Cal began to think that perhaps they had stopped too long to rest or climbed too slowly to make the trek in one day as they had hoped. He was suddenly struck by the alarming possibility that they had missed the right path somehow, and were wandering aimlessly, not toward Montego at all. It did seem surprising that through the whole day, they had still passed no other traffic in either direction. He was wondering just how cold it would get on the mountain overnight when he felt a soft hand on his arm.

He looked down quickly to see Elnora looking around with wide eyes. "We're being watched," she whispered.

"Are you sure?" he asked, keeping his own voice down. "I think maybe it's just the feel of this place." He had indeed felt a strange tingle in his spine that had increased in strength the further into the mountains they walked. He had assumed, with some excitement, that he was feeling that strange quality that King Cael had described.

Elnora shook her head. "I'm sure," she said, just as Jo drew close on her other side.

"She's right. I saw something too." He pointed ahead and to the side of the path nearest Cal. "Over there."

As he pointed, a figure seemed to detach itself from the rock up ahead in the lowering light. Cal blinked several times to assure himself he wasn't hallucinating. For a moment he had thought he was looking at a creature of legend, some kind of mountain troll or goblin.

The man, for man he was, wore a curious type of garb that Calinnae had never seen before. He could see how he had missed him. The varying shades of gray made the fabric blend with the surrounding rock, and the man's dark hair, although long, was braided behind his head and interwoven with the same gray fabric. There was something both wild and polished about the man's appearance, and for a moment Cal simply stared.

The man stared right back, his expression impassive as he took in every detail of the three travelers. When his eyes lingered on Cal's face, it took Cal a moment to place what was missing. Suddenly he identified it—he hadn't seen the tiny spark of recognition one usually expected when locking eyes with another human, even a stranger. Whether correctly or not, this man did not identify them as being of his kind.

It was his first glimpse of one of the mountain people, and it was instantly clear why hundreds of years of superstition had labeled them as magical, or in some way foreign to the rest of Kyona's residents.

As the silence stretched out, Jo stepped forward and addressed the man. "Hello," he said confidently. "We are travelers, hoping to make it to Montego before nightfall. Are we close?"

The man didn't respond, and Cal began to wonder if he could even understand them. If he could, he made no sign of it. But as they waited, half a dozen other silent watchers seemed to materialize suddenly, emerging from the rocks and forming a guard around the three companions.

Cal quickly sucked in a breath, and he heard Elnora stifle an involuntary squeak of surprise. He and Jo exchanged a look, silently gauging whether they should put up a fight.

Still no words had been spoken, but the man whom they had first seen turned and continued up the path in the direction they had been taking. The rest of the group also began to move, and almost without volition, the three travelers found themselves walking as well, keeping pace with the guard, which maintained a loose formation around them.

They looked warily at one another, but none of them said anything. Without intending to, Cal realized that he and Jo had formed a small guard of their own, flanking Elnora, who still walked with a slight limp. She drew even closer to Cal as they walked, and he resisted the urge to put a reassuring arm around her shoulders. Better to keep his hands free, just in case.

They walked on in this way for another half an hour, by which time twilight was setting in. They had seen no sign of Montego, and Cal assumed that either it must be further away than they had been led to believe, or they had indeed taken a wrong turn.

He was therefore taken completely by surprise when they rounded a corner and suddenly found themselves walking through an opening between crude stone gateposts. The ground in front stretched out in the longest flat patch they had seen all day. Stone dwellings were scattered around a large central space, some cut into the mountain, some built up from the ground.

There was no sign announcing the name of the town, but they weren't left long in suspense. One of their escorts peeled away from the group and disappeared into the gloom. He returned in a moment, accompanied by a tall, broad-shouldered man clad in the same gray garb. If he hadn't been so solidly built, he would have looked like an apparition, blending into the gray of the evening. His long grizzled hair was not confined in any way but flowed around his head like a mane. A wooden circlet, retaining the appearance of twigs rather than polished timber, wound around his forehead.

"Travelers," he said, his voice somehow both muted and strong, like his appearance. "Welcome to Montego."

CHAPTER TWENTY

"Thank you," said Jonan quickly. "We are honored to be here."

The man's eyes flicked to Jonan, and he looked him carefully up and down before speaking. Jo's words had clearly identified him as the leader of their group.

"I am Darius, chief of Montego. Perhaps you were surprised by your escort. We do not get many visitors here, especially in recent days. We like to know who comes and goes in our mountains."

The proprietary manner in which Darius said "our mountains" was not lost on Cal, and neither was the fact that his words had contained explanation rather than apology.

"Of course," said Jonan. "We are not looking to cause you any trouble." He looked around the central area. "We would be grateful for sanctuary tonight, however. We have traveled some distance."

Darius inclined his head. "You will be accommodated."

He spoke quietly to the man who had summoned him, who then disappeared once again into the town. When he had gone, Darius continued to observe them. Cal expected him to say something more, but he remained silent. It was strange, Cal reflected, how big a difference the setting could make. Had Darius walked through the streets of Nerita without changing his appearance at all, he would be an object of ridicule. But here, in his mountain home, his presence was commanding, even awe-inspiring.

The man who had left soon returned with two other citizens of Montego, a man and a woman. They gave quick nods in response to Darius's gaze, and the chief turned back to the three companions.

"These people have agreed to host you tonight," he said. Cal tried to give the new arrivals a grateful smile, but he was thrown by their passive expressions. "It is our custom to eat the evening meal all together here." Darius gestured back toward the open area, and Cal saw a large fire burning there. "Please join us."

"Thank you," said Jonan.

The local woman stepped forward. "Come," she said. The three of them started forward, but she shook her head. "Not you," she pointed deliberately at Jo and Cal in turn. "Just you," her eyes settled on Elnora.

"You can come with me," added the man beside her, nodding to the two boys.

Cal hesitated. He had not bargained on being split up. He could see that the dwellings were all small. Still, he didn't like the idea of Elnora being on her own.

But if Elnora was anxious about being separated from her companions, she didn't show it. "See you for the meal," she said quickly to the boys, then followed the woman around the edge of the central area.

Cal tried to see which dwelling she entered, but their own guide stepped in front of him, obscuring his vision. Cal noticed Darius watching him closely. He had the distinct impression that although his words might be few, the mountain chief did not miss much.

Their host led them in the opposite direction from where Elnora had gone, skirting the edge of the fire and stopping before one of the dwellings that was built up rather than cut into the mountain. As Cal had anticipated, space was limited in the man's home. There was a pallet in one corner where he clearly slept, and a small wooden table and chair. There was no area for cooking. Perhaps they ate all meals communally here.

A young girl arrived just after they did, bearing two extra pallets, which she placed inside the stone hut without a word. She and the man exchanged a nod of acknowledgment, then she left.

After they set up their sleeping area, the man gave Cal and Jo a long and measuring look. "I will get you fresh clothes," he said concisely. Cal attempted to protest, but the man was already outside.

"Not much into conversation here, are they?" muttered Jo, and Cal grimaced in response. Looking down at himself, he had to admit that a change of clothes would be welcome. He was still in the tunic he had changed into just before entering Alezae. He was glad that the smell of the marsh didn't cling to it, but it still had smears of both mud and blood from their encounter with Bryant's men, and in places the fabric had become blackened as they fled the fire.

It was no surprise that the clothes brought by their host were gray in color, but Cal was relieved to see that the design was a simple tunic and sturdy pants. The mountain chief might look impressive in his traditional garb, but Cal was certain that he and Jo would just look comical. The man also brought a bucket of water, allowing them the chance for a simple but much-needed wash.

The basic lunch they had shared seemed forever ago, and

Cal's spirits lifted as the smell of roasting meat penetrated into the dwelling, which sat surprisingly close to the central fire. Once he saw that they had donned their new clothes, the man beckoned Jo and Cal out of the hut without a word. As they approached the scene, Cal saw that the fire was built in a large fire pit. It was well maintained, and clearly enjoyed regular use. Large boulders, roughly hewn into flat surfaces, were strewn around it in a circle, forming the seating.

Many of the residents of Montego had already begun to gather for the meal. As seemed characteristic for these mountain people, there was little conversation. But Cal could see from the faces around him that people were relaxed and happy. Presumably the day's labors were over for most.

Their guide melted away into the crowd as soon as they reached the circle of boulders, and Cal and Jo were left to find themselves a seat. There was no sign of Elnora yet, but they chose a large slab of stone big enough to seat three. Perhaps the tone of Montego had settled on them, because they did not attempt conversation, waiting in companionable silence as the final preparations for the meal were completed.

Just as bowls started to be passed around, Elnora finally appeared. She had made it all the way across the circle and stood almost right in front of them before Cal recognized her. For a moment he just stared, forgetting even to greet her.

They were not the only ones who had washed, and been given a change of clothes. And if she had looked different when she adjusted her skirts to enter Alezae, it was nothing to how different she looked now.

The mountain people had dressed her in gray also, but it was a much darker gray than the tunic he was wearing, making her stand out boldly. Many of the locals seemed to blend seamlessly into their surrounds. It was almost as though their human forms were fading into mist and stone. But not Elnora. As she walked toward them, Cal was struck by the fanciful thought that the mist had solidified, and the mountain had taken human form, stepping out of the shadows.

The dress was cut in simple lines and seemed much more practical for a mountain hike than her previous one, closely fitted above the waist, with skirts just full enough not to restrict her legs. There were no embellishments and no pattern, just a smooth gray fabric of a type Cal didn't recognize. But its simplicity made it elegant rather than plain.

And it was more than just the new dress. Elnora's hair had been pulled back in a loose braid, a few golden tendrils waving loose and catching the firelight. The braid sat forward over her shoulder, and Cal saw tucked into its end a delicate white dianmon. None of the other women were wearing flowers in their hair, and he hadn't seen any dianmons close to Montego. He realized with a curious flip of his stomach that she was wearing the very flower he had given her that afternoon.

The memory of that moment only served to highlight how different her demeanor was now. With the filthy tattered clothing she seemed to have shed some of her fear and uncertainty. Her face was clean, and her eyes glowed with an excited light. Had he been surprised to realize he found her pretty when they were in Pravat together? Pretty didn't capture it at all.

Beautiful. She was beautiful. Not the dress, or the hair, but her. How had he not noticed it before?

"You look really nice, Elnora," said Jo admiringly, and Cal gave his friend an incredulous look. *Really nice?* What an inadequate description.

"Thanks," said Elnora, her voice a bit breathless. Her eyes flicked to Cal, and he realized that he still hadn't greeted her.

"Yes, really nice," he said stupidly. "Hi."

Jo was looking at him like he was insane, but Elnora smiled.

"Thanks," she said again. Her gaze took in their change in

clothes. "I see you two are mountain people now too." She looked around at the fire and the people beginning to eat, muted conversation arising sporadically. "I like this place."

Cal didn't respond, still feeling a little bit stunned, so Jonan stepped in, and the two of them discussed their impressions of the village. Jonan moved along so Elnora could sit between the two boys just as someone came past and offered them bowls of steaming food.

For a while their own conversation was as desultory as that of the people around them, the taste of cooked food making them realize just how hungry they were. Cal couldn't actually remember the last time he'd eaten a cooked meal, and the strips of meat and cooked beans and vegetables tasted even better than they smelled.

Calinnae had expected from the reserved manner of the mountain people that after the meal was finished, everyone would return to their homes. He was therefore surprised when Darius, having finished his food, stood up to address the assembled group.

"Friends," he said in his calm voice. "We have visitors tonight."

All heads turned toward the three of them, and Cal noticed that while many of the villagers wore expressions as placid as Darius's, those closer to his own age showed more curiosity. He remembered what Darius had said about receiving few visitors.

"We will celebrate."

Darius sat down, his speech apparently finished. Cal saw a small smile break through the man's calm reserve, and it was clear why. All around him people were starting to stir, smiling and talking quietly to each other. Again, it was the younger ones who showed the most enthusiasm. There was a flurry of activity as everyone hastened to clear up the remains of the meal.

"What do you think he means by celebrate?" asked Jonan.

Cal shook his head, nonplussed, but a pleasant voice answered for him.

"He means music and stories. And if we're lucky, dancing."

The speaker was a girl who looked a couple of years younger than them. Cal hadn't noticed her before, but looking over at her now, he saw that she sat on a boulder nearby, a number of other young people grouped around her.

"I'm Lilac," she said, extending a hand. "Welcome to Montego."

"Thank you," said Calinnae. He reached out and took her hand, attempting to shake it. She stared at him for a moment, then started to giggle, a number of the others joining in. Cal felt Elnora shift slightly beside him. He looked around in confusion and saw Jonan grinning at him.

"What?"

"I don't think they greet using handshakes here," said Jo, clearly deriving too much enjoyment from Cal's apparent blunder.

"What do you mean by music and stories?" Elnora cut in, addressing herself to Lilac.

"It's our tradition," the younger girl responded simply. "We pass our legends on through song and spoken word, and sharing music and stories is a common way to spend the evenings here. Plus," she added with a grin, "all mountain people love to dance."

"Really?" Cal hadn't intended his tone to be so openly skeptical, but it was hard to imagine these reserved and placid people dancing with any enthusiasm.

"Oh yes," said a boy sitting next to Lilac. "There's a saying in the mountains—we sing before we can speak, and we dance before we can sing."

As they had been speaking, the process of clearing away the meal had been completed. Everyone had returned to their boulders, a number of the villagers now bearing curious wooden instruments.

A sudden hush fell over the scene, as if everyone was responding to a silent signal. Cal felt the tingling sensation in his spine more strongly than ever. Some strange quality did indeed hover around this place and its people.

Before any of the instruments began to sound, Darius opened his mouth. His resonating voice seemed to weave its way around the circle of people as he began to sing, low clear notes rising in a hauntingly beautiful melody. Other voices quickly took up the sound, and the instruments joined almost as an afterthought, swelling the chorus.

Looking to his left, Cal saw that Lilac and her friends were all singing, their voices loud and their faces serious. There was no trace of self-consciousness that he could see. The music swelled around and through him, blending with the strange tingling until the two sensations were indistinguishable. For a mad moment, Cal felt the urge to open his mouth and sing himself, but he clamped his lips together firmly. The locals might feel no embarrassment, but that would not be true for him.

He looked at his companions. Jo was taking it all in with interest, the surprise on his face mirroring Cal's own thoughts. But Elnora was rapt, her eyes glinting in the firelight as she looked around the circle.

The communal song rose and fell for what felt like an age, everyone seeming to know when to let their voices rise to a swell, and when to drop to a gentle hum. Similarly, they all seemed to know when to peter out as the song eventually faded. It was hard to tell when it actually ended, because the notes seemed to hang in the air even after everyone's mouths were closed, as though they had been absorbed in the surrounding stone. Just as Cal thought the event was over, the various instruments started up again, this time without the singing.

"And now," said Lilac with a dreamy smile, "we dance!"

As one, all of the young people sitting with her surged up, laughing and jostling each other gently. All around the circle, people were getting to their feet. Most were not as openly merry as the young group, but gentle smiles could be seen on many faces.

As the three travelers watched, amazed, the demure towns-folk began to twist and glide gracefully, their movements as fluid and powerful as the flickering fire that cast their figures into silhouette. Watching them, Cal was reminded of his impression of the first man they had seen on the path—somehow both wild and polished. Even the chief had joined the dancing, his sure movements making his dance seem more graceful and less ridiculous than Cal would have imagined possible.

Lilac swirled back over to them, seeming older and more poised than she had when sitting.

"Would you like to join?" she asked, a smile on her face. "I can show you how."

Cal shook his head, trying not to look panicked. "No thank you," he said as politely as he could. He glanced at Jonan and saw a similar alarm in his friend's eye. He stifled a laugh. It would be almost worth being forced to dance in front of these people if it meant he got to watch Jonan in the same predica-ment. Almost, but not quite.

"Yes please."

He was surprised by the breathless voice next to him. Lilac reached out a hand and drew Elnora to her feet. Without a back-ward glance, she allowed herself to be pulled into the ring of firelight. Cal watched, spellbound, as she twisted and turned, following Lilac's lead and gaining confidence as she mastered the feel of the dance. After a while she spun back in their direction.

"Are you sure you don't want to dance?" she asked, a laugh in her voice and in her eyes. "It's not as hard as it looks."

Cal shook his head, his own eyes twinkling in response to the shining light in hers. "Not for you maybe, but I'm far too clumsy."

Receiving the same response from Jonan, she just laughed and returned to the throng. The truth was that Cal much preferred to watch her from where he was. It was undoubtedly a better view—he was mesmerized by the way she swung her body around, her arms over her head, her dress swishing back and forth.

Beautiful.

The surging mass of people seemed to ebb and flow like a tide, at times swallowing Elnora up so she was out of sight, at others pushing her gently back to the edges of the circle. Cal did his best to keep his eyes on her, looking for the way the firelight glinted off her golden hair, so much lighter than the characteristically dark hair of the mountain people.

He was watching her spin when it happened. One moment she was twirling in front of him, her pale braid fanning out behind her, the dianmon somehow still attached to its end, when suddenly as she completed the turn, her hair was as dark as anyone's, and she had grown several inches. She was clad in clothes that were the same fabric, but quite a different style, the skirt fuller, and the bodice higher. She moved effortlessly, more confident and skilled than any of the other people dancing around her. Snow fell gently onto her dark hair, only to slide off as she spun gracefully in a circle. She was wild, but safe. Exotic, but familiar.

Beautiful. My Jacqueline.

The thoughts came unbidden, right from his own mind.

With a start, Cal looked around him, returning to reality. Elnora swirled before him, still laughing, her hair as golden as ever, and her steps still clumsy compared to the experts around her. The night was mild, with the hint of summer. But the air hummed with that indefinable power, more strongly now than ever.

Cal blinked rapidly, trying to restore reason. What had just happened?

"You feel it, don't you?" said a quiet voice beside him.

He looked over to see an older man sitting on the boulder recently occupied by Lilac and her friends. The man spoke softly, clearly trying to attract only Calinnae's attention.

"Feel what?" he asked, a little too quickly.

The man smiled knowingly. "I can see that you do. There's a magic to this place. It affects some more than others."

Following the man's gaze, Cal saw Jonan still watching the dancers, his expression relaxed. He didn't seem to have noticed their conversation.

"Magic?" said Cal, trying not to sound too skeptical.

The man just smiled again. "Yes, magic." He gave Cal a measuring look. "You have mountain blood in you."

Cal shook his head. "I don't think so. My people come from the coast."

The man shrugged. "You may not know of it. Many in Kyona have mountain folk in their ancestry, without having any idea of it. Not all mountain people wish to stay here. Many have sought homes and families down on the plains over the generations."

He turned back to the fire. "You have mountain blood in you. I can tell."

Cal had no idea how to respond, but he felt intrigued. If he survived this journey, he would have to try to find out more details of his ancestry. It was tantalizing to think that he might have something of interest in his own lineage. Was there some reason he didn't know about to explain why the hidden heir to the throne chose to befriend his family?

He was almost nervous to return his gaze to the dancers. He wasn't sure about the man's talk of magic, but he was nevertheless shaken by whatever strange vision he had just experienced. But he needn't have worried. Everyone's forms stayed as they should, and it was only minutes before the music died down and the dancers drifted back to seats around the edge of the space. Elnora came to sit once again between the two boys, her face still alight with the joy of dancing.

When everyone was seated, Darius stood up.

"Friends," he said calmly. "It is through our stories that we know who we are."

"May our stories never be forgotten," chanted the rest of the circle.

Darius turned to the three outsiders. "Travelers," he said. "You are our guests tonight. To you I offer the honor of requesting a tale. Is there any story you wish to hear?"

Jonan cleared his throat. "Yes," he said, his clear voice carrying across the circle. "We would like to hear about the dragons."

CHAPTER TWENTY-ONE

"Dragons?" said Darius. His voice remained level, but his eyes showed his surprise. "I did not think anyone from the plains still believed the legends of dragons."

"They don't," muttered Calinnae, but at Elnora's reproachful look he fell silent.

Muttering had swept around the circle like a dry summer breeze at Jonan's words. But all eyes that had flicked to Jonan now returned to Darius as the chief continued to speak.

"Do you believe there are dragons in these mountains, traveler?"

Jonan met the man's gaze steadily. "I do."

Darius held his look for a long moment before answering. "It seems you have traveled far to hear these legends, young man. I will not deny you, although there is much I cannot share."

Cal could feel Jonan's excitement. Skeptical though he was, he also was intrigued to hear what Darius had to say.

"Dragons have long lived in these mountains," Darius began. "Their kind was here long before ours, and will be here long after. For generations they watched men on the plains with little more interest than we watch the movements of the wild elk. The people were suspicious of the mountains, sensing a powerful magic about them that, although they could not identify, instinct warned them to avoid.

"But then came a man more intrepid than the others, who sought a home in this great place. Dernoth."

Cal almost jumped as every citizen around the circle uttered a strange deep cry and thumped their chests in rhythm, one closed fist pounding twice over the heart.

"Our ancestor," continued Darius without pause. "Alone, he ventured far into the mountains. Stopping to drink one day from a mountain stream, he saw the dragon. It was a fearsome beast, as tall as five men, covered in scales like a fish, reflecting off the stream in purple and blue and green. Its mighty tail could wind around a boulder twice the size of a man and crush it to rubble.

"In that moment Dernoth prepared his spirit to meet his ancestors. But the creature locked eyes with him, and did not strike. The creature spoke with him, in the tongue of men, and Dernoth was stunned to hear its words. It was as curious about Dernoth as he was about it, and for the days that followed it returned again and again to the stream. Dernoth learned much in these exchanges, and the dragon was struck by Dernoth's unusual ability to sense the magic that dwells in these mountains. Dernoth sought the beast's blessing to settle in the mountains, promising not to attempt to search out the secrets of dragonkind.

"The beast agreed, and so Dernoth established Montego, and his descendants continue to make their home here, and in the other settlements that now stretch across this mountain region. Dernoth met with the dragon on occasion until he passed, full of years, to his ancestors. His sons and daughters claimed to have seen dragons, and to be able to approach them without fear, although never did another claim to have spoken with a dragon as Dernoth did. The sons and daughters of Dernoth's sons and daughters were said to have seen dragons only from afar. Their sons and daughters heard only whispers, and saw nothing with their eyes.

"It is a long time since any in Montego saw a dragon. But all of Dernoth's descendants can feel the magic that swirls in the mountain air. The tale of Dernoth and the dragon is our story."

"May our stories never be forgotten," the listeners chanted once again, then silence fell around the fire.

Cal had been spellbound by the chief's words, but now that the story was told, he didn't know whether to be disappointed or relieved. It sounded like a standard legend to him, a way to explain the origins of the community. It wasn't very convincing proof of the existence of dragons.

He looked over at Jonan. His friend was leaning forward, a slight frown on his face. He was clearly unsatisfied as well, but he didn't seem to be unconvinced in the way Calinnae was.

"You look like you have questions, young man," said Darius. The chief's eyes were also on Jonan. "You may ask them."

"Thank you," said Jonan, but it was a moment before he spoke again. "Are there no other stories of men encountering the dragons?"

"No others of Dernoth's descendants claim to have spoken with dragons," Darius repeated calmly.

"Yes, but..." Jonan hesitated. "What about others, not mountain people?" Darius waited, clearly unwilling to answer until Jonan revealed more of the thought behind the question. Cal could see that Jonan was trying hard to tread cautiously, his words hampered by the uncharacteristic desire to think carefully before speaking.

"What about, for instance, encounters between dragons and royalty?"

Another rustle went around the circle, and a man on Jonan's other side muttered audibly, "We recognize no royalty but our own."

Cal couldn't help raising his eyebrows as he looked at the man, who was tilting his head toward the mountain chief. Cal noted again the wooden circlet that Darius wore.

If Darius heard the man, he made no sign of it. "Royalty?" he repeated. He gave Jonan a level look. "Are you an envoy of King Filip?"

Darius's tone was mild, but at his words a hiss rose from the group, and Cal saw many pairs of narrowed eyes. And the mountain people were not alone. Cal and his companions also recoiled at the suggestion.

"I am no servant of Filip," said Jonan darkly. Cal had expected there to be surprise and maybe fear at Jonan's omission of the title, but on the contrary, the mood around the circle instantly lightened once again. Cal felt his own spirits lift with it. Whatever shadow the rest of the country was living under, these Kyonans were apparently not afraid of their false king.

"Then why do you ask such a question?" Darius probed.

Again Jonan hesitated before answering, and Cal saw him rubbing his chest distractedly, as though the heavy ring lying on its chain under his tunic sat uncomfortably.

"There is a royal bloodline truer than Filip's," said Jo at last. "We have heard whispers that this bloodline once had a friendship with the dragons. We would wish to see Kyona restored, and we believe that the dragons can help."

Again the reaction of the group was not what Calinnae had expected. Everywhere he saw people smiling humorously at each other, a few even chuckling lightly. Darius's expression remained grave, but his voice sounded indulgent as he answered.

"Dragons do not exist to help humans, young traveler." His

eyes lingered on Jonan's face. "Even royal ones. I would not wish you to set any hopes on their assistance."

"My hopes are my own gamble," said Jonan steadily. "All I ask of you is that you share any stories you may know."

Darius regarded him silently for so long that Cal thought he would refuse. But at last he spoke. "Very well. There are tales of another line beyond Dernoth's who had dealings with the dragons."

All around them, people settled back in their seats, ready for another story. Cal glanced down in surprise as Elnora leaned slightly against him. Her eyes were fixed intently upon Darius, and it was hard to tell if she was even aware of her gesture.

"One of the tales the dragon told Dernoth," Darius began, "concerned a friendship that had begun generations before between the dragons and the royal line of men. It was before the time of Dernoth's dragon that the friendship began, but it was continuing even when Dernoth lived, unknown to the rest of men. It began, the dragon said, at a time when Kyona knew great prosperity. The royal line was young, only a few generations old. But the king was wise, and had the love of his people.

"So worthy of admiration was the king, that the dragon-ruler, Qadir, sought him out."

Cal felt Jonan go still at the mention of the name they had heard before. He had to admit that even he was impressed that such a detail was consistent between the ancient account they had read in King Cael's records and the oral legends of the mountain people.

"I do not mean that the dragon-ruler went to the king in person," Darius was continuing. "The king lived in Kynton, and the dragons did not leave the mountains, even then. But Qadir visited the king in his dreams, and by his magic, he compelled him to come. The king could find no rest until he followed his yearning to visit the mountain. And here he met Qadir.

"The king came often for some years. It is said that the friendship that grew between Qadir and the king was such that the dragon-ruler even allowed the man to enter Vasilisa."

An awed murmur sounded on either side of the three travelers. Elnora looked around in confusion. "Vasilisa?" she whispered to Cal, but he just shrugged his shoulders. The name meant nothing to him either. He turned his attention back to Darius, who was still speaking.

"After a time the visits stopped, but it was not because the friendship had been severed. Dernoth's dragon told him that the king of men no longer needed to come to Qadir for wisdom, because the dragon-ruler had imparted wisdom to the king, such that he could find it wherever he needed it, not just in the mountains."

Cal's eyes met Jo's. That sounded a lot like the Esvalere, which King Cael claimed had been entrusted to his ancestor by the dragon-ruler.

"Dernoth was told by his dragon that although no descendant of the king of men had actually come to the mountains, as far as the dragons were concerned, the friendship continued strongly to that time."

Darius paused for a moment. "Just as the friendship between Dernoth and the dragons continues." He looked around the circle. "The tale of the kings of men and the dragons is our story."

"May our stories never be forgotten." The chant caught Cal less off guard this time.

It seemed that story time was over, as a few people started to drift away from the fire toward their dwellings. Many stayed behind, enjoying the warmth and engaging in quiet conversations with their neighbors, but it did not appear that Darius had any more official stories to share. Cal hoped Jo wasn't too disappointed. They hadn't heard anything of particular use as far as he could see.

Darius didn't sit back down, and Cal assumed he was going to return to his own home. He was therefore surprised when the chief drifted across the circle of firelight and joined a group of people sitting just to Jonan's right. Cal noted that one of the men was the one who had disclaimed allegiance to Kyona's royalty. The men moved along to make room for Darius, but there was no other acknowledgment of his arrival. It seemed that these people did not stand on ceremony with their chief.

Darius listened in silence for a moment to the conversation happening around him. When there was a lull, however, he spoke, addressing himself to the three companions still sitting silently on their boulder.

"Did you enjoy hearing our tales?" The attention of everyone in the small group turned to the three of them.

"Oh yes," said Elnora quickly. "I've never heard anything like it."

Darius smiled at her. "Some people present here would have been listening for the first time too. The story of our ancestor entering the mountains is familiar to us all, but the other story you requested is not one we often tell."

He looked thoughtfully at Jonan. "You may think our expression is mere form, but that story truly is part of our story as well, even though the king of men is not our ancestor as Dernoth is. The connection between the royals and the dragons forges a delicate but enduring connection between us and the royals as well."

"Yes," said Jonan, sounding eager. "I can see how that would be the case." Cal could tell he was hoping that he was about to get the answers he was convinced Darius held.

"That connection continued well after Dernoth's time,"

Darius was saying. "Those of the royal bloodline did sometimes come to the mountains. They could not sense the magic like Dernoth and his descendants could. But they knew of the dragons, and they took this place seriously." His expression soured briefly. "Not like the line that now sits on the throne."

Glancing around the group, Cal saw that the expressions of the others had also darkened. Clearly the crown had managed to offend this unpredictable people.

"Our stories say," Darius continued, "that one of the kings of men even lived in Montego for a time. That was generations after Dernoth had gone to his ancestors. This king loved the mountain people so much that he married the daughter of the chief at the time."

Cal started in spite of himself. Surely this man was speaking of King Cael and Queen Jacqueline.

"The crown and the mountains had never been joined in such a way before," said Darius. "But it did not last long."

"What do you mean?" Cal asked quickly.

"The king swore that his bride would be accepted by the rest of the country, and for a time she was. But in less than a generation, the prejudices and superstitions against the mountain brought an end to the union between us and Kynton. And brought ruin on the king also."

Cal supposed that it should be no surprise that the mountain people's chief interest was in the impact of events on their own circumstances, but it was strange to hear the ruin of King Cael's line added as an afterthought.

"What happened?" asked Elnora, her voice small. Cal looked away, suspecting that he did not need Darius's storytelling to know the answer to her question.

"We were not there," said Darius simply, and it struck Cal as he stared into the fire that Darius spoke of the mountain people as one entity, even though his tales spanned generations. "So we did not see. But a visitor came to Montego after the king had died. His queen, the mountain chief's daughter, had died a short time before. The king had been true to her, at least. He had grieved so over her death that he had no longer the strength to prevent his own ruin. It was their son who came to us, and told us some measure of what had happened."

Cal continued to watch the fire, his attention caught in its flickering light, his mind only half on Darius's words as the man began again to speak the legends of his people.

Jonathon looked up into the face of the mountain chief. Despite his advanced years, the man seemed as solid and as intimidating as the mountain itself had looked when he saw it from the plains below.

"Welcome, traveler, to Montego."

"Thank you Grandfather," said Jonathon, surprised at the stinging in his eyes. It had been months since he had fled Kynton, and the word "welcome" was not one he had heard during that time.

"You have done well to make it here," said the chief. "The snow has continued late this year."

Jonathon nodded. "It was not easy," he acknowledged, as he was led to the roaring fire that had been lit in the central space. He remembered happy evenings spent around that communal fire on the few occasions when his mother had brought him and his sisters to Montego. He again fought the tears that threatened to fall. "But I felt I owed it to you to come. I must add to your stories, though I take no pleasure from the tale I must tell."

"May our stories never be forgotten," said the chief quietly, in unison with those around him. Jonathon closed his eyes for a moment. If only he could forget.

Looking around the village, Jonathon sighed. "It feels like such a short time ago that my father and my sisters and I came here for her ceremony of farewell. Never did I dream that I would lose my father also, so soon after."

"Your mother's death was a blessing," said the chief gruffly. "To lose my daughter was pain I hoped never to know. But to watch as she saw her husband murdered and her son exiled would have been worse."

For a moment Jonathon was silent. He could never see his gentle mother's death as a blessing, but he did not take offense. He knew that it was not the way of the mountain people to express their emotions freely.

"It seems you know much of what I came to tell you," he said.

The old man regarded him steadily. "All of Kyona knows of your father's death, Jonathon," he said. "The country mourns."

"Not all of it," Jonathon said through clenched teeth. His grandfather disregarded his words.

"We are relieved to see you alive. We knew of the king's death, but we had heard nothing of your fate. Are your sisters safe?"

Jonathon knew his pain was clear on his face, but he could not hold it in. For a moment he shook his head wordlessly, trying to swallow the lump in his throat.

"Sarai is safe in Valoria with her husband," he said. "The usurper will not risk war with Valoria by seeking her out now that she is their princess also. Parmida..." he closed his eyes again, willing his voice to remain even. "Parmida was present when it happened," he whispered. "When I realized what was happening, and I rode after my father, to warn him, she insisted on following me. We were not there in time to save him. And she was struck down also, before my eyes."

How bitterly did he feel his failure. His mother, his father, his sister. So many dead because of his blindness. Never would he forgive himself.

The chief was silent for a moment, grief in his eyes. "And Avalyn?" he asked finally.

Jonathon took a deep breath, trying to pull himself together. "I cannot find her," he said in a voice that still trembled. "I have been searching, but I can find no word of her. Her betrothed also I hear nothing of. I can only imagine that they...I have no reason to hope they survived," he finished, his voice dull.

"I am sorry," said his grandfather after a long moment. "I will make inquiries of my own also. You know that you have sanctuary here, for as long as you wish."

Jonathon was shaking his head before the sentence was finished. "Thank you, but I cannot accept such an offer. I have no desire to bring danger on you all. You are my mother's people, and this is too obvious a place for me to hide."

"So you intend to hide?" Jonathon turned his face away from the disapproval in the elderly man's voice.

"What can I do?" he asked. "Do you have an army to offer me?"

"You have an army," said the chief sharply. "Your father's army is yours to command now."

"They are not loyal!" Jonathon bit back any further retorts. He was too weary to argue. "Well, not all of them. I was too blind to see what was under my nose—how can I expect to know who among them is true and who is not? And I am not fit to be king."

The chief only watched him in silence for a long moment. "How did this come to pass, Jonathan?"

"I hardly know," the young man answered. "I had no inkling of the darkness brewing within my own circle." He looked around the town again, the surroundings turning his thoughts inevitably back to his mother. "She would have seen it," he said softly. "She would have known. But of course, that's why they waited until she was gone."

"Did no one resist when your father was attacked?" pressed his grandfather.

"No one saw! They lured him out of Kynton with their lies, then they made it seem as though he was fleeing, the dogs." Jonathon spat on the ground.

"Fleeing? Fleeing what?"

"The usurper challenged him," said Jonathon angrily. "He accused him in front of the court. There were many there who should have spoken up against such conduct, but the traitors had done their work well. Just enough doubt had been sown to make everyone question their loyalties. I could see the uncertainty in their eyes. Their own king! He had always been nothing but good to his people." Jonathon covered his face with his hand.

"But what was he accused of? Your father was the most beloved king this country has seen in generations," said the mountain chief incredulously. "How could his people be turned on him so quickly?"

Jonathon took a deep breath. This was the part of the tale he had dreaded sharing. But it must be told. He knew how passionately the mountain people felt about their stories. They had the right to a full account.

"It began after Mother died," he said, his voice quiet. "The kingdom grieved at first, but somehow the grief turned into whispers. My father was not himself. He walked around the castle like a ghost for so long, people began to comment. They said his sorrow was more than was natural. Foolishness and superstition of course...how could he not grieve her loss, after the love they shared?"

For a moment Jonathon fought again to overcome his emotion. But he must continue.

"Old superstitions arose, about the mountains." He hesitated, looking at his grandfather's face. The man's normally passive countenance had begun to darken. "They said she had put a curse on him. So that he would not be able to rule effectively without her."

"And neither you nor your father took any action in response to this slander?" The chief's voice betrayed uncharacteristic anger.

"I heard nothing of these whispers until much later," said Jonathon quickly. "And you can imagine that everyone took care not to make any such comments in my father's hearing. Once he would have been much more aware of what was going on around him, but after he lost her...well, he wasn't the same.

"The whispers grew," Jonathon continued bitterly. "For so long I couldn't understand where they originated. It seemed so strange. I had heard no talk of these superstitions in all my years. I thought they had long been put to rest. But memory runs deep, it would seem.

"It was months before my father heard of any of this. His fury when he discovered that Mother's memory was being dishonored was terrifying, but I was almost glad. He had life in him again, for a moment. But then he discovered what they were saying about Thalia."

"Thalia?" his grandfather cut in sharply. "What does she have to do with this?"

"Nothing," said Jonathon, his voice choked from holding back tears. "And everything. Someone had spread a tale about her death. They claimed..." he chanced a glance at the old man, and it took all his courage to continue. "They claimed that Lord Lindor had been wrongly accused. That the collapse was not a murder attempt, but was caused by magic. Magic gone wrong." He paused. "Mountain magic—my mother's magic. And that's why she was never the same afterward."

"So," his grandfather's voice was deceptively calm, "they said that Jacqueline caused her own daughter's death?"

Jonathon nodded. "And that Father had blamed Lord Lindor—had him executed even—in an attempt to shield the real culprit. The look on Father's face when he heard those words..." Jonathon ground his teeth. "It was a clever lie. My sisters couldn't understand why he didn't defend himself. Why he wouldn't refute the allegations." Jonathon's head felt heavy. "He never told them all he told me about Thalia's death."

"And the people were convinced? Enough to believe he was not fit to rule?" The mountain chief still sounded incredulous.

"I hardly know," said Jonathon. "I don't think most of them

believed that he was unfit to rule, but the seed was planted. More importantly than the people—I think it was planted in his own mind. It wasn't necessary to really convince the people, just to spread enough confusion to create an opening. To create enough uncertainty that when he was publicly challenged, no one would know what to do." Jonathon could hear the hollow note in his own voice. "Then they could lure him out and strike him down."

He gave a bitter laugh. "They intended for me to be killed too, of course. They intended to end my father's line. And the lies they spread about both my father and me were supposed to create just enough doubt to make people wonder if our deaths were for the best."

"Lies about you? What lies?"

Jonathon shrugged the question off like an irritating insect. He was beyond caring about his own reputation. "Allegations that I had been unfaithful in my role as Border Protector. That I had turned a blind eye to the gathering aggression of Valoria, and that an attack was imminent. It was even hinted that the Valorian king knew of my parents' supposed crimes, and sought to punish the country. Just playing on people's fear that if our neighbor were to turn on us, Valoria could annihilate Kyona. But relations with Valoria have been good since Sarai's marriage. My father knew that, and I knew that."

Jonathon closed his eyes, the pain on his face making him look much older than his years. "He should have come to me," he whispered. "He should never have ridden out alone. I could have told him what he needed to know. Why he thought he had to see for himself that there was no invading army, I will never understand." His voice dropped even more, as he spoke to himself more than to his companion. "Perhaps that was what he meant by his apology."

"Apology?"

Jonathon started, almost having forgotten his grandfather's presence.

"Yes," he said quietly. "Parmida and I caught up to them in the Forest of Rune. We did not see the attack, but I saw them both on the ground. Father bleeding from his wounds, and the usurper," Jonathon spat again, "unconscious beside him. I thought he was dead, or I would have run him through myself." Jonathon's teeth were gritted, and he balled his fists again at the reminder that he had let his father's murderer escape.

"By the look of that coward's face and hands, Father gave a good account of himself before he was wounded." Jonathon took some tiny satisfaction from knowing that the scum would surely wear the scars on his face for the rest of his life. A constant reminder of the king he had killed.

For another long moment Jonathon was silent, then he continued. His grandfather had stopped asking him for details, but now that he had begun, he was somehow unable to stop until it was all out. "It was almost over when I arrived, but he knew my face. He said he was sorry, but I don't know what for. He never had the chance to explain."

Jonathon bowed his head. "He died right before me, and in my anguish, I didn't see the renegades coming. They killed Parmida before I could even draw my sword. But I did draw it." His voice was grim. "And many of them joined their ancestors also that day. But there were too many. At first I was so angry, I didn't care. I was ready to die beside my father and my sister. But when I saw that the traitor was not dead, that he had escaped..."

Jonathon trailed off, unable to fully explain even now what his thinking had been. "Well, I understood then the extent of the betrayal. I realized that he wished to rule in my father's stead. Suddenly I couldn't fight any more. I knew that if I died, my father's line would end, and so would Kyona's hope. I cannot explain it. But I knew I had to flee."

The mountain chief was silent, and Jonathon turned his face away. He knew what was coming next, and he couldn't bear to hear it.

"I know..." he began tentatively. "I know you will say that I *should not have run, that I should not hide. But I must—I don't know how to explain—"*

"It is not for me to say what you should and should not do," his grandfather cut him off. "You are my daughter's son, and you will always be welcome here as family. But the fortunes of the royal line are no concern of the mountain people. You must do as you see fit."

Jonathon stared at the elderly man with wide eyes. He had dreaded the expected recriminations, but this disinterest was even worse. After a moment, he turned his back altogether, unwilling for the other man to see the emotion on his face.

"Thank you for your welcome. I will be glad to accept your hospitality tonight. But tomorrow I must leave."

He would stay no longer in this place than he had to. Somehow here in the mountains his shame felt stronger than anywhere else.

"Where will you go?" asked his grandfather.

Jonathon shrugged. "Wherever I can find a safe road. I think I will head for the coast."

"Will you leave Kyona then?"

Jonathon's eyes stung as his answer rose to his lips with unnecessary passion. "Never."

Cal's awareness returned at the light touch of a hand on his arm.

"Cal?"

He started, and looked down to see Elnora watching him tentatively. He blinked as his eyes swept the circle. Most of the people had disappeared into the shadows, presumably headed for their beds. Cal had been staring into the fire for so long that his eyes struggled to adjust to the darkness. For a moment he felt a prickle of alarm, unable to find Jonan. But he spotted him just outside the ring of light, conversing quietly with Darius.

When had the mountain chief stopped speaking? Cal remembered being engrossed in his summary of what Cal knew to be Prince Jonathon's visit to Montego, but at some point he had ceased to hear Darius's words.

"Are you all right?" Elnora asked him softly.

Cal tried to shake off his stupor. "I think so," he said, his voice also quiet. He glanced at her, wondering how much to share. He didn't want her to think he was losing his reason, but in the flickering light of the fire, with the eerie quality of the mountain thick around him, nothing seemed too strange to say.

"I could see it," he finally ventured.

She looked uncertain. "See what?"

"The story. In the fire. I was watching the flames, and as Darius was talking, I could see it all happening. I could see Prince Jonathon speaking to his grandfather. I could even see his memories of what had happened in Kynton."

Cal shivered. It had been terrifying enough, seeing the sudden formation of shapes in the flames, without even counting the distressing nature of the events unfolding in front of him. But it had also been mesmerizing. He had always imagined the stories playing before his eyes with vivid detail, but this was different. This hadn't come from his own head, he was sure of it.

"I—I don't understand," said Elnora. She was looking at him with more uncertainty than ever, but to his relief she didn't draw away from him. If anything, she clung more tightly to his arm. Her touch was reassuring, but it wasn't enough to drive away the dreamlike feeling that still lingered on the edge of Calinnae's consciousness.

"Neither do I," he said simply.

He was spared extra attempts at explanation by Jonan's approach.

"Darius has agreed to help us," he said when he reached them.

Cal looked up blankly. "Help us with what?"

"With our journey. In the morning he'll provide us with supplies, and he'll point us in the right direction."

"The right direction? What direction is that?"

Jonan made an impatient noise. "We're here to try to find the dragons Cal, remember?"

Cal stared at his friend in astonishment. "You want to wander over the mountains looking for dragons? What kind of a plan is that?" He saw that his agitated tone had attracted the attention of the men still sitting on the boulder nearby, and he lowered his voice. "We'll be lucky to make it out alive if we leave the path."

Jonan made a frustrated noise. "Are we going to have this argument again? I thought you knew we came to the mountains looking for dragons."

"Looking for information about dragons! And we found it. You heard what Darius said. Even those who believe in the dragons say that no one has seen them for generations!"

"And I heard what else he said," Jonan retorted stubbornly. He glanced around quickly, then lowered his voice. "The dragons consider their friendship with the royal line ongoing. Maybe none of the mountain people have seen dragons in a long time, but we have something they don't."

"Jo, this is crazy—" Cal began, but his protests were cut off by one of the men sitting nearby. Calinnae recognized him as the one who had spoken up earlier.

"If I were you, I'd leave well enough alone." His voice was gruff. "That young king will get what's coming, and good riddance to him."

"What do you mean?" asked Cal warily.

"Filip," the man said the name like an insult. "If he survives the invasion, it'll be more than I would bargain for."

"What invasion?" Jonan's voice was sharp.

The man and his companions stared for a moment, their eyebrows raised. "Is that not why you're here?" one of them asked finally. "I thought you knew. It seems word of Kyona's decay has spread beyond the border. As have the rumors of the illegitimacy of Filip's line. The Valorians do not wish to see the chaos spread into their lands."

"So they're going to what, annex Kyona?" Cal could hear the note of panic in his voice.

The man just shrugged. "That's what I hear. Rumor is that the king of Valoria believes that if control is taken away from the Kyonan royals, the kingdom will fare better, and so will its neighbors."

One of the other men grunted his assent. "Daresay he's right," he said placidly.

Cal's shock began to build toward anger as he took in the casual nods of the other men in the group.

"But...how can you not care that our country is about to be invaded?"

The main speaker shrugged again. "Rulers come and go, lad. What business is it of ours?" He snorted. "When the prince puts his father in the ground because he can't wait his turn to rule, it's about time for a change. Maybe the Valorians will do a better job."

"But you're Kyonan! This is your land!" Cal hadn't realized he was on his feet until he found himself looking down at the villagers.

They looked up at him mildly. "We're mountain people—the mountains are our land," one of them answered. "What difference does it make to us whether outsiders consider our mountains to be part of Kyona or Valoria?"

"But…" Elnora said slowly. "What if the Valorians overrun the mountains? What if they try to drive you out, or levy taxes, or place controls on what you do?"

The men smiled grimly. "They can try," said the first speaker. "These lands are protected. We have lived here unhindered for many generations, and we will remain for many generations more."

"Protected?" said Cal. The anger in his voice surprised even him. "By what? Some kind of dragon magic?" He made an impatient noise. "Are you truly content to sit back and wait for things to fall apart, instead of doing something about it?"

Cal saw Jo giving him a strange look, but he ignored it. He was breathing hard, but it was difficult to maintain any passion in the face of the men's calm unconcern.

"You seem very convinced that you know what is and isn't true, young man," said one of the men in front of him. "But it is possible that you still have much to learn."

Without a word, Cal turned on his heel and strode toward the hut where he and Jo were being accommodated. He heard Elnora call him, but he powered on, too angry and unsettled to talk.

Jonan entered the dwelling just behind him. Their host was nowhere to be seen. Jo looked like he was going to ask Cal if he was all right, but one look at Cal's face seemed to change his mind. They had settled onto their pallets before he spoke.

"We're going to fix this, Cal. We're going to make things right."

Cal didn't answer. He had no desire to fight with his friend, and he couldn't see any other possible outcome of discussing Jo's maddening belief that finding dragons in the mountains was the solution to Kyona's problems.

After a few moments of silence, Jo spoke again, sleep starting to creep into his voice. "I was quite proud of you back there, Cal.

I think you stole my line. I've never seen you so unimpressed by the idea of watching and waiting."

Cal just turned onto his side, his back to Jonan. He was still too angry to want conversation. At least he and his friend were finally in agreement about one thing, though.

The time for waiting was over. It was time to act.

CHAPTER TWENTY-TWO

A number of the villagers gathered to farewell their guests the next morning, including Lilac and her friends, who waved merrily to Elnora in particular. Most of the residents had not witnessed the altercation that occurred after the storytelling time, and consequently the general mood was light. However, Cal couldn't quite shake his own sour mood.

He had even been curt with Elnora when she greeted him in the morning. He instantly regretted it when he saw the wistful expression on her face as she glanced around the central space. She would clearly love to stay longer in Montego. But he knew her better now than to suggest she stay behind in safety. He didn't want to offend her.

He summoned his civility enough to thank Darius for the supplies they had been given. He supposed the mountain chief couldn't be blamed for Jonan's mad determination. Still, he could have been a bit more discouraging.

"Legend says that Vasilisa is found north of here," the chief said when they took their leave.

"Vasilisa?" Elnora was once again the one to ask.

"Yes, Vasilisa. Some call it Dragon Nest, rumored to be the heart of the Dragon Realm." Darius looked them all over carefully. "I have no confidence that you will find what you are looking for," he said. "But it is not for me to stop you from making the attempt. You will be welcome back here should you choose to return to Montego."

Of course, that assumed they not only survived, but managed to find their way back, Cal thought blackly.

Jonan thanked Darius again, and the three of them turned to leave. Before they had taken a step, however, Darius reached out a hand and grabbed Calinnae's arm.

"Be on your guard," he said solemnly, "that you don't find what you are seeking only to lose something else. All of you." His eyes swept over the three of them, but came to rest on Cal's face, which was still set in grim lines. "You will be tested." His grip on Cal's arm tightened. "The mountains will test you."

Cal couldn't think of a response. It was all he could do to resist shaking the man's hand off like a petulant child. Fortunately, Darius held his gaze for only a moment longer before releasing him and stepping back.

The three travelers walked the length of the village before exiting at its northern end through an opening in the rocks leading to a small track. This was clearly no thoroughfare. Cal again felt thankful that it was not winter.

As it was, they were soon out of breath as the track wound up and down between steep crags. None of them seemed inclined to initiate conversation, and for some time they trekked in silence. The morning was fine, and there was a rugged beauty to their surroundings that Cal would have enjoyed had his mood not been so foul.

In many places, the narrowness of the track required them to walk single file. Jonan of course took the lead, and Cal insisted on bringing up the rear, so that Elnora could walk between them.

She gave him a long-suffering look, clearly intended to remind him that she didn't need looking after. He felt a bit guilty about the assumed chivalry. The truth was that he was still irritated with his friend and didn't want to stare at Jonan's back for hours on end.

As the fresh mountain air filled his lungs, however, his head began to clear a little. Their breaths might get shallower the higher they climbed, but the altitude came with its own reward. More frequently as the day progressed, he found that every glance back or to the side revealed incredible vistas. Once or twice he thought he caught the sparkle of sunlight on water in the distance on their right, and wondered if he could be glimpsing the Great River, which marked Kyona's eastern border with Valoria.

When they had been walking for a few hours, and Cal realized that his companions were still shooting wary glances at him, he felt ashamed of his grouchiness. He shook the stiffness out of his shoulders and made a point of smiling the next time Elnora looked back at him. Her answering smile held relief. A short time later, they found themselves walking across a grassy plateau, able to travel side by side for the first time in quite a while.

Elnora sidled up to him, her gaze sympathetic. "Are you all right, Cal?" she asked.

He let out a long breath. "Yeah, I'm fine. Sorry about earlier. I don't know what got into me."

"Me neither," said Jo, his usual impudence apparently restored by Cal's lift in mood. "You were a bear this morning."

Cal glared at him, expanding the gesture to include Elnora when she giggled in response to Jo's words.

"Now, that look he does all the time," Jo informed Elnora

wisely. "That's normal. But not the other stuff. Cal never stays in a bad mood this long. He's too even-tempered."

"Unlike some people," Cal muttered.

Jonan just grinned.

"But seriously," Cal said, not quite able to match the lightness in Jo's tone. "You heard what those men said last night. Surely I'm not the only one who's upset to discover our country is on the brink of war? We knew Filip was bringing Kyona to her knees, but now we're being attacked from the outside too?"

"We don't know that," said Jonan quickly.

"He's right, Cal," said Elnora, putting a hand on his arm. His muscles seemed to jump in response to her touch. "The mountain men said that they'd heard rumors, but it may just be talk. It would be a big thing for Valoria to actually invade. We shouldn't assume the worst."

Cal rolled his eyes. He couldn't help himself. "So you don't think the threat of an invading army is credible, but you both believe the legends about dragons without question."

Elnora smiled. "Don't look at me," she said, raising her arms. "I'm just along for the journey."

They both turned to look at Jo, and he put his hands out, laughing. "Hey, if one of you has a better idea..."

Cal stared unhappily at his friend. If only he could think of a more realistic way to overthrow Filip, he would be pushing harder against Jo's foolish plan. He was starting to reach his limit with simply following.

Jo took in Cal's change in expression, and his own eyes grew earnest. "This is going to work, Cal. I really think it is. Even King Cael wrote that there was a magic about this place, you told me yourself."

"He didn't call it magic," said Cal quickly, but Jo bent a stern look in his direction.

"Don't quibble, Cal. There's something here that's different from the rest of the country, and you know it."

For a moment Cal just frowned. He wanted to protest, but he couldn't deny the truth of Jonan's words. He thought about his strange visions the night before, and the tingling sensation in his spine that was growing stronger the further they traveled from Montego.

"There is something strange about this place," he said slowly. "I don't know how to define it."

"It's beautiful, for one thing," chipped in Elnora cheerfully.

"Yes, it is," said Cal abstractly, his gaze lingering on her face for a moment. "But it's more than that." He shook his head. "It's like the mountains are alive or something. Honestly, the whole thing makes me uneasy."

Jo leaned in closer to his companions, his eyes glinting. "Is that because—" his voice dropped to an eerie whisper, "—'the mountains will test you'?"

Elnora giggled again, and even Cal had to smile at Jonan's expression.

"Quit horsing around," he said without heat. "Do you want the dragons to overhear you?"

THREE DAYS LATER, Cal's desire to smile was long gone. Even the beauty of the mountains was beginning to pall on him. Rocks, rocks, and more rocks. Endlessly climbing one peak, only to descend the other side, only to have to climb upward once again —it was as maddening as it was exhausting. At first his lungs had blessed the downhill periods, but thanks to his complaining joints, he soon dreaded the descents even more than the climbs, and he constantly ached in muscles he hadn't previously known he had. The air was cold up near the peaks, even in summer, and his lungs often burned as he tried to take in enough breath to sustain his body throughout this interminable trek.

The sword banged against his leg as he walked, its extra weight an unwelcome burden. Half a day after leaving Montego Elnora had admitted, after persistent pressing by Cal, that its weight was slowing her down. So the three of them had taken to sharing the job of carrying it. If Elnora noticed that Cal always relieved her after a very short turn, she didn't comment on it, suggesting to him that she was struggling with the burden more than she had let on. He wished she would learn to ask for help.

The only positive to come out of it was that Elnora had agreed to teach them what she knew of swordplay during their breaks from the endless walking. It didn't take long, as she was far from skilled, but even those basics were an improvement for Cal and Jo. It seemed like a fairly large oversight on Elam's part that he never taught Jo at least how to wield a sword. But then that was only one of many oversights, Cal thought with a bitterness that once he could never have imagined feeling toward the gentle man.

Perhaps because of the physically demanding nature of the travel, tensions had steadily continued to rise. Jonan's joking mood the day they left Montego seemed like a lifetime ago—even their irrepressible leader had become almost taciturn. He tugged constantly at the chain around his neck, as if it was unbearably restricting, and the gesture never failed to fill Cal with an unreasonable irritation. In fact, Cal was in general more sullen than ever, and even Elnora was not her usual cheerful self.

Although he genuinely thought they were in danger of becoming lost in the mountains and eventually perishing from starvation or exposure, Cal was relieved to find that the strange fear that had crippled him earlier in their adventure had not reappeared. That relief was tempered, however, by his dismay at the other emotions that seemed to be constantly just below the surface now.

His resentment of Jo's leadership, that he had mostly been able to suppress at its first appearance, had steadily grown within him over the last few days. It was like a bubble expanding in his chest, now a permanent discomfort, waiting to be popped. He hated to admit it, but he had never felt more frustrated with his friend, or more envious of what Jonan had inherited.

The thoughts that swirled around his head scared him at times. The higher they climbed, the further his mind seemed to descend. It was all he could do to keep from snapping at his companions, and sometimes even that was beyond his reach.

"Stop shoving me, Jo," he said tersely, on the afternoon of the third day since they had left Montego. "I'm going as quickly as I can."

"It's steep here," Jo retorted. "You have to move further ahead, or Elnora and I won't have anywhere flat to put our feet."

"Well, I'll move as soon as I can move!"

"If you can't go more quickly, don't go in front."

"Of course," muttered Cal, "you can't stand the idea of anyone else taking the lead, can you?"

"What was that?" Jo's voice clearly showed that he had heard every word.

"Enough," snapped Elnora. "While you two are bickering, I'm still hanging off the slope behind you. Argue once we're on level ground." Her voice dropped to a mutter as well. "And don't complain about climbing until you've had to do it in a dress."

Cal almost smiled, but the impulse was brief.

He reached the top of the particularly difficult patch, and pulled himself up to find himself on top of a stony shelf. The path had been steadily dwindling, and these sections where they had to climb rather than walk were becoming more frequent. Not for the first time, the continuation of the path was not obvious. Cal groaned. He hated the tension of searching for the start of the path, and the anxiety of starting off along it again, never feeling sure that they had found the right way.

"Great, the path ends again."

"I'm sure it doesn't end," said Jonan shortly, pulling himself up behind Cal. "We just have to find where it keeps going."

"And then what?" asked Cal irritably. "It's not leading anywhere. What do you hope to find at the end of it? It's going to lead us off a cliff, or to a dead end."

"That's not what Darius said."

"Darius said he had no confidence that we would find anything!"

"He had to say that." Jo's voice was dismissive. "He couldn't give us a guarantee. But he believes in the dragons. You know he does!"

"Mountain superstition," said Cal. "This is a wild goose chase, Jo! We've been walking for days, and we have no more idea of where we are or where we're going than we did at the start."

"Well, feel free to turn back!" Jo's voice was rising to match Cal's. "No one's hunting you, you can go home. But I'm going on, and I'm going to find Vasilisa!"

Cal was dimly aware of Elnora pulling herself up onto the shelf, but he kept his eyes on Jo. "Oh really?" His voice was cool. "And how do I get home? And what will be waiting for me there? Soldiers occupying our homes—my mistake, *your* home, since mine was burned down with both of our mothers inside! I'm sure the soldiers would ask very nicely when trying to find out from me where you are."

Jonan winced, and Cal almost regretted his harsh words, but he was too angry to think before speaking.

"You think everything you do must be right, because you're the one with the royal bloodline, but if you hadn't made such a spectacle of yourself in Pravat, we could still be traveling unnoticed—"

"I don't think anything of the kind," said Jonan, clearly stung. "And I never told anyone they had to follow me. You're the one who worships the Bloodline, I don't think I'm better than anyone just because—"

"That's half the problem, you don't even value it! And stop tugging at that thing like it's strangling you!"

Jo glared at him, but dropped his hand from the chain. "I didn't say I don't value it," he snapped, "I just—"

"Over here!" Elnora's voice cut across their argument. Turning toward her, they saw that she had approached another rocky slope rising from the far side of the shelf. "I think I've found where the path continues."

"Just wait a minute, Elnora," said Cal, his unfinished fight with Jonan making his words come out more sharply than he intended.

"Actually, I don't particularly want to stand around waiting all day while you two squabble like small children," she said crisply. Both boys glared at her, but she just raised her eyebrows.

"Just give us a minute," Cal said. "You shouldn't be clambering up that cliff alone with no one to help."

Her eyes flashed. "How about you stop telling me what to do?" she said. "How many times do I need to tell you that I don't need you or anyone to look after me? I'm just as capable as either of you!"

"That's not what I meant, and you know it," said Cal, closing his eyes for a moment in frustration. When had everyone become so unreasonable? "I just meant that slope looks even more difficult than the one we just climbed. None of us should be rushing up it, it's a long fall if you slip. We just need to assess it to find the best way up before we—"

"This is exactly what I'm talking about," interrupted Jonan

triumphantly. "You complain about me taking the lead, but you're the one who's always telling everyone what to do, not me!"

"I am not! I'm just trying to help us avoid disaster, which is what would happen if we always blindly followed your insane instincts."

"Is that any way to talk to royalty?" said Jo mockingly, and Cal ground his teeth. The urge to hit Jonan rose up in him. They had sparred plenty, but never had Cal genuinely desired to hurt his friend, as he did now. Before he knew what he was doing, he had reached out his hands and shoved Jonan, hard.

The look on Jonan's face was as ugly as the thoughts jostling each other inside Cal's head. He had stumbled in surprise at Cal's push, but he quickly regained his balance, and lost no time in retaliating.

Cal grabbed the other boy's arm with unnecessary force.

"This isn't a joke, Jonan! This isn't some game where you try to outwit the other boys back in Nerita, or pull off some stupid prank without your mother finding out. People's lives are on the line, and not just the three of us!"

"Yes, I've heard quite enough about how many people are relying on me, thank you," said Jonan bitterly, shaking Cal off. "Is this what the rest of my life will be like? People criticizing and trying to control my every decision? You at the front of the line?"

"I wouldn't worry too much," Cal retorted. "At this rate your life won't extend much longer, so the great *inconvenience* of being the heir to the throne won't trouble you for long."

"Is that a threat?" Jo's voice rose dangerously.

"No, you idiot! You'll have no trouble getting yourself killed without any help from me! But if we're talking about a sound beating, it will do you good. And yes, I'll gladly be first in line!"

"As if you could!" mocked Jo, and Cal needed no further encouragement.

Forgetting the precarious height of the platform on which they stood, he lunged toward his friend. Jo's fists were instantly up, and he blocked Cal before he could get a good swing in. A second later, the breath was knocked from Cal's body as Jonan grabbed him around the waist, attempting to throw him to the rocky ground.

Cal swung his fist into Jo's side forcefully. Grunting in pain, Jo released his hold and stumbled back. For a moment Cal thought Jo meant to capitulate, but the honest truth was that he was glad when he saw the aggressive determination still alight in Jo's eyes. There was a release in physical expression of the anger and resentment that had been swirling inside him for so long. He wasn't ready to be done with the tussle himself.

He felt less glad a moment later, when he failed to block Jo's fist on its trajectory toward his head. Stars popped in front of his eyes, and he struck out blindly, not even sure what part of Jo's body he had just punched. For a moment the two boys scuffled wildly, heedless of their surroundings.

"Cal!"

Elnora's sharp cry ripped Calinnae's attention away. He instantly dropped his fists, and his heart seemed to fall into his stomach at the sight of Elnora clinging precariously to the rocks, high above them. She had climbed quickly, and was alarmingly far from the shelf on which they stood. At first he assumed that she had called out because she was stuck, and he had already taken a step in her direction before he realized that her eyes were fixed on something in the distance, to the east of them.

Before he could turn, however, he caught a flash of movement on the top of the slope Elnora had begun to ascend. He didn't get a good look, but something large had seemed to sweep across the top of the ridge. Elnora twisted quickly to look above.

Cal reached out a warning hand, as if he could bridge the distance, but it was too late. Her startled movement had dislodged her hold on the rock, as he had feared. Time seemed to slow, his shout mingling with her sudden scream, as she tumbled from the sky and fell as heavily as the stones that were coming down with her. She hit the rocky shelf with a horrifying thud and didn't rise, her body an unmoving heap at the base of the slope.

For a frozen heartbeat, no one moved. Then Jo and Cal both sprinted toward her still form. Cal was vaguely aware of Jo's shout, but his own terror seemed to have momentarily fused his tongue to the roof of his mouth.

He dropped to his knees beside her, his head swimming at the sight of the blood seeping from somewhere below her.

Not her head, not her head, he thought, even as his tongue became unstuck. "Elnora! Elnora!" he cried desperately.

There was no response.

Seizing her hands, he looked frantically for some sign of life. She couldn't be dead. Not just like that, in the blink of an eye. It couldn't be possible. After a moment of paralyzing fear he saw her chest rise slightly, and his blind panic subsided by an infinitesimal amount. She was breathing, but not deeply. But what did he do? He had no knowledge that could help him in such a situation.

He had warned her. He had told her not to climb up the cliff alone. Why hadn't she listened? Once again he had been given no control—once again his lack of authority had put them all in a bad situation. Needlessly, pointlessly running toward danger.

Anger at his own powerlessness rose within him, blending with his terror at the sight of Elnora's almost lifeless form, creating a strange and powerful sensation that tasted like fire in his mouth.

Through the haze forming in front of his eyes, he saw Jonan reaching a tentative hand toward Elnora.

"Don't touch her," he snapped, barely recognizing his own voice.

"I'm just trying to help!" said Jonan. His face was deathly pale. Cal had never seen his friend so shaken, but the sight did nothing to soften him. The rage growing inside him was taking control, twisting the face before him until he saw only an enemy.

"Well don't! I think you've done enough!"

"What's that supposed to mean?" Jonan's shock was giving way to his own anger now.

"This is all your fault! You have us wandering the mountains, chasing a wisp of smoke, all to satisfy your need for adventure!"

"My fault? You're the one who goaded her into climbing by telling her she had to wait for your help!"

"And was I wrong?"

"All I know is that someone who decided to wait for you would be waiting forever!" Jo's voice held a sneer that Cal had never heard there before.

"That's not fair!" Cal took a deep breath, trying to steady the storm raging inside him. How had they gotten here?

He and Jo had often argued, of course, but if someone had told him a month ago that he could feel this—almost hatred—for his best friend, he would never have believed it. He felt like a stranger in his own skin, hardly able to comprehend the terrible things he was thinking and saying. But then, at the same time, all of it was all too familiar, as if the worst parts of him had been gathered up and concentrated into one potent and destructive force.

"None of this is helping Elnora," he said, making an effort to pull himself together.

"You're not the only one who cares about Elnora," said Jo, clearly still angry.

Any attempt at reconciliation was instantly forgotten, as

something dark rose up inside Cal. "You have to have every-thing, don't you?" he said, his voice trembling. "The crown isn't enough—you have to take her, too."

"Listen to yourself," said Jonan in disbelief. "No one is taking anything."

"Really?" Cal shot back. "Then why is it that I've lost every-thing? You don't stop to think about the danger everyone around you is placed in because of the constant risks you take. My parents were murdered just for being friends with yours!" He saw Jo wince, but he couldn't seem to stop the words that were pouring out. "And you're doing everything you can to make sure I share the same fate!"

"I don't see anyone trying to murder you here!" growled Jo, gesturing around at the empty mountains. "And don't pretend that you care about Elnora. If it wasn't for me, you would've left her in Kerr. You don't really care about anyone, not her, not me."

"How dare you say that?!" raged Cal. "Everything I've done is to try to protect you, to try to keep you alive!"

"Yes, but not because of me! It's the Bloodline—that's all you care about!"

"And you don't care about it at all! You've been given the most precious gift, and you don't even want it!" Cal could feel his voice rising unnecessarily in volume, but he felt as though he had to shout just to hear himself over the pounding in his ears. The tingling sensation was growing stronger. No longer confined to his spine, it spread all over Cal's body, almost over-whelming his senses.

"Why don't you just say it, Cal!" Jo was shouting too, pain and rage and fear in his voice. "Go ahead, just say it!"

It should have been me!

The words smashed violently around inside Calinnae's head, dangerously close to breaking free. But he clamped his mouth shut, refusing even in his anger to utter them. He stared at his friend, noting with a hint of guilt that a bruise was already beginning to grow under one of his eyes. Jo was closer to him than a brother, and the look on his friend's face somehow broke through whatever darkness had been brooding over Cal's mind. Jo hadn't asked for any of this, and Cal suddenly remembered with blinding clarity who he did and didn't want to be. And his ancestry, or lack of it, had nothing to do with it.

The last true king had been brought down by a traitorous treasonous friend, and Cal was utterly unwilling to play that role in the story.

For a moment the two boys stared at each other, both breathing hard. Then Cal dropped his eyes. His rage had melted away as quickly as it had come. He no longer felt any hatred, or even anger, toward Jo. The face before him was once again that of his oldest, most trusted friend. Whatever inner monster he had just wrestled seemed to have conceded defeat. He felt unutterably weary, but at the same time strangely triumphant.

"You have my support Jo," he said. "Now and always. As the true king, without question. But even more so, as my friend." He looked Jo in the eye. "As my brother. I will always have your back."

"I'm glad I have your support," said Jonan quietly, also sounding weary. "Because I don't think I can do this without it."

"You don't have to." Once again Cal's gaze dropped down, his exhaustion tinged by fear as he took in Elnora's pale face. "And you're wrong," he added quietly. "I do care about Elnora. Very much—more than I know how to explain."

Jonan clasped his friend's shoulder bracingly. "I know," he said. "And I'm sorry. I shouldn't have said that, or what I said about waiting for you. You were right, it wasn't fair."

Cal shook his head. "It was fair. I've been waiting instead of doing all my life. But no more." He looked up. "You're a better man than I am, Jo. And a better man than your ancestors."

His eyes returned to the still unconscious Elnora, and he drew her head gently into his lap, disregarding the blood that stained his clothes. She wasn't bleeding freely, but something had clearly been injured when she fell. He smoothed a strand of hair off of her face, wishing desperately that his newfound determination to take action had given him the power to fix whatever it was. But he didn't know how.

"I'm just so afraid I won't be able to save her," he whispered. "What will I do if I lose her now?"

He looked up at Jo, willing his friend to have some answers, but something behind Jonan's head caught his attention. As his focus shifted to the distant view, he suddenly remembered that Elnora had been trying to tell them something before she fell.

He hadn't realized when he first pulled himself onto this shelf of rock, but they were on the tallest peak for a great distance around them. Between them and the eastern edge of the mountain range, the peaks dropped away gradually, revealing their first truly clear view of the Great River and the Valorian plains beyond.

For a moment, Cal remained frozen, his hold on Elnora tightening unconsciously as his eyes grew wide. If he had thought this moment couldn't get any worse, he had been terribly wrong.

Seeing his face, Jo turned his head quickly to see what Cal was looking at. For an endless second, the two of them stared wordlessly, too overcome by the enormity of what they saw to give it words.

"Not just rumors, after all." Cal's grim voice eventually broke the silence.

Jo didn't respond, his eyes as round as Cal's had been a moment before. Cal couldn't blame him. The sight of the army on the other side of the river was as impressive as it was terrifying. Row upon row upon row of soldiers must be gathered to create such an enormous shadow on the land. Cal almost thought he could see the glint of sunlight on steel, although he knew that in reality the spears were too far away for him to see any such thing.

Cal squeezed his eyes shut, holding Elnora closer as if for comfort. After everything they had done, after everything they had been through, it wasn't going to be enough to save Kyona. No matter the outcome of Jonan's claim, his beloved country would be overrun.

Darius's story about Jonathon's visit to Montego flashed through Cal's mind, and he had to bite back a bitter laugh. What irony. King Cael had been killed in an attempt to ascertain for himself the truth of the usurper's lies about an invading Valorian army. And Jonathon had regretted for the rest of his life that his father had not had enough faith in him to come to him instead, and accept his word that there was no truth to the claim.

Well, here was the army after all. They had just come generations late.

Cal's eyes remained closed, his hands cradling Elnora's head, when suddenly he felt the ground slipping away beneath him. Stifling a cry, he tried to open his eyes, but he could make no sense of what he was seeing. The mountains were melting away, trees springing up to take their place. The hard clear sunlight of the peak became dappled light as he rode frantically through the forest. He tried to remember how he had come to be on a horse, but his senses continued to swim as he was sucked further into whatever strange reality had claimed him...

KING CAEL THREW *everything into the ride, speeding through the trees with no company but the fury and terror that chased him.*

That they could make such accusations against Jacqueline still enraged him, but the anger was numbed by the memory of the scene he had endured that morning. A sliver of ice slid into his chest as he remembered his accuser's face, its shape all too familiar, as the young Lord Lindor accused his king of having his father put to death for a crime the nobleman had not committed. Cael's own regret condemned him.

Damian! *he cried in his heart.* Why did you put me in that position? Jacqueline! Why did you leave me far too soon? You would have seen this coming.

But he had seen none of it, too blinded by grief and regret, like an old fool instead of the strong king he was supposed to be. Jacqueline had even told him when Jon first brought Derek back not to let Derek too far into their circle. If only he had listened.

And if only Jacqueline were here now, to advise him. To tell him whether the doubt in his heart was the voice of justice, or just part of the lies of his enemies. Could it be true that he was not fit to be king? Could it be time for him to step aside and let Jonathon rule? Cael had become king too young. He had not wanted the same thing for Jonathon. But his heart swelled as he thought of his son. Jonathon was a better man than his father. His heart was as sound as his body was strong.

But at the same time he was afraid for Jon. Derek was as dangerous as his mother had been before him, and more so. Cael didn't know what the young man was planning, but he was sure it went beyond humiliating his father's old friend. The doubt Cael had seen in his people's eyes as Derek made his accusations in the throne room had shaken him to the core. What lies had Derek been spreading? What might be happening at the castle even now?

Cael had never felt so desperate for answers. And he didn't know where else to turn to find them. He felt the weight of the Esvalere in the bag slung over his back. Its physical weight was nothing to the consciousness of its presence. His whole body tingled so strongly that it made his senses swim.

It had felt almost like sacrilege, taking the sphere from its home in the secret chamber of the castle. But looking into it was no longer enough. He had hardly used it in recent years. He had doubted it, even blamed it—if it hadn't shown him what was coming before Thalia died, or given him any clue of how to pull Jacqueline from the malaise that had slowly eroded her will to live, what use was it to him? But perhaps if he had not been too proud to seek wisdom outside of himself, he would have seen Derek's plots before now. Maybe he was unfit to be king. Maybe the Esvalere would no longer even work for him.

But Qadir would know. Cael had never communicated with the dragon-ruler except through the sphere, but if he could reach Vasilisa, surely Qadir would receive him. Surely he would know what Cael should do.

But no one could accompany him on this ride. No escort, however loyal, could be allowed to see what Cael hoped to encounter. Even allowing another a glimpse of the Esvalere might be enough to bring the dragonwrath on him and his line. Cael shuddered at the thought.

Derek's preposterous falsehoods about the Valorian army had provided the excuse Cael needed to escape the castle. Of course there was no truth to it. Cael would never have allowed his daughter Sarai to marry the crown prince of Valoria if he had not been confident in the goodwill of the Valorian king. And Jonathon was a good Border Protector. He could never have missed such a thing. Cael could see that his guards thought it was madness for him to ride out alone to check the truth of the claim, but he was their king, after all. How were they to challenge him?

In his distraction, he failed to take note of the figure blocking the road in front of him until he was almost upon it. His horse reared in fright, and Cael was thrown from the saddle. Recovering himself, he turned toward the foolish pedestrian. His strictures on loitering in the middle of the road died on his lips when he saw who it was.

Derek.

He had been watching the king, then, since their standoff that morning. Cael cursed his own negligence. He had not intended anyone but his own guards to know that he had left the castle.

Derek drew his sword, the action slow and deliberate, his eyes never leaving Cael's.

"What is this foolishness, Derek?" said Cael in a hard voice. "I do not wish to hurt you. For your father's sake."

"Don't you dare mention his name in front of me," spat Derek. "Murderer."

"I am your king!" Cael's voice blazed with fury. "You will not speak so to me."

"Your time as king is over, old man," mocked Derek. "It is time for change."

"What do you hope to achieve, foolish child?" Cael almost felt pity for Derek, in his vain hopes. "Do you think because you have Jonathon's friendship, you will be able to direct his rule? He is no puppet. Having him as your king will not bring you more power than you have with me on the throne."

"Jonathon will never be king," said Derek with a sneer. "Your line will end with you."

Something in the calculating depths of Derek's eyes made Cael's blood run suddenly cold.

"What are you talking about?" he said. "Where is Jonathon?"

Derek shrugged. "I do not know where he is at this moment," he said. "But he is under watch at all times. He will join you soon enough."

"You seek the throne yourself," Cael whispered. "You think you can usurp his place."

"It is all but done." Derek gripped his sword meaningfully. "Only a few...practicalities remain."

"You fool," whispered Cael. "There is so much you do not know. You think that a man is made a king merely by seating himself on the throne, or placing a circlet on his head? My line has been entwined

with Kyona's lifeblood for countless generations. It will not be so easily dislodged."

"You won't be around to discover if that's true," said Derek without emotion. "I know what should have been mine from my childhood, and I will claim it."

"Your mother has filled your head with lies and fantasies, Derek," said Cael sharply. "The throne would never have been yours, and if you try to take it, you will bring great evil on yourself as well as on Kyona."

Derek didn't respond, merely crouching into a fighting stance.

"Enough, Derek," said Cael impatiently. "Do not make me fight you."

In a swift movement, Derek lunged forward. But Cael's movement was swifter. His sword had still been at his side, but it was in front of him in a moment, the clang of metal against metal thudding off the moss-covered trees surrounding them.

Derek took another swing, and Cael deflected it just as easily. He could see that the nobleman was well-trained, however. His heart sank before the determination in Derek's eyes. His hope for this to end without death began to fade.

"You are young," Cael said between parries. "You have your life ahead of you. Do not throw it away."

"Your words will not save you," panted Derek, as he lunged with furious force. "Nor will your honor. It is an insult to me that you refuse to fight back!"

Indeed Cael was unwilling to go on the offensive. Again and again Derek lunged, and each time Cael blocked and evaded, but made no move to riposte.

Derek pulled back, wiping the sweat from his brow with an impatient arm. The two men circled each other warily, the young aggressor looking for an opening.

"To the end he spoke of your honor," spat Derek. "It makes my blood boil to remember it. You, whom he had claimed as his closest

friend, were about to order his death, and still he would not say a word against you."

Derek raised his sword in a swift movement, and Cael faltered. In any other situation, he would never let an opponent rattle him with words. But this time was different, and Derek knew it. He took advantage of Cael's distraction and drove him back between the trees, continuing to press on the most painful of memories.

With more difficulty now, Cael resisted the attack, driven back against a large oak. Derek swung his sword downward. Dropping to one knee, Cael raised his sword to ward off the blow. The swords locked, and Cael rolled forward in a swift motion, disengaging and leaping to his feet once he was clear.

Derek snarled in frustration, but he made no immediate move to resume the fight, his chest heaving as he caught his breath. His eyes were on the point of Cael's sword, held out defensively in front of the king, who had retreated halfway across the clearing. Derek's own sword rested momentarily at his side as he continued his attack through other means.

"The night before you killed him, he told me to be loyal to the crown," he growled. "He told me to care for my mother. He told me he loved me."

Cael's throat was tight. "You dishonor his memory with your treason," he said, but his voice sounded hollow, his confidence wavering.

"Do not speak to me of his memory!" said Derek, his face looking almost insane as he raised his sword once again and lunged wildly. His breath was coming in pants, but he had clearly waited years to say these words. "I was ten years old when he handed me his signet ring."

Still Cael blocked him, but his arm was weakening. He was hampered by the pack on his back, but he didn't dare remove it—its contents were too precious. With an effort, he again disengaged his sword from Derek's, stepping neatly outside of the younger man's reach. Their eyes met, Cael's gaze willing his opponent to see reason.

"He would not want this, Derek," he said, his voice barely a whisper.

The two men again began to circle one another.

"I do not know what he would want," said Derek furiously. "I never got the chance to ask him—he was gone long before I was a man. But I will avenge him. And I will avenge my lost childhood. It was a lonely exile, and I had plenty of time to think about what my future would be."

"I am sorry for what you suffered, Derek," said Cael, trying to shake off the familiar grief and weariness that threatened to creep over him. "But it was not my doing."

"Not your doing!" cried Derek, incensed. "I told my father once that I wished I had not been the only child in our family. I asked if he had also wished for a brother or sister when he was young. Do you know what he said to me? He said that he had a brother—he had you."

Cael stumbled, and Derek was quick to make good on the opening. Lunging forward, he closed the distance between them, and with a practiced flick, he sent Cael's sword flying across the clearing into which they had maneuvered. Before Cael could react, the younger man had his sword pressed against the king's throat, driving him back against a tree.

"Derek," Cael whispered, not even conscious of any fear on his own account. "You must not do this. You do not understand the evil you will bring on this land if you spill my blood."

"Then you should have fought back when you had the chance," said Derek. "Because if you will not kill me, I will kill you."

Derek's movement was quick, but to Cael it seemed that every-thing slowed down. Derek pulled back his sword, and in that moment it felt as though Cael had known its thrust was coming for years. He barely felt the pain as the steel plunged into his abdomen, his mind strangely blank. He stared into the face of his attacker, and frowned in bewilderment. It was strange to see such familiar features so twisted

—*because he could not ever remember such an expression on Damian's face.*

"Forgive me, Damian," he whispered. "As I could not forgive you."

Derek pulled his sword out, and Cael slumped to the forest floor. He landed on his side, still clinging to consciousness, and his pack hit the ground along with him. He became aware of a dancing light, and for a moment his senses returned in all their sharpness. The pain of his wound was agonizing, but it was nothing to the terror that gripped him. The Esvalere!

He reached for it as it rolled away from him, but the gesture was futile. His strength was almost gone. Derek had seen the sphere, and he walked over to it, paying no heed to his dying sovereign, his expression curious.

As he reached out a hand to take what was not his, Cael found the strength to shout.

"No!!"

His cry was lost in the explosion of light and flame and pain that erupted at the moment Derek's hand touched the Esvalere. The young man was thrown back violently against a tree, jagged wounds criss-crossing his face and hands as though the Esvalere had splintered outward with great force. But the sphere was intact. Derek slumped to the ground, unmoving, and Cael tried once more to reach his hand for the object. If only Jonathon were here.

He could feel his life ebbing away from him when he heard a great rushing, and felt a mighty wind. He blinked furiously, trying desperately to clear the fog from his eyes for just one more minute as he looked up into the face of the great beast who had somehow, impossibly, folded himself into the clearing. Cael's eyes widened. Nothing he had seen in the Esvalere had prepared him for the sight of a dragon in reality.

"You have failed me, old friend," Qadir said. "I told you what would happen if you allowed another to wield my gift. I told you

generations ago." The dragon-ruler's voice held no anger, but a deep, ancient sadness.

"I...am...sorry," Cael whispered. "Please...my son..."

"Your son must suffer the consequences," said Qadir simply. "I would not choose to change such ancient magic." His eyes softened as they rested on Cael's face. "The dragonwrath will be unleashed—it is as must be. But I will be true to my word. I will hold the Esvalere for your son to claim, should he manage to overcome."

"Please," whispered Cael again, unable to bear the thought that after generations of faithful friendship, he had brought the dragonwrath on Jonathon. He coughed. He saw blood on his hand, but that didn't matter now. "What will...happen to him?"

Qadir shook his head. "You give me greater credit than you should, my friend. I do not know the future. I see only fragments. But your son will live—that I can see. Your line still carries the protection we gave it long ago. It will not end with you."

Cael closed his eyes, some small measure of relief defying the pain.

"Goodbye, my friend," said Qadir softly. "You go now where I do not follow. I envy you the knowledge you will find there. Be at peace."

With a mighty rush that shook the tops of the ancient trees as though they had been young saplings, the dragon-ruler returned to the sky, and the clearing was once again still.

Cael was still holding on, but he did not know what for. There was nothing now to keep him. Qadir had spoken of peace, and the thought calmed his frantically beating heart. What did the mountain people say? He would prepare his spirit to meet his ancestors. The mountain people. Jacqueline. He need not linger...

The sound of hooves, galloping wildly, penetrated to his consciousness. In moments he heard a familiar voice, its tones overlaid with anguish.

"Father! Father!"

"No! Father!" Another voice joined the first, and Cael felt his hands taken in a soft clasp, and the wetness of tears on his brow.

He opened his eyes and looked into the faces of his son and his third daughter.

"Father," Parmida wept. He had no words to offer her, but he gave her a gentle smile. What more did a man ask than to live a life of purpose and pass out of it surrounded by his children and mourned by those who loved him?

He turned his eyes to his son, and for a moment his vision darkened as he remembered what he had brought on Jonathon.

"Jonathon," he whispered.

"I'm here, Father," Jonathon choked.

"Jonathon, I'm sorry."

"For what, Father? You have nothing to be sorry for!"

"I'm sorry," Cael repeated. So much he had intended to tell Jonathon, but he had left it too late. He had not even told him of the dragons, hadn't even been willing to record those secrets in his writings. But there was no time now.

His children each clasped one of his hands, and with the last of his energy, he returned their pressure. "Goodbye," he whispered, as he fell back into the blackness gathering at the corners of his mind.

CAL FELL TO HIS KNEES, hard, gasping for air. Had he died? Was it over, then? For a moment he stared blindly around him, then realization came rushing back. He had not fallen to his knees, he had never left them. Elnora's head was still in his lap, and the blood slowly leaking onto his hands was not his own, but hers. Jonan was beside him, but for a moment Cal couldn't look at either of his companions, his heart still racing and his breath coming in gasps.

It had been just like the times he had remembered Elam's stories, but a thousand times more intense. He had been there. And this was a story Elam had never told. How could he, when

Jonathon did not witness what happened in that forest? The tingling sensation was so overwhelming that he had to fight to retain his consciousness. Cal blinked rapidly, trying to assure himself that the blackness was not gathering at the edges of his own sight.

Whatever strange vision he had just been shown, it was more than he would have ever asked for. To be fused to a man's consciousness right up until the moment of his leaving this life was not something he would wish on anyone. He was certain he would not readily forget the sensation of Derek's sword sliding into his torso.

But inexplicable as the experience was, Cal did not question the truth of what he had just seen.

"Cal." There was something in Jonan's voice that Cal couldn't identify.

"They're real." Cal stumbled over the words in his haste and shock.

"Cal!"

"Jo, the dragons are real!"

"I know." Jonan's voice was still unnatural.

"I know you already believed it, but I actually saw—"

"Calinnae!"

Cal finally gave his friend his full attention.

"What?"

Jonan didn't answer, just widening his eyes meaningfully as he stared at something over Cal's shoulder.

Cal turned around, searching for whatever Jonan was looking at. When he saw what had settled on the ridge above them, his heart stopped for a moment.

They had found the dragons.

CHAPTER TWENTY-THREE

Or to be precise, one dragon. A monstrous reptilian head was peering over the top of the ridge, and for a moment both boys could only stare stupidly, their eyes wide with shock.

The creature's gaze seemed filled with curiosity as he regarded the three figures huddled at the base of the cliff. After calmly watching them for a moment, the dragon came forward. It moved gracefully, its bulk swaying from side to side as the rest of its body came into view behind its head. Reaching the rim of the ledge above, the dragon spread its wings for a moment, apparently for balance, and Cal's breath caught in his throat.

From inside King Cael's head in his final moments, Cal had just seen how the sight of a dragon in the flesh had been so much more impressive than the reflections shown the king by the Esvalere. Cal knew how he had felt. The effect of seeing the creature with his own eyes was even more potent than watching through King Cael's mind. Not that it was the same dragon. Cal was sure he would recognize Qadir again after his vision, and this dragon was unfamiliar.

Cal's head swam with the tingling that he finally acknowledged to be magic. Naming it made it even more tangible. He could feel the strange quality rolling off the dragon in waves.

As Darius had said, the creature was indeed five times the height of a man. With its wings spread, it seemed impossibly huge, like they were looking up at a building rather than a beast. Its face was similar to a lizard's, but bearded ridges rose up on either side of its temples. Its back legs were thickly muscled, and it crouched almost like a cat, its smaller front legs resting on the edge of the rock. Its talons were as long and as lethal-looking as daggers, and sharp triangular plates rose evenly in a ridge that ran all the way from the back of its neck to the end of the enormous tail curled around its feet. Cal couldn't tell whether the scales that covered the creature were blue or purple or green. The sunlight caught on them, throwing out different colors as the dragon shifted.

Cal glanced at Jo. The expression on his friend's face would almost have been amusing, if not for Elnora's blood still seeping onto his lap, and the Valorian army still marching toward the border, and the real dragon sitting on the ridge above them, and, well, everything.

From the blank astonishment on Jonan's face, no one would guess that it had been him and not Cal who was convinced that dragons were real, and that they would find them. Until his strange vision, Cal had still thought Jo was wrong. But now that he knew the truth, he found it hard to remember that he had ever doubted.

"Greetings, wanderers."

Cal's head flicked back to the dragon in shock. Had it actually just spoken to them? Its voice was musical and not too deep, reminding him of the strange wooden instruments played by the mountain people.

The dragon's words were greeted by stunned silence, and after a moment it tried again.

"It has been a long time since I used the language of men. But I am sure I have it right. 'Greetings'. It is a pleasant sound."

Calinnae gulped, trying to pull himself together. Looking again at Jo, he saw that his friend was still frozen in absolute shock.

"Greetings," Cal returned. "I hope we do not trespass. I am Calinnae."

"Calinnae," mused the beast, looking at him carefully. "Well met. I am Elddreki. You begin to trespass, young wanderer. You are at the very edge of the realm open to men. But the mountain has not expelled you." He looked between the three of them. "Yet."

Cal swallowed. He wasn't sure what being expelled by the mountain would look like, but he had no desire to find out.

"Please," he said. "We mean no harm. Can you help us? Our friend fell, and she has not regained consciousness."

Elddreki looked down at Elnora, his eyes bright with interest.

"I imagine I can," he said, in his musical voice. His eyes seemed to laugh lightly. "It seems fitting that I should, as I believe it was I who caused her fall, although not intentionally."

He made as if to descend the slope, and Cal clutched Elnora more tightly, his heart swelling with hope. But after only a step the dragon paused, his head cocked to the side as if listening. A moment later Cal felt a rushing wind sweep across the plateau on which they stood. He closed his eyes against the sudden gale, and when he opened them his mouth once again dropped in astonishment.

Two more dragons had appeared, flanking Elddreki. They were both even larger than him, and their coloring was darker. One seemed to radiate more blue than purple, and the third had scales dominated by a dark green that did not appear in either of the others. But in form they were all much the same.

"Elddreki," acknowledged the blue one with a nod. "You located them."

"It was not difficult," said Elddreki, his eyes still on the trio of humans. "The concentration of power was growing stronger."

"Yes," nodded the third dragon. "We felt that last gathering of power also. It seems Qadir was right."

"He always is," agreed the blue dragon.

"Not always, surely," said Elddreki, his voice mild.

"What do you think they're saying?" Jonan's whisper startled Calinnae. "Do you think we should tell them why we're here?"

Cal stared at his friend, and was almost surprised to see Jonan's defensive stance. For all his talk of dragon quests, Jonan was afraid now that he was confronted with them. Looking back up at the three majestic beasts perched above them, Cal supposed it was a sensible response. But somehow, although he could never have explained it, he knew he didn't have to fear the dragons.

"You can't understand what they're saying?" he whispered back.

Jo stared. "Of course not. Can you?"

Cal didn't answer, feeling bewildered. They were surely speaking the language of man—hadn't Elddreki said so?

He felt Elnora stir slightly in his arms, and his eyes darted to her face, searching hopefully. But she made no further movement, and her breaths were as shallow as ever. The blood felt thick on his lap, and her face was terrifyingly pale. How long had she been unconscious now? He had lost all sense of time.

"Please," he said desperately, addressing himself to Elddreki. "You said you could help her."

The dragons all stilled, watching him silently for a moment.

"I did," said Elddreki eventually. "But not here. We will take her to Vasilisa."

Apparently the dragon was again speaking the human language, because Jo responded this time. "Are we not in Vasilisa, then?"

The three dragons all began to make a strange noise. For a moment Cal was alarmed, drawing Elnora closer to him protectively, but he suddenly realized that the creatures were laughing.

"No, young human," said the blue dragon, with a hint of amusement. "You have reached the very edge of the Dragon Realm. You have done well to make it so far, but Vasilisa is still many days travel from here as a man traverses. And no matter how skilled you might be at climbing these peaks, no such ability would help you reach it."

"Elnora doesn't have many days," said Cal. "Can't you help her now?"

The dragons all turned to him, and he swallowed convulsively. Their glowing yellow eyes were snakelike but enormous, and the effect of six of them trained unblinkingly on his face was unnerving.

"Indeed she does not," said the dragon with dark green scales. "But it matters not. She cannot enter Vasilisa."

"I did say I could help her," said Elddreki mildly. "Let us bring all three of them."

"Elddreki," said the blue dragon with an audible weariness. "Qadir said to bring the heir."

"And so we shall," said Elddreki calmly, as Cal and Jo exchanged a look in which astonishment mingled with excitement. It seemed they would not have to convince the dragons of Jonan's identity.

The other dragons did not seem convinced, but Elddreki's eyes were once again alight with interest as he studied Calinnae and Elnora. "Trust me," he said. "The situation warrants making an exception." He turned to his companions. "There are three of us, after all."

For a long moment there was silence as the other dragons seemed to consider his words. Then, with a sigh, the blue one shifted. "Very well." And before Calinnae knew what was happening, the dragon had unfolded her wings and swooped down upon them.

For a wild moment Cal considered pulling out the sword he still wore at his side, but he restrained the reflex. Instead he threw his arms up to shield his face from the mighty wind created by the dragon's wings. He didn't even realize the dragon's intention until he saw Elnora's form rising up between him and Jo.

"What are you doing?" he cried frantically, but his voice was lost in the gust. "Elnora! Where are you taking her?!"

None of the dragons responded, and before Calinnae could marshal his thoughts, the dark green dragon had swooped on Jo, gripping his shoulders in its claws. Jo's startled yell was swallowed up as the dragon shot into the air, reaching an impossible height in mere seconds.

For a moment the scene was still, as Cal blinked at the place where his friends had been moments before. The ground was still dark with Elnora's blood. He looked up to see Elddreki watching him, amusement in his eyes.

"What—?" Cal started, but before he could articulate a question, the dragon had unfolded himself from the rock in one fluid movement. Cal winced as the creature's claws gripped him, but to his surprise the hold, while firm, was not painful.

A second later, Elddreki streaked up into the sky, and Cal felt like he'd left his stomach behind. He kept his eyes tightly shut, but they still watered painfully as he gasped for breath in the still mountain air. Then, quite suddenly, the swift ascent ceased. Cal opened his eyes and let out a gasp of amazement.

They were high, much higher than he had expected. The sight of the distant ground made his head swim, but the vista was incredible. In the clear summer light he could see for leagues and leagues in all directions. He could see the Great River clearly, and could even dimly make out Bryford, Valoria's capital city, in the distance. His heart skipped a beat as he got a better look at the vast army camping on the other side of the river, but he turned his gaze resolutely away.

Looking back into his own land, he could see the great Forest of Rune sprawling between the northern end of the mountain range and the capital Kynton further west. South of the capital vast expanses of rolling pastureland stretched.

For the first few minutes Cal was mesmerized by the sight. But Elddreki was flying immeasurably fast, whizzing in seconds over terrain that would have taken them hours to trek through. He quickly caught up to the other two dragons with their burdens, and Cal found himself distracted from the panorama.

Jo's dragon held him firmly in the same manner that Elddreki held Cal, and Jo seemed secure, or as secure as possible when flying at breakneck speed hundreds of feet from the ground. But the third dragon held Elnora differently, with one clawed foot curled around her knees and one around her waist. The way her body hung limply, head lolling and limbs motion-less, filled Cal with terror.

Elddreki had said he could help her, but what if he was wrong? Or what if they were too late? Cal suddenly remembered what Darius had said about finding what they sought only to lose something else. In that moment Cal felt that if Elnora died, even if all of Kyona was somehow miraculously saved, it would be too high a price. For him personally, at least.

The journey was impossibly short for the distance they covered, and for the rest of its duration, Cal couldn't tear his eyes away from Elnora's inert form.

He didn't know what he expected to see as they approached Vasilisa, but no shining dragon city had appeared when the dragons began to rapidly descend. Visually the mountains had continued unchanged, but the further north they traveled, the thicker the air seemed to become with the magic that tingled in every fiber of Cal's being.

The dragons touched ground on a large patch of flat stone, so smooth that it could not have been natural. They were still high up in the peaks, but they were not at the summit of the mountain on which they stood. Considering the beasts' size, it was impressive how gently they were able to set their burdens down. Large cliffs rose up on two sides of the platform. On the southern end, the opening into a large cave yawned above them, tall and wide enough for a dragon to enter.

But it was the final end, toward the north, that drew Cal's gaze as soon as Elddreki let him go. The platform ended in a sheer drop, but from the middle of the space, a narrow walkway extended straight out, spanning a canyon so deep it looked bottomless. Despite the bright afternoon sunlight, the stone bridge disappeared into gloom only a dozen yards away from where it left the platform.

The other dragons set his companions down moments after Elddreki released Cal, then took off immediately. Jo shook his limbs out, a slightly shocked look on his face, but Cal didn't stop to talk to him. He sprinted straight to Elnora's side, once again kneeling down next to her prone form. If possible, she looked even paler. But at least she was still breathing.

"Wait here," Elddreki said. "We will speak for the extra two passengers before we enter Vasilisa."

"Wait!"

Elddreki turned at Cal's vehement exclamation, his expression faintly surprised.

"What is it?"

"Elnora! Aren't you going to help her?"

"I will be back," said Elddreki simply.

"But what if it's too late by then?!"

Elddreki smiled. "Humans are always in such a hurry," he said.

"You may have centuries to spare, but we don't!"

"I will be back," repeated Elddreki. Without another word he shot up into the sky and disappeared from view.

"Wait!" Cal called. "Come back!"

"Cal." Jo put his hand on his friend's arm.

"What?" Cal shot at him.

"I don't know, just…maybe arguing with a dragon isn't the best idea."

"But if they don't help her—"

"I know." Jo's voice was uncharacteristically gentle. He glanced around at the open plateau, then down at Elnora, whose face was directed straight up toward the sun. "Let's move her into the cave, where it's sheltered."

Cal nodded tightly. He wasn't sure what difference it would make, but doing anything was better than sitting and waiting, reminded every second that there was nothing he could really do.

Jo leaned down to help, but Elnora was so slight there was really no need for two of them. Cal lifted her easily in his arms, carrying her the short distance to the cave. As he walked he couldn't help thinking of the previous time he had carried her, and how she had clung to him afterward as she cried. Then he thought of her dancing with the mountain people in the unpredictable firelight, her hair flying, laughter on her face. A lump rose in his throat. She couldn't die. He wouldn't let her die.

But still she didn't stir. He knew nothing of injuries or healing, but he was sure this prolonged unconsciousness couldn't be a good sign. He carried her far enough into the cave that the light became dim, and placed her as gently as possible on the rough stone floor. He wished he had something to soften the surface, but he didn't even have a change of clothes anymore. It had all been lost with their rucksack to Bryant's gang, a lifetime ago.

He remembered how Elnora had squared her shoulders as she stood before the gang leader, ready to take whatever came. How she had saved his life when the trader captain had him by the throat, her hand steady as she held the man at sword point, despite the terror she had faced.

"You're strong, Elnora," he whispered. "Don't give in." For a moment he thought he saw her eyes flicker behind their lids, but then she was still again. He took one of her hands and held it between both of his own, noting in a detached way that his were still covered in her blood.

He sensed Jonan beside him, but neither said a word. How long they sat there he couldn't say, but it felt like an eternity before they heard the rush of wings and a soft call from outside the cave.

"I'll go," said Jonan quickly, getting to his feet. "You stay with her."

Cal nodded, the lump lodged in his throat making speech impossible. He couldn't tear his eyes away from Elnora's face as his mind whirled with a myriad of emotions, chief among them fear. As they had waited in the dim cavern, he had come to three crucial certainties. The two most pressing were, first, that Elnora was going to die without miraculous intervention and, second, that he would do whatever it took to save her.

A few minutes after Jonan left the cave, Cal was startled by a musical voice. "Let me look at her."

He whipped his head around to find Elddreki immediately behind him, his girth suddenly making the echoing cavern seem small and confined. How such a large creature could possibly move so silently was beyond him. Cal moved aside slightly, and Elddreki's head snaked past him as the dragon leaned toward Elnora's still form.

Those powerful muscles and sharp claws were alarmingly close, but Cal didn't lean away, maintaining his grip on Elnora's hand. He could feel the tingle of power radiating off Elddreki. He expected that the dragon would release some of that power into Elnora, but instead the dragon inhaled deeply, seeming to draw something out of Elnora in the process.

Cal again searched her face hopefully, but nothing happened.

"Hmm," said Elddreki. "She is injured more deeply than I realized. I am sorry, young wanderer."

"What?" Cal felt panic rising within him. "What are you saying?"

The dragon made a strange shrugging motion, and a ripple passed from his shoulders down his back, his scales seeming to rustle resignedly. "She stands in the doorway to death. She will enter soon."

"No!" Cal's shout bounced around the large cavern, magnified back to him. "No! You said you would help her!"

"I said I could help her," corrected Elddreki. "Not that I would."

"Well can you, or can't you?" demanded Calinnae.

The dragon met his look, watching him silently for a long moment. His gaze seemed to measure Calinnae.

"It is possible," Elddreki said eventually.

"Well how? What do we do?" Cal asked frantically. "I'll do whatever it takes."

Elddreki drew back his head and studied Cal with interest. "Anything?"

In his desperation Cal wanted to promise unconditionally,

but the part of his mind that was still functioning recognized that the dragon's words felt like a trap.

"How can we save her?" he asked more cautiously. "Tell me what I can do."

"Well," said Elddreki consideringly. "As I said, she is close to death. She cannot be pulled back without cost. Are you willing to make sacrifices to do it?"

"Of course I am," said Calinnae quickly. "I must save her."

"What would you give in exchange for her life?"

Cal gave a small cry of frustration. "I have nothing to give."

"Nonsense, young human. Everyone has something to give. Would you give, for instance, another life? The life of your friend?"

"What? What are you talking about?" Cal felt suddenly deeply uneasy.

"A life for a life, it is a simple exchange. Would you trade your friend's life if it could allow her to live?"

"No! I would do nothing of the kind," Cal said, his horror evident in his voice. Looking around the cavern, he realized for the first time that Jo hadn't followed the dragon back inside.

"Where's Jonan?" he asked sharply.

The dragon just looked at him evenly.

"Where is he?" Cal was on his feet without conscious thought, but of course the change made little difference to how high Elddreki towered above him.

"He is safe, little wanderer, do not fear."

Cal let out a long breath. Somehow, despite his uneasiness, he was confident that the dragon's words were true.

"What if I told you he was willing?" Elddreki pressed. "Would you then agree to exchange his life for hers?"

"I don't care how willing he is or isn't," said Cal, shaken. "There's no way I would agree to such a thing." As confident as he was in the truth of his words, some small part of Cal felt intensely grateful that he was not being asked this question a couple of hours ago, when he had been consumed by that blindly unreasoning anger toward his friend.

"Because of who he is? Because of his legacy?"

Cal looked up swiftly at the dragon, to find that Elddreki was watching him closely. So the dragons knew everything.

"Not just because of that," said Cal. "Even without that. How could I choose to kill my best friend?"

His gaze fell onto Elnora's deathlike expression, and he once again dropped to his knees beside her, suppressed tears threatening to choke him. There must be a way to save her. A different way.

Elddreki sighed. "I can see you care for her," he said. "But if you will not agree..."

"Why would you ask me to choose between them?" Cal choked out. "And why would it be mine to agree or disagree to such a bargain? No one should have that power."

"The power over life and death?" Elddreki said, his tone faintly incredulous. "Many people would give anything for that power."

"Well I'm not one of them," Calinnae spat. "I have no desire for control over anyone's life but my own."

Elddreki remained silent, but suddenly something clicked into place in Cal's mind. *My own.* "Wait..." he said slowly. "A life for a life...you said it's a simple exchange, didn't you?"

"I did," acknowledged Elddreki.

"Take mine," said Calinnae. "A life for a life."

"But I told you," protested the dragon. "Your friend—"

"Jonan's life is too important," said Cal impatiently. "And as I said, even if it wasn't, I could never in good conscience trade someone else's life." He turned away from the dragon, his eyes focusing once again on Elnora's face. "But I can trade mine. And I'm willing to do it, if it means she will live."

"Are you sure, young one?" asked Elddreki gently.

Cal swallowed hard, a thousand thoughts chasing one another frantically around his head. He pushed them all firmly to the side. He had died once already today, he thought shakily, inside King Cael's head. What was once more?

"I'm sure," he said, and was pleased to hear his voice coming out firm.

"Then I can help her," said the dragon, shifting purposefully.

"Right...right now?" asked Cal, his vision swimming.

"She doesn't have much time," said Elddreki.

Calinnae nodded. He lifted Elnora's hand, pressing it to his face for a brief moment. "You will explain to Jonan for me?"

"He will understand," said the musical voice.

Cal just nodded again, not trusting himself to respond. He closed his eyes tightly, trying to calm the swirling chaos within, as every unfinished thread in his short life clamored for his attention. He ignored it all.

"What do I have to do?"

"Nothing, young one," said Elddreki, and his tone made Cal look up into the beast's face. He wasn't sure what to make of the smile Elddreki wore. "You need do nothing. Just hold her hand."

That Cal could do. He turned back to Elnora and focused intently on her face, wondering if there would be any moment of crossover, just an instant in which he could see for himself that she had returned. She would help Jo finish what they had all started. The dragons would surely aid him in his quest to take back the crown.

Elddreki again leaned toward Elnora, and this time Cal felt the magic as Elddreki seemed to cast it out from himself in a net that came to rest over Elnora where she lay. The tingling passed from her into Cal's hands, so strong that he felt like he was being burned. But he maintained his grip.

Suddenly something powerful surged from Elddreki, and

Calinnae was blinded by a blazing light that erupted around Elnora. He tried with everything he had to cling to her hand, but the heat where they touched was almost unbearable. He let out a stifled cry as he felt himself falling backward, and for the second time in mere hours, saw the blackness rush forward to engulf his vision completely.

CHAPTER TWENTY-FOUR

But this time, even as his vision went black, he continued to feel the weight of the hand in his. After a moment he opened his eyes, blinking rapidly as he adjusted to the dim cavern after the flare of light. His eyes searched the space frantically. Nothing seemed to have changed. Elnora's form lay before him, still unmoving, and Elddreki was smiling at him.

"You did well, little human," he said. "You were brave." He regarded Cal with apparent satisfaction. "I like you."

"What happened?" asked Cal shakily. "What's wrong? Didn't it work?"

Elddreki just smiled more broadly. "It worked perfectly, young Calinnae. You just need to give her a few minutes."

Cal glanced quickly at Elnora and saw that her breathing had indeed deepened, and some color was returning to her face. Relief surged through him, but it was quickly replaced by confusion.

"I don't understand..." he tried. "I'm not—"

"Dead?" supplied Elddreki. "No indeed. And I'm glad. As I said, I like you."

"But..." Cal's head felt sluggish. "She's going to be all right?"

"Oh yes, she will be fine."

A horrible thought occurred to Cal. "Jonan?"

Elddreki chuckled. "He is fine, Calinnae."

"Why did you tell me I would die?" asked Cal, starting to feel indignant.

"Yes," Elddreki's tone was penitent, but his eyes seemed to twinkle. "I suppose it was a bit cruel of me to put you through all that. But Qadir wished me to do so, and as he is far wiser than I, I did as I was told."

"But what about 'a life for a life'?" asked Cal. "Was that all made up? Was she even going to die?"

"Certainly she would have died had I not intervened," said Elddreki comfortably. "That was no deception. But a life for a life was a stretch of the truth."

"A stretch?" repeated Cal incredulously.

Elddreki did his strange ripple shrug. "Perhaps it would be necessary had she already passed through the doorway. A magic more ancient than ours might be able to recall her if another life was paid in exchange. But it would not have helped in your case, because we do not meddle with such things. We do not change the past."

Elddreki's words stirred something in Cal's memory, but he didn't have any concentration to spare on it.

"She was not yet dead," the dragon was continuing. "Her injuries were grave, but certainly within my capacity to reverse." He chuckled again. "And I will not charge you a life in forfeit for my services."

"So all that was, what? A test?" asked Cal disapprovingly.

Elddreki didn't actually respond, but his indulgent smile spoke volumes. Cal wasn't sure whether to be angry or relieved, but a soft groan from Elnora drove all thought of the dragon's deception from his mind.

"I will leave you for now," said Elddreki, and with a rustle he was gone.

Elnora's eyes fluttered open, and she blinked even in the dim light. Cal squeezed her hand, his heart in his throat. It felt like it had been days rather than hours since he had seen those eyes.

"Elnora?" He wondered if she could hear the desperation in his voice. "Elnora, are you all right?"

She seemed to focus on his face with an effort, her gaze confused.

"Cal?"

"Yes, I'm here," he said, giving her hand another squeeze.

"What happened?"

He hesitated. A lot had happened. "You fell," he began. "You fell a long way, and you hit your head."

She sat up very suddenly, and her hand pulled out of his grasp in the process.

"I remember," she said, her eyes wide. "I saw an army across the river. Valoria is going to invade Kyona, Cal!"

"I know," said Cal heavily. In all that had happened since, he hadn't been willing to turn his mind back to that terrible revelation.

"And then something moved on the ridge above me, and I lost my balance," Elnora continued. She glanced around at the cave. "Where are we?"

"We're a long way north of where we were when you fell," said Cal carefully. "Elddreki and the others brought us here."

"Who's Elddreki?" Elnora looked bewildered.

Cal took a deep breath. "You missed a lot. I'll explain everything in a minute. But," he searched her face carefully, "are you really all right? You were unconscious for a long time. We—I was so worried about you." His voice dropped to a whisper. "I thought you were going to die, Elnora."

She finally met his gaze, her expression shifting in response to whatever she saw in his eyes.

"I'm sorry, Cal," she said quietly. "I shouldn't have been climbing up cliffs by myself. I was being stupid, but I just got so mad." She put a hand to her head. "I can't explain it. It was like I was my worst self."

"I know," said Cal quickly. "I know exactly what you mean. And I'm the one who should be apologizing. You don't have to answer to me, I was being obnoxious."

She smiled faintly. "Maybe, but you were right as it turned out." Her eyes widened as her hand traveled over the back of her head.

"What is it?" asked Cal anxiously. "Does it hurt?"

She shook her head. "No, it doesn't hurt. Actually," she clambered to her feet, and Cal copied the movement. "I feel great. Better than I have in ages. My hair just feels matted, like there was—"

"A lot of blood," Cal finished grimly. "There was."

Elnora's gaze swept over Cal's person, and her eyes widened again as she took in the blood all over his clothes. "Cal! Are you—?"

"I'm fine," he assured her quickly. "It's not my blood."

Her eyes were still glued to the sight, so he stepped closer, closing the distance between them and forcing her to look at his face as he took her hands again.

"Elnora." He hesitated. "You're truly all right?"

She nodded, her eyes still wide and her gaze locked on his as if hypnotized. He let out a long breath. Tentatively, he reached out a hand and touched her cheek. After her brush with death, everything about her seemed precious and delicate, and he wanted to shield her from a world that was proving to be more dangerous than he had ever imagined. But at the same time, he knew her to be strong. She wasn't fragile—she was more resilient than anyone he had ever met.

She was beautiful and brave and wonderfully alive.

Her body stilled completely at the touch of his hand on her face. His eyes roamed over her features, trying to read her expression.

"Elnora, I...I can't tell you how it felt. Thinking I would lose you." She remained silent, staring back at him out of eyes that seemed to penetrate into his soul.

"I thought I wouldn't get the chance to tell you."

"Tell me what?" Elnora asked, her voice breathless.

Cal paused, taking a moment to just look at her. She looked nervous, but he had never felt more certain of himself in all his life. His mind was clear—ablaze with his new determination to watch and wait no longer—and his heart was full of the final crucial revelation that had come to him while she lay unconscious.

"I love you," he said, his voice quiet but sure. "I love you, Elnora."

For a moment she looked merely stunned, then after a second that hung in the air between them like an eternity, she leaned toward him, face upturned.

Releasing her hand, he wrapped both arms around her waist and pulled her to him, pressing his lips to hers with a confidence he hadn't known he possessed. He had never kissed anyone before, but with Elnora it was as natural as breathing.

She responded instantly, and for a space of time that was both infinite and all too short, they were locked together, their lips needing no words to express the passion and fear and triumph of the days and weeks that had led to this moment. Cal pulled Elnora still closer as he felt one of her hands flat against his chest while the other made its way up his neck where her fingers could tangle themselves through his hair. The touch sent a different kind of tingle down his spine.

Eventually they had to pull back, but Cal immediately leaned his forehead against Elnora's, unwilling to relinquish this new closeness.

"You are the most incredible person I have ever met," he whispered, and Elnora gave a shaky laugh.

"I think you exaggerate."

Cal shook his head without breaking contact, his eyes closed and his heart too full to speak.

"I've been trying to hide all my life," Elnora said, her voice musical and soft. "I never thought anyone would really see me the way you do, Cal. I don't know how you found me inside whatever hiding place I'd built, but you did."

Cal smiled. "And I have no intention of losing you," he promised. "It's still hard to believe you could feel..." he tightened their embrace "...this toward me, though. I'm not sure what I can offer you to make it worth your while."

It was Elnora's turn to smile. "You don't see yourself either. You're...well, you're amazing. You're everything you should be."

He pulled back, looking at her seriously. "I'm hardly that. There are a lot of things I'm not. Not as brave as I should be, not as loyal as I should be...I mean, are...are you sure?" It was suddenly impossible to meet her eyes. "Jo, for example, is something that I will never be."

Still from inside the circle of his arms, Elnora stared sternly at him until he finally made eye contact again.

"What kind of a question is that, am I sure?" she demanded. "Do you think I go around kissing just anybody?" Cal laughed reluctantly, and she continued, her voice still scolding. "Jo and I have never seen each other that way, Cal, surely you can tell that." Her eyes softened. "From the very beginning, it was only you, Calinnae."

The sound of his full name in that soft voice was too much for Cal, and he couldn't resist leaning in once again. Elnora didn't seem to mind, and it was another blissful minute before Cal once again leaned his head against hers.

"It's a shame, really," he said.

"Why's that?" she asked, her voice sounding dazed.

Cal straightened his neck, looking at her with a warmth and admiration that brought a blush to her cheeks. "You would make an incredible queen," he said.

Elnora laughed in genuine amusement. "My ambitions are not so large, I promise you," she said. She placed a hand on his cheek, unknowingly mirroring his action when she had been unconscious. "You are more than enough for me."

Cal beamed down at her, his heart feeling like it would burst. He placed his hand over hers, feeling for the first time since leaving his home as though it might be possible for everything to turn out all right. He would have been happy for the moment to last forever, but Elnora looked around the cavern, as though only just noticing the glaring absence.

"Speaking of royalty," she said with a frown, "where is Jonan?"

"I don't know," Cal said, looking around also. "He was outside, but that was before Elddreki..." he glanced at Elnora's confused face. "Come on, let's go find him, then we can explain everything."

Taking her hand, he walked back toward the entrance of the cave. It was dim enough inside that he was vaguely surprised to find that afternoon sunlight still illuminated the platform on which the dragons had set them down. As soon as they exited the cave, he could see Jonan sitting on a large rock with his back to them, near the sheer drop at the plateau's northern edge.

"Jo!" he called, but his friend didn't turn around. Exchanging a concerned look, the two of them hurried forward. When they reached Jo, Cal felt slightly alarmed to see the dazed look on his face.

"Jo?" he said. "Are you all right?"

Jo focused slowly on Cal's face, his mind clearly still elsewhere. "Oh, Cal," he said. "Hi."

"Where have you been?" asked Cal.

"Here," said Jo. "That blue dragon..." Cal felt Elnora's hand tighten in his at the word, but he kept his attention on Jo. "She did something to me...she put me in a trance or something...I saw things, and I had to decide..." He trailed off.

"Are you all right?" asked Cal sharply. "What did she do?"

"Yeah," said Jo, shaking his head as if to clear it. "Yeah, of course I'm all right. I don't think she was trying to hurt me. It was more like she was trying to—"

"Trying to test you," finished Cal grimly. "Tell me about it."

Jo looked at him in surprise. "What do you mean?"

"Elddreki did the same thing to me," said Cal, his voice flat.

"What did he—?" Jo started, but Cal shook his head. He was sure that Jo was as curious about the details of Cal's test as Cal was about his, but Cal didn't want to discuss it in front of Elnora.

"Never mind that," he said quickly. "Did you pass?"

"I think so," said Jo, a touch of humor in his voice. "You?"

Cal grinned. "Well, I didn't get eaten, and he agreed to heal Elnora, so as far as I can tell..."

"Elnora!" Jo said, seeming to register her presence for the first time. "You're awake! Are you all right?"

"I'm great," she said, grinning back. "But it sounds like I have a lot of catching up to do. Would someone like to tell me who was going to eat who, and how we got here, and where here is, and—?"

"All right, all right," laughed Jo, raising his hands. "Cal, would you like to tell Elnora the story about how you finally admitted I was right?"

"What?" protested Cal. "I don't remember doing any such thing."

"I believe your exact words were, 'Jo, the dragons are real'," said Jo smugly.

"Oh. That. Well, yeah, I guess you were right about that."

Elnora stared between them, her eyes wide. "You saw dragons?"

The tale took a little while to tell. Jonan's astonishment at the account of Cal's vision about King Cael was almost as great as Elnora's at the discovery that while she was unconscious she had been carried through the air by an actual dragon at immense speed and high altitude for the equivalent of a journey of several days. If Jo noticed that Cal and Elnora's hands remained clasped throughout the conversation, he didn't comment on it.

They had just turned their thoughts to the question of what next when a mighty swishing sound heralded the return of Elddreki. The great beast landed just before them, and both boys couldn't help but grin at Elnora's round eyes and stifled gasp. It was clear that for her as well, hearing about it did not prepare you for seeing it yourself.

"Elnora," Elddreki greeted her, sounding pleased. Glancing at her face, Cal thought that pleased was probably not the right word for her reaction to being addressed by name by a monstrous, sharp-clawed dragon. "I am glad to see you awake and well."

His neck swaying, Elddreki leaned his head toward her. Although she clutched Cal's hand more tightly, to her credit she stood her ground. The dragon brought his face quite close to hers and gave a big sniff. Then he pulled back, making the same strange guttural sound that Cal had previously identified as laughter.

"It is strange to sense my own power coming from a human,"

Elddreki chuckled. "It will fade with time, but for now the potency is quite remarkable."

"Are—" Elnora's voice came out a squeak, so she cleared her throat and tried again. "Are you the dragon who healed me?" Elddreki inclined his head. "Thank you," breathed Elnora. "I don't know what else to say, but thank you."

Elddreki smiled indulgently. "Don't thank me, thank young Calinnae."

Elnora turned to him in confusion, but Cal was studying Elddreki curiously. "You are very comfortable around humans, aren't you?" Elddreki regarded him with apparent interest. "Are you...could you be Dernoth's dragon?"

Something glinted deep within Elddreki's eyes. "A dragon belongs to no man," he said sternly. Cal hastened to apologize, but Elddreki waved him off, his expression once again mild even as his claws swished alarmingly through the air.

"But I am indeed the dragon who spoke with Dernoth. I was very young at the time," he said, his eyes taking on a reminiscent gleam, "and I had not yet fully embraced the isolation we dragons choose to impose on ourselves. So young," he mused, apparently to himself. "My decision was not even made yet." The three humans glanced at each other, but no one was game to ask what decision Elddreki meant. After a moment the dragon shook out his body, his wings lifting slightly at the base to allow the movement. "I have not checked in on Dernoth in a long time," he said cheerfully. "I should do so again."

"But..." Having started, Jonan seemed unsure how to continue. "But he's...gone. Dernoth passed to his ancestors many generations ago."

"Gone?" repeated Elddreki, turning his great yellow eyes on Jonan with a look of faint surprise. "His descendants reside still in the mountains, do they not?"

"Well, yes, but—"

"As I said," cut in Elddreki comfortably. "I should check in on him soon."

Jo glanced at the others, but Cal just shrugged. He could no more interpret the odd ways of dragons than his friend could.

"I never thanked you," he said to the dragon. "For helping us, and for saving Elnora." He gripped her hand more tightly as he spoke.

Elddreki smiled at him again. "I am glad to help," he said.

Cal hesitated for a moment. "Thank you," he said again. "We were wondering, though...what next? How far are we from Vasilisa?"

Elddreki shook his head indulgently. "Always in such a hurry," he said. He looked up into the sky, and although Cal could see nothing, the dragon smiled. "But on this occasion," he said, "your timing is flawless. You ask what next—well, next Qadir wishes to speak with you."

As he said it, a thunderous rushing filled the air. It was considerably louder than the sound of Elddreki's approach, and a moment later, Cal was able to see why.

For a full minute after Qadir landed, all three of the travelers remained frozen, staring in undisguised awe. If they had thought Elddreki's size was immense, it was nothing to the sheer enormity of the dragon-ruler. He towered above them, as solid and impressive as the mountain itself. In shape he was like the other dragons they had seen. Unlike them, however, he had scales so dark as to be almost black. He moved with a grace that was both breathtaking and intimidating, his armored hide glinting in the fading sunlight. His magic was a hundred times more potent than Elddreki's—the ceaseless flow that emanated from him was almost suffocating.

Elddreki moved respectfully to the side as Qadir landed between the trio of humans and the narrow stone walkway leading off the northern edge of the platform. The dragon-ruler acknowledged him with a nod, but his gaze was fixed on the humans below him.

"Welcome, young king," he said, his voice managing to be smooth despite its depth. If Elddreki's held the music of a pleasantly bubbling mountain stream, Qadir's held the echo of a mighty underground lake, still and impossibly deep. "I am glad to see you again."

Once again the travelers exchanged bewildered looks, but no one spoke.

"Why have you come here?" asked the dragon-ruler.

"We have traveled a long way to seek your help," answered Jonan, his voice not quite as confident as usual. "We wish to see the throne of Kyona restored."

The great beast inclined his head. "I also would be glad to see such an event come to pass."

Encouraged, Cal spoke up. "Will you help us?"

Qadir regarded Cal steadily for a moment. "That depends on the nature of the help you seek," he said gravely. "Elddreki tells me you wish to enter Vasilisa."

"By your leave, we do," said Jonan.

Qadir looked down at Jonan through ancient eyes. "I do not wish to disappoint you, young traveler, but I will not grant your request. It has been a thousand years since a human was allowed to enter Vasilisa."

As the dragon spoke, he shifted slightly to the side, and Cal was suddenly able to see the narrow stone walkway again. He gasped in shock. The light was fading, and he had expected that the gloom into which the bridge disappeared would have deepened. But on the contrary, it had lifted altogether. The slanting streams of late afternoon sun now fully illuminated the scene before him, and he could only stare open-mouthed.

The walkway was long, but not as long as he had assumed. It spanned out across the chasm in a thin, slightly curved arc, and he could clearly see the far end. At the end of the arc, the bridge joined a mountain which, even from such a close distance, Cal could see to be the highest, most majestic peak in the mountain range. It stretched so far up into the sky that its pinnacle disappeared into invisibility. There was only one bridge to the mountain that he could see, and it ended in an enormous doorway. But dotted all over the mountain's surface were other openings and caverns that had no paths leading out from them, because the creatures who used them had no need of a track.

Dragons. Countless dragons were circling the mountain, coming and going on business of their own, taking off from openings, landing in monstrous stone doorways, flying in pairs deep in discussion, perching on the rocks to enjoy the last of the afternoon sun. Dragons of many sizes and colors, their wings causing a constant wind to whip around the peak, and their scales glinting like precious gems in the summer sun.

"Vasilisa," Cal heard himself whisper.

"Cal?" Jonan's voice was uneasy. "What is it?"

Cal turned to find both of his companions watching him with wary expressions. He gestured down the walkway, sure that any words of his would be inadequate to describe the sight. Jo and Elnora both leaned over to follow his gaze. They stared for only a moment before turning back to him, their expressions blank.

"What is it, Cal?" asked Elnora nervously. "What did you see? Is something coming along the bridge?"

Cal stared back at them, nonplussed. "You don't see it?" he asked. "You don't see what's at the end of the walkway?"

Jonan shook his head, confused. "What do you mean, Cal? It just disappears into darkness."

Cal looked up at Qadir to find the dragon-ruler watching their exchange in silence, his reptilian face revealing neither interest nor surprise. Elddreki on the other hand had a faint air of excitement about him.

"I cannot let you all enter Vasilisa," said Qadir, as if the conversation between the three companions hadn't occurred. "Such a happening would be without precedent."

"I thought that a king of Kyona was once invited here," said Cal quickly. "A long time ago."

"Indeed," said Qadir. "It was I who invited him."

"So why—" Jonan began.

"He was not any traveler," said Qadir calmly. "He was of a royal house of great nobility."

"But you will not let one of the same royal house enter?" challenged Jonan.

"I did not say that." Qadir's voice was as even as ever.

"You said—"

"I said that you could not all enter, not that none of you could. Only the true heir must be allowed to see inside Vasilisa."

Jonan looked at Cal and Elnora. Elnora nodded bracingly. As disappointed as Cal felt, he could hardly blame Qadir. He nodded also, saying softly, "Go ahead, Jo. We'll wait for you here."

Jo turned back to the enormous dragon, stepping forward. "I am ready," he said.

But Qadir shook his fearsome head. "No, young traveler. You may not enter."

"But—" Jo began, but he didn't finish his thought, the dragon once again cutting him off.

"As I said, only the true heir," he repeated.

Cal felt as confused as Jo looked. For a short time there was silence. As the moment stretched out, he glanced around at his companions and found to his consternation that they were both staring at him with expressions he could not read. He opened his mouth to ask them why, but before he could do so, he looked up and saw for himself what had caused their sudden scrutiny.

The dragon-ruler's eyes were also fixed firmly on Calinnae, their yellow hue seeming to gleam in the fading light. And when he spoke again, his gaze remained locked with Cal's.

"You, young king, may enter if you choose."

CHAPTER TWENTY-FIVE

"I don't...understand," said Cal stupidly.

"The true heir of Kyona's kings may enter Vasilisa," the dragon explained patiently.

"But...I'm not..." Cal looked hopelessly at his friends, but they both still stared blankly back at him. "Elam was..."

"Yes," acknowledged Qadir. "Elam was the direct heir of the last true king. We never lost track of Cael's line. It has continued unbroken, father to son, since the time the throne was corrupted. Assisted, I may add, by us. It is not blind luck that never has anyone in the Bloodline died before producing an heir."

"So then Jonan..." Cal petered off at the look on Qadir's face.

"Jonan, while valiant," Qadir inclined his head in Jo's direction, "is not Elam's true son. Can he feel the magic that is the foundation of this place? Could he understand the dragon-tongue? When the magic surrounds him, does it enable him to share his ancestors' memories? Can he, even now, see Vasilisa before him?"

Cal had no answer, his head reeling. What did the dragon-ruler mean by "true son"? It was true that he had always valued the stories more highly than Jonan, that he had a greater love for the land and its history. But he balked at the idea that by being more interested, or even more worthy, he could somehow buy Jonan's birthright from him. Such a suggestion would defeat the meaning of a True Bloodline altogether. And he had himself heard his and Jonan's mothers say that Jonan was the heir. Hadn't he? He cast his mind back, but he couldn't remember now the exact words that had been used, or whether names had been mentioned.

Was this a further test? Part of the challenges the mountain would make them face before deciding whether they would be allowed to pass, allowed to survive?

"I don't understand what you mean," he said faintly, "but I have no desire to take what isn't mine."

"I am glad to hear it," said Qadir sternly. His look softened slightly as he looked at Cal. "But you had already demonstrated the truth of this before young Elddreki brought you here."

Cal's mind flew back to his fight with Jonan, and the triumph he had felt when he overcame the ugliness within him that had wanted to declare that he was more fit than Jonan for the kingship. How long had Elddreki been watching them? And what part had the dragons played in the darkness that had seemed to grip them all the further they traveled into the mountains?

"I don't understand," he repeated simply.

Qadir sighed. "Humans are strange creatures," he mused. "They constantly deceive one another, even when their intentions are pure. Dragons do not lie to each other."

Some small part of Cal felt tempted to point out that this code of honor had not prevented Qadir and Elddreki an hour earlier from practicing on him a deception so brutal it had shaken him to the core. But he was too intent on Qadir's revelations, too desperate to understand, to allow himself to become sidetracked.

He looked up to find that Qadir was looking him in the eye. "Elam was your father, young Calinnae," he said. "You were born of his blood, and it continues to flow within you now that he has joined his ancestors. He and his wife chose for another to raise you in the name of maintaining a secret, the protection of which had long been given higher priority than it should."

Cal looked involuntarily at Jonan. Their eyes met, and all he saw reflected back was the same uncomprehending shock that filled his own mind. It couldn't be true. And yet...

So many things flashed through his mind in the space of a second. The familiarity of Elam's face as he sat before the fire, telling two young boys legends of a time long past, one of the boys listening with rapt attention, while the other could muster no enthusiasm for the recital. The way the stories had seemed to weave themselves around Cal's core, coming to him when he needed them, haunting his dreams, giving him a sense of purpose. Elam's inclusion of Calinnae in every lesson he ever taught his apparent son. The warmth Jonan's parents had always shown toward Calinnae, making him feel as welcome in their home as in his own. The depth of Cal's love for Kyona, which was so fierce it felt at times like physical pain. How Cal had seemed to recognize the face of King Cael in the stone effigy in Pravat. How he had felt the magic of the mountain flowing around and through him, growing stronger the closer they came to the dragons who claimed friendship with the royal line. How he had twice now peered into the mind of the long-dead King Cael.

He remembered how he had felt, when he overheard the truth about Elam's identity, that some part of him had always known it to be so. It was the same now. He had fought and struggled and wrestled with the revelation of Jonan as the true heir. The identity had seemed to fit Jonan so poorly because some part of Cal had recognized that the legacy belonged to him.

All of this passed through his thoughts almost instantly. He turned back to Qadir, blinking stupidly. It was as if he had been in the darkness all along, and now the light was too bright for him. He tried to find something, anything, to say, but his mind was blank.

"Come," said Qadir gently. "You will understand everything."

Cal took a half step toward the dragon, but checked himself at the thought of his companions. He turned back to them, still unsure what to say. Elnora was staring at him out of wide eyes. He couldn't read her expression, but it made him uncomfortable. He tore his eyes away from her face, forcing himself to look at Jonan. No word was spoken, but the turmoil in his best friend's eyes was eloquent.

"Jo..." he started. He had no idea how to continue, so was relieved when Jonan cut him off.

"Go Cal," he said, his voice sounding strange. "We need to finish this."

Cal nodded, then turned back to Qadir. "I am ready," he said, echoing Jonan's words earlier. How wrong they had been to think any of them were ready!

"Come," repeated the dragon, stepping fully aside to expose the beginning of the long stone bridge. Cal stepped onto it, feeling as if he was in a dream. He wondered what the others could be thinking. From what Qadir had said, all they would see would be Cal disappearing into the gloom, and he hoped they wouldn't be too alarmed.

Qadir lifted into the air and flew high above Cal, making his way toward the vast mountain at a pace that Cal suspected would be frustratingly slow for the majestic creature. Cal walked as quickly as he dared given the dizzying drop on either side of the path, and he was surprised at how rapidly the mountain reared up in front of him. In minutes he could see only a short way up its side, and in a few more minutes, he reached the end of the path. He emerged onto a broad platform similar to the one he had left.

Qadir awaited him, having already landed. Cal was grateful for his presence. No other dragons were on the platform, but Cal could tell that some had begun to take notice, numerous eyes following him from the sky or from perches on the rock. There was a strange gleam in Qadir's eyes as he watched Calinnae approach.

"You are like your father, young king," he said, sounding almost nostalgic. "You have his look about you."

"Truly? You think I look like Elam?" said Cal cautiously. He was still trying to wrap his head around the idea that Elam had been his father, and he had certainly never thought he resembled him greatly.

"No, I mean Cael. It's not that you look like him in features, precisely. But you have his look in your eyes. It makes me remember many conversations we shared."

Cal looked into the glowing yellow eyes before him and tried to comprehend the fact that the being with whom he was speaking had spoken in just such a way with King Cael hundreds of years before, and with King Cael's distant ancestor hundreds of years before that.

"Do dragons live forever, then?" he asked curiously.

A shadow passed over Qadir's eyes, but it was gone in an instant. "Some of us do," he answered simply. "But you did not come here to talk about dragons."

"I came to seek guidance and assistance," began Cal, but he fell silent at Qadir's smile.

"I think you came to seek something more substantial than that."

Cal hesitated for a moment, but the dragon's expectant expression seemed to invite him to be direct.

"Yes, Sire," he said. "I think you have something that belongs to me."

"I do," said Qadir solemnly. "It has been safe here in your absence. I have kept my word to you."

"To me?" asked Cal, bewildered.

"To your father, then," amended Qadir.

"King Cael was not—"

"I can call him your forefather if you prefer," sighed Qadir. "For creatures who know so little about almost every subject, humans are strangely determined that the words and actions of others must be correct according to their estimation."

"I am sorry," said Calinnae, chagrined. "I'm just trying to understand."

"I know, young king," said Qadir. "But understanding needs time to grow—you cannot acquire it all at once. You must remember that if you hope to wield the object of which we speak."

Cal nodded, hoping he looked humble, and not too eager. In truth, his excitement was building.

"Do you wish to see the Esvalere?" asked Qadir solemnly.

"Very much so," affirmed Cal, trying to match the dragon-ruler's tone.

Qadir glanced into the cavern from which the platform emerged. "It is a long way to the peak," he said. "Vasilisa is a wondrous place, full of sights you will never again have the opportunity to see. If you wish to make the trek on your own feet, I will not deny you, although there are some places you may not enter. It will take perhaps two days to reach the summit."

Cal swallowed. If he was tempted, it was only for a moment. He saw once again in his mind's eye the enormous army gathering on the far side of the river. He thought also of the companions waiting for him. There was much that needed to be said between him and Jo. And Elnora...well, he had a pretty compelling reason not to prolong his time at the Dragon Nest unnecessarily.

"I am honored," he began hesitantly, trying to be respectful, "by the extension of such a privilege to me. But—"

"It's all right, young king," said Qadir with a smile. "You needn't try to explain yourself. Elddreki has told me already that you are often in a hurry. We will travel there as dragons, not as men."

Cal expected that Qadir would seize his arms, the way Elddreki had done, but the dragon did not move toward him. Instead he opened his mouth and uttered a shrieking cry. It was all Cal could do not to cover his ears.

One of the many dragons who had been sunning himself on a rock nearby launched himself off his perch with an easy grace, swooping down onto the platform.

"I will take our young visitor to the Pinnacle Chamber," said Qadir to the newcomer. The dragon nodded curtly, then without a word took hold of Cal's shoulders and rose into the air, Qadir beside him. Cal could only suppose that the dragon-ruler was too elevated a personage to carry humans around like baggage.

They did not ascend quite as rapidly as Elddreki and the other dragons had done when they first carried Cal and his friends. But the mountain still streaked past alarmingly quickly. Cal caught tantalizing glimpses through cavern entrances, the flicker of fire, the reflection of water, the sparkle of what seemed to be precious gems. But before he had time to dwell on what he might be missing, the mountain began to taper in earnest, and looking up he could see the peak. The air was so thin that it was hard to breathe, and his head swam confusingly.

The dragon set him down inside a narrow opening that didn't look large enough for the creature to enter. Without land-ing, the dragon swooped away, descending once more to the lower levels. Glancing down after him, Cal stepped quickly back from the edge. He had never thought himself afraid of heights, but the sheer magnitude of the drop was terrifying. As soon as he vacated the opening, Qadir approached it.

Cal watched in astonishment as the dragon folded himself in through the entrance, somehow passing through a space that seemed impossibly small for his girth. Cal retreated further in to make room, shivering and rubbing his arms as he did so. Though it was summer, snow had appeared on the slopes of the mountain as they ascended, and his thin tunic seemed no protection at all against the bite in the air.

He cast a cursory glance around the chamber, and all thought of the cold disappeared. There was nothing remarkable about the cavern itself, the walls hewn from the same rough stone as the rest of the mountain, and no embellishments visible. But in the middle of the space, on a simple stone plinth, sat something very remarkable indeed.

The sphere glowed with an unnatural light. The flickering flames that seemed to be trapped within it danced and writhed, their light not only orange, but purple and green and blue, illuminating the cavern walls in uneven bursts that somehow combined to form a steady, pulsating rhythm. Almost more tangible than the light was the sense of magic that was also thrown out from the object, not leaping and twisting like the fire, but flowing thickly and steadily to wash the room with its power.

The Esvalere.

Cal stared, mesmerized. He had caught only the briefest glimpse of it in his vision of King Cael's death, and his whole being longed to race forward and grasp it, to search out its depths. But he held back, his awe reminding him that this was not a toy to be trifled with.

"I have waited a long time for you to come and reclaim your

gift," said Qadir quietly beside him. "I had almost forgotten the way your eyes light up when you see it." Cal glanced fleetingly at the dragon-ruler and saw that he looked pleased.

"Go ahead," said Qadir, his deep voice reverberating around the chamber. "You may take what is yours."

"But..." began Calinnae. "I don't know how to wield it. Do I —do I ask it to show me what I want to see?"

The dragon smiled. "No, young one, you do not speak to the Esvalere."

"Then how...?"

"You will learn with time," returned Qadir. "But open your mind to it now, see what it will show you. You can attempt to steer its direction if you wish, but do not expect to master it. We need a place to start, do we not?"

Nodding numbly, Cal moved forward. His steps were slow, and he felt like he was in a trance. But in moments he was in front of the Esvalere. He noted that the plinth had markings after all, some kind of runes that ran around the edge.

He had watched the Esvalere keenly as he approached, half expecting it to start showing him incredible sights, but the multi-colored fire continued to dance within it, as if trying to break free of its glass cage.

He reached a hand toward it tentatively, but hesitated before touching it. The memory of the explosion he had witnessed through King Cael's eyes when Derek touched the sphere was fresh in his mind. He remembered what the ancient account of the Esvalere had said about its power being unleashed in destruction and marking anyone who attempted to usurp it.

For a moment he felt afraid. What if Qadir was wrong about his identity? Or what if it really was still part of some elaborate test? But as he stared into the Esvalere, his hesitation vanished. He was still as confused as ever about the circumstances of his birth and childhood, but he found as he searched within himself that he didn't need anyone to tell him who he was.

Reaching out, he grasped the sphere firmly with both hands. The effect was instantaneous and many-faceted. The fire began to swirl frantically, blurring into a circular storm of flame and lightning and power. The orb grew hot to the touch, almost too hot to hold. No pictures appeared on the surface of the Esvalere as he had expected, but at once images flooded through his mind with dizzying speed and clarity. Words and impressions and sights poured across his consciousness, like boiling water being poured into an anthill, clearing everything before it. Answers poured into his understanding, creating more questions, which were chased off by answers hard on their heels. Much of it he couldn't take in, but already he could sense how in time he might learn to harness the flood and direct it into channels of his choosing.

All of this was secondary to the greater effect of touching the Esvalere. An overwhelming sense of rightness radiated out of the ball into every inch of his being. The sphere knew his touch, and celebrated in the reunion. Although he was no closer to articulating it, for a brief moment he fully understood the dragons' strange way of conflating generation after generation of a bloodline into one entity, one relationship. It seemed absurd and impossible that he had ever not known that he was a son of the great kings.

He neither left the Pinnacle Chamber nor remained there—it was more as though time and place no longer had restrictive power. He was nowhere, and yet with access to the Esvalere's power, he had the potential to be anywhere and everywhere. The future swirled wildly, full of promise and uncertainty, but the past streamed out behind him like a many-colored pennant rippling in the wind, his to explore and review at will.

As he had first touched the sphere, his thoughts had dwelt

on Qadir's unexpected revelation about his origin, and the Esvalere was instantly responsive to his unasked questions, engulfing his senses with information. In his mind's eye he saw the accidental slip of the tongue that had first revealed the identity of Elam and his wife Lynette to Nathan and Erryn, the couple whom Cal had known as his mother and father. He saw how from that revelation, at first the cause of terror and distress to the fugitive royals, a friendship had grown, creating in Nathan and Erryn a loyalty to the true crown almost as strong as that of the hidden heir.

He saw the delight of the two women when they fell pregnant one after the other. He saw Elam and Lynette's anxiety as whispers began to spread about the false royal house, and how they feared detection more than ever. As he sifted through the information, Cal inexplicably experienced the origin in his true father's mind of the idea of an exchange. He saw the agonizing wrestle of the four parents-to-be, as they tried to decide whether they could really make this sacrifice, and each give their child to someone else to raise. He felt a stab of grief so painful it was almost anger as he realized that the purpose of the exchange was to protect him, even at the cost of Jonan's safety.

He saw that they had only waited until Jonan was born, two months after Calinnae, to confirm that each couple had borne a son. Then they had left the seaside town where they had lived and settled in Nerita, where no one would know them, and no one would notice that a switch had occurred. He understood afresh the reason for the intense intimacy between the two families, each couple committed to living close to one another always, to maximize their involvement in the life of their true child.

He saw his journey with Jonan, and with Elnora once she joined them. Many things became evident that were not obvious to him at the time, and he shuddered to think how easily all might have been lost.

His searching thoughts having reached the present time in his own story, he turned his mind back to the distant past, and details swirled tantalizingly at the edge of his fingertips, tempting him to lose himself in exploration. It became instantly clear why the royal line had followed a tradition that had seemed shortsighted to the point of foolishness in passing on their history only orally. If each king had access to this kind of insight, it could hardly matter whether his father had remembered to tell him every detail.

But before he could begin down the path of his ancestry, Cal's thoughts flitted again to the army beyond the Great River. Instantly the flow of knowledge followed the course of his thoughts, and he saw that even now the army was beginning to march. He saw that they were less than a day away from reaching the broad ford that was hopelessly under-defended by Filip's soldiers, suffering from too little training and too much petty corruption to be effective.

He realized that while his connection to the Esvalere made him feel as if time had no meaning, in reality there was no time to waste. With an effort, he pulled himself out of the deep ocean of memory and truth, removing his hands from the sphere as he did so.

It took a moment for the world to right itself, but when it did he turned to Qadir. There was a look on the dragon's face that would almost have been amazement if it was on any other, less majestic, countenance.

"Well?" said the dragon-ruler.

Calinnae just shook his head, unable to articulate any of what he was thinking or feeling. But the dragon seemed to understand.

"I have lived a long time, young king. It is not often that

anyone surprises me, but you have done so. Your grasp of the Esvalere is far beyond what I expected. I do not think I have seen such an instant affinity for its use in any of your ancestors."

Cal was surprised himself, but Qadir's comments buoyed him.

"May I take it with me when I go?" he asked.

"You do not need to ask," Qadir affirmed, with an incline of his head. "It is yours."

Cal took off the rucksack he had been given by their rescuers from Alezae. He hesitated for a moment, looking between the sphere and the hardy but unembellished burlap sack.

"You need not worry," said Qadir, a smile in his voice. "The Esvalere is not fragile. Nor will it be offended. The nobility of something is not affected by its surroundings."

Cal nodded gratefully. He picked the sphere up, closing his eyes for a moment at the effort required to keep his mind from again delving into its depths, then placed the Esvalere into the rucksack. He tightened its strings securely, then returned the pack to his shoulders. As in the vision from King Cael, he found that his senses swam slightly from the nearness of the magical item. He hoped he would become accustomed, because he had a feeling he would need his mind and body to be sharp for what was to come.

"There's something I still don't understand," he said to the dragon-ruler. He supposed he could search for answers in the Esvalere, but he was afraid of becoming lost if he attempted to reenter its reality now.

"What is that?" asked Qadir, his voice as calm as ever.

"You told King Cael that his son, and his line, would suffer the dragonwrath, just as the ancient account said. But did they— I mean we? What does that mean? What is the dragonwrath?"

Qadir watched him silently for a long moment. "As to what the dragonwrath is, that is a more complicated question than I think you wish to have answered right now. It is many things, and in itself it is nothing. But as for your first question, yes, you and your ancestors have most certainly suffered under the drag-onwrath for generations."

"How?" asked Cal.

"Were you told the story of Lord Lindor's execution?"

Cal nodded.

"What of Lady Lindor's involvement in that scene?"

"You mean at the actual execution?" Cal clarified. "Just that she made a spectacle, throwing threats and accusations at the king before she exiled herself and her son."

Qadir sighed. "I suppose that even with the unnatural memory with which we gifted your line, it was inevitable that some details would be lost." Cal tried to process this information as the dragon-ruler continued. "She did more than threaten the king, she cursed him. In her arrogance she demanded that the king act to prevent the execution of her husband for a crime he did not commit."

"A crime *she* committed," muttered Calinnae, but Qadir continued without pause.

"When he failed to do so, she cursed him publicly. She said that he would suffer the pain she and her child were facing and more. She told him, 'you will see much pain—you will see but you will not act'. Words that have too long defined the story of the line of kings."

"But..." Cal's mind was reeling. "I don't understand. Did she have magic?"

"Certainly not," said Qadir shortly.

"Then what power could her curse have? And what does this have to do with the dragonwrath? No one but the true king had tried to look in the Esvalere—that didn't happen until years later. Why would King Cael be punished?"

Qadir regarded Calinnae thoughtfully. "I must remember

how very little you know," he said, and Cal tried not to feel offended. "It is true that at that time the dragonwrath was not unleashed, and Lady Lindor did not have any power granted by magic. But with or without magic, curses, like blessings, settle on their object, hanging around them like a cloak. What impact they will have, if any, is dependent on many factors.

"King Cael's choices could have taken a different direction, but well before the dragonwrath was released, he had begun to give power to the words of the curse, seeing pain and danger but failing to act."

Cal thought of Queen Jacqueline's warnings about the entrance of Derek into their lives, and King Cael's unwillingness to take action in response.

"After his wife's death," Qadir was continuing, "there was much that he should have seen, much action that he should have taken, but he did not."

Cal nodded slowly, the pieces falling gradually into place. Still the dragon-ruler continued to explain.

"The crowning offense was when, through his inaction, King Cael allowed another to usurp his place and take hold of the Esvalere. At that moment the dragonwrath was released."

Cal had been listening with rapt attention, but the dragon's next words brought him up short.

"You could say, perhaps, that in unleashing the dragonwrath I simply invoked the curse that already hung about your father, giving it a power and potency it could never have gained without dragon magic."

"*You* did?" repeated Calinnae, startled.

Qadir inclined his head. "Certainly. It was I who placed the enchantment on the Esvalere when I gave it to you, and I who acted to put it into effect when your oath was broken."

"But why would you do that?" demanded Calinnae, anger coloring his voice. "King Cael didn't intend for anyone else to see the Esvalere. He may not have been perfect, but he was a good man, and a good king!"

Qadir met his glare steadily. "We do not intend many things, young king," he said. "But a king's actions have consequences far beyond himself, and he must take responsibility even for things he did not design. You should understand this if you seek to rule."

"But—" Cal fought to master his frustration. "Why did you have to curse him? Did you want to open the way for generations of false kings to wreak havoc on our kingdom?"

"I am not responsible for your kingdom," said Qadir mildly. "You are. What I wanted or did not want has no bearing on the matter. I acted in line with my word, as I always will."

For a moment Cal continued to stare at the mighty beast in front of him, recriminations still swirling through his mind. But he remembered Jonan's earlier words, that arguing with a dragon might not be the best idea. And compared to Qadir, Elddreki was about as intimidating as a kitten.

"All right, so you wouldn't help him, but—"

"If by help him, you mean save him from the natural consequences of his own actions, then no, I certainly would not," interrupted Qadir in the same calm voice. Cal's jaw worked for a moment, then he pulled his emotions under control and continued.

"But will you help me now? Will you break the curse?"

Qadir smiled, but for once Cal didn't feel that the dragon was laughing at him with the expression. "I need do no such thing. You have already broken it."

"*I* have?"

"Well, not alone, by any means. It was yours to break the curse, but I think the credit must go as much to your noble friend as to you."

Cal felt a flicker of amusement at the description of Jonan as his noble friend, but Qadir was not finished.

"If you had not broken the curse, you would not be here," he said simply.

Cal thought for a minute. "That ancient account of the Esvalere," he mused, and was surprised at the amused smile that appeared on Qadir's face.

"How lightly you humans use the word 'ancient'," Qadir said. "I was already no longer in my youth when that record was penned regarding my dealings with my old friend."

The dragon fell silent, apparently not seeking a response, so Calinnae continued his interrupted thought.

"The record said that you would return the Esvalere if the heir could convince you that the dragonwrath had been lifted."

Qadir nodded gravely. "I am so convinced, young king," he said. "Or you would not now carry what you do."

"Thank you," said Cal, the weight of the Esvalere feeling solid and powerful against his back. "So will you help me reclaim the throne?"

"Have I not already done so?" Qadir asked with faint surprise.

"I am grateful for your answers," said Cal quickly. "And for the Esvalere. More than I can express. But...I still don't know how to defeat Filip."

Qadir shrugged, a much more dignified version of Elddreki's rippling motion. "You will figure it out, I am sure."

"But we don't have much time!" protested Calinnae. "There's an army marching on Kyona even now!"

"I see no reason for me to intervene," said Qadir unconcernedly. "I am glad to see our friendship renewed, but the fortunes of human kingdoms are no more my concern than they have ever been."

Cal wanted to groan in frustration. It was like the indifference of the mountain people, but so much worse.

"Surely you don't want to see Kyona overrun," he tried again. "And even if we can stop the army somehow, even if we can remove Filip, how will we convince people that I am the legitimate heir? Couldn't you come to Kynton with us, and—"

"Come to Kynton?" repeated Qadir, amusement mingling with indignation in his tone. "Certainly not. We do not leave the mountains."

"You left to come and reclaim the Esvalere," challenged Cal.

"And I did not do it gladly," said Qadir sternly. "Let us hope, for both our sakes, that you never again fail in your oath such that I must repeat the action." Something in his tone sent a shiver down Calinnae's spine, and he judged that it was time to stop arguing.

"Will you then return me to my friends?" he asked, his voice small.

"I will do more than that, young king," said Qadir graciously. "I will have you transported to the edge of the mountain region. In the Forest of Rune you will find the assistance you seek. But do not look for help from the dragons outside of the mountains. We will not come. It is many generations now that we have isolated ourselves from humans, and we are content to have faded into legend. I do not wish our presence here to once again become widely known."

"I see," said Cal, still subdued.

"And one more thing," said Qadir, his voice holding a smile. "I have something else of yours, that you may wish to reclaim."

"You do?" Calinnae looked up, startled. "What is it?"

"See for yourself," said Qadir, indicating a small alcove Cal had not initially noticed, across the room from where they stood. He made his way over and gave a soft exclamation of surprise when he saw what was resting on the small stone shelf inside the alcove. He pulled it out slowly, the ring of metal against the stone sending a small thrill through him.

"Was this King Cael's sword?" he asked reverently.

"It was," said Qadir.

"How do you have it?" Cal asked. He looked the sword over carefully. "Why do you have it?" He tried to remember if Elam's stories had ever included mention of a particularly special sword, but nothing came to mind.

"I took it when I retrieved the Esvalere," explained Qadir unashamedly. "It was of no further use to him."

Cal frowned. He opened his mouth, but hesitated, unsure how to say what he wanted to say, given that he was speaking to a magical centuries-old ruler of dragonkind.

Qadir seemed to know what he was thinking. "You may say that it was not mine to take, and strictly speaking you would be right. I would apologize, but," he smiled, for the first time showing his full set of razor-sharp teeth, "dragons do not apologize."

Cal swallowed and tried to look less intimidated than he felt. He did slightly resent what was effectively a theft, but on the other hand, had Qadir not taken the sword, Cal would undoubtedly never have possessed it himself.

"Was there a reason you wanted it?" he asked carefully. "Is there something unusual about it?"

"No reason, beyond sentiment," said Qadir.

Cal frowned again, feeling as though there was more the dragon wasn't telling him.

"It was always a good sword," Qadir continued, "but there was nothing special about it when King Cael wielded it. I think you will find, however, that having spent the last couple of hundred years resting in Vasilisa, and particularly in this chamber with the Esvalere, it has absorbed a substantial amount of magic. What the effect of this will be, I confess I do not know." Qadir smiled again. "You will have to experiment for me."

Cal hesitated for a moment. "Thank you," he managed eventually. It felt like he shouldn't have to thank Qadir for returning a stolen item, but on reflection he decided to err on the side of politeness. Qadir's smile still showed an alarming number of teeth.

"And now," said Qadir, "I sense you are eager to return to your companions." Cal nodded, and Qadir once again uttered an unearthly shriek.

Another unfamiliar dragon appeared surprisingly quickly. Cal nervously checked the strings of his rucksack and tightened his grip on the sword before stepping forward for the dragon to pick him up. In moments, Qadir and the second dragon were streaking away from Vasilisa, back toward the platform where Jo and Elnora waited.

CHAPTER TWENTY-SIX

he revelations of the Esvalere and his conversation with Qadir had so consumed Cal that he had forgotten his companions. During the short flight, he wondered anxiously what Jo would be thinking and feeling. It was dark now, but it was hard to gauge how long he had been gone, as his submersion in the Esvalere had seemed both instantaneous and eternal.

He wondered what Elnora and Jonan would have talked about in his absence. Had Elnora told Jo what had passed between her and Cal? For a moment Cal was distracted by the memory of her lips on his, and he felt suddenly eager to see her face again. Was she really alive and all right? Was she eager to see him? There was so much he wanted to talk over with her. He could hardly believe that such a short time ago he had told her, only half joking, that she should have chosen Jonan, because she would make such an incredible queen. And now it turned out she had attached herself to the heir after all. It was a good thing she was so tough, and so competent, he reflected. Some girls might be overawed by his identity, but he couldn't imagine Elnora being so easily daunted.

These thoughts quickly turned his mind to his worries about Jonan. Elnora had said that Jo didn't see her that way, but what if she was wrong? How angry and betrayed did Jo feel right now? Would he hate Cal for taking everything from him?

The plateau was empty when they landed, but a dim flickering from inside the cavern suggested that the others had lit a fire to shelter around. When the dragon released Cal, Qadir spoke.

"Rest here for the night. You will need your strength in the days that are coming. Do you have food?" Cal confirmed it, and the dragon gave a curt nod. "I will return in the morning, and set you on your path."

"Thank you," said Cal, only waiting for the dragons to lift off the rock before starting forward eagerly. When he entered the cave and saw the others, he was surprised to see that Elddreki was still with them.

"Cal!" said Jonan, the moment he came into view. "You're back!"

Cal nodded, suddenly finding he had nothing to say. But he didn't need to. Jonan jumped up and strode over to him, his step confident. He reached out, and Cal returned the gesture, clasping arms in a familiar greeting.

"Are you all right?" Jonan asked.

"Yes," said Cal. "Yes, I'm fine. What about you?" He looked carefully into Jonan's face.

"I'm happy to see you in one piece," said Jo. "Elddreki assured us that Qadir wasn't going to eat you or roast you, but it was pretty unnerving watching you disappear into the shadows with your dragon escort."

Cal smiled faintly. "Well, here I am, no harm done," he said, spreading his arms wide. His eyes were on Elnora. She had given him a brief smile of welcome, but she hadn't said a word. She sat next to the small fire they had built, hugging her knees in an unpleasantly familiar gesture. Cal frowned at the defensive posture, wondering what had made her retreat again. Was she uncomfortable to be sitting so close to a real live dragon? It would be a reasonable response.

And yet, after his time with Qadir, Cal found that Elddreki was now anything but intimidating. Contrary to expectations, the dragon did not return to Vasilisa once Cal joined his companions. He seemed to be quite content to chat with his new human friends around the fire, asking them about their lives and placidly answering their questions, his responses frustratingly cryptic. He announced that he would stay with them to protect them through the night. Cal wondered if this role was self-imposed, as Qadir had mentioned nothing about it. But he didn't ask.

The dragon's presence wasn't exactly unwelcome, but it was a barrier to candid conversation among the three of them. There was so much Cal wanted to say to both Jonan and Elnora, but it would have to wait. And perhaps it was for the best, given that he didn't know where to start. He was disappointed with Elnora's detachment. He wondered vaguely if it would be dishonorable to try to use the Esvalere to find out what she was thinking. Did her every nerve tingle the way his did when he glanced over at the corner of the cave where they had embraced such a short time ago? If so, she showed no sign of it.

When they settled down to sleep, trying to get as comfortable as possible on the hard stone surface, Elnora set herself up on the far side of the fire from the boys. Elddreki curled up across the entrance to the cave. Finding himself next to Jo, Cal took the opportunity to quietly recount to his friend the details he had discovered about their exchange as babies. He felt Jonan was at least owed that much explanation without delay.

Jo listened in stunned silence, his expression hard to read in the uncertain firelight.

"I can't believe it," he said at last. "I could never have imagined such a thing." He paused. "But at the same time..."

"I know," Cal agreed. "It's like you've always known."

"How strange that must have been," mused Jo. "For all of them. To be so close to your child, but not to raise them. Why would they do it?"

"It was your—my—Elam," said Cal. "His overabundance of caution. He came up with it as a way for the heir to hide in plain sight."

Jo was shaking his head in amazement. "I don't know what to think," he said finally.

"Me neither," said Cal.

"How did you find all this out?" asked Jo.

"I—I saw it, in the..." Cal trailed off, glancing at Elddreki at the entrance to the cave. He wasn't sure whether he should let the dragon hear that the others knew about the Esvalere.

When he looked back at Jonan, however, he saw that it was unnecessary to use the word. Jo's eyes were wide, a look of awe on his face. "You saw it?" he whispered. "You used it?" Cal nodded.

"What was it like?" Jonan asked, but Cal just shook his head.

"I don't know how to describe it," he said. "I wouldn't know where to start." Involuntarily his eyes flicked to the rucksack that he was keeping within arm's reach. Following his gaze, Jonan's eyes widened even more.

"Do you have it?" he asked, excitement and incredulity in his tone. "Is it in your pack right now?"

Cal nodded as surreptitiously as possible, casting another glance at Elddreki.

"Wow," breathed Jonan.

"Jo, you—" Cal hesitated. "I'm sorry, really sorry, but you can't look in it. It would be...disastrous."

Jo was silent for a long moment, but when he spoke, his tone was mild. "I realize that Cal, obviously. I wasn't going to ask to look into it. It's all just so amazing. I'm still getting my head around it."

"Me too," said Cal quickly. He paused. "Are—are you all right, though? I mean…" he trailed off, not sure how to put such a large question into a few words.

Jo clearly understood what he couldn't articulate, however. Cal took it as a good sign that his friend was not turning away from him, but seemed comfortable to talk.

"Honestly?" Jo said. "I don't know. It's a lot to take in. Everything has changed, and where in the kingdom I go from here, I can't imagine. But in another sense…it seems right."

He sighed. "I'm realizing how good a job you did of being in my position all this time. I didn't find it easy to suddenly find out I was someone important, but if I'm honest, it's no easier to go back to realizing I'm of no consequence after all."

"You are important, Jo," said Cal. "In ways I'm only just beginning to understand."

Jo smiled. "Thanks, but it's not quite the same, is it?"

Cal was silent, unable to deny it. As calm as Jonan seemed to be, he knew that there had to be a great deal his friend was leaving unsaid.

"By the way," said Jonan suddenly, reaching up to his neck. "This is yours now. Or, well, I guess it always was. But now we know…"

Cal hesitated for a moment, then reached out wordlessly to receive the chain Jonan was holding out. The heavy signet ring dangling from it was catching the firelight, glinting as it idly spun. Cal felt an undeniable eagerness to claim the object that had captured him at first sight, but the excitement was tempered by the awkwardness of the handover. Jonan's expression gave little away, but there was no denying that it was a strange moment. It was a physical expression of the astonishing exchange that had just happened, and it brought home more strongly than ever that his gain was Jonan's loss.

"I feel like I'm taking something from you," he said, in a stilted attempt to articulate the feeling.

"Nothing that isn't yours to take," said Jonan. He spoke lightly, but his expression was still veiled.

Cal pulled the ring off the chain and held it in his hand, staring at it for a moment longer. Then he slipped it onto his finger. It fit comfortably, in no danger of sliding off as it had been when Jo had briefly worn it. His friend's sudden laugh suggested that he was remembering the same incident.

"I guess it's no surprise that it fits you," said Jonan. "I never realized your hands were that much bigger than mine."

"Neither did I," said Cal, studying the effect of the ring on his finger. Not so long ago, he would never have imagined wearing jewelry of any kind, but it felt right, somehow. Like it belonged there.

"Do you want the chain?" Jo asked, holding it out. "It also belongs to you, after all."

Cal shook his head. "No, I don't need it. Rings are meant to be worn on your hand, not carried around your neck. You were right in the first place. This isn't something that should be hidden." He met his friend's eye. "None of this is."

Jonan nodded. He considered the empty chain for a moment, his thoughts impossible to guess, before slipping it back around his neck. Cal was surprised, but didn't comment.

Jo shifted his weight, settling in for sleep. "There's a lot I still have to figure out," he said, his voice betraying his weariness. "But one thing I can say for sure. I have your back, just like you have mine. You have my support, Cal."

"Thanks, Jo," said Cal softly, moved by this declaration.

He looked at Jo for a moment, then his eyes flicked across the fire to Elnora's still form. He somehow felt both hugely relieved and troubled at the same time. Neither of them had responded at all like he had expected.

The morning dawned as clear as the day before, the sun continuing to shine impartially down, as if everyone's worlds weren't being turned on end. Cal had watched it rise, having woken in the still pre-dawn and found himself unable to return to sleep. From the platform he could see Vasilisa appear from the darkness, as beautiful and surreal as ever. He didn't know what he found harder to comprehend—the fact that he was watching actual dragons circle through the early morning air, or the fact that twenty-four hours previously he had genuinely believed such creatures didn't exist.

He heard familiar soft footsteps behind him, and felt a warmth spread through him that had nothing to do with the morning sunshine. He turned as Elnora sat beside him, his eyes lighting up in response to her presence.

But there was no answering smile. For a moment she sat beside him in silence, her eyes staring unseeingly at the vista before them, which Cal knew would be shrouded in shadow to her eyes.

"Good morning," he tried tentatively.

"Good morning," she responded, her voice soft.

Cal looked sideways at her, trying to read her expression. He had fallen asleep the night before remembering the feel of her in his arms. In that moment, as he had pulled her close, he had felt so certain, but he couldn't deny that his confidence was wavering with her sudden aloofness. Did she regret what had passed between them? His face burned as he remembered telling her that he loved her. She had been responsive with her actions, but she had not actually said the same.

Be on your guard, the mountain chief had said, *that you don't find what you are seeking only to lose something else.*

With Qadir's revelations he had gained much more than he had thought possible. But was he now going to lose something equally as precious? Was it selfish to want everything? But having crossed that line with Elnora, how could he ever go back? He knew her friendship would not be enough for him now.

"How did you sleep?" he asked.

She smiled faintly. "Very little."

He hesitated. His whole reality had violently realigned since the same time the day before. His head was still reeling, and he had no idea how to process it all. He longed to open his heart to Elnora, to talk out all the complexities and exhilaration and fear that threatened to overwhelm him. He felt certain that she could help him to make sense of it, that they could be stronger together.

But her demeanor was anything but encouraging. Something was amiss. And although he didn't know how to fix it, he did know he had to try. The contrast could not have been more stark between the passion of their last moment alone together and the awkward tension of this silence.

"Elnora—" he began, but she cut across his words.

"What did Elddreki mean yesterday?" she asked.

Cal blinked, his thoughts thrown off course. "What?"

"When he said that I should thank you for him having healed me?"

"Oh," said Cal, suddenly even more uncomfortable. "It's not important."

"I'd like the opportunity to judge that for myself," said Elnora shortly.

"It was just his usual cryptic dragon way," he hedged. "He healed you, not me. I don't even know how he did it. Some kind of magic."

"That's not good enough, Cal," said Elnora, her voice curt. "I know you're hiding something, and I think there's been enough of that."

"What's that supposed to mean?" Cal asked with a frown, but Elnora shook her head.

"Don't change the subject. What happened while I was unconscious?"

Cal sighed, looking back toward Vasilisa. He had hoped not to let Elnora find out about the details of Elddreki's test. "Can't you just trust me that it's not anything you need to know?"

"No," said Elnora uncompromisingly. "I can't."

Cal looked at her unhappily, but there was no softening in her glare. "It was all just nonsense, really," he said. "Just a trick. Elddreki didn't need me to do anything, he was perfectly capable of healing you himself."

He paused, but Elnora's expectant expression compelled him to continue.

"He said that your injuries were too severe, that you were close to dying." Cal felt an involuntary shudder go through him at the memory of that moment. "That part was true." Tentatively, he placed his hand over hers where it was splayed on the rock, supporting her weight. She didn't pull away, and he wove his fingers around hers so their hands were interlocked.

"He said that to save you I would have to trade a life. He tried to convince me that I should trade Jonan's life for yours. I suppose that was the test."

"What?!" Elnora pulled her hand away. "What did you say?"

"I said no, of course!" Cal answered quickly. "I didn't even consider it, not for a second. I would never do such a thing."

Elnora let out a long breath, apparently relieved. "So when you said no, did he tell you it had been a test?"

"Well...yes. I mean not...not straight away, but he did tell me. Sort of."

"Cal," she said warningly. "Just say it."

"Well, he...he had said a life for a life. I knew it wasn't mine to trade Jonan's life, but..."

For a moment his words trailed away, then there was a sharp intake of breath as Elnora understood. "You offered your life?"

He didn't answer, but his silence evidently confirmed it.

"Cal, how could you?!"

He looked up in surprise. He hadn't wanted to tell her because he had thought it might make her uncomfortable, but he hadn't expected this anger.

He met her eyes and was surprised at the turbulence in them. A lot of emotions seemed to be trapped inside her, gaining potency the longer they were pent up. For a long moment he held her gaze, willing her to see his sincerity.

"How could I not?"

"You shouldn't have done that," she said, her teeth gritted.

Cal tried to take her hand again, but she pulled it away. "It doesn't matter, Elnora, none of it was real. We're both here, we're both fine."

"It does matter!" she said, unshed tears glazing her eyes. "You don't know what it means to live your life knowing people you love have died to keep you alive. You had no right to make that choice for me again."

Cal suddenly remembered Elnora's reaction to the story about Thalia dying to save Jonathon, her certainty that he would have felt guilty all his life, sure he wasn't worth it. At the time he hadn't known about her parents and her sister, and his heart twisted as he realized why that story had elicited such a reaction from her.

"Elnora—" he began helplessly, but she wasn't finished.

"Do you think I would want the guilt of knowing you were dead because I made a stupid decision? Being reminded the rest of my life that I caused the death of the real king, and the end of an ancient bloodline?"

"Well," said Cal reasonably, "I didn't know at the time that my death would have any effect on the True Bloodline."

"And if you had known?" Elnora challenged him. "Would you have chosen differently?"

Cal stared back at her for a long moment, considering his answer before uttering it, making sure he was convinced of its truth.

"No," he said at last. "It wouldn't have changed anything."

And it wouldn't have. He was certain of it. It was strange, because he had spent this whole journey trying to protect the Bloodline, valuing it above everything else. But somehow somewhere along the way he'd stopped believing that the protection of the Bloodline justified whatever action that took, even if it meant acting inconsistently with the legacy left by the great kings of the past. At the back of his mind he wondered if that was what Qadir meant by him having already broken the curse.

But the rest of his mind was occupied with trying to placate the beautiful, impossible, unfathomable girl in front of him, because her eyes were flashing fire in his direction.

"What were you thinking, Cal?" she demanded. "How could you be so irresponsible? I'm not that important."

"You are exactly that important to me," he protested. "Why are you so angry? It was my decision to make. Is my life not my own?"

She stared at him for a long minute. "Not anymore," she said at last, her voice once again quiet. With a fluid movement, she pushed herself to her feet.

"Elnora, wait!" Cal called, but she was already walking away.

He stared after her, nonplussed. Where was all this coming from? It was a complication he didn't need right now. He felt a spark of frustration, but it was quickly blown out by an icy gust of fear. What if she didn't forgive him for whatever offense he was supposed to have committed? He thought back to his reflections the evening before. Perhaps he had been wrong—perhaps Elnora was daunted by the reality of his lineage. But she didn't seem daunted. She seemed defeated, like she'd already lost a battle, one he had been sure she had the strength to fight. Surely she didn't think the revelation would change his mind about her? He couldn't have been more clear about where he stood.

He was still wrestling with the question when Elddreki approached. He watched the dragon unfold himself gracefully from the entrance to the cave, where he had curled up overnight.

"You look troubled, young king," Elddreki said, his gaze unnervingly perceptive.

"Things did feel less complicated when I woke up yesterday," Cal acknowledged dryly.

Elddreki smiled. "Do not be in a hurry, young one," he said. "You must give things time."

Cal shook his head, thinking of the army on the move. "Time is something we don't have," he said. "We need to leave."

"Qadir will come soon," promised Elddreki. He looked down at Cal's hand. "What do you have there? I didn't realize you carried a second magical object."

"What? Oh, this." Cal followed the dragon's gaze. He hadn't even realized that he had been absent-mindedly fingering the hilt of King Cael's sword, which sat on the stone next to him. "I don't think it's a magical object, exactly. Qadir said that it was an ordinary sword originally, but that because it has been kept in close proximity with magic for a long time there may be unexpected effects."

"Interesting," said Elddreki, his eyes alight with curiosity. "You should try it out."

"I have a feeling that I'll need to before this is over," said Cal grimly.

"Is that a second sword?" Jonan's voice startled Cal. He hadn't heard his friend approach.

"Yes," he confirmed. "Qadir gave it to me. It used to be King Cael's, apparently."

"Wow," said Jonan, impressed. He held up the sword Elnora had taken from the traders. "I guess that's why you left this in the cave."

"Where's your companion?" Elddreki asked Jo. "You will wish to be ready to depart when Qadir arrives."

"She's coming," said Jo, jerking his head back toward the cave. When Elddreki turned away, he took the opportunity to whisper to Cal, "What's wrong with Elnora?"

Cal grimaced. "I was hoping you could tell me. All I know is that dragons suddenly seem less mysterious than girls."

Jonan raised an eyebrow, looking unconvinced, but he was prevented from asking any further questions by the approach of Elnora herself. Cal felt a pang as she walked right past him, placing herself next to Jonan instead. He tried to catch her eye, but she was clearly avoiding his. She did, however, glance at the hand where he now wore the signet ring, and Cal was distressed at the expression on her face as she quickly looked away.

A moment later a mighty rush of wind heralded the approach of the dragon-ruler, accompanied by the dark green and blue dragons who had carried Jonan and Elnora the day before.

"Greetings, travelers," reverberated that deep voice. "Are you ready to depart the Dragon Realm?"

They nodded. Cal noticed that Elnora looked nervous, and he suddenly remembered that she had been unconscious on the previous occasion when she had been transported by a dragon.

"Where will you take us?" asked Jonan.

"To the northern edge of the mountains," answered Qadir. "The end of the mountain range marks the beginning of the Forest of Rune."

"And what then?" Jonan persisted.

Qadir fixed him with a calm look. "That is up to you."

"Aren't—" Jo glanced at Cal. "Aren't you going to help us take on Filip, then?"

"We do not leave the mountains, young traveler," said Qadir. "You must fight your own battle. But we wish you well."

"What good will that do us?" Jo began to protest, but Cal cut him off.

"So you haven't reconsidered, then?" he asked, addressing himself to Qadir.

"Certainly not," the dragon-ruler returned, unruffled.

"What if we can't defeat him?" Jo demanded. "Or what if we do, but we can't convince anyone that Cal is the true king? What will happen then?"

"Not all questions are mine to answer," said Qadir, his voice infuriatingly placid. "And you overestimate my ability. I cannot see the future."

Jo opened his mouth to argue further, but he fell silent at Cal's small shake of the head.

"Farewell," said Qadir.

"Farewell," Cal returned. "Thank you for your assistance." He hesitated. "And for your friendship."

Qadir inclined his head, the ghost of a smile on his reptilian face. "Indeed I have missed our conversations. It was good to see you again, son of kings."

Without further conversation, the other three dragons swooped on the companions, seizing them as abruptly as they had the day before. Cal heard Jo's sharp intake of breath and Elnora's stifled shriek, but the sensation had become almost familiar to him by now.

As before, it was Elddreki who carried him, and once again the other dragons were in front. Despite his anguish over her strange behavior, Cal couldn't help but enjoy the look of amazement on Elnora's face. The view was as impressive as it had been when he first saw it, and the further north they went the more clearly he could see Kynton in the distance, northwest of the hidden Dragon Nest.

Now that he knew it was his birthright, the city seemed to call to him with increased urgency and potency. He could almost feel his body leaning toward it, longing to claim it and restore it. But there was so much still to overcome before that could be achieved.

In an unbelievably short time, the mountains began to decrease in height and the sprawling forest drew closer. The dragons started to descend, and Cal barely had time to take note of where they were relative to the expanse of the forest before he found himself set on his feet. They were still within the mountains, but a track was visible nearby, winding the short distance from where they stood to where it disappeared into the trees.

The two other dragons deposited their burdens and immediately took off again. But Elddreki lingered, seeming reluctant to say goodbye. Cal wondered fleetingly what made him so different in temperament from his fellows.

"I wish you well in your quest, young travelers," said the dragon. He surveyed the three of them and smiled gently.

Following his gaze, Cal saw that Elnora looked windswept, her expression stunned from the recent flight, and Jo looked dejected. There was so much going on inside him that he couldn't have guessed what his own face showed.

"I can see that you are disappointed that Qadir did not agree to assist you further," said Elddreki, his eyes lingering on Jo's expression. He turned to Cal. "I would apologize, but—"

"Dragons don't apologize," finished Cal wryly. "So I've heard."

Elddreki's smile broadened. "Precisely." He looked between the three of them again. "Qadir is immeasurably wise. That does not mean he is always right. But he has reason for wanting to remain in isolation. Still..." The dragon's eyes had become fixed on Cal's new sword.

"Hold out your weapon," he said. Surprised, Cal obeyed.

Elddreki snaked his head toward the sword, then closed his eyes and inhaled deeply, as if trying to assess its substance.

"Very interesting magic," he mused, apparently to himself. "I confess myself curious also."

He took a deep breath, the motion slowly expanding his body from his throat down to his scaled chest. Cal heard a strange sound, like a deep rattling that emanated from the dragon's core. Then, without warning, Elddreki opened his mouth wide and released a white-hot tongue of fire which engulfed the sword completely.

All three humans cried out in shock, and it was all Cal could do to hold onto the sword. Just like Elnora's hand when Elddreki had healed her, the sword hilt burned hot against his palm as the whole thing was illuminated in blinding white.

As abruptly as it had started, the fire disappeared. Stunned, Cal stared down at the sword. For a short moment it glowed red with the heat, then the metal faded quickly back to its original state. He looked at the sword closely—as far as he could see, there was nothing different about the weapon. But as he gripped the hilt, he thought something felt slightly new about it, some essence radiating from it. It was new but familiar, although he couldn't quite place it.

Elddreki gave a low chuckle. "Now you are really taking some of me with you." The dragon's eyes flicked to Elnora, and Cal suddenly realized what was familiar about the sword now.

The signature of power coming from it was the same as the indefinable quality that had hung about Elnora since Elddreki used his magic on her.

"What did you do?" he asked, turning the sword from side to side.

"I added my own magic to whatever it already holds," said Elddreki simply. "It's not the same as steeping it in the heart of Vasilisa for centuries, of course. It won't linger for long, maybe a few days. But it's connected to me now. My fire is in it. You may find that...useful."

"What does that mean?" Jo asked, but Elddreki merely smiled at them all.

"Farewell, young adventurers," he said. "Until we meet again."

And without a backward glance, he shot up into the air, disappearing from sight in seconds.

"Why do they always have to be so cryptic?" Jo grumbled, adjusting the trader's sword, now strapped around his own waist. "I like a good mystery as much as the next person, but a bit of clear, uncomplicated communication would be nice once in a while."

"Tell me about it," said Cal, his eyes on Elnora. She was still refusing to meet his gaze.

"So why did the dragons bring us to the Forest of Rune?" Jo asked.

Cal shrugged. "I don't know. Qadir just said that we'll find assistance in the forest. Whatever that means."

"What else did he tell you?" Jo asked, as the three of them began to clamber down the stones, making for the winding track.

Cal recounted his experiences in the Dragon Nest. Jonan listened in fascination, and even Elnora couldn't entirely disguise her interest as Cal described the vast mountain, and the contents of the Pinnacle Chamber. He didn't describe everything he saw in the Esvalere, but he did his best to capture the sensation of wrestling with its flood of power.

They were both wide eyed by the end, and Cal felt suddenly uncomfortable with the awe on their faces as they looked at him.

"That's..." Jo seemed to struggle to find words. "That's a lot of power, Cal."

"I know," said Cal heavily. He could feel the weight of the responsibility as surely as he could feel the pressure of the sphere against his back. He glanced at Elnora and felt doubly uncomfortable at what he saw in her expression.

They had entered the trees a few minutes before, and the mossy trunks around them seemed to deaden their voices. The forest began abruptly, the trees almost immediately reaching an immense height. In the absence of a better plan, they continued to follow the track that had come down from the mountains and now wound between tree trunks, occasionally obscured by the undergrowth.

Elnora seemed to be making an effort to place herself alongside Jo rather than Cal as they walked. At first Cal hadn't fought her sudden aloofness, hanging back behind her and Jo as he had done when she wouldn't talk to him after her breakdown leaving Alezae. But as he watched her back, and saw the stiffness in her posture that showed him she was trying a little too hard to appear at ease, he reached his limit. They had come too far to slip back into awkward formality.

Something was clearly troubling her now, but he was confident that he had not imagined her eagerness as she responded to his kiss. The fire that raced through him at the memory energized him, strengthening his determination and clearing away any hesitation. She felt for him what he felt for her, and whatever the dragons might say about not being in a hurry, life was too short and too uncertain to allow something so important to fade away for lack of pursuit.

At the first opportunity, he maneuvered to walk beside her. Jonan's questioning look told him that he had not been as subtle as he had intended, but at a shake of the head Jonan dropped back willingly enough.

"What did you think of flying?" Cal asked Elnora, trying to smile naturally. The look she cast up at him was wary, but she couldn't seem to find a reason not to respond.

"It was...terrifying," she said. "But also amazing. I never imagined anything like it. It was like I could see forever."

"I know," he agreed. "It didn't seem real."

She sighed. "Nothing since I left Kerr seems real."

Cal decided that was enough of an opening. "Elnora," he said quickly. "I know you're angry with me. I don't really understand why, but I want to make it right. I never meant to upset you..." He trailed off as Elnora shook her head.

"I'm not angry with you," she said wearily. "I'm sorry about this morning. I—I was unfair. I didn't even thank you for—what you did."

"I didn't do anything," said Cal quickly. "I told you, it was just a trick."

"But you were ready to," said Elnora. "And I didn't even thank you." Her voice sounded choked, and glancing quickly down at her, Cal saw that tears were glazing her eyes. He started to reach for her but stopped himself, acutely aware of Jonan's watching eyes behind them.

"You don't have to thank me," he said instead. "I don't want you to. Are—are you sure you're not angry?"

"Of course I'm not," she answered, but her tone was subdued. Looking sideways at her, he saw that she truly didn't look angry. She just looked...sad. And weary. And no more ready to meet his gaze than she had been before.

"Elnora," he tried again. "What is it? What's wrong? Yesterday..." he glanced involuntarily back toward Jo and didn't elaborate. "What changed?"

She gave him an incredulous look. "What kind of a question is that? You don't know what's changed since yesterday?"

He met her look in exasperation. "Well...of course I do," he said. "But why—"

"Cal," Jo's sharp voice cut across their conversation.

"What?" asked Cal, not quite managing to keep the irritation out of his voice.

"The path is turning," Jo said. "Do we keep following it?"

Looking ahead, Cal saw that Jo was right. They had been following the path north for a couple of hours, but it had begun to bend toward the west. They all stopped, stepping off the path for a moment as they considered what was best to do.

Elnora stood quietly to the side, not taking part in the discussion. Cal's mind was only half on their conversation, his eyes continually flicking to Elnora. She had begun to wander idly further away from the path, toward a nearby clearing. Cal and Jo had just agreed that since west would lead them toward Kynton, it was as good an approach as any when he looked up and realized that she was no longer in sight.

He opened his mouth to call her name, but before he could speak, a stifled scream sounded from the direction in which she had disappeared. Without conscious thought, he started sprinting through the trees, calling for her, Jo at his heels.

He never made it to the clearing. He had taken only a few strides when something hit him hard from the side, and he was knocked to the ground. Before he could rise, he found himself pinned to the forest floor by a heavy weight, a vise-like grip holding his arms behind his back. He struggled for a moment without effect, then his vision went dark as a burlap sack was shoved over his head.

CHAPTER TWENTY-SEVEN

The next few minutes were a blur of sound and pain as Cal wrestled fruitlessly against the hold on his arms. His head had hit the ground hard when he was knocked down, and his senses were in a daze as he tried to take in what was happening around him. He was vaguely aware of being hauled to his feet and forced through the forest. He thought he heard both Jo's and Elnora's voices, but his hearing was muffled by the sack over his head.

Underneath the haze he was furious with himself. He hadn't even drawn the sword that had now been wrested from his grip. He could only be grateful that his rucksack was still on his back, but the power emanating from the Esvalere did nothing to help sharpen his senses. Its steady flow seemed to blend with the throbbing in his head, making it almost impossible to hold onto his awareness.

Whoever was pushing him along was not gentle. He stumbled and was pulled back to his feet a number of times, and before long he had aches all over his body to join the pounding in his head. Once he clearly heard Elnora cry out in pain, and the anger that rose up inside him helped to clear some of the fog enveloping his mind. He shouted accusingly, but his words were lost in the sack that was still over his head.

He had absolutely no sense of which direction they were headed, but judged that it wasn't more than ten minutes before he was pushed roughly to his knees. He attempted to struggle to his feet, but a sharp blow to the side of his head made everything spin for a minute. His hands were quickly bound behind his back with rough rope, then the sack was pulled abruptly from his head.

For a moment he blinked in the dappled light of the forest. A second later, Jo was pushed to his knees beside Cal, then Elnora on Jo's other side. They both looked as manhandled as he felt, and the sight of a long cut down Elnora's arm loosened Cal's tongue.

"Who do you think you are?" he spat, turning his head to face his captor. "What right do you have to attack travelers passing lawfully through these lands?"

The man didn't answer, or even look in Cal's direction. He was one of half a dozen positioned behind the three companions. They were dressed in the greens and browns of the forest, and looked like they were used to a rough life, from the set of their jaws to the state of their clothes. They had already shown that they knew how to move silently between the trees.

After a cursory look, Cal returned his attention to his friends.

"Are you all right?" he asked urgently, the question addressed to them both, but his eyes on Elnora. Jo grimaced but nodded. Elnora nodded also, a spark of defiance in her eyes. Cal relaxed slightly, remembering Bryant's gang. She had become so precious to him that he sometimes forgot that she was no stranger to perilous situations. Still, the sight of her bound and bleeding did nothing to calm the anger inside him.

He turned back to the men behind them. "What do you want

with us?" he demanded, closing his eyes for a moment as a surge emanated from the Esvalere, making his head swim.

Still they ignored him, their eyes fixed on the trees on the opposite side of the small clearing. He followed their gaze in time to see three more people, clad in the same camouflage colors, emerging from the foliage.

As with Bryant's gang, Cal had no difficulty identifying the leader. The man in the middle was young and strong, perhaps in his thirties, and those on either side flanked him protectively. Cal had almost forgotten what Elnora had told him back in Pravat about the reputation of the foresters, but it came back to him forcefully now. They were known as dangerous, and looking at the man in front of him, Cal had to agree with general opinion. The leader strode forward confidently, his gaze on the three travelers.

"Sir," said the man immediately behind Cal. "We found these three entering the forest near the mountains, like you said. They followed the path until it curved west, then we intervened."

"Intervened?" muttered Jo. "You mean attacked." Glancing at his friend, Cal saw the beginnings of a black eye. He wondered if he looked as hardened these days as Jo did. It was a long time since he had seen his reflection.

The newcomer's gaze shifted to Jonan, but he didn't comment on the interruption. The man studied the three of them carefully, his eyes lingering longest on Calinnae. Cal blinked stupidly, still feeling dazed. There was something familiar about the man, but he couldn't identify what it was. He was sure he had never seen him before. In fact, it wasn't his appearance that seemed familiar, more his...essence. Cal shook his head slightly as another pulse of power from the Esvalere seemed to enter his back and surge up into his head.

"You," said the man, his eyes on Cal. "Who are you, and what is your business in the forest?"

"I should ask you the same questions!" said Cal, his voice angry. "What makes you think you have authority to control who passes through the king's land?"

"You will show some respect," growled one of the men behind Jonan. He started toward Cal, but the leader stopped him with a casual raise of one hand.

"You call this the king's land," he said, his expression thoughtful as he looked at Calinnae. "But you are on our land now. We do not recognize the king here."

"You and half the country," muttered Jonan. It was clear that the leader had heard him, but if anything he seemed pleased by the interjection.

"Those are heavy words," said Cal. "I assume that you would not utter them if you could not back them up. What group do you represent?"

The man's smile widened slightly. "I think I will ask the questions, young man," he said. "I asked who you are."

Cal measured him for a moment. "I am Calinnae," he said. "I come from Nerita. My companions are Jonan of Nerita, and Elnora of Alezae. I would make a more formal introduction," a bite was in his voice, "but our hands are tied behind our backs, and we are on our knees under threat of violence."

"Indeed," said their interrogator crisply. "We cannot be too careful in such times. We are on the brink of war, after all."

"Are we?" returned Cal. "Then I can understand your desire to be careful. Less so your unprovoked violence against innocent travelers."

"Yes." The man's gaze lingered on the blood dripping slowly from Elnora's arm. "The force necessary to detain you was perhaps unfortunate."

Cal barely restrained a growl.

"I am Laramie," the man continued. "One of the leaders of the people of this area. And I wish you harm only if you are an enemy to our cause."

"And what cause is that?" Cal asked.

"The overthrow of the usurper who sits on the throne at Kynton," said Laramie simply.

For a full minute there was stillness in the clearing, as the three captives stared at Laramie in astonishment. It was Cal who eventually broke the silence.

"And who will take his place?" he asked slowly.

Laramie looked at him for a moment, then turned to the man standing behind him. "Blindfold them," he said curtly. "And bring them to base."

"Wait!" said Cal, but Laramie ignored him.

"And take his pack, it will be easier for him to walk without it."

"No!" Even Calinnde was surprised at the authority with which his voice rang across the clearing. The man whom Laramie had been addressing froze, even in the act of reaching for Cal's back.

"You have taken my sword, but you will not take my pack," he said, his voice confident. "Not unless I am dead first."

Laramie gave him a searching look. For a moment the clearing seemed to hold its breath, then the leader nodded.

"Very well, young man," he said. "You may keep your belongings. And your sword will be returned to you if you prove yourself loyal."

"Loyal to whom?" asked Cal, hoping his dry tone concealed his relief.

Laramie didn't answer, merely signaling to his followers. Within moments, Cal and his friends were back on their feet, marching again. The blindfolds were much better than the sacks

—at least Cal could breathe freely. And it was a good thing too, as the trip took at least half an hour this time.

Cal imagined that walking briskly while blindfolded would be difficult even on a smooth path. Through the dense undergrowth of a forest, it was a nightmare. Long before they arrived at their destination, every part of him ached. Finally, he was pulled to a stop.

"Welcome to our forest, Calinnae." Laramie's voice was so close beside Cal that it made him jump. The blindfold was suddenly whisked off his face, and he took in the scene before him with astonished eyes.

They were standing at the edge of an enormous clearing. The space was well defined by the tall wooden fence that rose up all around it. By the looks of the felled logs ringing the edges just inside the fence, the clearing had been enlarged, evidently a long time ago. The logs looked old, covered in moss and settled into the forest floor. Likewise, the wooden dwellings dotted throughout the clearing looked like they had not been constructed recently.

In between these buildings were tents made of animal hides, increasing the capacity of the space. The clearing itself was filled with activity, people coming and going in a ceaseless but ordered bustle. They were all wearing clothes in the forest hues worn by Laramie and his men, and as he watched them Cal noted that many were armed, men and women.

Everyone seemed to move with purpose and discipline, and there were no children or elderly people to be seen. Observing the movements of the forest dwellers, Cal realized that they were not looking at townspeople, like those of Pravat or Montego.

"They're—"

"An army," finished Jo quietly from close beside him.

Cal nodded, absorbing the scene before him. There were

signs around the clearing that the space was lived in, but he couldn't figure out if it was a forest community, a fortress, or a military camp. Perhaps all three.

"Come," said Laramie, leading the way toward a large tent in the middle of the camp. Exchanging glances that were now as curious as they were wary, Cal and his companions followed, their minders behind them. Just before reaching the large tent, Laramie veered to one side, and led them instead into a small tent just next to it. The space was not large enough to accommodate everyone. A number of the men continued on across the clearing, but at a word from Laramie, two remained outside.

Once inside, Laramie's gaze again fell on Calinnae.

"I will return in a moment with the other leader of this camp," he said. "But first—" His eyes flicked to Cal's pack then back to his face. "Would you like to tell me why power seems to emanate from your rucksack, Calinnae?"

Cal kept his expression stern, attempting to conceal his shock. "No," he said shortly. "I wouldn't."

"Very well," said Laramie, a hint of amusement in his voice. He glanced around at them all. "Wait here."

Without another word he slipped from the tent.

"What was that about?" asked Elnora in amazement. "What did he mean by power?"

Cal shrugged. He had no idea how to explain the potent presence of the Esvalere. "You don't sense anything?"

She shook her head. "Do you, Jo?" she asked, turning to Jonan.

"What? Oh, no, I have no idea what he's talking about," he said absently. "But never mind that. Cal," his voice had begun to take on a familiar hint of excitement. "Forget about waiting here. I have an idea for how to get away."

Even as he shook his head, Cal couldn't help the grin that spread across his face. "I'm sure you do, Jo," he said, resisting the urge to roll his eyes. "But I don't want to go anywhere. I want to find out exactly what this Laramie knows, and how."

"But—" Jo broke off, eyeing Calinnae suspiciously. "What are you grinning about?"

"You and your mad schemes," said Cal, his eyes twinkling.

"You haven't even heard it yet," protested Jo.

"I don't have to," Cal laughed.

"What is it?" Jo raised an eyebrow at the change in his friend's mood, but Cal just shrugged.

"Sorry, it's just...I didn't realize how stressed I've been. I've spent this whole time dreading you coming up with one of your crazy ideas, because then I'd have to figure out how to keep you alive through it. Stupid really, because you always manage to land on your feet somehow. I was trying to fight fate, thinking I could convince you to take the safe course. Now that I don't have to, I see how absurd it was to try to make you into someone you're not. Half of the events of my childhood only happened because of your dumb ideas. I guess...I guess I'm just glad to have my best friend back."

Jo was grinning in response long before the end of Cal's speech. "Likewise," he said, a laugh in his own eyes.

"This is all very nice," interjected Elnora. Cal noticed that although her tone was dry, she had a small smile on her face. "But there's a more pressing matter." She gestured to the tent wall, indicating the compound beyond. "What in the kingdom is going on here?"

"What's going on here," said a new voice, "is that we are preparing for war."

CHAPTER TWENTY-EIGHT

They all looked up to see a new face that was at the same time familiar. As Laramie entered behind him, the resemblance between them became even more marked. But that only partly explained the recognition Cal felt as he once again sensed some inexplicable connection with the stranger in front of him.

"This is Leander," said Laramie. "He also commands these forces." He turned to his companion, but his eyes remained on Calinnae. "Lee, this is the one," he said.

"Yes, I can see that," said Leander calmly, also looking at Cal with keen interest.

Cal met his eyes steadily. Once he would have felt unnerved by the combined effect of those two pairs of searching eyes. But he doubted that the boy who had grown up in a secluded fishing village would even recognize the person Cal had become.

"We would like to speak with you," Leander was continuing.

"Well, as you see," said Cal dryly, indicating his bound hands, "we are a captive audience."

"Really, Laramie," said Leander reproachfully. "Was that necessary?"

Laramie just shrugged.

"I would feel better about having a conversation if I didn't feel like a prisoner," persisted Cal.

The two leaders exchanged a glance, then with a sigh Laramie pulled a knife from his belt and cut the ropes. The three of them flexed their hands in relief, and Cal had to stop himself from going to Elnora's side when he saw her wince with pain as she rubbed her wrists. This wasn't the time to get distracted.

"So what do you want to speak to us about?" prompted Cal, shaking out his own hands. The gesture seemed to catch the attention of both of the men in front of him. He heard a sharp intake of breath, and looked up to see that both Laramie and Leander were staring at his hand. Or more specifically, at the signet ring he now wore there.

"Actually," corrected Leander, his eyes rising slowly to Cal's face, "it's just you we would like to speak to."

Cal shook his head firmly. Dragons he couldn't say no to, but these forest rebels were a different matter. "It's all of us or none of us," he said.

Cal could sense his friends' gratification, and the three of them drew closer together by an infinitesimal amount.

Laramie and Leander seemed to measure him with their eyes, but they didn't challenge his words. "Very well," said Leander at last. "What brought you to the forest? Our scouts say that you entered from the mountains. Very few use that road."

"We are making for Kynton," said Cal briefly. "We went to Montego looking for information, and our path from there to Kynton has led us through the forest."

"Montego?" said Laramie, surprised. "That's a long way south of here. You must have been trekking through the mountains for weeks."

"We..." Cal hesitated, exchanging brief glances with Jo and Elnora. "We took a shortcut."

"A shortcut?" repeated Laramie, frowning, but Leander waved a hand impatiently.

"Why are you going to Kynton?"

Cal sighed. "We don't know exactly," he said. Leander raised an eyebrow incredulously.

"It's actually true," chimed in Jonan, a laugh in his voice. Cal had to restrain a smile of his own. The further from the mountains they traveled, the more the old Jonan seemed to be returning, the one who never took anything seriously.

"This is not a joke to us," said Laramie. "We are on the edge of war."

"So we heard," Cal said. "Does that mean that you know about the Valorian army?"

They stared at him. "How do you know about the Valorian army?"

"We saw it," said Cal simply.

The foresters exchanged uneasy looks. "What do you mean? Our reports are that the army is yet to cross the Great River."

"That's right," said Cal. "From the mountains we could see the army across the river."

There was a moment of silence. "I think there's a great deal you haven't told us," said Leander shrewdly.

"About as much as you haven't told us," countered Cal. "I'll be candid when you are."

Laramie was looking at Cal through narrowed eyes, but Leander's scrutiny was more thoughtful than suspicious.

"As you wish, Calinnae," he said at last. "But first let me ask you one more question. Do you recognize me?" He glanced at Laramie. "Either of us?"

Cal hesitated, thinking of the strangely familiar essence that hung about them. "What do you mean?"

Leander seemed confused by the question. "I mean, have you seen our faces before?"

Cal shook his head. "No, I don't think so. Why?"

Leander sighed, running a hand through his hair before he responded. "Just that my brother and I—" he gestured toward Laramie, "had warning of your approach. We sent scouts to intercept you as you entered the forest."

"Warning?" asked Cal quickly. "From whom?"

"That I can't answer," said Leander smoothly. "No one who identified himself. We saw your face in a dream."

"What do you mean 'we'?" asked Jonan, perplexed.

Laramie shrugged. "It was not the first time we awoke to find that we had shared the same dream. Perhaps because we are twins? Who knows? But this time was different."

"Yes," agreed Leander. His eyes had not left Cal's face. "This time we saw you, Calinnae, entering the forest from the mountains. You wielded a sword, and you emanated power."

"Me?" Cal could only stare. "You saw my face?"

"As clearly as I see it before me now," affirmed Leander. "Tell me, Calinnae, do you know why Valoria marches against Kyona even as we speak?"

"Because..." Cal struggled to marshal his thoughts, his mind still in a daze. He had thought nothing would surprise him after the events of recent days, but the news that he had appeared as a vision in someone else's dream was hard to take in.

"Because," he tried again, "Kyona has fallen into decay, and news of it has spread beyond our borders. The country languishes under Filip's rule, and the Valorian king seeks to stop the deterioration by wresting the country away from the crown."

"That's right," said Laramie, his voice eager. "But maybe you've heard rumors...there are those of us who are aware that the country has already been wrested away from the crown. A long time ago."

"Yes," Cal agreed cautiously. "Everyone knows those rumors. But where do you come into this?"

"We have been building toward unseating Filip, and Hugo before him, for a long time," Laramie continued enthusiastically. "Waiting until we had the manpower. Waiting until the time was right."

"And do you?" Cal asked, feeling a stirring of excitement himself. "Have the manpower I mean?"

Laramie's face fell slightly, and it was Leander who answered.

"I will be honest with you, it was not our intention to act now. The Valorians have forced our hand. We are preparing for an attack on Kynton, but we do not have any certainty of success."

"But what do you hope to achieve?" Elnora asked, speaking up for the first time since the twins had entered the tent. "If you unseat Filip, do you think the Valorians will withdraw?"

Laramie and Leander exchanged a fleeting glance. "We have reason to hope so," Leander said.

"Surely not," Elnora persisted. "Surely the complaints about Filip are just a front, and Valoria wishes to annex Kyona for its own purposes."

"No, you're wrong," said Laramie quickly. "King Gresham does not wish for war with Kyona any more than we wish for it."

"That's a bit hard to believe. I saw the army with my own eyes," said Jonan dryly.

But Laramie was still shaking his head. "There is still honor in Valoria—they have not fully forgotten the old ties."

"You seem well informed," said Cal suspiciously. "How do you know what is in the mind of the Valorian king?"

The rebel leaders were silent, their eyes veiled.

"You've been in contact with him," said Cal slowly. "The

scouts who brought you the reports of the army were actually messengers."

Leander acknowledged it with a nod. "His Majesty was very interested in what we had to say about how Kyona has been impacted by the corruption of our royal bloodline. He seemed sympathetic to the suggestion that the land is under a curse as a result."

"So what is his army doing marching toward the crossing right now?" asked Elnora skeptically.

Leander sighed. "Our communication was too little too late. We could not promise him that we could resolve the...problem with our land to his satisfaction."

"But he is not against us," interjected Laramie quickly. "He will not throw his might behind us, but if we can unseat Filip without his help, he will withdraw, at least until he can see what the impact of the change might be. A great deal of bloodshed could be saved if we can avert this war."

"The impact of what change precisely?" asked Cal grimly. "If you overthrow Filip, who will sit on the throne? One of you?"

"Of course not," said Leander, his voice sharp. "We are not the heirs to the throne. But we believe that there is an heir." He was watching Cal closely. "The stories of the royal house—the true royal house—are all agreed on one point. The royal line has always been under a protection that is..." he glanced at his brother, "...not entirely natural."

He returned his gaze to Cal as he went on. "It is said that due to this protection no man in that bloodline ever died without producing an heir. We have strong reason to believe that the heir to the last king was not killed in the coup that overthrew his father. He escaped. And we believe—we are certain—that through him the line has survived. The Bloodline continues, and we have expended considerable effort trying to track it down. But it has been well hidden."

Laramie chimed in. "If we can bring Filip down, perhaps we can prevent war. We thought that a steward could perhaps be appointed until the true heir can be found."

There was a moment of silence. "I'm no authority when it comes to making plans," said Jonan, "but even I can tell that is a terrible plan."

Leander sighed again. "As we said, it was not our intention to act so soon. Even yesterday I had my doubts about the wisdom of an attack. I fell asleep frustrated about our fruitless search for the heir." He fixed his eyes on Calinnae. "But then I had a dream."

Everyone in the tent turned their eyes toward Calinnae.

"In the dream, Calinnae, you also wore a signet ring. Like the one I see on your finger now. Where did you get it, if I may ask?"

Cal exchanged a look with Jo. "It was my father's," he said at last. It still felt strange to speak of Elam as his father, but there was no need to bring these forester men into that whole history.

"And who is your father, Calinnae of Nerita?" asked Leander, his voice quiet.

Cal took a deep breath, and his eyes again flicked momentarily to Jonan before he answered. "His name was Elam," he said. "But he has passed to his ancestors."

"I am sorry for your loss," said Laramie gravely. "When did this occur?"

"Very recently," said Cal. "He was struck down by Filip's soldiers, who I believe came to our village specifically to seek him out. They also killed my mother, and Jonan's parents. My father was carrying this ring when he died."

The twins exchanged a meaningful look. "I am sorry," said Leander, speaking heavily and looking between both Cal and Jo this time.

"We heard rumors of this," he continued. "Our sources in the capital told us some time ago that Filip thought he had identified a descendant of the true kings. He accused this man of treason and sent soldiers to hunt him down. We were informed that he had been found and...removed, but that the soldiers have been unable to find and eliminate his offspring."

"And more recently," Laramie jumped in eagerly, "we have hardly needed our spies. The rumor has spread rapidly across the whole country that one of the two young men currently wanted for treason has been publicly claiming to be the descendant of the true royal bloodline. It was not difficult to imagine that this young man must be the fugitive heir of the man Filip sent his soldiers to execute."

Leander frowned at his brother. Perhaps he had caught Cal's and Jo's winces in response to the word "execute".

"I am afraid we are in some part responsible for what happened to your parents," Leander said. "The military activity across the border added an urgency to our inquiries in recent months. It seems we were careless, and news of our search reached Filip. He has always been paranoid—"

"With good reason," cut in Laramie dryly. "Have you heard the rumors about Hugo's death?"

"That the accident wasn't an accident?" said Cal grimly. "Yes, we've heard them."

"Well, there's little chance of proving it, but according to our men inside, very few in the castle doubt that it was Filip who removed his father. He has always been eager to rule."

"And to rule unchallenged," said Leander. "When he caught wind of our activities, he started inquiries of his own. I can only assume that he had access to information we did not."

Cal caught a hint of accusation in Jonan's eyes, but he could not fault the forest rebels for unintentionally endangering their families with the search. Elam had been hiding for a long time, and his concealment had come at great cost for many people.

"My father did not wish to be found," he acknowledged quietly. "But perhaps his caution overpowered his wisdom."

The air of excitement hanging about Laramie became more evident. Leander's expression gave less away, but Cal could see a gleam in his eyes.

"What did you mean about power coming from me?" Cal asked quickly, before they could begin questioning him again. He nodded at Laramie. "You said you could feel it coming from my pack."

"There is great power in this land," Laramie answered seriously. "Most people don't feel it, but we can sense it at times. Especially near the mountains."

"You sense it also, don't you?" probed Leander. When Cal didn't immediately answer, the rebel leader continued. "Let us speak plainly, Calinnae. You have heard our intentions, and if you are who we think you are, you know you have nothing to fear from us. So tell me—do you claim royalty in your ancestry?"

"I do," said Cal gravely.

"How far back can you trace it?" asked Laramie, barely containing his excitement now.

Cal shook his head in frustration. "I cannot trace it," he admitted. "My father did not confide in me. It was only after his death that I discovered, by accident, who he had been." He glanced again at Jonan. "That's a long story."

The twins again exchanged a look. "May we examine the ring?" Leander asked.

Cal nodded, and handed it over. It was strange, he thought, considering the short time he had worn it, how naked his hand felt without it.

Leander turned it over in his own hand, his expression almost reverent. "It's the royal seal, sure enough," he said to his brother in a voice that quivered with excitement. "See?"

"Yes," said Laramie eagerly, leaning in closer. "The true seal. I'd know it anywhere."

They turned to the three companions. "Let us show you," said Leander. "Laramie, the records?"

"I have them," said Laramie, pulling from his belt a scroll that was tightly furled and tied with a blue ribbon. He pulled a small table toward him and spread one of the sheaves open on it. "See there?" He pointed to the top of the page, and Cal, Jonan, and Elnora moved forward to see for themselves.

The records looked old, as old as some of the ones they had seen in Pravat. And at the top of this page, just as on the document Jonan had removed from the Hall of Records, there was a circle of hardened wax, with an intricate symbol impressed into it. A symbol that was already becoming familiar...

"Perfectly aligned," breathed Laramie, pressing Cal's ring into the indentation. "There can be no doubt that this is the royal signet ring of the True Bloodline. There was only one, and it could not be reproduced. That's why from the beginning the usurper's house had to use an altered crest."

The twins looked up at Cal, identical expressions of excitement on their faces. "Do you know what this means, Calinnae?" Leander asked, as he handed the ring back.

"This ring is all I have from my father," Cal said seriously. "I cannot prove my ancestry to you, or to anyone. But yes, I know what it means. And for reasons that go beyond this ring, I know without question that I am directly descended, father to son, from Jonathon, the only son of King Cael."

There was a moment of silence after this solemn declaration, as everyone in the tent seemed to stop breathing. Then Laramie and Leander both surged forward, and Cal found himself jostled as both men tried to clasp his arm at once, their words tumbling over him.

"Welcome, brother!"

"You have no idea how long we have searched for you!"

"I didn't think I would live to see this day!"

"How did you find us?"

Cal couldn't find the words to answer, torn between astonishment at their response and relief at the deep sense of belonging washing over him.

"Wait," he said at last. "How do you know I'm telling the truth? I mean, I am, but…how do you know I didn't just take this ring from the true heir?"

Laramie smiled. "Not many people, outside us in the forest, even know that this signet ring still exists. You would have been a well-informed thief to know that you should take it, or what to do with it once you had. And you would be lucky to have then found your way to us, the only people who would immediately accept it for what it is."

"The mere fact that you know the name King Cael is a count in your favor," Leander added. "And do not forget our strange dream."

Cal suddenly remembered the mountain people's legend about the first king to have friendship with the dragons, and how Qadir had visited him in a dream, compelling him to come to the mountains. And it had been Qadir who had said that they would find assistance in the forest, as well as insisting that they spend the night outside Vasilisa first. Perhaps the dragon-ruler had provided them with more help than he had let on.

"But in addition to all that," Leander was saying, his smile as warm as his brother's, "we recognized your signature as soon as we met you. Quite apart from having seen your face in our dreams. Do you not feel it also?"

Cal nodded numbly, unsure how to articulate what he had felt upon meeting the twins.

Leander clasped his arm again. "We are your kin," he said.

"Many generations may have passed, but our spirits recognize the connection yet."

"What do you mean?" asked Calinnae. "Are you also descended from Jonathon?"

Laramie shook his head. "If we were, we might have had some idea where to find you. But our ancestor lost contact with Jonathon at the time of the Corruption. She knew that he survived, because the usurper sought him, secretly but ferociously. She knew also the magical protection that was legendary in her house's history. The king always had a son, always only one son, the direct line never broken. When the usurper took the throne, our ancestor fled Kynton, but she stayed concealed not far away. The forest became our home, and has been ever since."

"Princess Avalyn," said Cal slowly. "So she did survive."

Laramie's smile was blinding. "She did. And in the tradition of her ancestors, she passed her stories down faithfully. We grew up knowing who we are, and longing for the day when our royal house would be restored. Our fathers before us not only built a home here, but worked always to prepare what resources we had to support our kinsman when he should come to reclaim his throne. We can trace our line directly from Princess Avalyn, and we have the records to prove it." He gestured at the sheaf still on the table. "These papers are the first of those records. That's why they have the seal of the true royal house."

"It is something of a problem that you cannot do the same," mused Leander thoughtfully. "The ring will be compelling for those who have seen the records that survived the usurper's purge—and there are more than you might think—but as you say, it is not conclusive. And not everyone will immediately understand its significance. We recognize your right to rule, but the rest of the kingdom may not be so ready to accept you."

Cal remained silent, wishing he had an answer to offer. If

only Qadir had been willing to accompany them. He could only imagine that the word of a dragon would carry a great deal of weight with any skeptical citizens.

Your right to rule. The words made Cal's head spin. He had not seriously questioned the truth of it since hearing Qadir's revelation, but somehow it felt much more real now that someone else believed it as well.

"There's no time to worry about that," said Laramie. "That is a problem that will have to take care of itself." He turned purposefully to Calinnae. "The real question is, will you march with us to Kynton? Will you challenge the usurper?"

Cal stared back into the rebel's eyes, and the hope and trust reflected back at him made him feel at once more confident and more ill-equipped than ever. But recent though the revelation of his identity had been, deep within himself he felt like he had been awaiting this question all his life.

"I will."

CHAPTER TWENTY-NINE

When the sun rose the next day, Cal was still attempting to catch his breath. It seemed lately that each dawn found his life dramatically different from the day before.

His declaration had been greeted with great enthusiasm by his distant cousins, and he had instantly been whisked away on a round of preparations and introductions. They had returned his sword immediately, with profuse apologies for its removal when they discovered that it had belonged to their royal forefather.

So much information had been imparted to him that he felt like his head was an overcrowded chest about to pop its hinges. He had been unsure how much of his adventures to recount to Laramie and Leander, and in light of Qadir's wishes, had decided in the moment to refrain from making mention of the dragons. As an unintended result, his achievements and discoveries sounded more impressive than they really had been, and he felt concerned that he was raising expectations he could not fulfill. But having opened the floodgates of their excitement, there was no stemming the flow.

Somewhat to his surprise, the rest of the camp seemed ready to take the twins' word for it that Calinnae was the true heir. He repeated the performance with the ring and the twins' ancient records so many times that he felt like a member of a traveling troupe, performing his act for audience after audience. Laramie and Leander also recounted their dream with unexpected matter-of-factness, and no one seemed to doubt its significance.

And it wasn't just that their faith in their leaders was absolute, although it obviously was. These forest people, descended from Princess Avalyn and those who had fled with her, had clearly grown up on stories as meaningful to them as Elam's stories were to Cal. They accepted the fact of the royals' connection to an unnatural power as readily as they accepted the significance of the legendary signet ring.

It was more than Calinnae could have ever hoped for, to find a large, well-equipped group with previous knowledge that would support his claim, waiting for him on his road to Kynton. But still, he found the people's tears and enthusiasm and declarations of loyalty overwhelming.

He barely saw Jonan and Elnora for the rest of the day. Multiple times he attempted to inquire after them, but Laramie and Leander assured him airily that they would be fine. It made him uncomfortable to be separated from them, and even amidst the chaos of preparation, he was acutely aware of his unfinished conversation with Elnora. But the pace at which the twins moved didn't allow him a quiet moment to seek them out.

Laramie did have the decency to look a bit sheepish when Cal asked acidly if his friends' injuries would be attended to, and for the next hour Leander continued Cal's tour alone while his brother hurried off to check on the others.

When the sun was low in the sky, and the camp began to prepare for the evening meal, Cal reached his limit. The twins wanted to fete him as the guest of honor at the meal, and Cal insisted he be allowed to speak with his companions before eating. He was directed to a small tent near the edge of camp.

When he strode in, they both greeted him with relief.

"I thought they'd never release you!" said Jonan. Elnora said nothing, but it was clear from her expression how overwhelmed she was.

Cal grasped Jo's arm briefly, then pulled Elnora against him, heedless alike of Jonan's raised eyebrows and Elnora's stiff posture. He continued to hold her firmly, and after a long moment, her body relaxed. She laid her head fleetingly against his chest before pulling resolutely away, wiping an arm across her eyes.

He frowned at the gesture, but like everything else, it would have to wait.

"What's happening?" asked Jonan. "I hear we're marching at first light."

Cal nodded. "They have people inside the castle, and the plan is to take the fight to Filip. They're relying heavily on the element of surprise, because they don't have the numbers. Filip has multiple garrisons stationed in the capital right now, in a belated attempt to respond to this Valorian invasion."

Jo gave a low whistle.

"They hope that we won't have to actually take them all out," said Cal, his voice betraying his skepticism. "They hope that there are a great number who might turn if they can be convinced of the legitimacy of my claim."

Jo's face looked skeptical as well, and Cal wondered if he was also picturing the soldiers they had encountered in Pravat.

"What have you been up to?" Cal asked quickly.

Jo shrugged. "Not much," he said. "They cleaned us up, and invited us to join the training exercises."

Looking at his friends properly, Cal realized for the first time that they were wearing different clothes. Like him, they were now dressed in the green and brown of the foresters. The clothes were practical and comfortable, but Cal felt no more like himself in them than he had in the gray of the mountain people. He would have preferred to ride for Kynton in his own clothes from Nerita, but they had never been returned in Montego. Remembering the state of them, he guessed that they had ended up in the communal fire.

Unlike the mountain people, the rebel women did not restrict their movement with skirts, and Cal noted irrelevantly that Elnora was just as stunning in the closely fitted green tunic and leggings as she had been in the simple mountain dress. He tried not to stare at the way the clothes hugged her form. Perhaps more stunning.

"Nice to be wearing clothes that aren't covered in blood for a change," he said.

Jonan gave a brief smile. "I wish we could have been here sooner. There wasn't much I could learn in such a short time, but I think I could be good at this if I'd had more training."

"I don't doubt it," said Cal, returning the smile. His look immediately became troubled as he took in the weapons both of his friends now wore. "We're not prepared for this though, any of us. We don't know how to fight a war. I don't want to drag you both into the middle of it."

"Don't think for a moment you can convince me not to come," said Jonan flatly. "Surely you know better than that."

Cal sighed. "I do," he said, "I really do." He looked at Elnora, almost pleadingly, but she shook her head firmly.

"Don't even say it, Cal," she said. "There's not a chance."

He stared at her unhappily. "I don't know if I can protect you," he said.

She raised her eyebrows. "I've never expected you to."

"Maybe not, but I expect it of myself," said Cal. "It's the least

I can do. I hardly think you would have left Kerr if you'd known you would be catapulted into a war."

"Actually," she said, "I would have." Her eyes met his, and something passed between them that filled Cal with a strange mixture of glorious fulfillment and hopeless longing.

She was so close he could have reached out a hand and touched her, but she was utterly inaccessible. How could she seem so completely as though she were a part of him, and yet so clearly not be his? If only Jo weren't here, he would close the distance between them, pull her against him, and refuse to let her go until she fully explained the wall she had put up between them since Qadir's revelation. Then he would kiss her until she forgot whatever stupid reason she had come up with to keep them apart.

But Jo was here, and there was an army waiting outside for him to lead them into an uncertain battle for which he was hopelessly underprepared. And although Elnora was apparently now unwilling to give him her heart, she was evidently determined to risk her life following him into a conflict with a doubtful outcome at best. Cal barely managed to restrain a groan.

But it seemed there was no more to be said. When they emerged from the tent for the evening meal, Cal was again whisked away. He found that he had no heart for the fuss being made of him, but he was sensible enough to realize the importance of accepting rather than rebuffing the enthusiasm of these people. He had no hope of success without them.

After the meal, Leander and Laramie took Cal with them into the large central tent, and discussed strategy for the following day until Cal's head hurt. He contributed very little, having no training or experience that could be useful. He only hoped that he didn't come across as unsuited for leadership as he felt.

When he was finally allowed to sleep, they tried to set him up in a spacious tent, but he resolutely refused. Instead he joined Jo where he had laid a pallet down by one of the fires dotted throughout the clearing. It seemed that the women slept in the wooden dwellings, and Elnora was nowhere to be seen.

Cal's weariness overcame his whirling emotions more quickly than he would have believed possible, and before long he had sunk into a deep and dreamless sleep.

And so, as the sun rose, he found himself dressed and ready, King Cael's sword strapped to his side, and the Esvalere pulsing with power in his rucksack. He had seen the curiosity burning in Laramie's and Leander's eyes when he had insisted that the pack must stay on his back even during the battle, but they had asked him no questions. It was hardly ideal, but he couldn't see what other choice he had. The memory was all too vivid in his mind of what had occurred the last time a king had ridden through this forest with the Esvalere in his pack.

For ride he would. He sat astride a beautiful roan mare, wishing not for the first time that he had spent more time in the saddle during his life in Nerita. Most of the group were on foot, but Leander had refused to countenance Cal's suggestion that the horse would be of more use to someone who had more riding experience. The forester clearly wanted Cal in front and visible, where his presence could inspire and encourage those following. It made Cal uncomfortable, but he supposed he would have to get used to it. Jo and Elnora were to walk, and the gulf that seemed to be widening between him and them only increased the surreal nature of the ride.

The army pushed on through the forest all day. The riders moved at a relatively slow pace to accommodate the majority on foot. But still, Cal could see that the group was being pushed hard to cover the ground as quickly as they did. He felt guilty to be riding, knowing that Jonan and Elnora must be exhausted to be marching so relentlessly immediately after their grueling trek through the mountains.

Even so, Cal thought he would have preferred to walk himself. In a very short time, he ached from the unaccustomed feel of the saddle, and every bone felt jolted by the time they finally stopped. It was already dark, as the plan had been to march until they were within reach of the capital. They were only an hour from the edge of the forest, Leander told him. As soon as they left the trees, they would be able to see Kynton before them.

It was hard to stop so close to their objective, knowing that the Valorian army would by now have crossed into Kyona, further south. But Cal couldn't deny that he badly needed to rest before confronting Filip. The bruises from his run in with Bryant's gang had started to fade, but he still carried the marks of his brawl with Jonan, not to mention the fresh injuries sustained while being forced through the forest by the rebels. Add to that the day of riding, and it was hard to locate any part of him that didn't ache.

He had seen no sign of either of his friends all day, and he wasn't able to find Elnora once they stopped, either. After another long session with the military leaders, as exhausting mentally as the ride had been physically, Cal slipped away and with difficulty located Jonan. Cal once again rejected the offer of sleeping quarters, instead settling in to sleep near his friend. Jonan told him that while everyone marched together, the women camped apart from the men, and Jo and Elnora had been separated as soon as they had stopped.

Cal sighed, glancing wistfully in the direction Jo had indicated. He had hoped to speak with Elnora again before the morning. "Is she all right?" he asked his friend quietly.

Jo shrugged, his face barely visible in the moonlight. No telltale fires had been lit tonight. "Honestly, I don't really know how to tell. She hasn't said anything, but she's seemed a bit off since we left the mountains."

Cal sighed again.

"What's going on with you two?" asked Jo. "It's like she's avoiding talking about you, but anytime you're vaguely close by, her eyes never leave you for a second." Cal was silent for so long that Jo prompted him again. "Cal?"

"I heard you," said Cal. "I just...don't know what to say."

"Well, did something happen between you?"

Cal let out a long breath. "Yes."

Jo waited, but Cal didn't elaborate. "Come on, Cal," he said in irritation. "Don't make me drag it out of you."

"Fine," said Cal shortly. "I told her I loved her. And then I kissed her."

There was a brief stunned silence, then Jo gave a soft exclamation of surprise. "Wow." He chuckled softly.

"What?" said Cal defensively.

"Nothing. I mean...it's not like I didn't know it was coming, it's just...I didn't realize you were so bold. When were you even alone together?"

"In the cave," said Cal shortly. "While you were being... tested or whatever it was."

"Of course." Jo's tone was thoughtful. "So what did she do? When you kissed her?"

Cal grinned in spite of himself, under cover of the darkness. "She kissed me back."

"Well, well, well," Jo sounded like he was holding back a laugh. "You two have been holding out on me."

"You don't...mind?" Cal tried to keep his tone light.

"What do you mean?" asked Jo. When Cal didn't answer, understanding seemed to dawn. "Cal, don't be an idiot! You're telling me you really can't tell that Elnora and I are not interested in each other that way? As if the two of you haven't been making eyes at each other ever since we picked her up in Kerr."

Cal let out a relieved breath. "That's what she said, too. I mean," he amended hastily, "the bit about you not being interested in each other, not the other part."

"Well, she's a smart girl," said Jo with a hint of amusement. "You should listen to her. She'll be a good influence on you. She might even be able to keep you from taking yourself too seriously."

Cal grunted in frustration. "I would love nothing more than to let her be whatever influence on me she likes, but she'll barely look me in the eyes now."

"Hmm..." mused Jo. "I guess the whole identity swap thing is a lot to take in." His tone was mild, but Cal couldn't miss the weight behind his words. "For all of us."

"I guess," Cal agreed unhappily. "I don't really know why it would change how she feels, though. It's not like she's not strong enough to face whatever might come at us now." He grimaced. "More successfully than I will, probably. She's weathered more than either of us has."

Jonan considered his words for a moment. "That may be so," he said at last. "And I don't know that it would change how she feels. But maybe what she thinks."

"What do you mean?" asked Cal, but instead of answering, Jo gave vent to a huge yawn.

"Don't ask me to unravel her mind," he said. "You'll have to ask her. And if we're going to be able to stand on our own feet tomorrow, we both need to sleep."

Cal couldn't disagree, but it didn't stop him feeling unsatisfied.

.   .   .

He woke quite suddenly in the darkness. He knew that the plan was to leave a couple of hours before dawn, but looking at the stars, he was pretty sure it wasn't time yet. He glanced at Jo's form nearby. From the heavy rise and fall of his chest, his friend was still fast asleep.

Cal sat up and hugged his knees for warmth in the chill night air. His mind was a chaotic whirl. He could hardly believe that he was only hours away from marching on the capital and declaring himself the true king. It seemed like a lifetime had passed since he and Jonan fled Nerita, but in reality it was only a short time ago that he had been just another boy growing up in the small coastal town. Well, not quite just another boy. Their superior education had always set him and Jonan apart. But he had never felt out of place. They had always had each other.

And now they were marching to war. Would he live to see another night? Would the rebels' spies inside the castle be able to unlock the portcullis as planned? Would they be able to convince any of the soldiers to turn on Filip? Even if everything went as they hoped—which seemed unlikely—there was still the problem of convincing the rest of the country to accept Cal as their king.

He leaned back, looking up at the stars. In his mind he traced the journey that had brought him to this point, trying to recapture all the interweaving threads revealed to him by the Esvalere. He couldn't remember all the details, but he knew that as he wielded it, he had become aware of so much that he had missed when actually living through the adventure. Even now he could feel its pulse at his back, its power leaking out to cover him like a blanket. It wasn't giving him the clear images and insights it would if he were to touch it with his hands, just reminding him potently of its presence.

It was tempting to pull it out, but he didn't dare do so in such a crowded place. Even if everyone between him and the distant sentries appeared to be asleep.

He thought about what Qadir had said about the dragonwrath. King Cael had been cursed to see evil but not to act. How accurately that captured the inaction of Jonathon's line, all the way down to Elam. All the way down to Calinnae, Cal realized with shame. He thought of the humiliating fear that had seemed to grip him with unexpected force any time either he or the Bloodline—as he understood it—was in danger. The instinct to do whatever it took to remain safe had been so strong. It had felt like a physical presence, restraining him from taking the decisive action that came so naturally to Jonan.

It had thrown Cal because he had never been fearful as a child. He realized that the fear hadn't begun until after Elam died. Perhaps it was only with the death of his father that the curse had passed to him. When he pictured that fear as an embodiment of the curse, it made much more sense. It had seemed like its own force, somehow coming both from outside of him and from deep within his core. The evil brought to the country by the false king's rule hadn't been enough to break through it. He had seen evil but not been willing to act. Hadn't Jo told him, immediately after their parents' deaths, that the inaction of the true royals had been a betrayal? And all Cal could do was encourage Jonan to go into hiding himself.

Qadir had said that Jonan shared the credit for breaking the curse. Cal had always thought Jo reckless, but it seemed that from the very beginning, his friend could see things Cal could not. Cal searched through his memory, trying to remember all the instances of that crippling fear. On reflection, he didn't think he'd felt it since they rescued Elnora from the trader vessel. Was that when he had broken it? Taking his warning from King Cael's failure to intervene when it still might have made a difference, Cal had pushed his fear aside and put his life on the line to do what needed to be done.

But that had been an easy decision, really. It had been to save Elnora. Feeling what he felt now, Cal could hardly believe that he had hesitated even for a moment.

His eyes followed the direction of his thoughts, straying over to where the women were camped. He could see nothing in the darkness, but some fancy made him feel as though her presence was calling out to him across the intervening space.

Even as he told himself that he would never locate her amidst the sleeping forms spread across the forest floor, he found that he was already walking, picking his way quietly around groups of pallets.

He soon realized that all the people sprawled in sleep before him were women. He searched fruitlessly for a familiar shape. Then suddenly, glancing up, he glimpsed her through the trees ahead. Of course she wasn't sleeping. It seemed the most natural thing somehow that if he was awake, she would be too.

She was sitting on a fallen tree a short distance away. Her back was to Cal, but there was no mistaking her outline, or the loose braid down her back that glinted in the moonlight.

He approached her quietly, treading carefully to avoid waking anyone. She started when he came alongside her, but stilled instantly on recognizing him.

"What are you doing here?" she asked softly. "They separate to sleep."

"I know," he said, sitting beside her. "But I couldn't sleep. I came to find you."

"Oh," she said. He waited, but she didn't add anything.

"I didn't see you all day," he tried again.

"Yes," she acknowledged. "You have other responsibilities now."

He reached out a hand and tucked a loose strand of hair

behind her ear. She closed her eyes at his touch, but said nothing.

"Not anything that's more important than you," he responded softly.

She kept her eyes closed. "Don't do this, Cal," she said tersely.

"Do what?"

She rose to her feet, stepping away from him. "Remind us both of how hard this is." She spoke as though her point was obvious, but still Cal was in the dark.

"What does that mean?" he asked, standing also and closing the distance between them.

"It means that no matter how much I might want to be with you—"

"And do you?" Cal interrupted. "Do you want to be with me?"

"Of course I do!" she cried softly, turning to face him. "You know I do."

Cal wasn't even conscious of leaning toward her. He was only conscious of the way her face looked in the moonlight, unshed tears making her eyes glisten as they looked up into his with sadness and longing.

Then she was in his arms, and he was kissing her much more passionately than he had in the cave, making a mess of her hair as one hand reached up to cup the back of her head, his breath ragged and his lips insistent. And she was returning his kiss with an intensity that savored of desperation, her arms around his neck and her body pressed against his where they stood.

For a long moment they remained molded together, Cal pulling her so tightly against him that her feet almost left the ground. He had never felt more full of life and fire, and the knowledge that he might be riding to his death in mere hours only heightened his eagerness to hold her close.

Of course it was Elnora who pulled away. Cal would have made the moment last forever if he could. She was breathing hard as she turned her face away from his, and her voice came out choked.

"You should go, Cal. It's cruel to remind me what I'm losing."

"Why do you think you're losing anything?" Cal demanded, attempting to turn her face back toward him. She pushed his hand away.

"I mean it, Elnora," he said firmly. "Why?"

"Because," she said, turning to look at him at last, her face full of steely determination. "Because we're going to succeed. We're going to reclaim what's yours by right."

"And that's bad?" Cal asked, perplexed.

"Of course not!" she said. "That's why we're all here."

"Then why do you look like someone's plunged a knife into your side?" Cal insisted.

"Because—" Elnora met his look, her expression anguished. "Once we set things right, you can never be mine."

"Why not?" Cal protested.

"Because you'll be king, Cal," Elnora said impatiently.

"And what does that have to do with anything?" Cal asked, torn between the desire to finally understand her sudden withdrawal, and wanting to be done with all this talking so he could kiss her again.

She looked at him incredulously. "Do you really think the people of Kyona are going to accept me as queen?"

He traced her cheekbone with his thumb, letting it travel all the way down to her lips. "They would be mad not to."

"Be serious, Cal," said Elnora, her voice not entirely steady.

"I am being serious," he said. "I'm an unknown kid from a

fishing village. I think they're as likely to accept you as queen as they are to accept me as king."

She shook her head. "It's not the same. This is your birthright. You're supposed to be king."

"And we're supposed to be together," said Cal firmly. "I'm as sure of that as I am of anything."

She was silent for a moment. "I'm touched, Cal," she said at last. "Truly I am. Not very long ago there was nothing I wanted more than to hear you say that. But things have changed now."

"Not as far as I'm concerned," Cal persevered stubbornly.

"Especially as far as you're concerned," Elnora insisted. "It seemed like a stretch even when I thought you might become the king's close adviser, but I thought maybe it wasn't impossible...but when you're actually the king? You have to be realistic, Cal. You're just not free anymore to fall in love with an orphaned street rat from the dirty docks."

Cal stared at her. "Is that how you see yourself?"

"I'm not looking for a compliment, Cal," she said quickly. "My point is you won't be allowed to choose me. It would never work."

"Shouldn't I be allowed to do whatever I want if I'm king?" asked Cal indignantly. He was starting to understand Jonan's irritation at all the times Cal had told him that being the heir meant he had to act differently from how he wanted to.

"Of course not," said Elnora crisply. "I don't know much about court, but even I know how these things work. I imagine you'll be expected to make some kind of political marriage, or to marry someone from the nobility to help legitimize your rule."

"Elnora," said Cal seriously, taking her hands and holding them tightly when she tried to pull away. "I don't care what other people expect of me. Not in this. I care what I expect of myself. And I expect myself to choose someone I can trust to be the one standing beside me."

He released one of her hands, but only so he could run the back of his fingers gently along her cheek, following the line past her jaw, his hand coming to rest cupped around the back of her neck.

"Someone who is as brave as she is beautiful, as kind as she is smart, and as strong as she is precious to me."

"Oh Cal," she whispered, tears again in her eyes. "If only it could be that simple."

"It is that simple," he said firmly. "You're the only one for me."

She shook her head, but he was already leaning back toward her, one hand still curled around behind her head, and the other reaching for her waist. If words couldn't convince her, maybe actions would. He was certainly willing to try kissing her out of her absurd dejection.

Before he could do so, however, he was startled by a loudly cleared throat. Elnora jumped guiltily away from him, the flush that rose to her face visible even in the moonlight. Cal retained a hand on her waist, refusing to let her go so easily. He glared at the forester who had interrupted him, and the poor boy looked terrified.

"I'm sorry, Sire," he said nervously. "The leaders sent me to look for you. We're riding soon, and you're wanted in their tent."

"Well, they can wait," returned Cal, unable to fully keep the snap out of his voice.

Elnora shook her head. "Go, Cal," she said. "This is what we're here for."

"I don't want to," he said stubbornly.

She smiled sadly. "You have things to think about beyond what you want," she said. "We both do."

He sighed. "Fine," he said, not very graciously. He released her, but before turning away, he caught her gaze and held it, his voice serious. "The only barrier between us is the one you've created in your head, Elnora."

She didn't respond to his words, but she put a gentle hand on his arm. "Be careful out there, Cal," she said anxiously. "He won't give up without a fight."

He nodded. "You too," he said, a thrill of fear going through him at the thought of her in the battle. "I really wish you would stay clear until it's over, one way or the other."

She just shook her head, her half smile at odds with the tears still gathered in her eyes. "Go," she said.

He hesitated for another moment, but the messenger hovered intrusively close by. There was nothing to be done except follow him away from Elnora and back through the trees.

When he reached the makeshift tent where Laramie and Leander waited for him, he felt anything but prepared for battle. Every nerve tingled with the memory of Elnora's body pressed against him, but his heart was troubled at her persistent stubbornness. And his mind was distracted, wanting the chance to speak to Jonan again before they faced whatever the day might bring.

Unfortunately, it quickly became evident that he would get no such opportunity. The plan was to reach Kynton before dawn, trusting their men inside to take out the relevant sentries and raise the portcullis. Cal respected the twins for their intention to ride at the head of the party and be the first inside rather than staying at the rear. But the downside was that it meant imminent departure, with no chance to exchange last words with his companions.

The rebels were clearly well used to sleeping rough, and in an impossibly short time the first group was ready to depart. Cal and his kinsmen led at the front. When Cal had emerged from the tent to walk the small distance to his horse, he found that rebels lined his path, closing their fists over their hearts in a salute reminiscent of the mountain people's gesture.

He felt a certainty of purpose rise up within him as he acknowledged the tribute, and for once he didn't protest about the horse or the fanfare. He wanted to be at the front—he wanted to reach Filip before anyone else.

Riding through the dark was not as difficult as he expected. They took the main road boldly, and as they got closer to the forest's edge, Cal knew that the absence of any soldiers was a good sign. It seemed that their scouts and their men inside the castle had played their part. Nothing hindered their progress, and in less than the allotted hour, Laramie indicated to Calinnae that he should stop. He could see nothing in the darkness, but he knew that they must be very close to where the trees opened onto a short stretch of grassland.

They inched forward, and sure enough, within moments the road became a wide clear track across the field. From behind the tree line, Cal caught his first glimpse of a sight he had often longed to see.

Kynton.

From their vantage point, they could see the turrets of the royal castle rising above the mighty stone wall that circled the capital. Cal knew that the city itself sprawled out on the southern and western sides, but that the castle marked the eastern edge of the city, at which they were now looking.

Even in the moonlight, it was impressive. The darkness robbed its waving pennants of color, but the castle was still formidable, its battlements rising gracefully from the gently sloping grassland around it. It wasn't far away, barely more than a stone's throw. The road that ran out from the portcullis bent around to the south, but a decent-sized path branched off to run due east across the short distance to the forest, marking the beginning of the trail they had followed for two days now.

Cal heard a soft curse beside him, and turned in surprise to see Laramie scowling at the castle. Looking back at the capital he realized why. He had been so lost in admiration of the sight before him, that he had failed to note the most important detail.

The portcullis remained firmly closed. Something had gone wrong inside.

CHAPTER THIRTY

The twins drew their horses together, Cal in the middle, as they debated what to do. Since they had arrived at the edge of the forest earlier than expected, they had waited almost half an hour in the hope that the spies they had long ago placed inside the castle would still do their work. But the portcullis hadn't budged.

"We can't wait any longer," said Leander.

He was right. The sun would begin to rise in another hour, and any chance of entering the capital unseen would be long gone.

"Yes," Laramie agreed. "We have no other choice now. Someone must scale the wall and attempt to raise the portcullis from within."

"But surely the wall can't be climbed," Cal protested.

"It can by an agile climber," shrugged Leander. "Ordinarily the sentries would make it very difficult to enter undetected in such a way, but we know that's no barrier in this instance."

"I don't think we really know anything," said Cal dryly. But Leander had a point. They had observed carefully as they waited, and no sentry was patrolling the eastern wall.

Clearly their spies had at least partially succeeded in their mission.

"If someone makes it over the wall," Leander was continuing, "they may find the whole area undefended. If our men managed to take out the sentries before something went wrong, perhaps they also took out those at the gatehouse. It should then be a simple matter to raise the portcullis."

"That's a lot of ifs," Cal said heavily, but he had no better idea to offer.

"I can climb the wall," said an unexpected voice. All three riders started, looking down at the slim figure that had appeared next to their horses. Apparently while they tarried, the main force, traveling on foot, had caught up.

"No," said Cal flatly. "Absolutely not."

"You know I can do it, Cal," said Elnora calmly. "You've seen me do it before."

"That was different," said Cal. "We climbed up creepers at Pravat—here it's just the stone wall."

"Cal." Elnora spoke as if Cal was an unreasonable child. "I grew up in a street gang, remember? I'm pretty handy when it comes to things like climbing and sneaking into places, and going undetected."

Laramie was regarding Elnora with interest. "That's good to know," he mused.

"No," growled Cal, glaring at the older man. "Don't even think about it, we're not sending her. She may be good at sneaking in, but she's not trained in fighting. Surely any number of these people can climb that wall, and be better equipped to defend themselves once they're over it."

"Some of them could, but not as many as you might think," said Leander mildly.

"I'm pretty sure I can," chimed in another voice cheerfully, and Cal groaned.

"Jo, don't encourage this," he said wearily. "Neither one of you is climbing that wall."

"Well, someone has to," said Elnora reasonably. "And it sounds like we might not need to defend ourselves on the other side. If the spies have taken out the sentries, I mean."

Leander gave her a pointed look, but she just shrugged. "No offense, but if you didn't want to be overheard, you should have been a bit more aware of your surroundings. I told you, I'm pretty good at going undetected."

"And you know I can climb, Cal," said Jonan. "Much better than you can, and you had no trouble at Pravat."

It was all true. But it didn't make Cal any happier.

"It's not a bad idea," mused Laramie, apparently oblivious to Cal's glare. "If they really can scale the wall, they'd have as good a chance as anyone of raising the portcullis. Better, even. They don't carry themselves like foresters. They could probably pass as civilians. Just a young couple out for a moonlit stroll."

Cal's scowl deepened. "Except for their forester clothes," he said tartly.

"Surely someone can lend us traveling cloaks to cover up these clothes," said Elnora dismissively.

"And traveling cloaks will make it so much easier to climb the wall," said Cal sarcastically. He shook his head, his voice firm. "You're not soldiers. One of the foresters who's good at climbing can go. Someone who can fight whatever guards they meet once they're over."

"Calinnae," said Leander, his voice reasonable. "I think we should consider this offer. The very fact that they're not trained fighters makes them a good choice."

"How can it possibly—" Cal began, but his indignation turned to anger as he caught Leander's meaning. "They might be expendable to you," he growled, "but they aren't to me."

"No one said they were expendable," said Leander patiently. "But numbers are heavily against us, as you know. We are not such a large force that we can afford to spare trained fighters to do a job untrained civilians could do for us."

Cal opened his mouth to protest further, but Elnora cut him off.

"Listen to him, Cal," she said. "He knows what he's talking about. You're central to all this, but Jo and I have just been passengers since we reached the compound. We want to do our part, and this is something we have as much chance as anyone of doing."

"I agree, Cal. So stop wasting time," rebuked Jonan. "It'll be daylight before we get inside if you keep coming up with reasons why you don't think this will work."

"He's right," said Leander quietly. "If you trust their loyalty, I don't see any reason to refuse this offer. If we can't get the portcullis up, the fight is lost before it begins."

"Of course I trust their loyalty," Cal spluttered. "That's not the issue. We have no idea what they'll find in there, and I'm not about to let them risk their lives—"

"We are all risking our lives," said Laramie simply, "including your friends. Whether they go first or come behind, you cannot guarantee their safety."

Cal wanted to protest, but he couldn't deny the truth of Laramie's words, not when that very thought had haunted him ever since he had agreed to challenge Filip.

"We want to help, Cal," said Elnora softly. "We've both already left everything behind to help your cause. Don't tie our hands now."

Cal stared at her unhappily, his gaze taking in Jonan as well. His friend was reckless and restless, and Cal had no reliance on Jonan thinking about his own safety once inside the walls. And

Elnora...everything in him rebelled against the idea of sending her into danger. If he somehow survived all this but never again got to hold her in his arms...it was hard in that moment to imagine what the point of it all would be. But looking between the four faces turned to him, he could see that however much they might acknowledge his royalty, he could not prevent this from happening.

"Fine," he said, his voice a growl as he dismounted.

"What are you doing?" demanded Laramie, startled.

Cal glared at him. "Climbing the wall with them."

Four heads were being shaken frantically at him. "No, you're not," said Leander firmly. "We need to stick to our plan. You're needed here, at the front of the contingent."

"But—"

"No, Cal," interjected Jo. "You stay here, out of sight. Elnora and I will climb the wall without you and come back and let you know how it all goes."

Cal opened his mouth indignantly, but then he caught the grin lurking behind Jo's solemn expression. He rolled his eyes. He supposed he shouldn't be surprised that there was literally no situation too serious for Jonan to make a joke out of.

For a moment he met Jo's challenging stare, then he ground his teeth in frustration. "You're right," he conceded. "It is absolutely maddening being on this end of it."

Jo's grin broke free, and he clapped Cal on the shoulder. "Don't worry, Cal," he said. "We'll make it over the wall, and we'll raise the portcullis." He winked. "Or die trying."

"That's not funny," said Cal sharply. But looking into Jo's eyes he could see that Jo fully understood what was happening. Cal couldn't blame him for not wanting to share a serious moment with Leander and Laramie watching on in interest, so he just clasped Jo's arm and let his eyes add weight to his inadequate words. "Be careful."

He turned to Elnora, and suddenly he couldn't master a single word. *Don't do this*, his eyes begged her, but he could see her determination as she steadily returned his gaze. He reached a hand toward her but let it fall. She also said nothing. He remembered her telling him that she didn't like to say goodbye, and panic seized him at her silence. How did she manage to be so calm? How did she behave so naturally in front of their audience, as if the two of them hadn't been locked in a passionate embrace only a few hours ago?

He could taste her lips on his as she turned away from him, but still he had no words as he remounted his horse and watched the two figures move stealthily through the trees. At a word from Leander, someone had brought them cloaks, and the dark fabric made it even more difficult to follow their forms as they crossed the short stretch of grass between the forest and the wall.

Cal was focused on their progress, every muscle stiff with anxiety, so he was taken by surprise when Leander spoke to him.

"A lot will change if we succeed, Calinnae. For your friends as well as for you."

Cal looked over at the rebel leader questioningly.

"For example," Leander elaborated gently, "even now it is not a good idea for others to hear them speaking to you so casually. These people don't want you to be 'Cal'. They want you to be their king."

Cal knew that Leander meant well, but he couldn't help his expression hardening. "And I am willing to be who they need me to be," he said. "But as far as I'm concerned, Jonan is my brother, and I will not ask him to use a title."

Leander gave him a long look. "And the girl?" he asked. "Is she a sister to you?"

"Absolutely not!" returned Cal with unnecessary vehemence. He saw Leander's raised eyebrow, and he met the other man's look steadily, remembering Elnora's words a short time before. "I hope she will be something even closer," he said. "With even more right to call me by my given name."

Leander's eyes narrowed slightly as he continued to stare thoughtfully at his kinsman. Cal stared unblinkingly back, neither breaking gaze nor allowing his expression to soften. Just let anyone dare to tell him Elnora was unsuitable for him while she went ahead of the army, risking her life for the sake of his claim.

For a long moment, the two men held each other's gaze, each seeming to assess the other's resolve. To Cal's satisfaction, it was Leander who looked away first, his voice thoughtful as he spoke.

"Hmm. If she means so much to you, perhaps we should not have sent her into a perilous situation. Her presence in the battle may be a distraction you can ill afford. We should have kept her safe in the forest until the fighting is finished."

"I wholeheartedly agree," said Cal grimly, turning his attention back to his friends who had now reached the wall. "But she wouldn't hear of it." Glancing back at Leander, he saw the older man again raise an eyebrow. Cal shrugged. "You don't know what we've been through to get to this point. I would have demanded she stay, but in truth she has as much right as anyone to see this thing through. Plus," he added with a wry smile, "I'm not king yet."

"Yet," agreed Leander, his own smile expressing the grim determination of someone ready to die in an attempt to make it happen.

In the darkness, it was almost impossible to see the two figures as they began to scale the wall, so much taller than Pravat's. Cal could just make out two black patches inching up the stone surface, but he couldn't tell which one was which. He had to remind himself to breathe as they climbed higher and higher. At least there was still no sign of any sentry.

When the figures reached the top and disappeared over the edge, Cal heard two other relieved exhales to match his own. He was reminded that the forester twins had as much to lose as he did. The wait felt interminable, Cal's heart in his mouth. But apparently Jonan and Elnora met no resistance, because it was in fact a remarkably short time later that Laramie gave a startled gasp.

"The portcullis!" he said.

Cal strained his eyes toward it eagerly, his heart leaping when he saw it begin to move.

"Your friends did well," said Leander, his voice steady but his eyes excited.

"What now?" Cal asked, any nervousness forgotten in his eagerness to get inside and ascertain that Jo and Elnora were all right.

Leander glanced up at the sky, where the very first hints of dawn were beginning to show. "Now we avenge our kin," he said forcefully. He and Laramie raised their swords in one fluid movement.

Cal drew King Cael's sword from its sheath, wielding it for the first time. He felt a sense of power flowing from it into his hand, less potent than the Esvalere, but reassuringly strong all the same. He wished fleetingly that he had been able to train properly in sword fighting, but it was too late to worry about that now.

At the twins' signal, Cal felt at his back the gathering tension of their small but determined army preparing itself for the final approach. Even as he looked at the fortress ahead, and knew the uncertainty of the fate that awaited them there, he felt his spirits lift. With his forefather's sword in his hand—the dragons' magic leaking from it—his kin at his side, and his people at his back, he felt strong beyond his imagining.

When the portcullis was almost fully raised, Leander

brought his sword down in a swift arc in front of him, his battle cry ringing through the trees and echoing back from the foresters behind him.

"Kyona!"

Cal's voice joined the many others as they surged forward. There was no time to waste—even as they burst out from among the trees, Cal could hear the alarm bells starting to ring throughout the city. But they covered the short stretch of turf in minutes. Cal was almost glad that time was too short to sneak gradually through the gate as originally planned. The rush of courage that came from this reckless charge would probably serve them better than stealth and silence.

The sound of pounding hooves filled the air, and the stampede of human feet wasn't far behind. Cal urged his horse forward, outstripping the twins just before he passed under the open portcullis. He slowed slightly, his eyes searching frantically for Jo and Elnora as he took in the numerous bodies sprawled on the ground near the gatehouse.

Clearly a fight had taken place between the foresters' spies and the guards before the arrival of the army. That the spies had managed to take down all the guards before any could raise the alarm was miraculous, but it looked like none of them had lived to tell the tale, or more importantly, to raise the portcullis as intended.

Cal felt a sick swoop in his stomach at the sight of the blood-stained flagstones and the bodies of good men who had died to win him the throne, but he turned his thoughts resolutely away. He had chosen willingly to shoulder his burden, and he could not afford to dwell on the ramifications now.

With the horde of people rushing in through the gateway behind him, he could not stop his momentum. He had almost passed the gatehouse when he saw two familiar figures tumble out of its doorway. He felt a powerful release of tension in his chest as he cried out a wordless greeting.

Jo raised an arm in acknowledgment, but there was no chance to stop or talk. A small measure of Cal's anxiety returned as he saw both Jonan and Elnora pull out their weapons and join the throng of foresters. But he remembered Leander's warning and willed himself not to become distracted.

His role was to make for the throne room, and with the pulse of the Esvalere at his back and his ancestors' memories chasing one another through his mind, he hardly needed the careful instruction he had received from Laramie to find his way. He was an exiled king returning to his own, and his determination had never been stronger.

But as he rounded a corner, Laramie and Leander hard on his heels, he drew up short. A squadron of soldiers was racing forward to meet him, some still strapping on weapons as they came. The foresters who had infiltrated Filip's ranks had done their work well in incapacitating those on watch on the eastern wall that night. But the final approach of the rebels had roused the rest of the guard.

Making a split second decision, Cal wheeled his horse around, heading back to the courtyard that stretched out from the gatehouse where Jonan and Elnora had emerged. He suspected that he would have to fight sooner or later, but there were other ways to reach his destination, and it seemed smarter to try those first.

Laramie and Leander followed his lead, and their horses pounded across the cobblestones, back the way they had come. When they reached the courtyard, Cal saw that they couldn't try a different route. Squadrons of soldiers were appearing from all directions, converging on the open space, called to action in the chill pre-dawn. Already the cries of men and the clang of weapons had begun to fill the air.

Cal scanned the melee purposefully, trying to find the best route, but he could see no easy way through, and soldiers continued to pour into the square.

They were outnumbered, and they were surrounded.

CHAPTER THIRTY-ONE

Cal knew he should keep his mind on his mission, but he couldn't help his eyes roaming over the scene before him, trying to locate Jonan and Elnora. They were nowhere to be seen, but that didn't mean anything. In the dim light he could hardly make sense of the chaotic activity before him. He had never seen battle before, and his head reeled at the violence unfolding in front of his eyes.

His mind in a whirl, he tried to assess the best exit to make for, but he was distracted by the sight of a young forester nearby. The boy was younger even than Cal, and he was defending himself desperately against a large soldier. Cal urged his horse toward them, swinging his sword down as he went. The soldier didn't even see him coming. Cal's sword plunged straight into his back. Unused to riding as he was, Cal was unseated by his own momentum, and he toppled to the ground, scrambling to his feet as quickly as he could.

The soldier keeled over forward, and Cal tried to ignore the churning in his stomach as he pulled his sword out of the dead man's back. He remembered fleetingly his thoughts when he had considered killing the deckhands back in Alezae, but he hardened himself. Lindor's treason had brought great evil, and Kyona would not be restored without cost.

The young rebel looked at Cal, his eyes wide as he stuttered his thanks. Cal nodded absently, but his attention was already elsewhere. His horse had disappeared into the chaos, but it made little difference. The square was too crowded for an inexperienced rider like him to maneuver through it successfully. Of course, that meant that he had no advantage over the other fighters. He was now in the thick of the battle in earnest. He couldn't even see Laramie and Leander anymore.

The sun was rising now, and the scene it illuminated was grim. Soldiers were everywhere he looked, more continuing to arrive from the garrison he knew to be located on the other side of the city. The only reason the rebels hadn't yet been overrun was that the confined space in the courtyard prevented Filip's men from making full use of their superior numbers.

Cal raced to the aid of another beleaguered forester, but the fact that either of them survived was thanks only to the intervention of a third rebel who dispatched the attacking soldier with a practiced thrust. Another of their comrades on his other side was not so lucky. The soldier who had felled the man was taken down by the same rebel who had helped Cal, but it was too late for the sandy-haired young fighter whose name Cal would never know. Cal stumbled over the man's body as he swung around, looking for the next threat. He glanced down, but wished he hadn't, turning his eyes away from the fallen fighter.

Cal tried to remember what little swordplay Elnora had showed him in the mountains, but his mind struggled to focus, and his body wasn't practiced enough to perform the actions without clear mental direction. Cal thought suddenly of the fight he had witnessed between King Cael and the young Lord Lindor. He had been inside the king's head, and each block and parry had seemed to come so naturally.

Despite the frantic fighting around him, Cal closed his eyes for a brief second. He tried not to think, but instead to feel, drawing on every story he had ever heard of the old royals' exploits. The Esvalere hummed potently at his back, and as he attempted to call forward the memories of his long-dead kin, he felt a blaze of power surge into his hands from another direction.

The sword!

In the turmoil of the battle, Cal had forgotten that he wasn't fighting with an ordinary weapon. He had no experience of wielding a sword to draw on, but his mind flew to his one attempt at wielding the Esvalere. The magic that clung to the sword was not as concentrated as the Esvalere's power, but its signature was the same. Not stopping to think it through, Cal raced forward into the fighting once again, his sword held before him.

He made no attempt to instruct his arm on how to fight with the sword, instead turning all his efforts toward harnessing the weapon's power much as he had wrestled with the flood of magic that had poured out of the Esvalere and into his mind. The blade seemed to dance in front of him, cutting down a soldier who was about to run a forester woman through.

Cal turned to find another soldier rushing at him with a spear, and he swung his sword forward without conscious thought. It wasn't that the sword acted of its own volition—Cal was fully in control of his movements. His decisions just seemed to bypass his mind, the power he was harnessing passing straight from intention into action.

His sword connected with the spear's long handle. Cal tensed his arm in expectation of the impact, but his blade sliced straight through the wood, severing the spear as though it had been a stalk of wheat. He felt power pulse from his weapon as it destroyed its inferior brother, and turning that power to good account, he whipped the sword up toward the spear's bearer. The soldier's startled expression lasted only a moment before Cal's sword entered his chest.

Cal didn't pause, turning to a nearby struggle between a middle-aged rebel and two burly soldiers. He raised his sword to meet that of one of the soldiers, deflecting the thrusts threatening to overwhelm his fellow fighter. The soldier turned his full attention to Cal, who deflected another thrust with a flick of his wrist. He pressed the soldier forward, his own sword raining down blows as he went on the offensive.

For a brief moment, Cal seemed to lose track of who he was as he tried again and again to get under the man's guard. He was Cael, and he was Jonathon, and he was Calinnae. He was no individual in particular, but he was all of them as he channeled the power of his royal line into his movements.

The soldier faltered under the light in Calinnae's eyes, and he was given no chance to regroup. Cal's sword drove straight through a weak parry, dispatching the man in an instant.

Looking up, Cal caught sight of a familiar golden braid flicking through the air on the other side of the courtyard. Full awareness came rushing back as he remembered that whatever blood ran in his veins, he was still just one man. He might represent a legacy, but his own experiences, and setting, and people were as important to him as any other man's would be.

He sprinted toward Elnora, barely even aware of the damage as his sword cut through any soldiers in his way. She was battling furiously, but she was clearly outmatched. It was all she could do to deflect the sword of the large man pressing her back, each time managing only just to hold off the killing blow. Cal was still only halfway across the space when he saw the man pull back his arm for a powerful swing.

Cal's cry of rage and warning was lost in the melee, but as he watched through wide eyes, another blade joined Elnora's, repelling the thrust aimed for her heart. Jonan was bleeding from one cheek, but he seemed otherwise whole and unharmed.

Relief warred with terror in Cal's mind as he continued to race toward them. Cal knew that after his disclosures of the night before, if Jonan died defending Elnora, it would be as much for Cal's sake as for hers, and Cal didn't think he would be able to live with it. The two of them fought well together, but they were still struggling to hold off the well-trained soldier who pressed forward more relentlessly than ever.

With a shout, Cal reached them. His eyes met Elnora's for a brief moment, and he saw there the same mix of relief and fear that still coursed through him. The soldier turned to him purposefully, but Cal was ready. His face was set in grim lines as he raised his sword, the clang of metal adding to the din around them.

Jonan and Elnora fell back for a moment, panting. Cal hacked at his opponent with unremitting energy, the power that flowed into him from the Esvalere and out of him through the sword lending unnatural force to his blows. The man fell back a step, and Cal lunged, realizing too late that it was a feint. He was barely able to leap out of the way as the soldier brought his own sword whipping up toward Cal's chest. The man pursued his advantage, and Cal parried with an effort.

He saw his friends run forward, attempting to join the fight again. He was distracted for a moment as he realized that Elnora was limping. His eyes were drawn to a gash in her leggings just below the thigh, and the blood running from the wound down her leg. Anger suddenly blazed through him with such ferocity that he struggled to master the surge of power that came with it.

His sword was still locked with his opponent's in the carry through from his last deflection. Barely pausing, his hand flashed up in a riposte aimed for his adversary's heart. The man was quicker than he expected, raising his disengaged sword in front of him. The two weapons met, but the metallic clang that Cal expected didn't come. Instead, Cal's sword continued with barely a check, its blade blazing white hot for a moment as it passed through the soldier's weapon. The lesser sword splintered into fragments, the shards of metal exploding outward with a loud bang.

Jo and Elnora threw their arms over their faces, their shouts of surprise drowned out by the sounds of battle. Cal fell back a step himself, breathing hard, his eyes wide with astonishment. No fragments of blade had come in his direction. He could see cuts on Jo's and Elnora's upraised arms, but to his relief the injuries looked superficial.

The soldier had not fared so well. He was sprawled on the ground, a jagged piece of metal protruding from his chest. One glance was enough to see he would not be rising.

"What in the kingdom was that?" demanded Jo, his eyes on Cal's sword.

"Never mind that," said Cal quickly, his eyes darting between them both. "Are you all right?"

"Still standing," said Jo. "What are you doing here, Cal? Aren't you supposed to draw out Filip? We can't hold them off for long."

Cal glanced around him, taking in the battle scene. Jo was right. All around him rebels were dead and dying, alongside soldiers just following the authority of the only royalty they had ever known.

He needed to finish this.

But it was evident that the battle was going badly. Soldiers pressed in on the rebels from every direction, with the exception of the eastern wall through which they had come. The portcullis was still up, and the path was clear to a retreat. But Cal's heart swelled as he realized that no one was moving toward the gateway. These hardy forest fighters were not going to flee. He admired them for it, but he also felt a thrill of horror as he wondered how much blood he would have on his hands by the end of this day.

It was clear that even if he could fight his way through to get out of the square, and leave the battle behind while he sought out Filip, the band of rebels would not emerge from this clash. His eyes were drawn to Laramie and Leander, still mounted, fighting on the other side of the courtyard. Not far away from them was the start of the path they had initially tried to take, the most direct route toward the throne room. Cal felt his resolve strengthen as he noted that it was blocked by only a thin line of soldiers. Perhaps if they could break through, the remaining rebels could escape the bloodbath the square was turning into. The twins had wanted the confrontation to be as public as possible, after all.

He raised his voice in a shout, but the sound was lost in the clash of weapons and yells of the fighters. Glancing around, he saw an upturned cart nearby and leaped up onto it. He raised his sword high. He wasn't sure if it was his imagination, a result of the power he felt crackling from the sword down his arm. But he could have sworn that the blade glowed with a white flame for a second as he shouted again, his voice somehow carrying this time over the tumult.

"With me! With me!"

He saw many heads turn toward him, and he didn't wait for further acknowledgment. Jumping down from the cart he ran toward the exit, his sword wreaking destruction before him. He could feel both Jonan and Elnora at his back, and the numbers of their little band seemed to swell as they passed through the courtyard.

He thought he heard Leander's voice cry, "To the heir!", but he didn't stop to see where his kinsman was. The soldiers blocking the exit turned toward him as he approached, but he could see them falter beneath the fire in his face. The rebels fell on them with ferocity, and quickly broke through.

Cal sprinted down the cobblestones, his army at his heels. The soldiers gave chase, but they had clearly not expected their adversaries to flee further into the city, and their surprise gave the rebels a head start. Glancing back, Cal saw Laramie and Leander riding to catch up with the rest of the force, cutting down the front runners among the soldiers as they came.

Cal was confident of his direction as he ran, and soon he found himself taking the steps up to the castle doors two at a time, his fellow fighters spreading out around him in the temporarily wider space. The few guards stationed at the entrance to the castle were quickly overwhelmed, and the rebels passed through. With Cal at their head, they surged up the broad stone staircase that rose from the entry up to a wide land-ing, then split into two before reaching the level above. Once at the top of the stairs, it was a short distance to the throne room, and Cal knew the way as surely as if he had grown up in the castle, even though he had never been there before.

The entrance to the throne room was protected by a dozen guards, but the sight was a welcome one as far as Calinnae was concerned. It suggested that the twins had been correct about where their quarry would be found. For a moment the scene descended into chaos, the rebels' sprint turning once again into a fight. Dispatching a guard with a quick thrust, Cal pushed his way through the mass of people to the heavy wooden door. He raised his sword before him, taking a moment to direct its power before slashing at the wooden beam placed across brackets, holding the door closed.

The sword sliced through the wood, leaving a charred trail behind. Placing his free hand against the door, Cal pushed with all his might. It swung violently open, and rebel and guard alike seemed to fall into the room as their struggle continued, the chaos intensified by the soldiers from the square, who were jostling at the rear.

Cal took in the scene in the throne room at a glance. He felt a grim satisfaction when he saw the significant number of courtiers who seemed to have been shepherded from their beds in the early morning to shelter in the large room with their supposed sovereign. The more witnesses the better.

Turning his eyes to the end of the long room, he saw that the ornate wooden throne on its raised dais was occupied. The sight of Filip sitting on the seat of King Cael filled Calinnae with a rush of something too intense to be called anger, or any other mere emotion. It was power, raw and unharnessed, flowing from the Esvalere, and the sword, and his own core.

The usurper jumped up from his seat at Calinnae's entrance. From where Cal stood, his chest heaving and his sword momentarily at his side, Filip's expression was impossible to read. Half a dozen guards moved to flank Filip, their eyes on Cal.

Ignoring the shocked cries and screams from the courtiers, Cal gripped his sword with both hands and ran toward the throne, shouting an inarticulate challenge as he went. One of the guards stepped forward to meet him, and Cal ducked beneath the man's sword, the power that coursed through him giving him unnatural energy and agility. Steel clashed against steel as the man came at him again, but he was driven back, no match for the force of Cal's attack.

Cal heard a shout on either side of him, and looked up to see that Laramie and Leander had joined his struggle against Filip's guards. They were formidable fighters, each battling two of the guards, and holding their own. Impressive as the sight was, Cal's eyes slid past the twins and locked on the man cowering behind the guards.

Taking advantage of a moment of distraction, Cal raised his foot and kicked the soldier he was fighting, hard, in the stomach.

The man stumbled, and Cal raised his sword high. This time he brought it down hilt first, crashing it onto his opponent's head and knocking the man senseless.

They were so close to their real target, and with Filip in sight, Cal was finished with needless bloodshed. Quick as lightning he darted forward, seizing the usurper's richly embroidered clothing. The room seemed to still as Cal pressed the tip of his sword to Filip's throat.

"Call off your soldiers," panted Cal.

"You upstart," growled Filip, "how do you think this will end? You'll never make it out of here alive, you or any of your forest rabble."

"Call them off, or I run you through," Cal said deliberately. Filip hesitated, apparently trying not to swallow with Cal's sword so tight against his throat. Cal looked up and saw that the rebels, Jonan and Elnora included, were fighting desperately to defend themselves against the mass of soldiers still pouring through the doorway.

"Call them off!" Cal shouted, pressing down with the sword until it punctured Filip's skin.

"Stand down!" Filip rasped. "Stand down, all of you!"

The room instantly stilled as the soldiers lowered their weapons. Everywhere combatants drew back, breathing hard as they took advantage of the respite.

Cal held his arm steady, his eyes locked with Filip's. His every nerve hummed with energy as he stood in the halls of his fathers, facing down the representative of the line who had wrested everything from them.

"Who do you think you are?" Filip spat at him, even as his eyes seemed fixed involuntarily on the signet ring Cal wore. "How dare you raise arms against your king?"

"I know who I am," said Cal, his clear voice carrying throughout the room. "As do you. You had my father killed for his identity, so do not pretend that you do not know the legitimacy of my claim. How dare *you* sit on that throne? I am a descendant of kings—you can claim nothing but treason and murder from your ancestors! They tried to wipe my line out, but we have persevered."

"My ancestors," raged Filip, "did what needed to be done. They saved the kingdom from a bloodline unwilling to take the action that was needed."

"And what action are you taking now?" demanded Calinnae. "With every day that passes, the deterioration of our country progresses. I have seen it with my eyes. Your soldiers terrorize Kyona's citizens, slave traders raid our coasts freely under the crown's protection, and even now the vast armies of Valoria march through our lands, driven to intervene by the decay you have allowed to seize our country. And what are you doing about it? Hiding in your castle! Taxing your subjects so heavily that the poor can barely survive, and executing whoever in your court dares to question your greed and violence!"

"I am not to be questioned!" Filip's voice rose sharply. "Especially not by some forest brat who dreams of power."

"I do not come from the forest," said Cal steadily. "I am Calinnae, son of Elam, and I challenge you. I am descended father to son from Jonathon, son of King Cael, whom your forefather murdered in cold blood. You and your fathers before you have taken what was not yours for too long, and Kyona suffers for it. I challenge you, usurper!"

CHAPTER THIRTY-TWO

The shocked silence in the room gave way to murmurs as Cal spoke. His ringing challenge was met by a shout from the forest rebels, but he was more interested in the response from the rest of the room. The nobles huddled in one corner of the vast space were watching with wide eyes, and even some of the guards seemed to falter for a moment, lowering their weapons slightly.

But Cal's distraction cost him. He had taken his eyes off Filip to scan the room, and he didn't see the quick movement until it was too late. Cal had been foolish to imagine that Filip's obvious reluctance to join the fighting arose from any lack of prowess with a sword. Unlike his opponent, he had actually been raised as a royal, and it should not have been a surprise to find him well-trained.

With a quick flick of his wrist, Filip brought his blade up, its razor-sharp edge barely missing Cal's face as it engaged with Cal's own sword. It was all Cal could do to keep his weapon from leaping from his hands as its point swung out in a wide arc.

He didn't need to be experienced in sword fighting to antici-pate the riposte that would follow Filip's deflection. Maintaining his grip with an effort, Cal dropped to his knees, rolling forward under Filip's arm in a fluid motion, just as King Cael had once done in a duel of his own. Cal leaped to his feet behind Filip's position, but his opponent had already turned to face him, not to be so easily outmaneuvered.

"Do you think you can best me, you worm?" Filip sneered. "You will die as ignominiously as your father."

Cal felt a flicker of anger rise up within him, but he tried to master it, aware that Filip was trying to bait him to distract him from their fight.

"My father died honorably," he said, his voice not quite level. "As did my mother. The shame rests with the murderer, not his victims." He met Filip's eyes steadily. "Your father would say the same, don't you think?"

The flash of fear and rage that raced across Filip's face was enough to convince Cal of the truth of his suspicions. He had no intention of publicly charging Filip with the crime of killing his father. He had no proof, after all. But the knowledge drove away any remaining hesitation about striking the false king down.

He raised his sword before him, but his attention was suddenly torn between his adversary and the scene behind. With Filip's successful evasion of the sword against his throat, hostilities had resumed in earnest throughout the rest of the room also. Cal brought his sword up mechanically to meet a thrust from Filip, but his eyes were focused on the other side of the hall, where Jo and Elnora, separated by the crush, were both coming under heavy attack.

His second parry was clumsy, and he felt the burn of Filip's sword as it sliced shallowly along his arm.

"Calinnae!" Leander's voice reached authoritatively across the space between them. "No distractions!"

Cal knew Leander was right, but it was hard to think straight as people continued to fall all around him. Turning back to

Filip, he saw that he was too late to heed the warning anyway. His quarry had fallen back a step, two soldiers appearing in front of him to intercept Calinnae's attack. Cal wanted to scream his frustration with himself. For a moment he had felt so close to having Filip in his grasp.

But his anger turned to icy fear at the calculating look on the face of the larger of the two soldiers before him. The man had clearly witnessed the whole exchange, and his eyes darted shrewdly from Leander to Calinnae, then along the trajectory of Cal's gaze. They rested for a pregnant moment on Elnora, who was still bleeding from her leg, her back pressed against the far wall as she fought one of Filip's men, assisted by a grim-faced forester.

This time Cal didn't hesitate. Focusing all his attention toward drawing on the power that flowed through and around him, he gathered his fear and anger into a potent energy. Its raw force exploded out of him as he brought his sword to bear on the thickset soldier.

The man staggered back under the impact of Cal's blow, but he managed to bring his sword up to meet Cal's, its blade raised in a horizontal shield in front of his face. For a long moment their blades remained locked together, Cal focusing all his force in an attempt to destroy the man's weapon as he had done the sword of the soldier in the square.

But Cal still knew very little about how his sword's unusual properties worked, and either this soldier or his weapon was made of sterner stuff. With a roar, the soldier raised his other hand, gripping the end of his naked blade, blood running freely down his hand as he maintained his defensive position.

Cal could feel the power running out of him, and he knew that the man must have incredible strength to continue holding off Cal's sword. Cal frowned in concentration, trying to make sense of the dissonant note that seemed to have crept into the power swirling around him, almost as though another strain had been introduced.

They grappled for an interminable moment, then with a final shout, the soldier threw Cal's sword off, disengaging with a quick motion. Cal fell back, panting. While he had tussled with the brutish guard, Laramie and Leander had raced forward to deal with the other soldier defending Filip. Cal's opponent did not immediately attack, looking warily at the three determined men now ready to take him on.

"That's Yaeger," muttered Laramie in Calinnae's ear. "Chief of Filip's Royal Guard. His soldiers are more afraid of him than of Filip. Even if any of them wanted to side with our cause, they would not do so with him still in control."

Cal nodded tersely, indicating that he understood the importance of incapacitating this Yaeger. Filip still hung back behind the man, obviously trusting in his chief's ability to defend him. The three challengers dropped into a fighting stance, raising their swords almost in unison.

Another soldier ran up, ready to assist his chief, but he stopped several paces short as Yaeger waved him away.

"I can handle these three," the chief guard grunted. He jerked his head back toward the far wall. "Get her! The one against the wall!"

The soldier looked around, confused, but he never even had the chance to identify Elnora. With a wordless roar of fury, Cal leaped forward and ran the soldier through where he stood, his distaste for all the bloodshed forgotten. Yaeger met Cal's eyes, the glint in his own revealing that Cal had confirmed his suspicion.

"Get that girl!" he shouted to the room at large. His words were swallowed up by the tumult of the battle, but a few heads turned questioningly in his direction. He sucked in a breath, clearly ready to shout again, but Cal didn't give him the opportunity.

The fury racing through him was so powerful as he rushed on the man, that he felt fire in his hands. Whether it was passing from the sword to him, or from him to the sword, he couldn't tell.

Yaeger was ready. The guard raised his sword, and when the weapons met, a sizzling bang sounded throughout the room, causing the briefest of lulls before fighting resumed. But Yaeger's will was too strong to be easily overcome, and he disengaged his sword quickly, falling back several paces to regroup. Cal lunged after him, a red haze before his eyes, but he was pulled up by Leander's voice close beside him.

"We will deal with him! Do not forget your true end in all this! Filip!"

Cal snarled in frustration, every muscle in his body straining to pursue Yaeger, to silence him forever before he could pass on to anyone else his deadly knowledge of how to incapacitate the young challenger to the throne.

But Leander was right. Filip was the only way to end this, and while they had faced off against Yaeger, the young ruler had edged his way further back, now standing against a tall curved window to the left of the dais.

Cal glanced over at Elnora again. She was still standing, still fighting, and apparently oblivious to the lethal notice she had attracted simply by having value to him. Jonan, still looking miraculously uninjured, was some distance away from her, but Cal saw that the same serious-looking forester he had seen before remained at Elnora's side. Cal blessed the man internally, then turned resolutely away. He may wish that he could be fighting alongside his friends, but he had a bigger purpose here.

Filip.

Cal turned to the twins. Laramie's eyes were on Yaeger, but

Leander was watching Cal expectantly. Cal gave a tight nod, and a moment later, the twins raised their swords in a synchronized motion, falling on Yaeger with a ferocity that required his full attention. Cal sprinted forward, curving around the three fighters. Yaeger saw his target and roared, but he was unable to break free of his furious struggle with the rebel leaders.

Filip's eyes widened as Cal raced toward him, and he raised his sword defensively. Still sprinting, Cal swung his own sword toward his enemy with such force that Filip's arm was thrown wide, both swords flinging sideways, but remaining in the grasp of their owners. Cal's momentum carried him forward, and as his body turned with his sword, he thrust out a shoulder, catching Filip in the chest.

The force of the impact knocked Filip backward off his feet, and Cal was unable to pull himself up in time to avoid joining him. Both men crashed through the window in front of which Filip had been standing, broken glass splintering in all directions.

Knowing they were one story above ground, Cal braced himself for the fall, but they merely fell through the window onto level ground. Springing to his feet and brushing shards of glass from his clothes, Cal saw that they had emerged onto the top level of a stone courtyard. The edge of the platform on which they stood was twenty feet away, running perpendicular to the wall of the throne room. There was no sheer drop, however, as a broad stone staircase ran right along the length of the platform, leading to the courtyard's lower level.

Although he had never seen it before, some part of Cal recognized the setting with a jolt. The lower courtyard was empty now, but it was easy to imagine a large scaffold constructed there, with King Cael watching from the raised second level. Was this also where Filip executed anyone who dared to disagree with him? Cal turned to his adversary with renewed energy.

Filip had leaped up as well, and as they continued to duel with deadly determination, Cal was dimly aware of movement on the lower level of the courtyard. Enormous double doors led out of the throne room much further along from the window that had been smashed, wide stone steps flowing from the threshold down to the lower courtyard.

As if the exodus of the two leaders had been a signal, the doors had been thrown open, and the other fighters were spilling out, many racing down the steps to take up defensive stances where they could have the advantage of the increased maneuvering space.

Cal fought untiringly, energy continuing to flow through him from the Esvalere and the sword. But he couldn't match Filip in training. Again and again the usurper king blocked Cal's attacks, and Filip's own lunges had the force of desperation. Cal tried hard to keep his focus concentrated on his own battle, but a collective shout from the level below drew both his and Filip's attention away from their fierce struggle.

The cry was a jumble of voices, the soldiers' raised in jubilation and the rebels' in dismay. It took only a glance to see why. What appeared to be multiple squadrons of soldiers were approaching the courtyard from a broad road running in from the west, where the garrison was located. The morning sun was at Cal's back, and he had a devastatingly clear view of the number of fighters about to pour into the space.

His heart sank within him. Locked in his own fight with Filip, it had felt like if he could only defeat him—and even that he had not come close to doing—the fight would be won, and the rebels would prevail. But there was no guarantee that the soldiers would stop resisting if Filip fell. And it didn't matter whether they would, because as far as the survival of the rebels was concerned, Cal had run out of time to force a victory.

Those closest to the western entrance to the courtyard turned resolutely toward the new threat, but it was clear to Cal that they had no hope. The dwindling rebel force was moments from massacre. Even as he watched, he saw Jonan go down to a ferocious blow from the fist of a soldier who mercifully seemed to have lost his weapon. Cal breathed again as Jo scrambled backward, relieved that his friend was still alive. But for how much longer?

Before Cal could act, his eyes were drawn to a new figure, leaping purposefully down the steps, eyes scanning the crowd below. The two lithe figures who appeared in the doorway behind reassured Cal that Yaeger had broken free from Laramie and Leander rather than defeated them. But his relief was short-lived, as he realized with a jolt of horror what Yaeger's object was.

His cry of warning was stillborn in his throat as his eyes caught a flicker of movement, and he pulled his sword up just in time to protect himself from Filip's renewed attack. He parried with vicious force and made for the stairs, but Filip appeared in front of him, forcing him back with short, well-aimed lunges.

Again Cal tried to disengage, and again Filip pressed him. There was a gleeful light in Filip's eyes, and Cal realized with a surge of rage that his opponent had also seen Yaeger's intention, and was ready to make full use of his adversary's inevitable distraction.

The rage threatened to turn to despair, but Cal mastered it, letting it swell inside him into a white hot fire of defiance. His fury wasn't limited to Filip, or even to Filip's bloodline. He raged against the fact that evil thrived in his land, and those who wished to overcome it were constantly beset and overpowered at every turn. He raged at the inaction of his ancestors, at the sadism of the slave traders, at the indifference of the mountain people, at the self-imposed isolation of the dragons who withheld their powerful magic.

Why are we alone in this?! No words left his mouth, but he felt as though his spirit shouted directly into the skies.

His eyes, however, were on the carnage below. Even as he watched, he saw that Yaeger had almost made it to his quarry. Elnora, who seemed to be catching her breath from whatever altercation she had just escaped, looked up toward Cal, starting in surprise as she found his gaze on her. Even across the distance, a spark of connection seemed to jump between them before Cal looked frantically back at Yaeger. Elnora turned to follow the direction of his gaze, and her eyes widened at the sight of the Chief Guard making straight for her with deadly purpose.

To Cal's wrath and horror, Yaeger looked directly up at him before he attacked, satisfying himself that he had succeeded in diverting Cal's attention. Cal pushed forward against his own opponent with renewed vigor, but he still couldn't break through. He knew how dangerous it was to allow his focus to be so divided, but despite Filip's continued offensive, Cal couldn't seem to tear his eyes from the scene below him.

Elnora raised her sword defensively, but even from where he stood, Cal could see her exhaustion. It was miraculous that she managed to deflect the blow at all—there was no chance of her entirely holding off the powerful thrust Yaeger aimed straight toward her heart. All her energy went into her parry, and Yaeger's sword was forced a few inches off course, plunging into Elnora's shoulder with horrifying force.

Cal could have sworn he felt the steel enter his own flesh as Elnora's scream of pain cut through all the pandemonium between them. With a shout, he brought his free hand to meet the other on his sword, and the pulse of power that burst from him knocked Filip off his feet without any physical contact.

His shout swelling to a scream of raw emotion and willpower, Calinnae raised his sword above his head, its point rising directly toward the sky. Every eye in the courtyard seemed to be drawn to it, and Cal's hands burned furiously as the sword glowed white-hot with power. Suddenly, the steel burst into flames, and a mighty rush of wind swept the courtyard. Everywhere the combatants, soldiers and rebels alike, threw their arms up over their faces.

For a moment Cal's senses swam as he wrestled with the power surging from his weapon. White flames enveloped it, but whether they were streaming from the sky into the sword, or from the sword into the sky, it was impossible to tell.

The wind was still whipping furiously around Cal when shocked screams rent the morning air. A vast shadow fell over the courtyard, a monstrous shape blocking out the sun as its outline stretched from one end of the courtyard to the other. Cal realized that every face was turned toward him, full of terror and awe and disbelief. Even the windows of the throne room were lined with spectators, many commoners seeming to have joined the courtiers gathered there.

Magic radiated through and around him. Cal didn't need to turn his head to know what he would see in the sky behind him, but he did anyway, his sword still held aloft.

The mighty silhouette of the dragon might cover the sun, but the fire pouring from between its jaws to connect with the burning sword in Cal's hand was light enough. The expressions on the faces below him communicated eloquently how impressive was the sight of the enormous reptilian form rising up behind the slim figure of the young king. All fighting ceased, and even Filip, still on the ground at Cal's feet, stared in undisguised amazement at the beast before him.

With a final swish of his mighty wings, Elddreki came to land on the platform beside Cal. The chain of fire between him and the sword receded, although small tongues of flame still licked the weapon.

"Greetings, young king."

The dragon's voice rumbled clearly across the courtyard, somehow sounding less like music and more like a battle cry than the last time Cal had heard it. Cal remembered that after meeting Qadir, he had thought Elddreki no longer intimidating.

He had been wrong.

He would have guessed that the dragons would be shown to best advantage in their mountain home, but in fact Elddreki's presence was more impressive outside the Dragon Realm.

Elddreki's gaze was calm as it rested on Calinnae's face. "I came in response to your call, my friend," he said. Cal could feel the ripple of shock and awe emanating from the watching crowd, but Elddreki spoke as if he was having a simple conversation with Cal alone.

"I thank you," Cal said, trying to speak gravely to hide his breathlessness.

"I have followed with interest your quest to reclaim your birthright," Elddreki continued, his majestic voice reverberating into every corner of the space. "I am glad to see you restored to the birthplace of your fathers, young king."

"I am king here!" Filip cried, surging to his feet at last, desperation in his voice.

Elddreki turned a cold stare toward him at the interruption, as though Filip was an impertinent child.

But unlike the rest of the population of Kynton, Filip wasn't looking at Elddreki. His eyes were on Calinnae, and pure hatred shone from their depths.

"You will not take my throne from me!" he cried, picking up his sword from where it had fallen on the flagstones.

Cal raised his own sword in a defensive gesture almost without thought. For a moment he knew only incredulity as the blades rang together, fire still flickering from Cal's weapon. Certainly none of Filip's soldiers seemed willing to continue the fight when a dragon had appeared from out of legend and aligned himself with their opponents. But then, Cal supposed that Filip had nothing more to lose.

And for his own inscrutable reasons, Elddreki chose not to intervene. Filip rained down blows on Calinnae, his sword flashing up and swinging down in repeated attempts on his opponent's skull. Cal blocked each one with ease.

Suddenly he switched gear, going on the offensive himself, forcing Filip back as he lunged for the heart. Gone was Calinnae's impotent rage at being alone in this fight, and in its place was a certainty of purpose beyond anything he had ever felt, lending meaning and power to every movement of his arm.

Filip's confidence seemed to waver as Cal's grew, and he failed to adequately deflect a blow aimed for his heart. Cal's sword plunged into his adversary's shoulder instead, just as Yaeger's sword had pierced Elnora. The memory filled Cal with anger once again, and he followed up his advantage as Filip fell to the ground with a cry. Pulling his sword free, Cal disarmed Filip with a swift stroke, the would-be ruler's sword spinning a short way across the stone floor.

In a moment Cal's knee was on Filip's chest, his sword pressed against his throat, as it had been at the beginning of this fight.

"Time to answer for your crimes," he growled.

But before he could strike, he looked into his enemy's eyes, and what he saw there rattled him to his core. Filip didn't look fierce, or evil, or even defiant. Cal knew that he was all of those things, but deeper, beyond the twisted impostor he had grown into, Cal saw something much more primal, and much more familiar.

Fear.

Filip was afraid. He was afraid of death, and afraid of Calinnae, and afraid of the consequences of his choices. For a moment Cal's thoughts spun away from him. Time ceased to pass as he stared into those eyes, and the powerful familiarity of this place he had never been to before washed over him. Everything else seemed to freeze, but the Esvalere continued its steady ebb and flow of power, as Cal suddenly saw the same courtyard through different eyes.

KING CAEL STOOD on the platform, his kingly bearing hiding the anguish in his heart. The scaffold on the lower level was a hideous blot on an otherwise pleasant prospect. His wildest, darkest imaginings could never have come up with a fate more terrible than this. He didn't know what ripped his heart apart more—the knowledge that he was about to execute his best friend, or the painful truth that in spite of his grief for Damian, he could not rid his heart of the hatred and anger and resentment that had become intermingled with every happy memory of the friendship.

He saw Organza in the crowd below, her face white and furious as her former friends among the nobility refused to acknowledge her. Jacqueline was not here. She had refused to be present, and Cael only wished he could have done the same.

His expression was blank as Damian was led into the courtyard and up the wooden steps. His former friend did not resist the hold of the guards. Some part of Cael wanted to sprint down the stone steps before him and draw his sword in Damian's defense, coming to his rescue as they had done countless times for one another in their past escapades. But who would he defend him against this time? Cael himself was the authority that had decreed that his friend must die.

And even more distressing—another part of Cael had no desire to save Damian. The memory of Thalia's sweet laugh still haunted him, and a part of himself he didn't care to confront too closely wanted to see someone pay an incalculable price for the darkness that Damian had brought into their lives.

Cael tried to remove all emotion from his voice as he addressed the prisoner with the customary words.

"You are leaving to join your ancestors. Do you have any last requests?"

Damian met his eyes across the empty space, his face expressing all the anguish Cael was keeping tightly inside. "Only one," he said.

"Name it." Cael's voice was terse.

"Only this. Forgive me, Sire. Forgive me, Cay."

Cael turned his face away, but he knew that Damian's expression would remain burned in his memory forever.

"You should have asked for anything else," he said, his voice heavy. "Because that request I cannot grant."

CAL LET out the breath he had drawn in as he first looked into Filip's eyes. In the space of that breath he had left his own mind and returned to it. As he looked at Filip, he realized for the first time how young the false king was. Perhaps two years older than Calinnae himself. Barely a man. How had he not seen it before? Filip had so much blood on his hands, but he had probably been raised to what he had become as much as Cal had. And like Cal he carried the weight of generations, the curse of his ancestors' errors.

Cal could see no contrition in Filip's face, no plea for redemption. But as he saw the fear in the other man's eyes, he found himself drawing back. He experienced again the terrible anguish of soul that King Cael had felt in this same courtyard, that rending of his heart after which he had never been the same again.

Cal felt suddenly weary of it all. A few months ago he had never even seen death, and now he had so much blood on his own hands. What the effect of that would be on him, he couldn't yet measure. And while he knew that justice demanded Filip's death, he found himself rebelling against the realization that some part of him took pleasure in the thought of that death.

No. Perhaps a king might be called upon to fill the role of executioner, but any king who delighted in that role was not fit to hold it. He would not start his reign with the same action that had marked the end of the golden days of the reign of the last true king.

He pushed himself to his feet, stepping back from Filip. He could feel the tension throughout the still courtyard. The other man's eyes showed first surprise and then derision as he grasped Cal's intention to show mercy. In a swift motion, he seized his sword from the ground, whipping it up toward Cal. Cal felt neither surprise nor alarm, only a sense of disappointment that he would have to kill Filip after all, as he again raised his own sword.

But the weapons never met. Filip's startled half-cry was drowned by the shocked shrieks of the watchers as Elddreki's head shot out. He seized Filip between his powerful jaws and with a movement that managed to be both swift and unhurried, he flung him like a straw doll across the raised platform. Filip hit the far wall with a dull thud, and slid to the ground, his head lolling sickeningly to the side on his clearly broken neck.

CHAPTER THIRTY-THREE

For a moment there was absolute silence in the courtyard, shock on every face. Cal felt stunned himself as he turned to Elddreki.

"Why did you do that?!" he demanded.

Elddreki did his strange ripple shrug. "I could see that you didn't really want to kill him," he said. "Whereas I," his voice was bright and cheerful, "didn't mind at all."

"But—" Cal's mind was reeling.

"He would have caused you trouble all your life if he had survived, Calinnae," said Elddreki, his stern tone at odds with the lively interest in his eyes as he scanned the scene before him.

Cal raised an eyebrow. "I thought dragons couldn't see the future," he said.

Elddreki grinned at him, the gesture showing all his teeth, and Cal heard a faint ripple of alarm pass through the watching crowd.

"I don't need to in order to predict that," Elddreki was saying, his eyes still on the chaos below. "You seem to have made quite a stir."

Cal laughed weakly. "*I've* made a stir?"

He heard racing footsteps and turned to see Laramie and Leander sprinting up the steps toward him. Their faces expressed their shock as their eyes flicked briefly to Elddreki, but apparently even a dragon could not deter them from their long held purpose.

Leander seized Cal's arm and raised it into the air. "The True Bloodline is restored!" he shouted, his voice carrying almost as much as Elddreki's had done. "Long live the king!"

The resultant shout shattered the silence that had settled over everyone at Elddreki's entrance. The remaining forest rebels were cheering themselves hoarse, some openly weeping. Many of the soldiers looked uncertain, but most of them had thrown down their weapons. Glancing up at the windows into the throne room, Cal saw mixed reactions on the faces of the nobles, some joining the cheer while others seemed still too stunned to decide how to react. The commoners, on the other hand, cheered with all their might.

Cal glanced involuntarily at Filip's crumpled body. He could see no tears being shed for the former king. He thought of King Cael's last thoughts, how he had felt peace as he passed out of life surrounded by his children who loved him and mourned him. The young Lord Lindor had thought he had defeated the king and replaced the royal bloodline with his own, but Cal knew which position he would rather be in.

As he looked out over the crowd, Cal saw that some of the soldiers were trying to inconspicuously make for the edge of the courtyard.

"You need not flee," he called, and silence fell again. "Any of you. You were deceived into believing Filip had the right to command you. The whole kingdom was deceived. I do not wish for vengeance—I wish only to see Kyona restored."

The cheer that greeted his words was louder than the first, some of the soldiers joining in, relief evident on their faces and on the faces of some of the nobles. Cal felt confident in his words. He could only imagine that the process of determining who he could and couldn't trust would be long and tortuous, but he had no desire to start massacring those who had followed Filip. Even any who would prove to be his enemies were probably better kept close for now, instead of letting them flee freely across the country.

"Well done, King Calinnae," said Leander beside him, his eyes shining fiercely. "You have come into your own."

"Thanks to you," said Cal, trying not to show how startled he was at the sound of the title. "And I will not forget it, as long as I live."

"It seems there is a great deal you didn't tell us, Your Majesty," said Laramie, his wide eyes on Elddreki, who was watching their exchange with his usual interest. "I think our task of convincing the kingdom of your lineage just became considerably easier."

"Yes, I tried to make it clear enough for even the thickest of humans," said Elddreki conversationally.

"Thank you," said Cal, holding back a laugh at the stunned looks on the twins' faces as they realized they were being addressed by a dragon.

"I am glad to help, my friend," said Elddreki pleasantly. "Speaking of which, where are your friends from the mountains? Does Elnora still smell of my magic?"

"Elnora!" Cal cried, the dragon's words jolting him out of his thoughts. His eyes scanned the crowd frantically, trying to find her. "She was injured—she may need your help again."

He felt sick as he remembered how Yaeger's sword had plunged into her. He had seen nothing of her fate after that, and he couldn't face the thought that anything worse had followed.

Cal's alarm deepened as Elddreki shook his head. "No my friend, I am afraid not. An injury sustained in my mountains is a different matter entirely from a wound suffered in battle out here in the realm of men."

Cal started for the steps, his eyes still searching for any familiar form in the milling mass of people below. He had also lost sight of Jonan.

"Wait, Sire," said Leander quickly. With an effort, Cal forced himself to look back. "With your permission, we will take charge of the clean up. The wounded will need to be treated, among many other things."

Cal nodded, his relief evident in his voice. "Please—I would be grateful."

"You need to meet with the nobles, Sire," continued Leander. "Without delay."

"I will do so," returned Cal, his eyes hard. "But one delay you will have to tolerate." He hesitated for a moment, glancing back at the dragon.

"I will wait, Calinnae," said the dragon, inclining his head.

Cal nodded his thanks and without another word took off down the steps. The crowd parted before him, and he tried not to dwell on the uncomfortable sensation of hundreds of eyes watching him in awe. He jogged toward where he had seen Elnora, but as he passed the step leading up to the double doors, he veered off course for a moment, a glad cry on his lips.

"Jo! Are you all right?"

Jonan had been sitting on the steps, but at Cal's voice he pushed himself quickly to his feet, swaying for a moment before hurrying forward to clasp his friend's outstretched arm.

"Cal! I can hardly believe it's over! Are you in one piece?"

"I am," said Cal, holding back a laugh that threatened to become slightly hysterical. "Are you?"

"I'm fine," Jo assured him. Cal frowned as his friend swayed once again, but Jo waved dismissively. "It's nothing, I'm fine. I took a pretty hefty blow to the head, and I'm still not sure which way is up, but no harm done. Pretty lucky that Elddreki showed up when he did!"

"Yes, but never mind that now," said Cal quickly. "Where's Elnora?"

Jo sobered instantly. "I don't know," he said. His eyes took on a stricken look. "I tried to stay close, but I lost her in the battle, Cal, I'm sorry."

Cal shook his head. "You don't have anything to be sorry for." He turned his gaze back to the crowd. "But I need to find her, now."

"Go," said Jonan. "I'll catch up."

Cal took off back into the crush before Jonan finished speaking. He couldn't see far through the mass of people, and he hoped he was going in the right direction. Many of those in the throne room had started pouring out into the courtyard, and Cal was jostled along with everyone else. The crowd no longer parted for him, people not immediately recognizing who he was.

His sense of direction did not fail him. He had pushed his way halfway across the courtyard when he finally found her. She was propped against a barrel, her sword on the ground next to her. Her face was white, and her eyes were closed, but she was breathing. Cal inhaled deeply himself, feeling like he was able to properly get air into his lungs for the first time since remembering that she was unaccounted for. The grim-faced forester he had seen with her before was kneeling next to her, apparently speaking in a quiet voice as he pressed a wad of material to her shoulder. The garment was soaked with red, and the sight made Cal's head spin.

"Elnora!"

He was still some distance from her when he called out. Her head snapped up at his voice, her eyes flying open and finding his instantly. She struggled to her feet, despite the protests of the man assisting her.

"Cal!" she cried, reaching toward him.

But she had more eagerness than strength, and she winced, one hand flying to her shoulder as her injured leg seemed to wobble beneath her.

He sprinted the last few strides and caught her in his arms as she swayed. "Whoa, easy there!" he said, gently lowering her back to a sitting position and kneeling beside her. He put a hand against her cheek, searching her face anxiously as she once again closed her eyes. They sprang back open quickly, however.

"That was unbelievable, Cal! Are you all right?"

"Am *I* all right?" he repeated incredulously. "What a stupid question!"

She smiled faintly, closing her eyes for another long second. Anxiety rose up in Cal at how pale her face was.

"Elnora, what can I do?" he asked desperately, but she shook her head.

"I'm fine Cal," she said, a hint of stubbornness in her voice. How he loved that stubbornness.

"No, you're not fine!" he said grimly. He looked at the forester, who stood nearby with the blood-soaked makeshift bandage. The man nodded curtly.

"She's lost a great deal of blood, but the bleeding has slowed now. It's a clean wound from what I can tell. My guess is that she'll recover more quickly than you think. She's strong, this one."

As if he didn't know it.

"See," said Elnora. "Like I told you, I'm fine."

He scowled at the blood all over her clothes. "This is not my idea of fine. You've taken way too many hits for me today."

"Don't be silly," she protested faintly, but Cal squeezed her hands.

"I saw the sword go into your shoulder," he said, his voice coming out shaky. "I thought he would kill you."

"He certainly intended to," she said dryly. "Whoever 'he' was. I don't know where he came from, but he seemed quite determined to reach me."

"It was because of me," said Cal in a strangled voice. "He was the Chief of Filip's Royal Guard, and he was targeting you because of me."

"What do you mean?" Elnora asked, clearly confused.

"He saw me watching you, earlier in the battle. I couldn't help myself—I was checking to see if you were all right, and he figured it out." Cal clenched his teeth together, still angry at the thought of it. "He figured out that attacking you was the surest way to distract me."

Her eyes were round. "I'm so sorry, Cal," she started, but he cut her off, seizing her good arm bracingly.

"Elnora!" He could see that she was startled by the anger in his eyes, but he didn't soften his glare. "Don't you dare apologize for such a thing! If you're going to apologize for being important to me, you may as well apologize for breathing."

She swallowed, but didn't immediately respond. Cal looked around, frowning. "Where is he anyway? The Chief Guard." Elnora shook her head, and when Cal looked to her new friend for confirmation, he just shrugged.

"I didn't see where he went," the man admitted. "After that dragon showed up, I lost track of everything else."

Cal pursed his lips. He would have to take care. No matter what he'd said to the crowd before, Yaeger was one soldier who would not be receiving clemency. His thoughts were pulled back to Elnora as he felt her light touch on his arm.

"You did it, Cal," she whispered.

He tightened his hold on her. "We did it, you mean," he corrected.

She shook her head, and he thought her smile seemed faintly sad all of a sudden. "No, it was you. You were incredible. I don't know how you did...whatever it was you did up there, but I'm not surprised. I never doubted for a second that you could see this through."

"The dragon didn't hurt," he said lightly, trying to hide the warm glow that spread through him at her praise.

"No, the dragon didn't hurt," she agreed with a laugh.

It was a musical sound, and his heart swelled as he heard it. For a long moment he just looked at her, taking in every detail. Already color was starting to return to her face. He was torn between elation at her survival and terror at how close he had come to losing her.

Glancing around, he realized that those in their vicinity had figured out who he was, and they had gathered quite an audience. He hadn't even noticed Jo standing nearby, but his friend gave him a reassuring nod when they locked eyes. Jonan seemed to have recovered his balance.

"Can you stand if I support you?" Cal asked Elnora gently. She nodded, and he helped her carefully to rise. This time she was steady on her feet. He drew her against him, but she pulled back. From the look in her wide eyes, she had only just noticed how much attention was on them.

Disregarding her sudden stiffness, he put his arms around her and pulled her close.

"Cal," she began to protest, then corrected herself hastily. "I mean Sire, or should it be Your Majesty? Everyone is watching."

"Don't you dare," he growled quietly. "If I ever hear you call me 'Sire' again, I'll summon a dragon to come and eat you."

Her involuntary chuckle quickly died. "The kingdom's eyes are on you, Cal," she said seriously.

"Yes, I know," he returned, his voice calm. She tried again to pull away, but finding his arms unyielding around her, she gave up the struggle and instead buried her face in his chest.

Cal held her for a long moment, part of him wishing he could keep her hidden safely there forever. But he knew how crucial were the next minutes and hours and days, for the country as well as for him. His dramatic confrontation of Filip in the throne room had been no accident—he had innately understood the importance of the timing and the setting, and this was no different.

He rested his head on the top of Elnora's for a moment. "As wonderful as this feels," he said quietly into her ear, "you shouldn't hide your face. I want them to see who their queen will be."

Her head came slowly up at his words, and he could see surprise and hope and resignation and longing warring in her eyes. "Cal, we've been through this."

"Yes," he agreed. "We have. I've given some thought to what you said, and I realized something about our conversation in the forest." She looked at him questioningly, and he smiled down at her. "I forgot to tell you again that I love you."

However uncertain she might still feel about how the kingdom would receive her, the look in Elnora's eyes told Cal that her heart was open to him again. As he leaned toward her, the warmth and love in her gaze seemed to break through her barriers, and she responded to his kiss with enthusiasm.

A cheer went up around them, picked up by others further back who surely couldn't see the couple and likely had no idea what they were cheering about.

Cal held Elnora tightly as he kissed her, trying to avoid her various injuries. He drew back quickly, mindful of their setting. He could only hope that the look he gave her as their eyes again met would communicate all the passion he had not allowed his lips to express in such a public embrace. The look she sent back at him somehow managed to be both shy and blazingly triumphant, before she again laid her head against his chest.

"Why are they cheering?" she asked breathlessly.

He grinned. "Because they're an excitable crowd." His arms tightened around her. "Sorry about all that," he muttered into her hair, even as he continued to grin. "I'm sure you'd prefer something more private, and so would I." He pulled back and met her eyes seriously. "But I really did think about what you said. And I thought the best way to make sure no one tries to tell me I'm not allowed to be with you is to not give them a say in the matter." He touched her cheek gently. "We come as a pair, the decision already made. As far as anyone here is concerned, I never existed apart from you."

She seemed unable to find words, but her eyes said enough.

"I'm afraid I need to go now," Cal said regretfully, stepping back and acknowledging the eager crowd with what he hoped was a kingly nod. "There are a great many people I should speak to while the moment is fresh."

She nodded quickly. "Of course. I'll be fine."

Jonan appeared alongside them. "Don't worry Cal, I'll look after her. By which I mean, I'll make sure she gets her various life-threatening injuries attended to instead of telling everyone who asks her that she's fine."

Cal smiled ruefully as Elnora sent a mock glare in Jonan's direction. He knew he needed to leave, but he wished he could make the moment stretch forever, not ready to let go of the easy companionship shared by the three of them.

"Go Cal," prompted Jo. "The action's over—go take care of the politics." Cal's smile turned into a grimace at the "better you than me" look that Jonan directed toward him.

When he turned away, he found Leander waiting for him close by. Laramie was presumably engaged in overseeing other practicalities. The forester's eyebrows were slightly raised, and Cal met his look evenly, a challenge in his own expression.

Leander smiled. "You are full of surprises, Your Majesty." He gave a sudden laugh. "I cannot fault your aptitude for seizing the moment. Your ability to sense and exploit the mood will serve you well in the challenges to come."

Cal smiled wearily. "I suspect the challenges to come will require many skills I do not possess. I am trusting you to assist me."

"I will gladly do that, Sire," said Leander bracingly. He smiled with sudden warmth. "And I like her. I am glad that she survived Yaeger's attack."

"Yes," said Cal darkly. The thought of the guard still made his blood boil. "Unfortunately no one seems to know where Yaeger is. I think he may have slipped away."

"That is troubling," acknowledged Leander. "I will have some of our people search for him, but for now you have other duties to attend to."

"Yes," sighed Calinnae. "I suppose I do."

CHAPTER THIRTY-FOUR

Dealing with the nobles was so draining that Calinnae thought he'd rather have another duel with Filip. But he understood the importance of these conversations without Leander needing to explain it. He smiled at the thought of Jonan attempting this part of the adventure. It was reassuring to remember that tact was just as important as bravery for a king.

He knew it would be a long road ahead, but he felt optimistic by the time the sun reached its zenith and Leander finally released him. It was daunting to see that the instability that had worsened throughout the country during Filip's rule was reflected in the court. But how could it not be? And Filip's violence and paranoia had paved the way for his successor to win over the nobles. The prospect of a sovereign who wasn't inclined to execute anyone who questioned him was appealing for a court that had become increasingly fearful.

The signet ring was once again of great interest, the exercise with the ancient records being repeated for nobles and commoners alike. The latter group was by far the most impressed by it, but even the courtiers seemed struck, as much by the surviving records as by the ring itself. By the end of his interviews with them, many of the nobles were already hinting that they had suspected Filip of killing his father, and had known for years that his actions had brought a curse on the land. Cal hid his smile at these wise declarations. It was amazing what people had "always known" after someone else had proved it to be so. But as Leander said quietly in his ear, if the nobles were trying to impress him, it was a good sign.

Cal was no fool—he knew that a tumultuous transition was ahead. But there was hope for Kyona, and for now that was enough.

Cal had made a point of taking time to mingle with the commoners, the foresters and even some of the soldiers. Fortunately pretty speeches were not as important here, and it was a welcome break to communicate his goodwill without words. He found that it was just as effective to clasp a hand, bow his head in grief over the dead, or even just nod reassuringly.

His biggest concern throughout the morning was Elddreki. It felt unnatural to keep a dragon waiting on his convenience, but Elddreki looked comfortable enough, sitting with his tail curled around him on the top level of the courtyard, deserted except for his gargantuan form. And impolite as he felt at the delay, Cal suspected that the dragon's continued presence, and the apparent interest with which he watched proceedings, had a large part to play in the cooperative response Laramie was receiving from even the soldiers to his efforts at organization.

Cal was just making his way toward the broad stairs when he heard a familiar voice call his name.

"Jo!" he said joyfully. "I'm glad you found me. I was just going to talk to Elddreki."

"Yes," said Jo. "I thought I'd come. Elnora is sleeping. The physician who tended to her wounds is confident she'll make a full recovery."

Cal let out a long breath. "Thank you," he said.

"So," said Jo as the two of them mounted the steps. "Looks like you two are ready to settle in and grow old here, then?"

Cal laughed. "Hopefully not too quickly. But yes, I think we've landed where we're supposed to be." He looked sideways at his friend. "Haven't you?"

Jo shrugged. "I think I'm better at flying than landing. I was never as eager as you were to see Kynton."

"Well, something tells me you don't want to go back to Nerita," said Cal dryly.

Jo laughed. "Definitely not."

They had reached the top of the steps, and they both turned their attention to the dragon who was waiting patiently for them.

"Elddreki," Cal began. "I apologize for keeping you waiting so long."

"Long?" echoed Elddreki with the ghost of a smile. "Perhaps to you. I was quite content to wait for one morning."

"Well," Calinnae pushed on, "I can never thank you enough for your intervention. You saved many lives, and I don't think we could have succeeded without you."

Elddreki nodded graciously. "I am glad to strengthen the friendship between dragons and your royal line," he said. "And do not underestimate your own efforts. You did very well."

Cal didn't respond, looking out at the aftermath of the battle and thinking about how many people had lost their lives.

"It's a shame you couldn't have come earlier," said Jonan, voicing the thought Cal was too polite to say.

"Calinnae didn't call me earlier," said Elddreki calmly.

"I wasn't aware that I called you at all," said Cal. "Or that I could do so."

"I did tell you that the sword was connected to me."

Cal barely refrained from rolling his eyes at this fresh example of the gulf between what dragons and humans considered to be clear communication.

"Qadir said very clearly that we shouldn't expect help from the dragons outside the mountains," he said instead.

"As I told you when you left the mountains," answered Elddreki, his tone mild, "Qadir is wise beyond calculation, but he is not always right. There are decisions that even he...I will not say regrets, but perhaps questions."

"So he questioned his decision to remain hidden from humans?" asked Cal.

Elddreki chuckled. "No, indeed, young king. Of that one he was certain. My decision to come here was not made under his direction."

Cal raised his eyebrows. "He won't be happy that you have exposed your existence." He glanced around at the courtyard. Many people had moved elsewhere in the hours since the battle, but there were still dozens of figures dotted around. And most of them continued to shoot furtive glances in Elddreki's direction every minute or so. Cal looked back at the dragon. "I don't think you'll be able to convince anyone that dragons aren't real anymore."

Elddreki smiled indulgently. "It is not a matter of convincing. If we truly wish to fade back into legend, we need only decide not to emerge again for half a dozen or so of your generations. This is no great feat." He continued speaking serenely, apparently oblivious to his listeners' expressions. "But it is true that I have taken it upon myself to usher in a new era of interaction between us and humans. Qadir will likely be displeased."

"You don't seem too concerned about what he'll do," said Cal cautiously.

Elddreki looked at Cal with faint surprise. "Certainly not."

He smiled. "It is a very human trait to worry about what the future will bring. Perhaps that's why humans are always in such a hurry." He was silent for a moment, apparently deep in thought. "Or is it that humans worry about what is coming because they are hurrying toward it? An interesting question."

The dragon's eyes glazed over, and Cal and Jo exchanged a look. Elddreki looked like he was settling in for a lengthy contemplation of the human mind.

Jonan cleared his throat. "So you're not worried that he'll banish you, or kill you or whatever?"

Elddreki turned his placid gaze upon Jo. "I hadn't thought about it, young one, but since you bring it up, I am confident that he will do neither of those things." Elddreki chuckled at some joke of his own.

"Can dragons even die?" asked Jo curiously.

"Oh yes," said Elddreki in the same calm tone. "But more relevantly, no they certainly cannot."

Jo evidently had less restraint than Cal, because he actually did roll his eyes. "A cryptic answer. What a surprise."

Cal couldn't help but laugh.

"I will return to the mountains now, I think," mused Elddreki. "I wish you well in the days to come. I am confident you will overcome any obstacles."

"Thank you," said Cal gravely. "Will I be able to communicate with you again?"

Elddreki inclined his head. "If you wish it. As you become more familiar with the object you carry, you will understand how."

"Thank you," Cal said again. "I also am glad to strengthen the friendship between our peoples."

With a final stately dip of his head, Elddreki shot into the air, disappearing from sight almost instantly. A wind whipped briefly but violently through the courtyard, accompanied by involuntary cries of shock on all sides.

"You're quite good at this diplomacy thing, Cal," said Jo admiringly.

Cal grinned. "Well that makes one of us."

Jo looked as though he was about to give Cal a shove, but at the last second he glanced around at their elevated position, in full view of the courtyard, and seemed to think better of it.

"Just don't let it go to your head," he said sternly.

Cal was still grinning. "Not much chance of that, with you around," he said.

Jo hesitated. "About that..."

"Your Majesty?"

Cal turned to the messenger approaching them on the stairs, swallowing his irritation. He supposed he would have to get used to such interruptions. He cast his friend an apologetic look, but Jo waved him off.

"We'll talk later," Cal promised.

He couldn't help but glance back as he followed the messenger down the stairs. It somehow made him both happy and sad to see his friend gazing off into the distance, a familiar faraway look in his eyes.

To Cal's disappointment, "later" seemed to get further and further away. He was kept occupied for the rest of the day, and he was in such a state of utter exhaustion when he finally fell into bed at the end of it, that he didn't even question what room he was in. It was certainly too late to seek out either Jo or Elnora.

He had managed to pay Elnora a quick visit in the afternoon, to ascertain for himself that she really would fully recover. She had been asleep, but he had spoken to the physician. He had also received Laramie's promise that upon her release from the infirmary she would be accommodated in accordance with her status as his betrothed. He knew Elnora would care little about the opulence of her quarters, but he wanted her position to be clear to the court from the beginning.

It wasn't until the next morning that he even remembered that he had sustained a sword wound himself. Shallow though the cut was, his arm did sting furiously when he awoke. His new title notwithstanding, he was scolded like a small child by the head physician for not having had the wound dressed immediately. The physician fussed around him, assuring him that he was fortunate to have escaped infection. Cal took these strictures with good grace, deciding that he liked the old man.

Any hope Cal might have had that the new day would bring an opportunity for private conversation with Jonan quickly dwindled. The only private moment he had all day was when he woke in the chill of pre-dawn in whatever room he had been directed to the night before. He had been too tired at the time to appreciate it, but this bed was surely the most comfortable he had ever slept in. The room was richly decorated, and it was tempting to just lie there, enjoying the soft mattress and plump pillows after so many nights of rough sleeping.

But he knew he needed to take the opportunity to do something that had pressed on him ever since the battle finished. He had lost track of how many times a servant had offered to relieve him of his rucksack, and he had begun to see some odd looks in response to his continued refusal.

Assuring himself that he was alone, he gently upended his bag, letting the Esvalere roll out onto the bed. He took a moment to admire its dancing light. It was as mesmerizing as ever.

He took a deep breath before placing his hands on it, but the rush of magic and images was still overwhelming. He thought he caught a flash of an interaction between Qadir and Elddreki after the dragon's return the day before, but it was gone before he could make sense of it, swept away in the rush of information. He saw details of the battle that had passed, his heart jumping into his mouth as he witnessed a number of near misses for both Jonan and Elnora that he had not observed in real life. He even saw his home in Nerita, familiar and unfamiliar images flashing into and out of his mind.

He realized that the Esvalere was responding to the things closest to his heart, but he knew that if he explored all of it now, he would lose track of time in the real world, and he couldn't afford to do so. So he focused on trying to direct the tide. He delved for a moment into King Cael's mind, and saw what he wanted to see—the king making his way through this same castle, his steps sure and his route familiar to him.

With an effort, Cal took his hands off the Esvalere and scooped it back into his bag. He was relieved to see that it was still dark. Slipping out of his room, he hurried through the castle, hoping desperately that Filip, and all Lord Lindor's other descendants, had not found the secret chamber in the intervening years.

He followed the route taken by King Cael, ending in a lower level he had not known was there the day before. Cal had passed a few servants already astir on the upper levels, but no one else was down here. He reached the alcove he was looking for. His heart leaped when he saw the stretch of wall. He reached out and pulled at the hidden catch. Despite the intervening centuries, the stonework remained sturdy, and the secret door slid smoothly open.

The hidden chamber was not large, but it had a sense of grandeur all the same. Just as in the Pinnacle Chamber, the presence of the Esvalere had surely left a mark here. Cal could feel the residue of its magic all around him, and he felt the sphere itself pulse rapidly, as if overjoyed to be reunited with its resting place. Cal felt confident that no one had been here since King Cael's death, but there was no sign of decay or disuse, not even cobwebs appearing in the corners. There was no time to explore now, but Cal promised himself that he would spend many hours here in the years to come.

He reverently placed the Esvalere on the raised plinth in the middle of the room and stepped back, an immense weight lifting from his shoulders. He hurried back up through the levels of the castle, hesitating wistfully as he passed the infirmary. It would be so nice to slip in and have the chance to talk privately with Elnora while everyone else still slept.

But he knew that their relationship was likely to face some opposition at court, and that Elnora would feel the impact of that more than he would. He didn't want to risk starting any whispers. He supposed they would have to consider the proprieties now. No more stolen kisses in caves and moonlit forests. The thought was deeply depressing.

By the time he realized what his day would entail, Cal was half wishing he'd ignored his common sense. It seemed that he would get no opportunity to see either Elnora or Jonan that day. He had almost forgotten the fairly large problem of the Valorian army in the chaos of the battle the day before, but of course that was a situation that couldn't wait. He found a few minutes before departing to send a squadron riding for Nerita, with instructions to end the military occupation.

Had things been less tense, Cal would like to have gone himself, to ensure that his parents—both the ones who shared his blood, and the ones who raised him—had been properly buried and honored. He would certainly make a pilgrimage to visit their graves at the earliest opportunity. He wondered if he would be able to convince Jonan to go with him. His friend was not exactly eager to return to the fishing village, he knew.

But in the meantime he set off that very morning, accompanied by a squadron led by Laramie and one by Leander, to intercept King Gresham. The army was camped mere hours from Kynton, and Cal's blood ran cold at the sheer size of the Valorian force. Certainly this was not a king to make an enemy of.

But Laramie and Leander had not been deceived in their dealings with him. When he heard the account, King Gresham was indeed willing to withdraw. He did not seem as astonished as Cal had expected to hear that a dragon had truly been present in Kynton.

The middle-aged king invited Calinnae to have private speech with him in his tent, and they spoke for some time. Cal felt that he learned a great deal about the foreign sovereign in that conversation, but he was confident from King Gresham's shrewd questions and piercing gaze that the Valorian learned much more about Calinnae. The thought made him nervous.

As they rode back for Kynton in the fading light, Cal asked Laramie if he had sensed a familiar quality about the foreign king. Laramie smiled, and answered with one word—Sarai. Suddenly Calinnae understood. Just as the twins were descended from King Cael's daughter Avalyn, King Gresham must be descended from King Cael's daughter Sarai, who had married the Valorian crown prince. He was distant kin to Calinnae as well, and he had Queen Jacqueline's mountain blood in him. No wonder he had not been more skeptical about the dragons.

Cal arrived back in Kynton, once again unutterably weary. No one seemed able to tell him where Jonan was, but he persisted this time in visiting Elnora in the infirmary. He was not surprised to find her restless and insistent that she was well enough to get up.

He just smiled fondly at her as he sat on the edge of her bed, and infuriated her by deferring to the physician's opinion that she should rest for another day. She seemed to forgive him when he wrapped his arms around her, though, holding her close for a long moment despite the anxiously hovering medic. There were so many things he had wanted to say, but he found in the moment that he felt no urgency to do so. They would have the rest of their lives for that.

It had been decided that a coronation should take place as soon as possible, to avoid further unrest. But apparently such events required some preparation, a matter Cal was very happy to leave to others. He was told that it would be another week before the official ceremony could occur. In the spirit of capitalizing on the current enthusiastic mood of the populace, Leander had suggested that they have a less formal celebration the following day.

Cal had agreed to it, but maintained a healthy skepticism about what "less formal" signified. He knew it was important to mark such occasions, but as he lay in his bed that night, he wished all the fuss could be over so he could attend to matters he cared more about. He thought his first point of order would be a visit to Pravat, to once again commence restoration of the Hall of Records. He was eager to see Aurelius, partly to assure himself that the elderly record keeper was fully recovered, and partly to gain access to the valuable records that he was determined to fully explore himself.

After that, Cal thought grimly, he would have to take strides toward rooting out the hideous slave trade flourishing in the south of the country. He thought he would quite enjoy another confrontation with Bryant, given his change in circumstances. He would like to see the look on the man's face when he discovered that the orphaned street girl he had exploited and attempted to sell into slavery would soon be his queen. He would pay for his treatment of her, Cal promised himself, as would Yaeger. The continued mystery as to the guard's whereabouts was a source of unease to Cal, but there was little he could do in the short term.

Thoughts of Elnora softened Cal's mind as he drifted into sleep. After all, there was much to look forward to as well as much work to be done in the days to come.

CHAPTER THIRTY-FIVE

As predicted, the morning's celebrations were full of pomp and ceremony. On his limited sleep, Cal found being fussed over exhausting, but he maintained an appropriately gratified facade. When he was released from the morning's events to prepare for the midday meal, his spirits lifted upon the discovery that Elnora was to be allowed to leave the infirmary to join the festivities. His expectation of enjoying the meal increased exponentially, and he had a spring in his step as he headed for his chambers.

He didn't even feel as ridiculous as he had expected when he donned the outrageously elaborate ceremonial outfit laid out for him, now that he knew he and Elnora could laugh about it all together later, and remind each other of the disheveled appearance they had become so used to. It was certainly an impressive contrast, he thought, when he took in the finished effect in the long looking glass in his chambers. The embroidered embellishments all over the clothes made it hard to find himself under it all, but he was actually quite taken with the traditional Kyonan blue and gold.

Surveying his reflection critically, he was pleased to see that when his face wasn't smeared with blood and grime, he actually looked a tiny bit regal. Some of his bruises were fading, but he still looked much tougher and more solid than he had when he left Nerita. The physical hardships of his journey had developed muscles he hadn't known existed, and he thought that even the lines of his face somehow communicated his increased mental and emotional resilience.

He had retained no concept of dates while he traveled throughout the country, and he had realized with surprise only the day before that his birthday had passed since he left home. He was eighteen now, and he found that he did somehow feel like a man.

Cal went to collect Elnora himself, wanting to arrive at the meal together. She emerged from the infirmary as he approached, and his steps faltered at the sight of her.

"What's wrong?" she asked quickly, taking in his wide eyes.

"Wrong?" he repeated, a smile dawning as he looked her up and down.

She had been dressed as befitted her new station, and the contrast in his appearance was nothing to the change in hers. He felt like she had been covered in blood half the time he'd known her, but now...she was the most beautiful thing he had ever seen. Her sweeping gown was a pale gold that blended well with the golden embroidery on his own clothes, and it clung to her in all the right places before fanning out majestically. Her hair had been tied up in an elaborate style, making her look older.

He thought fondly of the ragged street urchin who had beckoned him to safety that night in Kerr.

"Absolutely nothing is wrong," he assured her, closing the distance between them with confident steps. "You're just so incredibly beautiful that I forgot how to walk properly."

She rolled her eyes at him, but he could tell that she was pleased. She looked him over as well, and her eyes grew slightly rounder. "You look pretty amazing yourself," she said. She reached out and tentatively touched the embroidery on his chest. He placed his hand over hers, trapping it in place as she looked up shyly into his eyes. "You look very kingly."

He smiled down at her, his eyes blazing. "I feel like I somehow got everything I could have ever wanted, and I'm still trying to figure out what I did to deserve it."

"Don't be silly," she scolded, softening the rebuke by laying her head gently against his chest as she reverently touched his signet ring. "You deserve to be king more than anyone I've ever met."

He put his arms around her. "That's not what I was thinking of, actually."

She kept her head where it was, and he wondered if she could hear the way his heartbeat sped up at her nearness. He wondered if that would fade with time. He hoped not.

With a sigh she drew back. "This dress is ridiculous," she said. "It has a train!"

Cal grinned knowingly at her, and she colored slightly. She could say what she liked, but he could tell she was enjoying looking so beautiful. And who could blame her? Far from needing to convince the court of her suitability, he was thinking he'd better marry her as quickly as possible before someone else tried to cut him out.

"The bandage doesn't really help the look," she was saying ruefully.

He shook his head, reaching out to gently touch her bandaged shoulder. "Yes it does. It shows that you're a fierce warrior as well as an elegant lady."

She gave a startled laugh. "No one has ever called me a lady before. Or elegant."

He laughed back. "Well, don't get too used to it, My Lady,

because before you know it they'll be calling you a queen instead."

Her eyes glazed over for a moment as she tried to take that in. "Honestly, the thought is a bit overwhelming," she admitted.

Cal's smile was rueful. "I know the feeling," he said.

He offered her his arm, and he could tell that she felt the surreal nature of the moment as much as he did, as they walked into the banquet hall together, their steps stately and their elaborate clothes proclaiming their new status. King Cael's signet ring on his hand felt heavy but secure, like it was resting where it was supposed to be. Surely it had only been the day before that they had been fleeing through the streets of Alezae, covered with ash and lucky to escape enslavement or death.

The meal itself was delicious, especially after surviving so long on trail fare. For the first time Cal felt a stirring of genuine excitement about the practical realities of a privileged royal lifestyle.

But much more gratifying than the food was the delight of witnessing Elnora's graceful presence. She sat beside him, and the strength with which she gripped his hand under the table told him that she was nervous. But her bearing didn't communicate it. She appeared poised and confident.

It reminded Cal of how her demeanor had seemed to change in Montego when she shed her filthy garments for the elegant garb of the mountain people. He recalled the way her eyes had lit up as she danced in the firelight, and his heart swelled at the memory. He was determined to do all he could to ensure that her life in the castle held that kind of joy. His own life would surely be much more joyful with her by his side. Truly she would make an excellent queen.

Somehow, incredibly, he was able to extricate himself from the midday meal cleanly, nothing expected of him for an hour or so. He was torn, part of him wanting to remain with Elnora, but she sent him off, knowing that he had been troubled by Jonan's absence from the day's proceedings so far.

He wasted a quarter of his free hour wandering the castle looking for Jonan, and trying to avoid being waylaid in the process, but eventually he ran him to ground.

Calinnae walked up to his friend, who was standing on the battlements looking out.

"Hello."

"Hello," said Jonan, looking up and smiling as he watched Cal awkwardly trying to lean on the wall in the huge robe someone had put on him during the course of the meal. He eventually gave up and draped it over the wall.

Cal let out a long sigh. "Well, we made it."

"Yes, we did."

Cal looked sideways at his friend. He looked peaceful and contented. More so, in fact, than Cal could ever remember seeing him. He could almost believe that Jonan was resting in some new inner peace, not even thinking about the future. Almost.

"You're doing the sideways glance thing Cal, what is it?"

"Well, it's just...I never expected it to turn out like this. I have no idea what you're thinking or feeling, Jo. I mean..." for a moment he struggled for words. "I got the crown and the girl."

Jonan let out a ringing laugh, a sound more triumphant than all the trumpet fanfare of the morning. "You can keep what's yours, Cal." He flashed his friend a grin. "I was only in it for the dragons."

Calinnae smiled slowly, feeling a sudden wave of release. "It was all thanks to you, you know," he said.

Jo was still looking out across the fields. "What do you mean?"

"You did as much as I did to break the curse," Cal went on. "Qadir said so himself."

"He did?" Jo turned startled eyes onto his friend, and Cal nodded.

"I was cursed to see and not act, just like all my ancestors. But you...you were the free, wild, reckless best friend I've always known. Without you, I would have made the same mistakes as all my fathers before me."

"I hardly think I can claim credit for all your decisions, Cal," said Jo mildly. "There were lots of times you were the one who figured out what to do."

Cal shrugged. "I think the curse weakened the further along we went, and the more I chose to take action. But in the beginning, it was all because of you. If I had known I was the heir, I would have chosen to run and hide for sure, to protect the Bloodline. I even tried to convince you to do it. But since I believed you were the heir, I was committed to following your lead." He flashed his friend a grin. "However crazy I thought your instincts were."

Jonan grinned back. "We did have some near misses, didn't we?"

Cal shook his head. "The biggest near miss was how close I was to giving in to the dragonwrath. Like you said, I would even have left Elnora in Kerr if you hadn't suggested we invite her to come with us."

Jo grimaced. "Don't remind me of what I said. Can't we just agree to forget everything we both said during that awful fight?"

Cal smiled, but shook his head again. "No, because you were right. Kyona would have waited for me forever if you hadn't been there to give me a push. This is your victory as much as mine."

Jo was silent for a long moment, his gaze turning back to the distance beyond the castle walls.

"That's kind of you to say," he said at last. "You're a good man Cal, and a good friend. You'll make a better king than I ever would, and I truly don't envy you the job. But this isn't my victory, it's yours."

Cal sighed. He wasn't surprised, but his heart felt the wrench all the same. "By which you mean to say, you're not sticking around."

Jo shook his head. "There's more for me out there, I can feel it."

"Haven't we had enough adventure for a lifetime?" Cal asked dryly.

Jonan laughed, clapping him on the shoulder. "Spoken like the tired old man in a young man's body I've always known you to be. There's no such thing as enough adventure. Plus, like I said, this has been your adventure all along. I want to find my own."

"If I'm a tired old man, you're a stubborn child," said Cal. He gave Jo a playful but forceful shove, after a shifty glance around to make sure no one was watching.

Jo shoved him back without hesitation. "What a pair we make then, hey?"

"What a pair," Cal repeated with a smile. He turned to watch the summer sunlight sparkling far across the vast expanse that was his home, as his breathing quickly fell in step with that of his companion.

THE REST of the day was filled with formalities, and the evening's feast passed in a blur. Exhausted as he was, Cal again rose early the next day, finding that there was too much on his mind to allow him to sleep deeply. He knew that Elnora was now free from her sickbed, and thought he might try to find her before the day's duties began. On inquiry, a servant directed him to a large rose garden located on the other side of the castle from the throne room.

Sure enough, her slim figure could be seen wandering the rows, running her fingers lightly over the blooms. Cal hovered in the doorway for a moment, enjoying the sight. She was of course not wearing a ceremonial dress this time. But her graceful form was just as striking in the simply and elegantly cut white gown, her loosely braided hair creating a golden crown all her own as it caught the early morning sun. While he watched, another figure approached from a different doorway. Jonan had a rucksack slung over his shoulder, and he clearly hadn't seen Cal.

"Well, don't you make a pretty picture among the roses?" he teased as he approached Elnora.

She smiled up at him, her tone as cheeky as his. "Sorry Jo, I'm already spoken for."

"So I hear," he laughed. "And now I know Cal is such a fearsome fighter with that magic sword of his, I won't dare to challenge him for your fair hand."

She laughed too. "As if you ever dreamed of doing such a thing."

He smiled back at her with the easy familiarity of friendship, making no attempt to chivalrously deny it. "What are you doing out here so early, anyway?"

She looked dreamily around her. "Actually, I was just wondering how such enormous and beautiful roses managed to grow under an oppressive reign like Filip's. What about you?" She turned back to him and seemed to see his rucksack for the first time. "You're leaving." It wasn't a question.

Jonan nodded.

"Does Cal know?"

He nodded again.

She sighed. "He'll miss you so much. You're not even staying for the coronation?"

"No, I like to leave before things get anti-climactic."

Elnora laughed, and Cal could have sworn the roses bloomed a little more. "You're really relieved, aren't you?"

"That I don't have to be king? Yes." His look dared her to challenge this declaration.

"So am I."

Jonan raised his eyebrows in mock offense. "And I thought you were a friend to me! You don't think I'd make a good king? That crown might've made a man out of me, you know."

"A man?" Elnora shook her head. "You have the rest of your life to be a man."

Jo grinned and clapped her on the shoulder. "Look after Cal for me would you?"

"I'll do my best."

Elnora's sigh of satisfaction told Cal as clearly as words that this was the happiest goodbye she had ever said. After Jonan disappeared, Cal moved forward with soft footsteps, slipping his arms around her waist and resting his chin on top of her head.

"He's gone, I see."

"Mmm. Did he even say goodbye to you?"

Cal grunted. "Last night. I tried to convince him that he should stick around for a while, come back to Nerita with me before leaving. He laughed in my face."

Elnora chuckled. "Of course he did."

"And of course he wouldn't let me send any guards with him," Cal continued. "I had to practically force him to take a few coins. I don't think even he knows where he's going. I don't even know if I'll ever see him again."

She turned to face him. "Oh, I'm sure he'll drop in from time to time."

He smiled down into her face, his arms tightening around her. As he leaned toward her, he couldn't help but reflect that there were some advantages to Jonan making his own path. At least now he might have a hope of the occasional moment alone with Elnora.

CALINNAE SHIFTED his weight from one foot to the other to keep his feet from falling asleep. He tried to imagine Jonan at this coronation and almost laughed out loud. As he felt the weight of the crown go onto his head, he looked out over the seemingly endless vista of green fields and golden wheat, rivers and forests. And the sky went on forever.

SOMEWHERE BEYOND THE sight of the king, a ship was just sailing out from the quay. The young man nobody recognized was standing on the deck, looking out over the living mystery of the sea to the bobbing horizon beyond. Breathing in the fresh salt air, he leaned into the wind and smiled.

NOTE FROM THE AUTHOR

Thank you for reading *Heir of the Curse*. I hope you enjoyed reading it as much as I enjoyed writing it! I would be so grateful if you would consider leaving a review on Amazon—it would really make a difference!

To find out what happens next in both Jonan's and Cal's stories, check out *Captives of the Curse*, the second book in the Kyona Chronicles, where more adventure, fantasy, mystery, and romance await.

You can find a bonus chapter for *Heir of the Curse* on my website. If you join up to my mailing list at deborahgracewhite.com, you'll also receive *Dragon's Sight*, an 8,000 word prequel to *The Kyona Chronicles*, told from Elddreki's perspective. That will also allow me to keep you updated on new releases, specials, and giveaways.

Again, thanks for entering the world of *The Kyona Chronicles*! I hope to see you back again.

ACKNOWLEDGMENTS

The idea for this book was born when a thirteen-year-old me took a high school elective called 'dragon art'. The elective confirmed what I already knew—illustration was out as a career option for me. To be honest, writing professionally seemed no more realistic at the time, but that didn't stop my imagination from ticking away with the beginnings of a story. I did some scribblings here and there over the next few years, but it was more than fifteen years, one law degree, and two children later before I actually sat down and wrote the story that would become *Heir of the Curse*. So to that high school science teacher who cheerfully ran a session on art even though it was seemingly irrelevant to your subject—thank you!

More to the point, though, my wonderfully supportive husband deserves a huge thank you for his patience and enthusiasm in pursuing this project with me. Ray, you are incredible, and without you I can't see this dream ever becoming a reality. Thank you for being endlessly interested in my work, and for all the times you pick up the slack because the world of fantasy and words has stolen my attention away from duties nearer to home.

My two excessively lovable children also merit thanks and

appreciation for putting up with my abstraction. Happily for me —perhaps not for them—they're too young to articulate their frustration in my moments of distraction. To both of you, I hope one day you get the joy out of reading that I have, and that in providing one more novel for you to devour, I pay back in small measure your patience with me now.

Thank you to my beta readers, Andrew—always the quickest to finish and provide helpful feedback—Mum, Dad, Adrian, Tamara, Jana, Cherilyn, David, Ali, and Mel. Your feedback has been invaluable, and this book is most definitely a better product because of your input.

And a double thank you to Mum for your line editing, and to Dad and Mel for your copy editing and enormously helpful advice and assistance with the practicalities of publishing. I would have been lost without you.

Karri, the talented artist who created such a beautiful cover, you captured exactly what I wanted, and I couldn't be happier. Rebecca, your map is a hundred times better than my imagination could have painted it.

To you, the reader, thank you for giving me the privilege of being an author.

And most importantly, to God, from whom all creativity flows. Thank you for blessing me with immeasurably more than all I could ask or imagine, and for giving me a tiny spark of your creative nature.

ABOUT THE AUTHOR

I've been a reader since I can remember, growing up on a wide range of books, from classic literature to light-hearted romps. The love of reading has traveled with me unchanged across multiple continents, and carried me from my own childhood all the way to having children of my own.

But if reading is like looking through a window into a magical and beautiful world, beginning to write my own stories was like discovering that I could open that window and climb right out into fantasyland.

I cannot believe how privileged I am to actually be living that childhood dream and publishing my own novels. I do so from my hometown of Adelaide, Australia, where I live with my husband and our three little ones.

I've never outgrown my love of young adult stories, and my first series, *The Kyona Chronicles*, is a young adult fantasy series of four novels and two novellas.

Feel free to email me at deborah@deborahgracewhite.com and introduce yourself! Or subscribe to my mailing list at deborahgracewhite.com for free giveaways, sales, and updates.